"*Don Phillips has captured the spirit of the Yorktown Campaign. The dialogue of the participants combined with well-researched sources result in both an entertaining and educational book about one of the most important and inspiring events in American history.*"

—John Short
Park Ranger, Colonial National Historical Park
Yorktown, Virginia

"*Wow! Talk about the little guy winning big. After fighting for six years with few victories, America's ragtag army finally won it all. In this splendid book, author Don Phillips vividly demonstrates how courage, perseverance, and the pursuit of a dream can result in great success.*"

—Rudy Ruettiger
Business Leader, Motivational Speaker
Subject of the motion picture *Rudy*

"*So often sports metaphors are used in leadership. But this time, George Washington's leadership at the battle of Yorktown will be used as a metaphor for leadership in sports. This outstanding story, so eloquently told by Don Phillips, is destined to become a classic.*"

—Mike Cragg
Associate Director of Athletics, Duke University

On the Wing of Speed

On the Wing of Speed

✦

George Washington and the Battle of Yorktown

Donald T. Phillips

iUniverse Star
New York Lincoln Shanghai

On the Wing of Speed
George Washington and the Battle of Yorktown

Copyright © 2006 by Donald T. Phillips

iUniverse Star
an iUniverse, Inc. imprint

iUniverse books may be ordered through booksellers or by contacting:

iUniverse
2021 Pine Lake Road, Suite 100
Lincoln, NE 68512
www.iuniverse.com
1-800-Authors (1-800-288-4677)

Cover image of George Washington owned by Picture History, used by permission.

ISBN-13: 978-1-58348-198-1 (pbk)
ISBN-13: 978-0-595-82964-4 (ebk)
ISBN-10: 1-58348-198-2 (pbk)
ISBN-10: 0-595-82964-3 (ebk)

Printed in the United States of America

PART I
PRELUDE

1

It's mid-morning. A rather handsome, two-story farmhouse is barely visible in the dense fog that has risen from the Hudson River. There's a solid layer of snow coating the ground. Nearby trees are barren of leaves, their branches gnarling and creaking in a light, chilly wind.

The surrounding small plain is filled with tents and wagons, but there is minimal activity. Several grooms are tending to a few gaunt horses. A dozen or so sentries are strategically stationed along the perimeter of the camp where a thick forest begins. Some stand at attention, their rifles at shoulder arms. Others have their hands wedged into the fronts of their pants, rifles clasped tightly under their armpits or resting against a tree. Most stomp the ground to keep their feet warm. Some feet are wrapped in old gray rags.

Two officers walk past the farmhouse. The snow crunches beneath their boots.

Inside, George Washington sits alone in an upstairs room—at a table near the window. The door is closed. Logs are crackling in the fireplace.

Resting on the table is a leather-covered wooden chest, the interior of which is lined with green wool. Inside are knives, forks, plates, cups, and bottles of various sizes. Set out on the table are a couple of miniature brushes, a file, a tin of myrrh, and a folded towel of homespun linen.

Washington's coat is off. His face is very near a small rectangular mirror leaning against the chest. A flickering lantern is inches away. His left hand holds his upper lip. In his right hand, moving back and forth in short strokes, is a small metal file.

Washington is cleaning his teeth.

Every now and then the file touches his inflamed, swollen gums. His head jumps, and he groans. His gums give him constant trouble. They are red, painful, and almost always bleeding. He has only eight permanent teeth left. Three are loose and most of the rest are black and rotting, but Washington refuses to have them pulled, because he would have a terrible time eating. Elsewhere in his mouth are old root fragments left behind by teeth that have fallen out. From these alone, the pain is sometimes excruci-

ating. At regular intervals, he pulls the file out of his mouth, takes a swig of water, swishes it around, and spits the bloody water into a bowl resting on the table. Then he goes back to the scraping.

Outside the perimeter of the camp, three uniformed riders are waved through by the sentries. They ride to the farmhouse at a full gallop, one rider leading the other two. The front rider jumps off his horse and rushes up to the door. The others wait with the horses.

Washington hears the noise outside and immediately grabs two bridges of false teeth from the folded towel and slips them into his mouth. With a small set of pliers, he carefully uses gold wire to connect the bridges by half-hitching them to the teeth still rooted in his mouth. His unusually large hands make the delicate maneuvering look awkward, yet he has performed this task so many times that both bridges are in place within moments. Then he moves his tongue around the interior of his mouth, smacks his lips, pulls his head back, and looks in the mirror.

Washington's face has marks and wrinkles consistent with his forty-nine years. He has light bluish gray eyes, a straight, thick nose, and perpetually sunburned cheekbones. There is a small scar on his left cheek caused by an old abscessed tooth. His lower jaw juts out ever so slightly and there is an uneasy set to his lips. His graying auburn hair is brushed straight back from his forehead. It is long enough so that when tied in a short ponytail it half-covers his ears and bobs on the back of his neck.

Presently, there is the sound of boots rapidly ascending the stairs, then a knock at the door. "General Washington, sir," a firm voice calls out.

"One moment," he responds.

Washington quickly pushes his files, brushes, myrrh, and mirror next to the bowl and covers them all with his towel. He rises, takes several steps across the room, and opens the door. The general's six foot two inch frame towers over the diminutive Alexander Hamilton standing in the hall.

"Sir, Major Fishbourne is here with an urgent dispatch from General Wayne."

Washington looks at Hamilton, furrows his eyebrows, and cocks his head. His expression asks for more information.

"There's been a mutiny in the Pennsylvania line, sir. Near Morristown."

"I'll be right there," he says firmly.

Washington closes the door and goes back to the table. Still standing, he takes several pinches of myrrh from the tin, mixes it in his cup of water, takes a sip, gargles, spits the water into the bowl, and wipes his face. Then he reaches for his coat. It is dark blue with buff facings and plain metal buttons. There is a silver tasseled epaulette on each shoulder—the only hit of military rank on his entire uniform. His knee pants, also buff colored, are tucked into his black boots. He puts on his coat and pulls down the cuffs of each sleeve. Standing tall now, Washington stiffens his back. He opens the door, strides out of his room and down the staircase to the ground floor.

Present in the main room are the general's aides-de-camp—Washington's staff, or his "family" as he refers to them. All are young officers—well educated, extraordinarily competent, even brilliant. There is Alexander Hamilton of New York, Tench Tilghman of Maryland, and David Humphreys of Pennsylvania.

All stand when Washington enters the room. Snapping to attention with a crisp salute is Major Benjamin Fishbourne. He looks tired and worn out. He has had a long ride.

"General Washington, sir. I have important news from General Wayne."

Washington returns the salute. "Yes, Major. Welcome. Please take off your coat and sit down. Gentlemen, can we get a cup of warm tea for our friend?"

"Of course," responds Colonel Humphreys, who immediately walks back to the kitchen.

"Thank you, sir," replies Major Fishbourne.

Colonel Tilghman takes the major's overcoat, as Humphreys returns quickly with some piping hot tea, steam rising from the cup. Fishbourne places his cold hands around the cup and takes a sip. All are now seated.

"Well, Major," says Washington, "what is your news?"

"Sir, I beg to report that there has been a mutiny in the line. Nearly half the regiment is marching to Philadelphia as we speak."

"When did this occur?"

"January first, at night, sir."

"Go on, Major. We will listen."

"Yes, sir. At about ten o'clock, two guns were fired, and a skyrocket was thrown from the encampment. These were signals to start the mutiny. Soldiers began running from their tents with their arms and knapsacks. Our officers immediately rushed in and began ordering the men to lay down their arms and go back to quarters—which they would do while we were present, but as we moved on down the line they would run off. Soon the soldiers assembled in crowds and became violent. Lieutenant White was shot through the thigh. Captain Tolbert was shot through the body. He is very ill. Colonel Butler was also shot through the body. He is dead. A number of mutineers were killed."

Washington winces, then pauses. "Were any officers involved in this revolt?" he asks.

"No, sir. Only enlisted. They were led by the sergeants."

"Continue, please."

"Yes, sir. At about one in the morning, the mutineers began turning all soldiers out of their huts. Those who would not participate were forced to run and hide in the woods or else be beaten or shot. At two o'clock, they marched off, in regular platoons with fifes and drums playing."

"Where was General Wayne during all this?" inquires Washington.

"Sir, when the revolt began, General Wayne rode straight to the scene. Guns were immediately pointed at him. He opened his coat and yelled: 'Here! If you mean to kill me, shoot me at once.' But the men did not shoot. They said their quarrel was not with him but with Congress. General Wayne spoke with them a long time. He exhorted them to lay down their arms and said he would do all in his power to satisfy their grievances. But as the men were heavily liquored up and on empty stomachs, they could not be reasoned with."

"Were most of the sergeants drunk, also?" asks Washington.

"Yes, sir—clearly."

"And where is General Wayne at this moment?"

"Sir, he is following the mutineers to Philadelphia. He met them as they were marching off and tried to get them to stop, but they would not. He begged them not to go to the enemy."

"And what was their response?"

"Sir, they said it was not their intention to go to the enemy, and that they would hang any man who would attempt it."

"Good!" exclaims Washington.

"General Wayne stated that he would not leave his men—and if they would not allow him to march in their front, he would follow in the rear."

Washington clenches his jaw and nods his head slightly. "And that, Major, is why Anthony Wayne is a general in this army!"

"Indeed, sir."

"Can you estimate how many participated in the mutiny?"

"Sir, when we arrived the next morning to draw provisions, we found that near half the men of our regiment had refused to take part and remained behind. That means approximately 1,200 marched on. And curiously, sir, they did not take any part of what was left of our provisions."

"And why do you find that curious, Major?" asks Alexander Hamilton.

"Because, sir, when men get little, they want more."

"I suppose," says Washington. "Our troops have been starved for years. But it does not surprise me that they would not take food from the mouths of the soldiers who stayed behind."

"They had come to the end of their rope," adds Tench Tilghman. *"They'd simply had enough."*

"I'm sure the liquor played a large part," says David Humphreys, *"and on empty stomachs, too."*

"All true," responds Washington. *"But they are accountable for their actions, drunk or sober. And clearly, this is a disturbing situation. It sets a dangerous precedent, for I fear when others hear of this mutiny it will inspire them to take like action."*

"It must be quelled immediately, sir," says Hamilton.

"Yes," replies the general. *"Major Fishbourne, you will return to General Wayne tomorrow. You will pass to him my advice that as opposition by force was not successful in the first instance, it will most likely not work now—at least not while the mutineers are together. I think it would only keep alive their resentment and drive them to the enemy en masse. I would recommend that General Wayne cross the Delaware with the mutineers, ascertain their principal grievances, and promise to faithfully represent their concerns to Congress. I will provide you a written dispatch stating as much."*

"Yes, sir," replies Major Fishbourne.

"In addition," continues Washington, *"I will ride directly to Philadelphia to help quell the revolt. In the meantime, Major, we offer our amenities to you, what few we have."*

"Thank you, sir," responds Major Fishbourne. *"I have two men with me."*

"Of course, sir. We will see that they also receive all courtesies. Colonel Humphreys, will you please see to the major and his men?"

"Certainly, General."

After Humphreys and Fishbourne leave, Hamilton and Tilghman stay behind to confer with the general.

"Sir," says Tilghman, *"I wonder if it might not be advisable for you to remain here rather than ride to Philadelphia."*

"Oh?" responds Washington, who flashes a glance at Hamilton.

"I agree, General," says Hamilton. *"In the regiments encamped here, there is a dire want of flour, clothing, and virtually everything else."*

"Yes, that is true."

"Well, sir," continues Hamilton, *"once word reaches our troops, as it surely will, it might be better if you were present for any possible action."*

"Hmmm," mutters Washington, raising his hand to his chin.

"If the troops here attempt to mutiny as well," continues Hamilton, *"it would provide the enemy with an opening. And as the river is free from ice, circumstances are favorable for an attack."*

"I see."

"Also, sir," says Tilghman, "General Wayne is most certainly able to handle the situation. Perhaps a letter of encouragement and support to him…"

"And one also to Congress," interrupts Washington.

"Yes, both would do nicely, I believe."

"Very well, gentlemen. I agree. A trip to Philadelphia will be postponed for the time being. I compliment you on your sound advice."

"Thank you, sir," says Tilghman.

"Thank you, sir," adds Hamilton.

"Colonel Tilghman, would you be able to work with me this moment on several communiqués?"

"Certainly, sir."

"Very well."

Hamilton excuses himself as Washington and Tilghman retire to a small room on the lower floor. It is equipped with a table upon which there is a lantern and a variety of writing supplies. Tilghman takes a seat behind the table and pulls out pen and paper. Washington takes off his coat and lays it over the back of a chair, but remains standing. He begins to pace back and forth.

"Shall I address this to General Wayne, sir?" asks Tilghman.

"In a moment," replies Washington. "Let's first compose a circular to the governors of the New England states, as such: 'It is with extreme anxiety and pain of mind that the event I have long apprehended has at length taken place.' Colonel, you will next please fill in some of the details of the mutiny."

"Yes, sir," replies Tilghman.

"'This event,'" Washington continues, "'has resulted from the total want of pay for nearly twelve months, for want of clothing at a severe season, and for want of adequate provisions. All are beyond description. In my opinion, it is in vain to think that the army can be kept together much longer unless some immediate and spirited measures are adopted. I send General Henry Knox to you with specific requests for the welfare of our army.' Colonel, you may fill in additional words as you feel necessary."

"Yes, sir."

"Now, a letter to General Knox."

Tilghman pulls out another piece of paper and nods that he is ready.

"General Knox, as you are acquainted personally with the governors of the states of Connecticut, Rhode Island, Massachusetts, and New Hampshire, you will proceed to them forthwith with the accompanying dispatches. You will generally represent the alarming crisis to which our affairs have arrived. You will press upon them our dire need of food and clothing—especially shirts, vests, breeches, and stockings to carry our

soldiers through the winter. You will request a sum of money equal to three months' pay for every soldier in their state regiments assigned to this army. You will also point out the need for a speedy adoption of measures recommended at this time—and inform the governors that you will call upon them on your way back to the army to learn what has been done in regard to our request. I wish you a more pleasant journey than can be hoped for."

Washington pauses until his aide has stopped writing. Tilghman finishes and looks up.

"A letter now to the president of Congress," says Washington, who begins to describe the events surrounding the mutiny. "I enclose a copy of a letter I have written to the four eastern states in preparation of a major requisition for provisions, supplies, and payroll. I ask for your help in this endeavor. Matters have now come to a crisis, and it will be dangerous to put to further test the patience of our troops."

"That will do for now, Colonel Tilghman," says Washington as he grabs his coat and takes a step toward the door.

"What of General Wayne, sir?" asks Tilghman.

"Let's work on that letter this afternoon," Washington responds. "I want to think a bit more on my words to him."

"Yes, sir."

"Oh, and when you finish, please summon General Knox. I'd like to update him on the mutiny and present orders to him in person."

"Yes, sir."

Washington leaves the room. Tilghman stays behind to complete first drafts of the letters.

◆   ◆   ◆

The winter of 1780–1781 was a desperate time for General George Washington and the troops of the Continental Army. They were now in a worse situation than they had been during the harsh winter of 1777–1778 when encamped at Valley Forge, Pennsylvania.

Their numbers were alarmingly low. In 1778, with renewed hope and supplies from a new alliance with France, the army's strength had swelled to nearly 17,000 men. Two years later, it was only 8,000 strong. And now, Washington was in command of a mere 3,500 regulars encamped in and around the Hudson Highlands of New York.

He had moved his headquarters to New Windsor in November 1780 so that he might keep a closer eye on the enemy. Fortunately, Britain's North American commander, Sir Henry Clinton, was in no hurry to take action. With a force of some 7,000 British regulars, he was in firm possession of New York City, he had an abundance of food and supplies, and his men were safe and warm. Clinton was content to ride out the harsh winter right where he was.

Washington, on the other hand, was fighting for his life. He lacked almost everything needed to sustain an army. He was low on artillery, guns, ammunition, tents, entrenching tools, blankets, and hospital supplies. He was out of every conceivable article of new clothing a soldier might need. And he was having serious trouble feeding his men—constantly writing letters to the governors of the surrounding states begging them to supply beef cattle, poultry, vegetables, and salt.

Because he had no money to buy anything, Washington had been forced to seize food and supplies from surrounding landowners. And American citizens were angry at having their hard-earned wares taken from them to back a cause that seemed increasingly hopeless. They were getting tired of the war and becoming apathetic to its outcome. After all, they had supported the conflict for nearly six full years and didn't have much to show for it. American victories were few and far between. The Continental Army appeared to be right back where it had started, and the British seemed to be in a stronger position than ever before. As a result, George Washington's leadership was now under serious scrutiny. The previous June, for instance, without consulting Washington, Congress appointed a new general, Horatio Gates, to command American southern forces—and the commander in chief had deeply resented the move.

Overall, there seemed no place to turn for immediate relief. The French were reluctant to provide additional money and supplies after having seen their earlier contributions go for naught. The United States Treasury was empty. The value of Continental paper money had collapsed—giving rise to the popular phrase "not worth a Continental." And the Congress in Philadelphia had no power over the states to draft men for the army or levy taxes to fund the war. The truth was that nearly everyone had serious doubts that the fledgling nation could survive much longer.

But George Washington refused to give in. He continued to produce a torrent of letters to Congress and the state governments about "the alarming state of our supplies." "The absolute want of pay and clothing, along with the great scarcity of provisions, are too serious a trial for men," he wrote in one letter. "Recruits cannot possibly join the army before they are clothed," he grumbled in another. "I think I am giving you a general," he said when he promoted Rhode Islander

Nathanael Greene, "but what can a general do without men, without arms, without clothing, without stores, without provisions?"

Washington had sent Greene south in October with hopes of halting a string of British victories there. In May 1780, American General Benjamin Lincoln had been forced to surrender Charleston, South Carolina, after holding out as long as he could against a siege conducted by 14,000 British troops under the command of Lord Earl Cornwallis. In what turned out to be the worst defeat of the Revolution for the Americans, more than 5,000 troops had been captured. It was this loss that precipitated Congress's appointment of Horatio Gates as southern commander.

But only a few months later, in August 1780, a disastrous defeat at Camden would give the British total control of South Carolina. During that battle, Cornwallis (outnumbered by a two-to-one margin) had made the bold stroke of charging directly into the center of the American line where Gates had placed untrained militia rather than experienced Continental soldiers. The militia quickly threw down their arms and fled. General Gates, who had positioned himself in the rear of the fighting, panicked when he saw the massive retreat and hundreds of British regulars charging straight toward him. He galloped away as fast as he could, leaving his troops without a leader. By nightfall, he was in Charlotte, North Carolina, some sixty miles to the rear. Three days later, he ended his personal retreat in Hillsboro, North Carolina—more than 180 miles from the battlefield in Camden. When it was all said and done, Gates had lost all but 700 of his 4,100 men—and Cornwallis had lost none of his 2,000 troops.

That's when George Washington sent Nathanael Greene south to replace Gates. Congress, of course, did not offer any objections, even though Greene was an unproven commander—a thirty-three-year-old Quaker from Rhode Island who had no military experience prior to joining the army. What Greene did possess, however, and Washington knew it, was an uncommon ability to lead men. Buoyed by Washington's confidence in him, Greene quickly rode south and implemented vast changes to restore the demoralized army to fighting form. Among other things, he was to beg, steal, and borrow so that his men were properly clothed and fed. Then he unashamedly and repeatedly reminded them that they had a purpose in this war. "You are fighting to be free," he told them.

As if the fall of 1780 had not been bad enough with the losses at Charleston and Camden, Washington also had to face the shocking defection of one of his best generals—his friend and personal protégé, Benedict Arnold. In command of the garrison at West Point, Arnold had become incensed at being passed over for promotion. In retaliation, he had offered his services to the British Crown. They were immediately accepted and, for more than a year, Arnold had been relaying to British General Henry Clinton in New York detailed information of American maneuvers. On September 21, Arnold had given Major John Andre, Clinton's adjutant general, a secret letter confirming that the British would pay him a huge sum of money in return for surrendering West Point to the British. That move, if accomplished, would secure the Hudson River for the British navy. But Andre, who tried to pass through the American lines dressed as a civilian, was captured and the incriminating document discovered hidden in one of his boots.

After being shown the letter, Washington immediately sent a detachment to arrest Arnold. But the traitor was tipped off in advance and quickly fled to the safety of an anchored British warship in New York Harbor. Later, Arnold sent his former commander a personal letter admitting his guilt.

George Washington took this treasonous act personally. And it was a betrayal that would gnaw at him for the rest of his life.

"This is treason of the blackest dye!" he exclaimed in disgust to Alexander Hamilton after reading Arnold's letter. "Whom can we trust now?"

Despite a last-minute personal appeal from Major Andre to be shot as a soldier rather than hanged as a spy, Washington rejected the request and ordered Andre hanged. Such a decision, he knew, would send a piercing message to Benedict Arnold that, should he ever be captured, hanging would be his fate, also.

2

General Washington's Winter Headquarters
New Windsor, New York
January 1781

General Washington is seated at the center of the writing table. A stack of papers along with an inkwell and quill pen rest in front of him. Washington is leaning back in his chair, chin in hand, looking at and listening to David Humphreys, also seated and reading a just-completed letter.

Charles Watts, soldier in the Tenth Massachusetts regiment, was tried for absenting himself from his regiment without leave and attempting to go to the enemy. The court, after maturely considering the evidence, finds the prisoner guilty of a breach of Article I, Section 6, of the Rules and Articles of War, and sentences him to suffer death—more than two-thirds of the court agreeing. The commander in chief confirms the sentence but is pleased on the intercession of the officers of the regiment to which the prisoner belongs in his behalf to pardon him and directs his release from confinement.

Humphreys places the letter in front of the general who signs it and puts it on top of eight other letters completed this day.

"The last, Colonel?" asks Washington.

"Yes, sir."

"Very well. Is there any news of General Knox and his progress with the governors?"

"None, formal," responds Humphreys. "However, there is scuttlebutt that he has persuaded several to contribute liberally."

"Excellent!" says Washington. "Let's draft a brief note to the general complimenting him on his accomplishments."

"Even without confirmation, sir?"

"Yes, Colonel. If true, it is most deserved. If not, it may spur him on to try harder."

"Yes, sir." Replies the young aide as he jots down a few notes.

Tench Tilghman briskly walks in holding several papers. "We have two dispatches, sir," he says excitedly. "One from General Wayne and the other from Governor Jefferson."

"What does Wayne say?" asks Washington tensely.
"He relates that the mutiny is at an end, sir."

◆   ◆   ◆

In the weeks following the rebellion of the Pennsylvania line, the mutineers were forced to halt at Princeton because all boats on the Delaware River had been seized by order of Congress. That prevented them from descending into Philadelphia. Anthony Wayne subsequently had been held under guard by his own rebellious troops at a local tavern.

In the meantime, General Henry Clinton got wind of the American mutiny and immediately ordered British Grenadiers, Light Infantry, and three battalions of Hessian Grenadiers to prepare for a march into New Jersey. Clinton also sent two emissaries to meet with the Pennsylvania insurgents and offer them a deal. If they would lay down their arms, Clinton would pardon them on all past offenses. They would also be paid any money due them by the American Congress and would not be required to serve in the British army unless they chose to do so.

But Clinton's plan backfired. The mutineers, who had long since sobered up, took the emissaries prisoner and informed General Wayne that they were no "Benedict Arnolds," that their intentions were honorable, and that their "attachment to that country for which they had so often fought and bled" was unalterable.

◆   ◆   ◆

"The mutiny is at an end?" asks Washington with a smile. "Good news, indeed. What details?"

"General Wayne explains, sir," continues Tilghman, "that the two emissaries from General Clinton are to be tried and, if found guilty, hanged as spies."

"Excellent!" snaps Washington. "That will certainly shut the door against any further negotiations with the enemy!"

"General Wayne goes on, sir," says Tilghman.

"Yes, please continue."

"Governor Joseph Reed has been appointed by Congress to lead a New Jersey commission to redress grievances. I have explained to him that our soldiers are not devoid of reasoning faculties, nor are they callous to the first feelings of nature. They have served their country with fidelity for near five years, poorly clothed, badly fed, and worse paid. Each case will be examined individually, and it is anticipated that some

soldiers will be discharged. I believe, however, that many will elect to reenlist until March."

"General Wayne concludes, sir," says Tilghman, "it is my honor to inform you that the mutiny is over."

"Good! Very good," responds Washington. "I am much relieved. Now, what has Governor Jefferson to relate?"

"I'm afraid the news is bad, sir," Tilghman replies. "The governor reports that Benedict Arnold has been granted a command in the British army and, with a force of some 1,500 men—including Lieutenant Colonel Simcoe's Queen's Rangers and the light infantry and grenadiers of the 80th Regiment—has invaded his state."

"Good God!" exclaims Washington rising to his feet and pounding his fist on the table. "That traitor is in Virginia?!?!?"

"Yes, General," says Tilghman, who refers to the letter without reading verbatim. "Governor Jefferson reports that Arnold landed at Hood's Point near Jamestown where he quickly overran the local militia. Six miles upriver at Westover, his troops destroyed an iron foundry, a gunpowder factory, and several machine shops. Then he marched on to Richmond and, without opposition, occupied the city."

Washington is now pacing back and forth in front of the table, running his right hand through his hair from the forehead back.

"Arnold next wrote a letter to Jefferson offering to spare Richmond if the governor would allow him to seize tobacco without resistance," continues Tilghman.

"And how did Jefferson respond?" asks Washington.

"Sir, the governor called Arnold 'the greatest of all traitors' and told him to pound salt."

"Good for Jefferson! Good!"

"Arnold then ransacked Richmond, sir. He burned many public buildings and private residences. The traitor has now moved on to Portsmouth where, Governor Jefferson reports, he is preparing a winter encampment."

"Jefferson is also besieging us for troops and supplies, I suppose?" asks Washington.

"He is, sir," responds Tilghman, "although not with as much fervor as before."

"Well, I'm sure that's because he well knows of our condition here."

"And because he has been refused before, sir."

"Yes, Tilghman. Well, thank you for your summaries," says Washington, who turns toward David Humphreys, still sitting at the table. "Colonel Humphreys, have you time to begin a letter to Governor Jefferson right now?"

"Of course, sir."

"If that is all, sir…" says Tilghman who, after receiving a nod from the general, takes his leave.

"To His Excellency, Thomas Jefferson, Governor of Virginia," begins Humphreys.

"Yes," says Washington, now dictating. "I am much obliged for your letter giving me an account of the enemy's incursion into your state. There is no doubt that a principal object of Arnold's operations is to make a diversion in favor of Cornwallis in the Carolinas. I am apprehensive that you will experience more such depredations in the future; nor should I be surprised if the enemy were to establish a post in Virginia until the season for opening a campaign begins.

"Our situation in this quarter precludes any hope of affording you further assistance at the moment. To oppose our southern misfortunes and surmount our difficulties, our principal dependence must be on the means we have left to us in your quarter. I hope it is some consolation to you that I believe, among all our distresses, that these are more than adequate to get the job done. I am also persuaded that you will not be diverted from the measures intended to reinforce the Southern Army and put it in a condition to stop the progress of the enemy in that quarter. I have the honor, etc."

"I wonder if General Greene is aware of Arnold's presence in Virginia," says Humphreys.

"I'm certain Jefferson has sent him a communiqué to that end," responds Washington. "That'll be one more evil added to Greene's challenge."

General Nathanael Greene's Encampment
North Carolina/South Carolina Border
January 1781

Thomas Jefferson had indeed updated Nathanael Greene. But the new southern commander was unable to help defend Virginia from the ravages of Benedict Arnold's army. After his appointment as southern commander, Greene had ridden directly to Charlotte, North Carolina, to take command of an army of only 2,500 men of which fewer than 1,500 were fit for duty.

"The appearance of the troops was wretched beyond description," he wrote a friend after his first inspection. "The wants of this army are so numerous and various that the shortest way of telling you is to inform you that we have nothing! We are living on charity."

Greene was well aware that forces under Lord Cornwallis included more than 13,000 British regulars, Hessians, and American loyalists. Undaunted by those numbers, however, he confidently proceeded to take command and create a fresh plan of action.

After consulting extensively with his officers, Greene elected to divide his army into two parts—delegating a significant portion to Brigadier General

Daniel Morgan, a wily veteran whom Washington had sent south thinking he could be of use to Greene. Hoping to confuse the British by having two active armies in different places, General Greene believed that once Cornwallis committed himself to pursue one army, the other could approach the British from the rear. Accordingly, Greene assigned 300 ready-to-fight Maryland, Virginia, and Delaware soldiers and cavalrymen to Morgan with orders to march into western South Carolina and gather militia along the way. Then, realizing the need to regroup, Greene marched his remaining troops southeast to Cheraw, South Carolina, for refitting and training.

In response to this move, however, Cornwallis shrewdly split his own forces and detached 1,200 troops under cavalryman Banastre Tarleton to take on Morgan. Tarleton's reputation was one of lightning-quick strikes, mad dashes, and barbaric cruelty. Every South Carolinian, for example, well knew that Tarleton's British Legion had massacred dozens of American soldiers as they surrendered at the Battle of Waxhaw's Creek in May 1780. Such brutality had earned the dashing young cavalryman the moniker "Bloody Tarleton."

Morgan had progressed sixty-five miles southwest of Charlotte when he received intelligence that the British troops were approaching. Despite having been joined by more than 500 local militiamen, the Americans were still heavily outnumbered. And Morgan was experienced enough to realize that untrained militia were no match for British regulars and cavalry. Seeking a good defensive position, he quickly concentrated his troops on a large piece of elevated pasture known locally as "The Cowpens." Then he stayed up all night and devised a new and innovative battle plan.

The biggest problem Morgan faced was the tendency of American militiamen to break and run when under heavy fire—just as they had done at Camden. The British, he knew, counted on such a retreat and regularly planned their own strategy to take advantage of it. Determined to avert a catastrophe, Morgan decided to place his militia in two front lines, order them to fire no more than two volleys, and then run to the rear behind the Continental regulars.

That night, getting no sleep and battling almost-crippling arthritis, Morgan went among his men from campfire to campfire and explained what he wanted them to do and why it would work. "Remember, boys," he told them, "just hold up your heads, give them two fires and you're free."

At sunrise on January 16, 1781, Morgan placed expert riflemen on the point followed by the rest of the militia. Behind them and out of sight, he placed the seasoned Continentals—and to the far rear were the cavalry. As predicted, when the battle began, Tarleton ordered a frontal bayonet attack. The militia responded with their two shots and retreated. The redcoats, thinking they were winning, charged wildly into the center of the American line. Suddenly and unexpectedly, however, they were cut down by heavy fire from the entrenched Continentals. General Morgan then outflanked the British by sending the militia around to the left and the cavalry around to the right. Within minutes, the entire British force was surrounded. Rather than be slaughtered, most promptly surrendered.

Colonel Banastre Tarleton, however, fought savagely and, with a few of his dragoons, cut a path out of the encirclement and beat a hasty retreat to the east. Morgan's cavalry followed along for nearly twenty-five miles before giving up the chase. When it was all said and done, Daniel Morgan had captured or killed nearly 80 percent of the British contingent sent against him that day.

Word of Morgan's victory spread quickly through the thirteen states and provided a much-needed shot in the arm for the American cause. The mere thought of Tarleton retreating and running for his life resulted in hoots and hollers from troops everywhere. Washington, at New Windsor, heard about it when Morgan's report was passed to him through a dispatch from General Greene. "Eight hundred stand of arms, one hundred dragoon horses, two standards, two fieldpieces, thirty-five wagons, a traveling forge, and all their music are ours," Morgan had proudly reported. Not only that, he went on, but British casualties amounted to "100 killed, 200 wounded, and 600 captured" while the Americans suffered twelve killed and sixty wounded."

Washington responded with letters of praise and commendation. "I wish to congratulate you on the brilliant and important success of General Morgan," he wrote to Greene (observing the formal chain of command). "Please thank Morgan and the gallant troops under his command for their brilliant victory."

General Washington's Headquarters
New Windsor, New York
January 1781

Any time Washington might have had to savor Morgan's victory at Cowpens was short-lived. Another dispatch soon reached New Windsor reporting that 200 members of the New Jersey brigade had staged a mutiny of their own. "The troops have marched toward Trenton," the message read. "They are much disguised with liquor, but no blood has been spilt. The mutineers claim they have the same grievances as the Pennsylvania line."

As more details poured in, Washington realized this new insurrection had been spurred on because no real punishment had been doled out after the Pennsylvania mutiny. "This spirit will spread itself through the remainder of the army if not extinguished by some decisive measure," Washington noted. And then he immediately ordered General Robert Howe to take 600 men from West Point, march to Trenton, and "compel the mutineers to unconditional submission." Washington further stated that Howe should "grant no terms while they are with arms in their hands or in a state of resistance" and that, if successful in achieving a surrender, he should "instantly execute a few of the most active and most incendiary leaders."

Washington next sent out two more letters. He asked the governor of New Jersey for the help of the militia in quelling the mutiny and, additionally, requested that no compromise be made with the mutineers. His second letter was to the committee created by Congress to deal with the mutinies. "I beg leave strongly to recommend that no terms be made with them," he urged. "I am now taking the most vigorous coercive measure to put an immediate stop to such horrid proceedings."

After these letters were sent out by dispatch riders, Washington became restless and began to think more and more about the consequences that might result if this mutiny were not handled forcefully. Then he startled his aides by announcing that he was going to ride directly to the scene to personally oversee the situation. The next day, the general and a small travel contingent rode to Trenton along mountainous roads through rough winter weather. When heavy snows made the roads impassable, Washington borrowed a sleigh from a local resident and took off cross-country through the woods.

Once at the scene, Generals Washington and Howe armed their troops with artillery and surrounded the huts of the mutineers. After being ordered to surrender within five minutes or suffer the consequences, the insurgents gave up without resistance. But Washington immediately made it clear that he would allow no negotiations. Fifteen of the 200 were identified as ringleaders, instantly tried, and found guilty. Twelve of the fifteen were sentenced to comprise a firing squad that would execute the other three. The first two executions took place separately as the shooters wept openly. Washington then pardoned the third condemned man.

After decisively settling the matter, the commander in chief urged members of the New Jersey Congressional Commission to give the fullest hearings to all complaints. "The mutinous disposition of the troops is now completely subdued and succeeded by a genuine penitence," wrote Washington. "Having punished the guilty and supported authority, it now becomes proper to do justice. I hope this will completely extinguish the spirit of mutiny, and that we can now render the situation of the army more tolerable than it has heretofore been."

When Washington returned to New Windsor a couple of days later, he sat down with Alexander Hamilton and, together, they composed "General Orders" to all the troops in the area. In this several-page document, Washington and Hamilton recounted recent events including a detailed account of the New Jersey mutiny. And then, knowing it would be read aloud, they made an eloquent plea for the troops to remember what they were fighting for.

We began a contest for liberty and independence ill provided with the means for war, relying on our own patriotism to supply the deficiency. We expected to encounter many wants and distresses, and we should neither shrink from them when they happen nor fly in the face of law and government to procure redress. There is no doubt the public will do ample justice to men fighting and suffering in its defense. But it is our duty to bear present evils with fortitude—looking forward to the period when our country will have more in its power to reward our services.

History is full of examples of armies suffering with patience, extremities of distress which exceed those we have suffered—and this is the cause of ambition and conquest—not in that of the rights of humanity, of their country, of their families, of themselves. Shall we who aspire to the distinction of a patriot army do less?"

3

General Washington's Winter Headquarters
New Windsor, New York
January 1781

It is barely sunrise. Alexander Hamilton reports to headquarters as usual. He bounds onto the porch of the farmhouse, pausing long enough to stomp the snow off his boots, then bursts through the door and springs up the stairs to the small writing room. His work this day will include drafting two letters for the general—one to the president of Congress providing an update of events and another to British General Sir Henry Clinton, proposing a prisoner exchange.

Hamilton has been with Washington for nearly the entire duration of the war—first as an artillery officer and next as aide-de-camp. Everyone knows that Hamilton has earned his reputation as one of Washington's most trusted advisers. Some say he is also the brightest. But on first sight, it is hard to believe. Standing barely five feet seven inches tall with narrow shoulders, he looks more like a young boy than a seasoned veteran who has just turned twenty-six years old. He has a freckled baby face with piercing violet-blue eyes. His forehead is high and his sandy brown hair is curly and cropped short.

A few months earlier, Hamilton had taken some time off to marry Elizabeth Schuyler in Albany, New York. Now his ambitious mind was turning toward the future. He wanted to start a family, study law, and make something of himself. He longed to distinguish himself in battle, but General Washington had repeatedly turned down his requests for a field command.

On this particular morning, Hamilton is not in a good mood. He is stewing about Washington's stubbornness—and brooding about the fact that he has not received a promotion in nearly four years. He is also irritated that Washington had, the day before, reprimanded him for a couple of minor errors he'd made in a letter.

It doesn't help the situation that, on this morning, George Washington is in one of those gray moods the staff notices on occasion—where he appears somber, sullen, and perturbed about something. The stage, therefore, is set for a confrontation between the two. And it comes unexpectedly when, later in the morning, Hamilton finishes writing his drafts and goes to deliver them to Tench Tilghman.

On his way down the stairs, Hamilton passes Washington heading upstairs.

"Colonel Hamilton, I would like to speak with you," says the general.

"Yes, sir," comes the response. "I'll be with you immediately."

Assuming that Hamilton is going to drop off the letters to Tilghman and be right back, Washington waits on the upstairs landing. Hamilton, on the other hand, assumes that Washington will simply go into his room and attend to other business. So when he reaches Tilghman in the downstairs writing room, he takes several minutes to discuss some important details.

On his way back, Hamilton runs into his young friend, the Marquis de Lafayette, in the hallway. Although Lafayette is a general and Hamilton a lieutenant colonel, the two greet each other without regard to rank. They embrace, kiss each other on the cheeks, and begin conversing in French.

Marie Jean Paul Joseph Roch Yves Gilbert du Motier, Marquis de Lafayette, one of the wealthiest young men in France, is heir to the estates and manor houses of Auvergne-Vissac, St. Romain, Fix, and Chavaniac. His habit of always dressing in an impeccably handsome uniform offsets an ungainly, pudgy frame. He has thin red hair that is rapidly receding. His face, with a long, pointed nose, seems slightly misshapen. He is only twenty-three, but he's been in America for more than four years—and has earned the respect of nearly everyone he's met.

In 1777, Lafayette appeared before Congress with a pot of money and an offer to serve without pay and without a command. In response, Congress appointed him a major general. When he showed up at Valley Forge, Washington was impressed with the nineteen-year-old's demeanor, passion, and gift for inspiring the troops. "The moment I heard of America, I loved her," Lafayette told Washington. "The moment I knew she was fighting for freedom, I burned with a desire of bleeding for her."

In a very short time, the commander in chief was treating Lafayette like a seasoned officer. And when the young man was wounded at the battle of Brandywine, Washington had told his surgeon to "treat him as if he were my son, for I love him as if he were." In turn, Lafayette (whose father had been killed in a European war) viewed Washington as an adopted father.

Alexander Hamilton, who was the only aide-de-camp who spoke fluent French, had become fast friends with Lafayette. Both young, both bright, both energetic, capable, and confident, they looked out for each other. Lafayette had particularly encouraged Hamilton to ask for a command of his own—and had lobbied Washington to make it happen. He had even nominated Hamilton for the position of adjutant general although the appointment ultimately went to Colonel Thomas Pickering.

Now meeting in the hall, Hamilton and Lafayette chat excitedly in French for several minutes. When the marquis mentions he has been summoned by Washington to discuss Benedict Arnold's presence in Virginia, Hamilton suddenly remembers that the general wants to see him, so he excuses himself and briskly walks back to the front of the house and up the stairs. He finds the commander in chief impatiently pacing back and forth on the landing.

"Colonel Hamilton," *snaps Washington,* "you have kept me waiting at the head of the stairs these ten minutes."

Caught completely off guard, Hamilton reacts defensively. "Certainly, General, that was not my intention," *he responds.*

"I must tell you, sir, that you treat me with disrespect—and I do not appreciate it," *says Washington, his voice now clearly resonating along the walls.*

"And I don't appreciate your tone, sir," *Hamilton barks back.* "Perhaps, it's best for me to tender my resignation."

"Very well, Colonel—if that is your choice."

"That is my choice, sir," *responds Hamilton, who then spins around and stomps down the stairs.*

Washington, in turn, marches into his room and slams the door.

Downstairs, Lafayette has heard the ruckus and rushes over to meet Hamilton, who immediately begins venting his anger. Hearing the shouting, Tench Tilghman walks out to see what is going on.

Tilghman and Lafayette quickly escort their friend to the back writing room and try to calm him down. They give him a cup of tea and explain that General Washington isn't himself, that something is obviously bothering him, and that when he calms down he will surely have a change of heart. But Hamilton assures them both that it does not matter what the general does now because he has had enough and intends, once and for all, to go somewhere else.

About an hour later, Lafayette and Tilghman call on Washington to discuss the matter. The general has, by now, calmed down and deeply regrets his burst of temper. He has thought about Hamilton's service at Trenton, at Valley Forge, and how his young aide has loyally stood by him when others would not.

"Will you please go to Colonel Hamilton in my name," *Washington asks Tilghman,* "and assure him that I have great confidence in his abilities and integrity. Please also tell him that I would like to meet personally with him to heal this difference—which could not have happened except in a moment of passion."

While Lafayette stays to confer with Washington about Benedict Arnold, Tilghman goes downstairs to relay the general's message to Hamilton.

"Please tell General Washington that I have made up my mind on this matter and will not change it," *Hamilton replies matter-of-factly.* "But also assure him that I will stay on until a French-speaking aide can be found."

Tilghman returns to the commander in chief's office just as Lafayette is leaving. When he explains Hamilton's negative response, Washington winces and puts his left hand to his cheek. Trying to mask the shooting pain from one of his infected teeth, the general makes a muffled sound and responds in a hollow voice.

"I see," he says. "I am sorry to hear it."

◆   ◆   ◆

The Marquis de Lafayette appeared on American soil well before Benjamin Franklin was able to persuade France to declare war on Great Britain. Lafayette became involved because he was inspired by America's fight for freedom against great odds. On the other hand, the king of France and his prime minister, Charles Gravier Count de Vergennes, got involved because they saw an opportunity to gain revenge against Great Britain for defeating them during the French and Indian War. But in forming an alliance with the Americans, they were careful not to allow the infant nation to become too powerful. The Americans had to be maneuvered so that, in the end, France could reap the bounty of large North American land domains.

Initially, the French supplied George Washington with abundant provisions, munitions, clothing, and money—most of which arrived at Valley Forge during the harsh winter of 1777–1778. That aid, more than anything else, resulted in a great renewal of the American cause. With new hope, thousands of volunteers poured into Valley Forge—and within six months, a refortified and reenergized force marched out of the once-withered encampment. But now, more than two years had passed without significant help from France. Finally, in July 1780, a fleet of eight ships of the line, two frigates, and two bomb vessels arrived off the coast of Newport, Rhode Island. On board were some of the finest military forces in the world—nearly 6,000 French troops under the command of veteran Lieutenant General Count de Rochambeau. This was three-quarters of the promised force. Another 2,000 men had been left behind, because there were no ships to transport them. In addition, the balance of the French Navy headed to the Caribbean Sea to protect France's assets in the West Indies.

For months, Washington and Rochambeau communicated mainly through dispatches. Washington related vague generalities about what might be done in a joint venture. Rochambeau, in turn, placated the American commander in chief. "I come wholly obedient," he said, "and with the zeal and veneration which I have for you and for the remarkable talents you have displayed in sustaining a war which will always be memorable."

The truth is that neither general actually wanted to make a move. Rochambeau was reluctant to act without being at full strength. And Washington, waiting for supplies and reinforcements, did not want the French commander to find out just how weak the American army really was for fear he would return to France. During this period of inactivity, a superior British fleet moved in position to blockade the French ships from leaving Newport. Then the landlocked French troops began to drain what was left of America's limited food supplies.

Finally, on September 20, 1780, the two commanders traveled to Hartford, Connecticut, for a brief personal meeting. Communicating mostly through an interpreter, Washington proposed that the French fleet make a dash for Boston Harbor where they would be both more useful and more secure. In addition, he suggested that the French and American armies redeploy in the vicinity of New York City. Such a move would serve two purposes: First, it would prevent Sir Henry Clinton from sending too many forces south to join Benedict Arnold; and second, the combined force would be ready to take action en masse if an opportunity presented itself. To the first proposal, Rochambeau politely explained that the French fleet was much weaker than the British who were blockading them and that they could not possibly take the risk of trying for Boston. Regarding joining the American army near New York, Rochambeau was both reluctant and evasive. He indicated he did not wish to move until his additional 2,000 troops arrived, but he said he would like to think over the idea in more depth. Having made the first step at building a personal relationship, Washington returned to New Windsor and Rochambeau to Newport.

Over the fall and into winter, as the two commanders continued to communicate by dispatch, Rochambeau came to realize the true condition of the American army and its nation's situation. In letters to his superiors in France, he wrote that General Washington had only 3,000 men, and that the government was "in consternation" because paper money had fallen to an almost worthless state. "Send us troops, ships, and money," Rochambeau wrote, "but do not depend on these people or upon their means: they have neither money nor credit; their means of resistance are only momentary and called forth when they are attacked in their own homes."

After waiting months for his additional 2,000 troops and hearing nothing from the French government, General Rochambeau sent his son (an officer serving under his command) to France with a personal letter to Prime Minister Vergennes. The general requested more money, more supplies, and the immediate deployment of his promised troops.

French Ministry
Paris, France
Late January 1781

Rochambeau's son, the Viscount de Rochambeau, received a cold response from the prime minister who was not inclined to provide any more help whatsoever to the American cause. As a matter of fact, Vergennes was fed up with the American Revolution and had recently devised a plan to end the war. He had proposed that a summit of European nations be held in Vienna. Emissaries from the Netherlands, Sweden, Russia, and Austria-Hungary would act as mediators while representatives of France, Britain, Spain, and the American colonies would negotiate final terms. Vergennes was then going to present the idea of a final settlement based on the current status quo in America. At that point, the British controlled Georgia, the Carolinas, New York, and most of Maine, Vermont, Michigan, Wisconsin, Minnesota, Illinois, Indiana, and Ohio.

After floating his idea across the English Channel, Vergennes received word back from British Prime Minister Frederick Lord North that Great Britain was "very interested" in the proposal and would be inclined to accept it.

4

General Washington's Winter Headquarters
New Windsor, New York
February 1781

It is mid-evening. Washington, Lafayette, and Hamilton are seated around the dining room table in the New Windsor farmhouse with old friend and former aide-de-camp, John Laurens, who has just arrived at the encampment. They have completed a relaxing dinner, reminiscing about old times and catching up on events since last being together. Some food still remains on the table. Empty plates have been cleared away. Washington picks up a pitcher of ale and tops off each man's mug.

"A toast," *he says lifting his drink,* "to the good health of our friend John Laurens."

"Here! Here!" *responds Lafayette and Hamilton as each takes a swig.*

"And to your good health, also, gentlemen," *responds Laurens with a drink of his own.*

After a brief pause, General Washington's face turns serious. His eyes fix on Laurens. The others realize it is now time to get down to the business at hand.

"Colonel Laurens, when you reach Paris, I would like you to engage in a somewhat different approach with the French than we have previously taken."

"Yes, General?" *asks Laurens.*

"Yes. Rather than requesting only French troops and supplies, I would like the majority of what you ask for to be a sum of money equal to the procuring of such resources. If aided in this way, we shall be in a condition to continue the war as long as the obstinacy of the enemy may require."

"You must concentrate their thoughts on providing a few items rather than many," *adds the Marquis de Lafayette.*

"And it is much easier to simply write a check than to mobilize men and procure supplies," *says Alexander Hamilton.*

"Certainly," *confirms Laurens.* "I understand."

"Good," Washington says. "Now we know that our French friends are hesitant to provide additional resources, so I suggest we concentrate on the presentation you must make."

"Indeed, sir, I agree," responds Laurens. "That is why I am here, of course, to seek your advice and counsel."

◆   ◆   ◆

Congress had unanimously elected John Laurens, twenty-six-year-old native of South Carolina, to be a special minister to France. His mission: travel to Europe and convince the Court of Versailles to provide additional aid for the American cause.

It was a good choice. Educated in Geneva and London, Laurens was well suited to the task. He had a bright mind and spoke fluent French. Slender, good looking, and passionate, he made a good first impression and was able to think quickly on his feet. And despite his young age, Laurens was a seasoned veteran. He had become Washington's aide-de-camp in 1777 and had served at Brandywine, Germantown, Valley Forge, and Monmouth, where he was wounded. In May 1780, he'd been among the 5,000 soldiers captured when Charleston fell to the British and had spent six months as a prisoner of war. After being freed in a prisoner exchange, he was sent back to the south to serve under Nathanael Greene. While there, Laurens conceived a plan to enlist slaves in the Continental Army and grant them freedom in return for their service. While it was a good way to add reinforcements to the American line, the idea had not been well received in southern circles—even though Laurens used his own money to purchase clothing, food, and arms for an all-black regiment.

When Congress asked him to accept the appointment to go to France, Laurens suggested his good friend Alexander Hamilton as a better choice. But the members of Congress were more familiar with Laurens because his father, Henry, had served as its president. After leaving office, Henry Laurens had been appointed minister to Holland but was captured on board ship in the Atlantic by a British vessel and was being held prisoner in the Tower of London. Congress suggested that John Laurens could take the opportunity to negotiate his father's release via a prisoner exchange. Faced with that possibility, the young man accepted the appointment and, as ordered by Congress, had traveled to New Windsor to consult with the commander in chief.

Washington asked the Marquis de Lafayette to sit in on the conversation because of his obvious familiarity with French government officials. The general had also included Alexander Hamilton, with whom he had recently made amends, because he knew Laurens and Hamilton were good friends. Washington had it in the back of his mind that, as Laurens spoke French, he might be a replacement for Hamilton upon returning from France.

◆   ◆   ◆

"Regarding your presentation to the Court of Versailles," Washington says, pulling a piece of paper from his vest pocket, "I have made some notes of suggestion."

"I'm very interested to hear them, General," responds Laurens.

"I have jotted down twelve key points."

Laurens leans forward in his chair, arms resting on the table.

As Washington starts to speak, Hamilton pulls out a pen and paper and prepares to take notes. Lafayette, too, is leaning forward, his chin resting on his hand.

"Point 1," begins Washington. "The following facts have brought this country to a crisis: the diffused population of the states; the difficulty of drawing together its resources; the temper of a part of its inhabitants; the lack of a sufficient national wealth as a foundation for revenue; and the almost total extinction of commerce. All these things have contributed to the fact that this country has exceeded is natural abilities to carry on the war.

"Point 2. Some errors have been committed in the administration of our finances. It is impossible, by an internal means alone, for us to extricate ourselves from these embarrassments, restore public credit, and furnish the necessary funds to support the war effort.

"Point 3. It is impractical to maintain paper credit without hard cash on hand.

"Point 4. The seizure of provisions from local citizens, as I have had to do, is now regarded as burdensome and oppressive to the people. It has excited serious opposition.

"Point 5. The instability of our currency and our deficiency of funds has impaired the public credit.

"Point 6. You should make a point of mentioning our soldiers—their sufferings, their want of clothing, want of provisions, and want of pay.

"Point 7. There is danger that our citizens, apprehensive of future sufferings and little accustomed to bearing heavy burdens, may imagine they have only exchanged one tyranny for another.

"Point 8. Today's absolute necessity of an ample supply of money will effectuate once and for all the great objects of our alliance—the liberty and independence of these United States.

"Point 9. Next to a loan of money, we believe that a constant naval superiority on these coasts is most important. It would interrupt the enemy's regular transmission of supplies from Europe and reduce them to a difficult defensive position. This superior-

ity (combined with an aid of money) would enable us to convert the war into a vigorous offensive. And, of course, there would be advantages to the trade of both France
and America."

"If I may comment on that point, General," interrupts Lafayette.

"Of course, my dear Marquis."

"Colonel Laurens, I believe you should point out to my countrymen that with a
naval inferiority, it is simply impossible to make war in America. If we had possessed
a naval superiority this spring, a great deal might have been achieved with the army of
Monsieur de Rochambeau."

"Excellent point," exclaims Alexander Hamilton, furiously writing down everything that is being said.

"Also," continues Lafayette, "English detachments under the arch-traitor Benedict
Arnold are now ravaging the South. Under the protection of some frigates, a corps of
1,500 men are repairing to Virginia without our being able to get to them. We simply
must have naval superiority for the next campaign and money enough to place the regular army and 10,000 militia in the South.

"I see," responds Laurens. "Yes, of course, I see."

"Point 10," continues George Washington. "An additional supply of troops would
be extremely desirable. Count de Rochambeau and I believe 15,000 men would suf-
fice for the next campaign. Remember my earlier point, though, and do not belabor
this issue."

"Yes, sir," says Laurens.

"Point 11. The United States will be able to repay what it borrows once independence has been established.

"Point 12. In addressing the restlessness of the American people, this is what I
advise you say, because I know it to be the truth: The people are discontented, but it is
with the feeble and oppressive mode of conducting the war, not the war itself. They are
willing to contribute to its support, but they are unwilling to do it in a way that renders private property precarious. A large majority are still firmly attached to the independence of these states, abhor a reunion with Great Britain, and are affectionate to
the alliance with France."

"You should also tell them," says Lafayette to Laurens, "that the Continental troops
have as much courage and real discipline as the English. They are more accustomed to
deprivation, more patient than Europeans. And the recruits we are expecting have
seen more gunshots than three-fourths of the European soldiers."

Now appearing somewhat restless, Washington stands up, which signifies to the
others that the dinner meeting is at an end, and they too rise from their chairs. "My
dear Colonel Laurens," he says while reaching out to shake the young man's hand, "I

am delighted that this mission has fallen upon you. You are capable of placing our concerns before the Court of France in a more full and striking point of light than by any written communication I could send. Your integrity and independence of character, your exemplary honor and candor, I'm certain, will serve our cause well in this instance."

"Thank you, sir," replies a somewhat embarrassed John Laurens. "Thank you, indeed."

"Is there any other service we might be able to render you?" asks Washington.

"Sir, I wonder if you might commit to writing your twelve points so that I may study them on my voyage to France."

"Certainly, certainly," says the general, turning to Alexander Hamilton. "I believe we can accommodate your request."

"Absolutely," responds Hamilton. "We'll have it ready before you leave tomorrow."

"Excellent!" says Laurens. "My sincere thanks."

"Very well, sir. We shall see you in the morning," says Washington, who quickly exits the room.

Lafayette and Hamilton stay behind for a few moments to speak with Laurens. Lafayette shakes his friend's hand and wishes him the best. Hamilton goes up, drapes his arm around Laurens's shoulder and kisses him affectionately on the cheek, to which Laurens reacts uncomfortably.

In the back of the farmhouse, General Washington slips on his overcoat and goes out the door. Hastily traipsing across the backyard with snow spraying from his boots, he reaches the wooden outhouse where he fidgets with the latch, opens the door, and goes inside.

Near the North Carolina/South Carolina Border
February 1781

Following the battle of Cowpens, Generals Nathanael Greene and Daniel Morgan reunited their armies some thirty miles to the east near Catawba, South Carolina. They were forced to pull together, because Morgan could barely handle the six hundred British regulars and cavalrymen he had captured. After conferring about what to do next, the American commanders decided to head north to deposit their prisoners in Virginia. They also realized that while having to guard what amounted to a small British army, they would become extraordinarily vulnerable in the event of another major battle. So they sought to avoid conflict at all costs.

It was a good thing, too, because when Lord Cornwallis heard about Tarleton's loss at Cowpens, he took immediate action to rescue his six hundred men. In a daring move for an eighteenth century military leader, Cornwallis ordered nearly all his food, baggage, tents, wagons, and supplies burned, so his army could become more mobile and quick-moving. Then, joined by Banastre Tarleton and what was left of the cavalry, he took off in hot pursuit of Greene and Morgan.

Both armies crossed the Catawba River and headed into North Carolina—the Americans staying barely one step ahead of the British. The terrain they were traveling was severely hampered by a series of east-west running rivers and streams. Unfamiliar with the territory, Cornwallis was continually choosing the wrong places to cross—at the Catawba, at the Yadkin, and at the Deep River. The Americans, though, guided by local militia, knew exactly where to cross and what areas to avoid. Over the next two weeks, although he tried valiantly, Cornwallis was simply unable to catch Greene. Finally, on February 14, 1781, the Americans crossed the Dan River into Virginia. But when Cornwallis arrived the next day, he not only found the waters swollen from winter flooding, but had to face the fact that Greene had taken all available boats with him to the Virginia side. Frustrated and weary, the British commander decided to march his men to Hillsboro, North Carolina, for some rest and recuperation.

Nathanael Greene, meanwhile, took his British prisoners into central Virginia for interment and subsequently set about refitting, resupplying, and preparing his troops for a new offensive. Ten days later, on February 23, 1781, the entire American force recrossed the Dan River into North Carolina and began a cautious movement toward Hillsboro. Greene had developed a well-thought-through plan to harass Cornwallis without ever engaging him in a major conflict. Over the next several weeks, he intended to march back and forth, nibbling at the British army, ambushing them and then running away, and making strategic use of his new cavalry headed by Colonel Henry "Light Horse Harry" Lee. This was a campaign of harassment he had learned from George Washington.

General Washington's Headquarters
New Windsor, New York
February 1781

"Colonel Laurens is off on his journey in the proper state of mind, I trust?"

"He is, General," Lafayette replies. "I rode with him for several miles beyond the perimeter. His attitude is positive and optimistic. I believe he will do as well as anyone may do, given the circumstances."

"Indeed. Have you heard any more rumors about this supposed plan of Vergennes?"

"No, sir, nothing more. Perhaps it is just that, a rumor."

"Perhaps so," Washington agrees. "However, we cannot take that chance. If true, we only have a limited amount of time before France withdraws all support."

"Yes, sir," replies Lafayette. "But with delays in communication, formulating a concrete plan of action, organizing everyone—I would suppose we have at least a year or more."

"That depends, of course, on how far this rumor has been taken—and if a truce is actively being planned."

"Yes, General," replies Lafayette. "But Vergennes is a politically adept and cautious man. He will take his time. And I suspect, also, that the king does not yet completely support the idea."

"Oh?"

"Yes, sir. He is a kindly man with a soft heart," says Lafayette. "I explained this to Colonel Laurens. I told him that if he encounters stout resistance by Vergennes…"

"Which he most certainly will if there is any truth to this plan," Washington interjects.

"Yes, sir. If that happens, he should appeal for a direct audience with his majesty."

"Benjamin Franklin should be able to help with that," Washington thinks out loud. "I will send him a letter to that effect. Let us suppose for a minute, my dear marquis, that plans are indeed under way for a settlement based on territories occupied at the time of the truce."

"But, sir," replies Lafayette, "I just don't believe…"

"Yes, I know," interrupts Washington. "But just let us assume it is true. If so, it could explain a number of recent events."

"Well, sir, I guess it could explain Rochambeau's reluctance to take action."

"Uh-huh. He could be under orders from Vergennes to move only if he is at full strength and can assure success. But, I think, more likely, it explains why Arnold was given a command and sent into Virginia."

"Oh?" asks Lafayette in surprise.

"Yes. Virginia, intersected as it is with large navigable rivers, is greatly exposed to those kinds of predatory expeditions. There is simply no remedy against such a thing except naval superiority."

"Yes, that is true, but…"

"I believe Sir Henry Clinton understands this. I believe he thinks he can take control of Virginia in relatively easy fashion and in short order."

"And if they gain control of Virginia before…"

"Exactly," says Washington. "They will control the entire South."

"Mon Dieu! The entire South."

There is a brief lull in the conversation as both generals reflect on the possibility.

"I think it probable the enemy will push their operations into Virginia," says Washington finally, "and that makes our affairs there extremely important."

"I have seen this look on your face, before, General. You have a plan."

"I do," responds Washington with a smile. "And it involves you, sir."

"I stand ready for America, sir."

"Good. Here is my proposal. You are aware that a few weeks ago a storm broke the British blockade of Newport."

"Yes, sir," replies Lafayette. "Several of the British ships were damaged, and they had to retire to New York for repairs."

"As soon as I heard this news, I sent a dispatch to Rochambeau suggesting that, as his ships now enjoy an advantage, Commodore Destouches and his fleet ought to proceed to the Chesapeake along with a thousand troops and as much siege artillery as can be spared. Once there, they will provide the naval superiority needed to capture Arnold."

"Destouches will need help by land," replies Lafayette with a wink.

"Indeed, sir, and that is where you come in," says Washington. "I would be grateful if you would lead a detachment of light infantry from here along with a Continental regiment formed at Morristown from the Jersey troops. Combined, they will amount to about 1,200. Once your two battalions rendezvous, you will proceed with all possible dispatch to Head of Elk, Maryland, where you will then convey down the bay to the point of operation—mostly likely Hampton."

"Is that where I will find Destouches?"

"Yes. I have just received a dispatch from General Rochambeau that his ships will sail on the ninth of March from Newport."

"Excellent, sir! I am glad to hear my countrymen are taking action at your request."

"When you arrive at your destination, you must act on your own judgment as circumstances direct. I would suggest you immediately open a correspondence with Baron Von Steuben who now commands the Virginia Militia. He will be ready to act in conjunction with your detachment."

"Certainly, sir."

"Your primary mission is to work with Von Steuben and Destouches to capture Arnold. With nearly double his number and a naval blockade, you stand a good chance of success. Of course, if he should fall into your hands, you will immediately execute him."

"The traitor deserves nothing less, sir."

"You are also at liberty to concert a plan with the French commander for a descent into North Carolina—to cut off the enemy, possibly intercept Cornwallis, and reinforce General Greene. This, however, I think ought to be a secondary objective and only attempted in case of Arnold's retreat to New York."

"I understand, sir."

"Do you have any questions?"

"None, sir," replies Lafayette, as he and Washington rise.

"Very well, then. You must be off immediately."

"Yes, sir. I look forward to our next meeting, mon pere."

Washington embraces Lafayette. "Godspeed, son. Godspeed."

As the marquis leaves, General Washington walks to the downstairs writing room where Alexander Hamilton is working.

"Colonel Hamilton, have you some time to work with me on a few dispatches?"

"Now, General?"

"They are important, Colonel," replies Washington. "We are to begin a joint offensive with the French Navy in Virginia. Letters to Von Steuben and Jefferson are of the essence."

"Of course, sir," replies Hamilton. "I am ready."

"Very well," says Washington, who explains to Hamilton all he had just said to Lafayette.

"First to Major General Von Steuben," Washington begins as Hamilton writes. "A French naval squadron, including a sixty-four and some frigates, is moving to the Chesapeake Bay. Convinced as I am that a naval operation alone will probably be ineffectual, and the militia alone would be unequal to the reduction of Arnold in his works, I have detached a corps of 1,200 men from this army commanded by the Marquis de Lafayette. It will, I hope, arrive at the Head of Elk about the sixth of March to embark there and proceed down the bay to Hampton Road or the point of operation. You will make appropriate arrangements with respect to the militia. When the French squadron appears, you will immediately open a correspondence with the commanding officer acquainting him with my intentions and your preparations."

"Very good, sir," says Hamilton. "I have it."

Washington waits while his young aide pulls out a fresh sheet of paper. "The second letter is to Governor Jefferson, as such," he says. "The Chevalier Destouche, command-

ing France's squadron in the harbor of Newport, promises to dispatch a ship of the line of sixty-four guns and three frigates to the Chesapeake in hopes of finding there and destroying the fleet under the direction of Arnold. I have also put a respectable detachment of this army in motion. It is commanded by Major General Marquis de Lafayette and should arrive at Head of Elk by the sixth of March where they will fall down the Chesapeake in transports. Baron Von Steuben has been alerted to assist and join forces. With the highest sentiments of respect, etc. Do you have all that, Colonel?"

"I do, sir," replies Hamilton. "And it should make the governor very happy."

"Yes, he has been requesting such help for a long time," responds Washington. "However, I fear greatly for his safety."

"Sir?"

"Yes. If I were Arnold, and I know him well, I would head straight for Monticello and try to capture the author of the Declaration of Independence. Such a move would greatly harm the morale of our cause."

"Should we perhaps include such a warning in this dispatch, sir?"

"No need, Colonel. I'm certain Jefferson is already thinking of it."

"Very well, sir. Is that all?"

General Washington pauses and looks out the window for the longest time before responding. "One more letter, I think," he says finally.

Hamilton pulls out another sheet of paper and looks up at his commander in chief.

"This one to General Henry Knox—and please mark it 'private.'" Washington begins, "Sir, if we can have naval superiority through the next campaign and an army of double the force of the enemy early enough in the season to operate in that quarter, we ought to prefer it to every other object, as the most important and decisive. Applications have been made to the Court of France in this spirit, which is to be hoped will produce the desired effect."

Washington pauses again. Hamilton finishes writing and looks up. The duration of the silence seems unusually long, and Hamilton cocks his head wondering what would come next. Finally, the general continues.

"It is incumbent on us, General Knox, to make every necessary preparation on our part for a siege on New York. Therefore, I request that you prepare a plan for artillery emplacements to that end. You are well acquainted with New York and its defenses. You can, therefore, judge the means requisite for its reduction by a siege.

"In your calculations, you will estimate the force on our side at about 20,000 men; the remainder with a proper siege and field apparatus are to be supposed to be furnished by our allies. The enemy's present force of regular troops at New York we believe to be near 7,000. You may rely upon all the assistance and support it will be in my power to give, etc., etc."

Hamilton finishes writing and looks up. "Sir, if I may comment?"

Washington nods.

"Well, sir, are we not taking for granted the agreement of the Court of France? Once Rochambeau hears of your direction, as surely he will, may he not think it somewhat presumptive?"

"The French have sat idle for too long. And we no longer have the luxury of standing around. Time is of the essence, now. We must begin to force the issue. We must make something happen. I am willing to take the risk of offending Rochambeau—although, after having met him, I believe he will not react that way. I detect in him a slight impatience with his government. I think he is a man of action."

"Very well, General," *says Hamilton.* "I understand and am with you. I will prepare these letters for your signature today."

"Thank you," *responds Washington.* "And there is one more thing I would like for you and Tilghman to prepare."

"Sir?"

"I'd like you to prepare for an expedition. We are going to visit the French in Newport. We will stay no less than a week. We are going to see to it ourselves that the French ships sail south to join Lafayette. And while there, we will work on our relationship with Rochambeau to prepare him to plan a siege of New York this summer."

"Very well, sir," *Hamilton excitedly responds.* "I'll get right to it."

5

Connecticut/Rhode Island Countryside
Early March 1781

General Washington is riding east at a full gallop—his party of about a dozen trailing twenty or thirty yards behind—except for Billy, who consistently rides two horse lengths behind. It's early morning, there's a crisp chill in the air, and the general's reddish, windblown face is showing the effects of a hard ride.

Washington is in the second full day of the 200-mile journey to Newport. Because he lingered at the home of his friend Colonel Andrew Morehouse, the general is trying to make up for lost time. He wants to reach Hartford by the end of the day—some thirty-five miles away. That shouldn't be a problem, since he rode forty miles from New Windsor the first day. But anything can happen along the way. He must stay ahead of schedule and keep on time. That's why he's galloping. Mustn't fall behind, not ever.

Washington has crossed the New York state line and is coming up on the Housatonic River. There's a bridge there—Bull's Bridge—but its 110-foot span is nearly forty years old and quite rickety. Many of the baseboards have been broken by heavy wagons from the nearby iron foundry, which, for years, have traveled across it on a daily basis. When Washington reaches the bridge, he finds it enveloped in a dense fog rising from the river. But he does not slow down. He proceeds onto the bridge at a full gallop. About halfway across, his horse steps into a hole. The loose and weakened boards give way, and the horse's front legs crash through. Its chest hits the bridge full force, and the horse falls fifteen feet down and into the middle of the river. With the spring of a deer, Washington leaps from the saddle before his mount falls. He lands on the bridge about ten feet forward of the hole—tumbling a couple of times but catching himself on the edge of the bridge and rising to his feet. Walking back and peering into the hole, the general sees his horse tangled in some tree branches in the river. Billy is on the scene and prepared for such a mishap. Washington quickly takes the reins of his extra mount and leaps in the saddle. As the rest of the party rides up to the scene, the general shouts for them to attend to his fallen horse. He then turns and gallops away. Billy follows. Hamilton quickly orders two men to stay behind to rescue the horse—and he and the rest of the party ride on in an effort to keep up with their leader. When Hamilton reaches the other side of the Housatonic, the fog lifts and he strains his eyes to make out how far ahead Washington has ridden. All he can see is the back of Billy's horse far off in the distance—snow flying from its back hooves.

◆   ◆   ◆

Billy is Washington's slave. He is about twenty-eight years old, a mulatto with light-colored skin and a large athletic frame. Washington had purchased him fourteen years earlier for the tidy sum of sixty-one pounds and made him his valet and huntsman.

Billy was an outstanding equestrian, one of the few people who could keep up with General Washington when he was on the move. He had been with his master for the entire war—except for several months in 1776 when he was captured by the British and held until a prisoner exchange could be worked out. Mostly, Billy stayed in the background attending to the general's private needs and looking after his horses. Over the years, the two men had formed a strong bond. Washington depended on Billy and trusted him implicitly. To a friend, he had written that Billy was loyal and faithful and had "followed my fortunes through the war with fidelity."

◆   ◆   ◆

From Bull's Bridge, the two ride at a full gallop for another twenty-three miles—until they reach a tavern at Litchfield, Connecticut. There they stop to rest their horses, get something to eat, and wait for the rest of their traveling party to catch up. Then it is another hard ten-mile ride until they reach Hartford where they spend the night. The next day they ride all the way to Norwich and stay the night in the vicinity of Westerly—then it's on to Narragansett, Rhode Island. On March 8, six days after beginning their journey, they arrive in Newport—having ridden an average of thirty-four miles each day.

When Washington disembarks from the ferry that carried him over the bay to Newport, he is met by nearly the entire French army. Soldiers have lined both sides of the road all the way from the wharf to the Count de Rochambeau's house where Washington is to stay. The French troops are excited. This is the first opportunity they've had to see "their general"—the hero of America whose courage and perseverance against overwhelming odds have sustained the Revolution for six years. Rochambeau himself is at the pier to meet Washington and escort him through the honor guard. Because neither general speaks the other's language well, the interpreters chat back and forth the entire way.

At night, the city of Newport is illuminated with candles in the windows of every house. A ball is held in General Washington's honor, and he surprises everyone with his handsome, noble, and gracious demeanor and his excellence at dancing. Overall, the French are extraordinarily impressed.

"I have never seen anyone more naturally and spontaneously polite," notes one officer. "He asks questions, listens attentively, and answers in low tones with few words."

"He has not the imposing pomp of a person who gives orders," observes another. "A hero in a republic, he excites another sort of respect which seems to spring from the sole idea that the safety of each individual is attached to his person. The goodness and benevolence which characterize him are evident in all that surrounds him, but the confidence he calls forth never occasions improper familiarity."

◆   ◆   ◆

In the days following all the pomp and ceremony, Washington made a concerted effort to get to know as many of the French officers as possible. He held numerous formal meetings, dined with them regularly, inspected their legions, and complimented them often. And Washington got to know the French commander well.

Jean-Baptiste-Donatien de Vimeur, Count de Rochambeau, he learned, was a scarred veteran of almost forty years of European warfare—including fourteen sieges. Now fifty-six years old with thinning gray hair and an imposing paunch, he called himself Papa Rochambeau when around his men. And while Washington astutely observed that several of the French officers saw their commander as disagreeable and a bit unreasonable, he noticed that Rochambeau was also tactful, dignified, astute—and unfailingly polite toward the Americans.

In subsequent formal discussions, Washington again pushed the idea of laying siege to New York. This time, Rochambeau was more receptive to the idea and began to discuss its merits. While they were mulling over the matter, a dispatch rider arrived with word that the Marquis de Lafayette, along with his 1,200 troops had reached Head of Elk, Maryland, and were rapidly embarking on transports. Much to the amazement of Washington and Rochambeau, Lafayette had wasted no time in marching his troops more than thirty miles a day to get to the Chesapeake ahead of schedule.

This news spurred both generals to get the promised French ships supplied, loaded with troops and artillery, and headed south. It took several days before they were finally under way—and General Washington stood on the side of the pier waving to them as they set sail. He had accomplished his mission in Newport. Now, he believed, they had a good chance to capture that arch-traitor Benedict Arnold.

On March 13, Washington and his detail headed back to their headquarters in New Windsor—although not with as much haste as they had come. They made stops in Bristol, Bolton, Hartford, Farmington, Litchfield, and at the Morehouses'. At almost every stop, people came out to greet them. Arriving in Providence after nightfall, a throng of children carrying torches crowded around them to a point where no one could move.

"Look here, boys," Washington shouted to his aides. "We may be beaten by the English—but here is an army they can never beat!"

Guilford Courthouse, North Carolina
Mid-March 1781

Nathanael Greene's campaign of harassment against Lord Cornwallis in North Carolina was turning out to be more like a game of cat and mouse. "To skirmish Cornwallis is my only chance," Greene wrote to a friend. "To guard against a surprise, I rarely ever lay more than two days in a place. Skirmishes happen daily—and the enemy has suffered considerably."

One of the officers who came up with several secondary victories was the handsome twenty-year-old "Light Horse Harry" Lee who led a crackerjack band of cavalrymen mounted on fine plantation horses. At Haw River, the Americans, dressed in green dragoon coats, approached 400 British Loyalists who were on their way to join Cornwallis. Colonel Lee then audaciously passed himself off as British Colonel Banastre Tarleton (whose cavalry was well-known for their crisp green coats). When the Loyalists relaxed and put down their weapons, Lee's Legion rode in among them with sabers drawn and killed, wounded, or captured the entire division.

On March 11, General Greene was reinforced by a large contingent of Virginia and North Carolina militia and a smaller Continental regiment from Virginia dispatched by Governor Jefferson. Although the American numbers now swelled to more than 4,000, most of the men were untrained militia who had not been battle-tested. And the hero of Cowpens, General Daniel Morgan, had retired from the scene due to crippling arthritis. Still, Greene realized that he now outnumbered the British commander and made the crucial decision to make a stand against the British in a place of his own choosing. He selected the isolated Guilford County Courthouse—a modest building situated in a small field surrounded by dense forest. There, he set up his defenses and waited for the enemy to approach.

On the morning of March 15, when informed of the American position, Cornwallis hurriedly marched his army twelve miles and, allowing no time for rest, ordered an immediate attack. Even though his forces numbered only 1,900, they were the cream of the crop—tough British veterans. Emerging from the woods, Cornwallis noticed that Greene had aligned his troops just as Morgan had done at Cowpens. Untrained militiamen were located forward in two lines. Behind them were the Continental veterans. And on the right and left flanks were the cavalry.

Learning from Tarleton's mistake, though, Cornwallis tried a different approach. He ordered Tarleton's Legion to attack the American cavalry on the flanks and then launched an artillery bombardment from his three light field guns. After the center had been softened up, the British regulars advanced. The American militia countered with two rifle volleys and then turned and ran to the rear. But rather than stopping at the Continental line, they continued to retreat into the forest. Sensing an opportunity, Cornwallis quickly ordered attacks on both flanks. The Americans were thrown back and their middle began to collapse. General Greene, however, rallied his troops. The sheer fact that they outnumbered the British two-to-one made a significant difference.

The ensuing battle was long and bloody. Finally, the British became weary and began to retreat. When Cornwallis observed a major American push to seize the field, he stunned his artillery officers by ordering them to fire into the middle of the battlefield. The resulting barrage killed many more British soldiers than Americans. But it did the trick. Greene was forced to order an immediate retreat, and the battle was over. Cornwallis occupied the field overnight but at an enormous cost. British casualties were 532 killed and wounded—more than one-quarter of Cornwallis's entire army. Even Banastre Tarleton was wounded—having lost two fingers on his right hand. American casualties were lighter—seventy-eight killed, 183 wounded.

For several days after the battle, Greene stayed within striking distance of the British. But Cornwallis decided to withdraw his force to Wilmington on the coast of North Carolina so he could rest his troops and rethink his overall strategy. And General Greene was glad for the time to recoup. "We have little to eat, less to drink, and lodge in the woods in the midst of smoke," he wrote in a letter to Congress. "Indeed, our fatigue is excessive. I was so much overcome the night before last that I fainted. The militia are leaving us in great numbers to return home to kiss their wives and sweethearts."

General Washington's Headquarters
New Windsor, New York
Late March 1781

When George Washington arrived back in New Windsor, his hopes were high. He had personally seen to it that Commodore Charles Rene Destouches (the Chevalier Destouches, Rochambeau's officer in charge of the French naval detachment) had set sail from Newport in charge of a squadron of eight ships loaded with 1,200 men. He had sent the Marquis de Lafayette south and received word that his young general was in position at Annapolis to join up with the French on the Chesapeake. The combined force had a good chance to capture Benedict Arnold and reclaim Virginia for the Americans. At that time, Washington was also heartened to know that Nathanael Greene had eluded Cornwallis successfully and was building the strength of his army.

But all that changed on March 30, 1781, when the commander in chief received two key pieces of news from separate dispatch riders. The first communiqué related the events of the battle at Guilford Courthouse on the fifteenth. Washington was understandably distressed. The only good part of the news was that Cornwallis had lost so many soldiers. That would, at best, delay his incursion into Virginia. But then he received word that on March sixteenth, the day after Guilford Courthouse, a sea battle had been fought along the Chesapeake capes, and the French had not fared well.

It turned out that a British naval force, under the command of Admiral Marriot Arbuthnot, had learned of the French Navy's intentions and set sail from Gardiner's Bay, New York, headed toward the Chesapeake. With superior sailing, Arbuthnot had reached the bay before Destouches and forced a daylong battle. The two forces were evenly matched with eight ships each. The British, however, had heavier guns and were able to outmaneuver the French with their quicker copper-lined hulls. Destouches was forced to head seaward, while Arbuthnot, in turn, established a position at the mouth of the Chesapeake Bay. Having suffered casualties of seventy-two dead and 112 wounded, and believing that his damaged squadron could not break the British line, Commodore Destouches reluctantly sailed back to Newport.

And so, in addition to the loss at Guilford Courthouse, Washington was faced with the bad news that the French had not disembarked their land troops and that they did not have naval supremacy in the Chesapeake. Rather, the British had entered the bay and rendezvoused with Arnold. Moreover, having received news of the engagement, Lafayette had loaded all his troops back on the transports and returned to the safety of Maryland.

Washington was beside himself—pacing back and forth on the lower floor of the New Windsor farmhouse, his heels pounding harder on the wooden floorboards with each successive step. All his work. All his planning. His ride to Newport. His personal attendance to seeing the French fleet sail. It seemed now that they were worse off than before. Virginia was defenseless—its Continentals now in North Carolina with Greene. Lafayette was stranded in Maryland. And Arnold was free to ravage the state as he pleased.

"What now?" Washington was wondering when Tench Tilghman came in with yet another distressing report.

"Sir," said Tilghman, "General Clinton has dispatched an additional 2,500 British regulars under the command of Major General William Phillips. They are headed south toward Virginia."

6

General Washington's Headquarters
New Windsor, New York
Early April 1781

The seasons are changing at New Windsor. Temperatures are rising and snows are melting. Things are soft, muddy, sluggish. Some days provide glimpses of bright sunlight, but most are still filled with dreary gray skies. This particular afternoon the clouds are low. It is raining lightly. There is a mild fog.

General Washington and David Humphreys are in the downstairs writing room working on correspondence. They have been there for some time. Humphreys is at the table, pen in hand. Papers are spread all around him.

Washington is sitting near the window—his right boot resting on the sill and his chair tilted back slightly. His left hand is up to his face, chin in palm, index finger pointed up near his left eye, other fingers curled under his nose and covering his mouth. He is staring outside, half listening to the raindrops softly patting the window-panes, half listening to Humphreys reading letters and asking how to respond.

"This complaint was signed by Lieutenant Colonel James Mellen and six other Massachusetts field officers," says Humphreys. "They're upset that they were not chosen for the light infantry."

Washington closes his eyes, lowers his chin slightly, and shakes his head in annoyance.

"All right, all right," he says. "Let's respond, as such: 'No one who considers the good of the service can blame me for taking officers who were eligible to command and unoccupied by other duties to accompany the detachment. These and only these were the reasons why no more than one field officer was taken from the line of Massachusetts. I conceive it to be a right inherent with command to appoint particular officers for special purposes—but shall take this occasion, once and for all, to observe that I am not conscious of exercising a partiality in favor of one line, one corps, or one man, more than another. I never did, nor will I ever hurt, intentionally, the feelings of any officer unless I can be justified upon general principles, and good is to result from it.'"

"Very well, sir. I've got it," says Humphreys, who turns and picks up several other pieces of paper. "We have some orders of execution for desertion to be signed. One is a

Joshua Taylor of the Third Connecticut Regiment for joining the enemy and taking up arms in the British service. A second is from West Point—one John Walker, convicted of deserting and reenlisting by the name of Robert Maples for three years and taking a bounty of $200 and deserting again. A third is from the Massachusetts line—Nathan Gale, for repeated desertion."

"All were tried and convicted according to standard procedure?" asks Washington.

"Yes, sir."

"No extenuating circumstances?"

"Apparently not, sir."

Washington pauses.

"Very well," he says. "Let the sentences be carried out."

"Sir, Miss Mary Dagworthy is also due a note of thanks for the stockings she and the other ladies made."

"Ah, yes," responds Washington. "Let's reply as such to Miss Dagworthy: 'Madam, I have had the pleasure to receive your favor and have given directions to deliver the…' How many pairs were there, Colonel?"

Humphreys pauses to pick up the original letter. "There were 380, sir."

"'…to deliver the 380 pairs of stockings for the use of the troops of the state of New Jersey,'" continues Washington. "'This gratuity of the ladies, I am persuaded, will be very acceptable at this season. Please pass on to them our deepest gratitude.'"

Once done writing, Humphreys picks up another piece of paper and reads from it. "Sir," he says to Washington, "I have taken the liberty of issuing an impress warrant for teams to be gathered by the quartermaster general of the army to transport flour to the troops near Ringwood."

"Very well," replies the general. "The existence of the army and the preservation of the country depend on such measures. What friend to his country is there who would not approve of its being carried into execution by military coercion?"

"Indeed, sir," responds Humphreys. "May I add that statement to the warrant?"

"If you believe it will help."

"Very well. I will add it."

"I think it is time for another letter to the Congress," says Washington.

"Yes, sir," replies Humphreys, pulling out a new sheet of paper. "I am ready."

Washington stares out the window for a few moments before starting to dictate.

"I think it my duty to inform Congress," he begins, "that there is great dissatisfaction at this time in the York line for want of pay; near sixteen months, I am told, is due to it. If it were practicable to give a small portion of their pay, it might stop frequent desertions and avert greater evils that are otherwise to be apprehended.

"*In addition, all the little magazines in the garrison of West Point, which we had laid up against an emergency, are entirely consumed. Nor is there a mouthful of bread or flour at the garrison for tomorrow. If the states will not or cannot provide me with the means, it is in vain for them to look to me for the end and accomplishment of their wishes. Bricks are not to be made without straw.*"

"*Do you have all that, Colonel?*" *asks Washington.*

Humphreys quickly finishes writing and looks up. "*I do, sir. Anything more?*"

"*Yes. End with this. 'In the wake of the failed French naval expedition off the Chesapeake capes, I sent letters of thanks and admiration to Rochambeau and Destouches for their fine effort. I would suggest that Congress send similar letters. Although our plan has unluckily failed, they deserve the highest applause and warmest thanks of the public for the boldness of their attempt to carry it into action. Shortly after the event, Sir Henry Clinton at once dispatched Major General William Phillips and 25,000 troops to Virginia, where they arrived on March 26th. That arch traitor, Arnold, will apparently escape the hangman's justice. The world is disappointed at not seeing him in gibbets.'*"

With that final word, Washington rises from his chair and puts his hand on a stack of papers on the edge of the writing table.

"*These are my personal letters?*" *he asks.*

"*Yes, sir,*" *responds Humphreys.*

"*Very well,*" *says Washington as he picks up the papers.* "*I will work on these upstairs. Thank you for your good work today, Colonel. I know you are overtired, because Tilghman is ill.*"

"*I believe his fever has broken, sir.*"

"*Good. I will look in on him.*"

"*Sir, take care not to get too close,*" *warns Humphreys.* "*Tench would not want you to pick up the sickness from him.*"

Washington nods and exits the room. He walks down the hall, through the main room, and up the stairs. Holding the papers in his left hand and using his right, the general slowly and quietly opens the door to Tilghman's room. He does not want to awaken his aide should he be sleeping. But Tilghman is awake already, on the bed lying sideways. As Washington pokes his head in the door, Tilghman manages a smile.

"*Are you feeling better, Colonel?*"

"*Yes, sir. Thank you, sir. But please don't come any closer.*"

"*Of course. I have already been so advised by Humphreys.*"

"*I am still a bit weak, sir,*" *says Tilghman,* "*but I'm sure I'll be able to resume duties by tomorrow morning. I am sorry for the inconvenience, sir.*"

"No, no. You must get well. Of course, we all look forward to seeing you on your feet again—especially Humphreys," says Washington with a wink and a grin. "Do you need anything? Tea, perhaps?"

"Thank you, sir. But I am fine."

"Very well, Colonel. I'll see you in the morning." Washington closes the door, turns, and walks back down the hall to his own room.

The general plops his papers on the table, positions his chair near the window, and begins to read some of his personal correspondence. The first letter he picks up is from his old friend Benjamin Harrison, now a member of Congress representing Virginia. The substance of the letter is brief and to the point. "The last assembly proposed to apply assistance for your mother," Harrison has written, "who they said was in great want, owing to the heavy taxes she was obliged to pay. I took the liberty to put a stop to this, supposing you would be displeased at such an application."

With a pained look, Washington drops his hand holding the letter to the table.

"What?" he says out loud.

Then he pulls out pen and paper and dashes off a letter to Harrison.

"My dear sir," he writes, "a year or two before I left Virginia, I did, at my mother's request, but my own expense, purchase her a house in Fredericksburg near my sister. I have also provided to her an annual expense ever since. From where her distresses can arise, therefore, I know not, never having received any complaints.

"She has not a child that would not divide the last sixpence to relieve her from real distress. I would feel much hurt at having our mother a pensioner while we had the means of supporting her. But, in fact, she has an ample income of her own. I request that all proceedings on it may be stopped or, in case of a decision in her favor, that it may be done away and repealed at my request. Yours, etc."

Washington next picks up a letter from Lund Washington—his cousin and the resident manager of his plantation at Mount Vernon. The British, Lund reported, had recently sent a flotilla of six vessels with twelve to eighteen guns each and a half-dozen smaller craft up the Potomac River. They temporarily occupied Alexandria and burned several plantation homes. When a British sloop-of-war dropped anchor in front of Mount Vernon, about twenty of Washington's plantation slaves fled to it. In an effort to regain the slaves, and fearing that the British detachment intended to burn Mount Vernon, Lund went to the ship with a friendly greeting and refreshments. Then, in return for sparing the plantation, he consented to provide a consignment of sheep, hogs, flour, and cured ham from the smokehouse—and he agreed to let them keep the twenty slaves.

When Washington reads this, his face flushes red with anger, and he just keeps shaking his head, no, no, no, no. The anger shows in his return letter to Lund.

"That which gives me most concern," he writes, "is that you should go on board the enemy's vessel, furnish them with refreshments, and commune with a pack of plundering scoundrels. Your action was exceedingly ill judged. It is a bad example of communicating with the enemy and will be a precedent for others. It would have been a less painful circumstance to me to have heard that in consequence of your noncompliance with their request, they had burnt my house and laid the plantation in ruins.

"I am, however, thoroughly persuaded that you acted from your best judgment and believe that your desire to preserve my property and rescue the buildings from impending danger were your governing motives. But in contemplating the loss of all my Negroes and the destruction of my houses, I am prepared for the event."

After writing these two painful letters, Washington pauses to look out the window for the longest time. The sun is going down now. It is dark, cloudy, still raining.

His thoughts drift back to Mount Vernon, to Martha, to his stepchildren, and to the new grandchildren he has never met. He longs to see them all, to tend to the everyday business of plantation life—the horses, the crops, the daily rounds.

Washington picks up his pen and replies to a few more letters. The first one is to a friend in New York declining a request to visit him in Albany. "Thanks for your kind invitation," he says, "but the distresses of the army are too great and complicated for me to think of private gratification." In another letter, he pointedly states that there was "not a single farthing in the military chest" and "I have not been able to obtain any money for my own expenses or table for more than three months."

Then he begins to think about rumors of the Vergennes plan becoming more widespread. The French minister had been openly communicating with George III, he had heard. And the king of England seemed amenable. The British were now in possession of Georgia, the Carolinas, Virginia, and New York. If the truce were signed today, it would be a disaster. The last six years would have been wasted—all the time, all the effort, all the American lives lost. The truth is that Washington can see no way such a European settlement could be overturned if ever enacted.

Morale in the colonies is not good, either. Washington has just received word that citizens in Philadelphia had tarred a dog, plastered its body with worthless Continental currency, and paraded it through the streets in protest. And business owners were threatening to close their establishments if they were not paid in gold or silver. The commander in chief realizes what this all means, of course. There will be no infusion of cash from the bankrupt United States government.

"In the hours of our deepest distress and darkness, our affairs have been brought to an awful crisis," Washington writes to a colleague. "The hand of providence, I trust, may be more conspicuous in our deliverance. The period for that deliverance may be too far distant for a person of my years. My morning and evening hours, and every

moment unoccupied by business, are filled with thoughts of retirement—and for those domestic rural enjoyments which, in my estimation, far surpass the highest pageantry of the world."

Later that evening, before retiring, Washington records personal thoughts in his diary. *"Instead of having magazines filled with provisions, we have a scanty pittance,"* he writes. *"Instead of having our arsenals well supplied with military stores, they are poorly provided. Instead of having the regiments completed, scarcely any state in the Union has met an eighth of its quota in the field and little prospect that I can see of ever getting more than half. Instead of having the prospect of a glorious offensive campaign before us, we have a bewildered and gloomy defensive one—unless we receive a powerful aid of ships, land troops, and money from our generous allies."*

Usually, the last thing he does every night before going to bed is to write in his diary. But on this night, Washington pens one last letter. It is to his young friend John Laurens, upon whose shoulders, he believes, rests the American cause. If Laurens is not successful in his mission to France, all will be lost.

"My dear Laurens," Washington writes. *"We cannot transport the provisions from the states in which they are assessed to the army, because we cannot pay the teamsters who will no longer work for certificates. Our hospitals are without medicines and our sick without nutriment. All our public works are at a standstill.*

"If France delays a timely and powerful aid package, it will avail us nothing should she attempt it hereafter. We are at the end of our tether—and now or never our deliverance must come."

PART II
THE DECISION

7

Lieutenant General Sir Henry Clinton's Headquarters
Harlem Heights, New York
Mid-April 1781

It is early afternoon, the sun high in the sky. A large white, two-story mansion radiates atop a steep hill. Visible from miles around, it rests at the center of a vast estate that stretches across the entire island of Manhattan—from the Hudson River to the East River. A soft warm wind flutters leaves on the tall trees. New daffodils spring from green grass, and birds chirp ballads of spring.

Half a dozen armed British soldiers stand guard on the mansion's front portico—their bright red coats and shiny black boots contrast sharply with the mansion's four white pillars. Inside, the lower floor's nine rooms are furnished with fine Chippendale and Baroque furniture. Imported rugs rest on polished wooden floors. Works of art hang on freshly painted walls. A harpsichord is the centerpiece of the main room.

Two smartly dressed black servants holding wine trays walk across the foyer into an elegant dining room, their heels clicking crisply on the floor. Seated at the head of the table is Sir Henry Clinton, supreme commander of His Majesty's royal forces in North America. The only other person seated is Mrs. Mary Baddeley, Clinton's mistress. She is eight weeks pregnant, although she has not yet informed the general of this fact. The two are taking the noon meal together.

Four servants—two black slaves and two white military staff—stand at attention in each corner of the room. The two servants who have just entered fill the diners' wine glasses—the general's with a freshly opened bottle of red cabernet, Mrs. Baddeley's with a white Riesling. Clinton takes a sip of his wine and frowns.

"This is sour!" he barks. "Take it back and bring me another."

"Right away, Your Excellency," responds a white servant, who motions for the black servant to withdraw.

Mrs. Baddeley takes a sip from her glass and indicates to Clinton that it is fine. The two go back to eating, but there is no conversation between this couple, who met six years earlier in Boston. Mary had been married at the time to a British noncommissioned officer whom Clinton quickly transferred to the southern war zone. The man soon died of swamp fever leaving Mary a widow. She had stayed with the general, even with the knowledge he had five children back in England and his wife had recently died.

Sir Henry Clinton was far from a ladies' man. At age fifty-one, he was small and paunchy—his round face dominated by an unflattering hooked nose. It was Clinton's wealth and position that attracted Mrs. Baddeley, especially the fact that he had been knighted by the king and was generally regarded as a hero—first at the battle of Bunker Hill (1775) and later for having laid siege to Charleston, South Carolina (1780). That clash resulted in the capture of American General Benjamin Lincoln and his entire army—unquestionably one of the great British victories of the American Revolution. Shortly afterward, Clinton had withdrawn to New York and left Major General Lord Earl Cornwallis in charge of the southern campaign. For almost a year now, he had been living in the lap of luxury while Cornwallis fought swamp mosquitoes and contended with the deprivation of military life in the field.

While Sir Henry and Mrs. Baddeley are dining, a courier arrives at the house and presents several dispatches to Clinton's aides. In the back study, Captains F. Dawkins and J. Gurwood eagerly pour over the communiqués, both of which have been sent from Lord Cornwallis. He has not been heard from in more than a month.

"My God," says Dawkins at last. "Can you believe what His Lordship has done?"

"It is both bad news and unwanted news," replies Gurwood.

"I do not wish to present these to the general. Here," says Dawkins handing one dispatch to Gurwood, "you do it."

"No, no! Indeed not! I had to tell him of the loss at Cowpens. Now it is your turn."

"But he is certain to throw a fit!"

"I know!"

Captain Dawkins rolls his eyes and dejectedly plops down in a chair, resigned to his fate. "Damn!" he says in disgust.

At that moment, Sir Henry Clinton walks into the room. He has heard the courier enter the house and, wondering what the news might be, has abruptly ended his meal. "Did I hear you utter a profanity, Dawkins?" he asks. "You know I do not approve of profanity from my staff!"

Startled, Dawkins jumps to his feet. "Sir, we have two dispatches from Lord Cornwallis—the second written ten days after the first."

"I see. And what does his royal highness have to say?" says Clinton facetiously.

"Which letter would you like me to relate first, General?" asks Dawkins.

Clinton only glares at his aide.

"Sir, if it pleases you, I will begin with the one dated earlier."

"God Almighty, Dawkins!" screams Sir Henry with impatience. "Do I have to read the letters myself to find out what's in them?!"

"Yes, sir. Er, I mean, no, sir—sir. Lord Cornwallis reports that he has engaged the rebels at a place called Guilford Courthouse in North Carolina. He claims victory, sir, but…"

"And when did this battle occur?" asks Clinton.

"On the fifteenth of March, sir."

"The fifteenth of March!?" screams Clinton. "What is the date of that letter you are holding, Captain?"

"April tenth, sir," responds Dawkins.

Sir Henry's face is now flushed with fury. "He waited almost a month to make this report?"

"Apparently, that is the case," Dawkins replies meekly.

"And of course the communication was delayed two more weeks," says Sir Henry, "and now I have to make a decision in regard to a battle that is nearly six weeks old. That man Cornwallis will be the death of me yet!"

"He states that the battle has been a triumph, sir. 'I have had a most difficult and dangerous campaign,' he writes, 'and was obliged to fight a battle 200 miles from any communication against an enemy seven times my number. It ended happily, however, in our completely routing the enemy and taking their cannon.'"

"I have never before received information that Greene had seven times His Lordship's number of troops," says Sir Henry. "Seven times? Is that what it says?"

"It is, sir. Seven times."

"Not possible. Not possible," repeats Sir Henry.

"Lord Cornwallis goes on to report, sir, that his force has been reduced now to 1,000 effectives. Therefore, he has retired to the coastal area of Wilmington to rest and refit."

"One thousand?" asks Clinton. "Does it indeed say 1,000?"

"It does, sir."

"The last time I heard from him, he had more than 3,000 men," states Sir Henry, shaking his head incredulously. "And what of Greene and the rebels?"

"Apparently, Greene has led his troops back into South Carolina and reclaimed the state, sir."

Sir Henry just stares straight ahead, at first giving his aide no reaction. Finally, he speaks. "Hmmm. His Lordship has lost an army, lost the object for which he moved it, and buried himself on the seacoast of North Carolina. With this, he claims a victory. I think another such victory would ruin the British army."

"Sir, I would like to read the opening of His Lordship's second letter to you as it is written," says Captain Dawkins, "if that meets your approval, sir."

Clinton nods affirmatively.

Dawkins clears his throat nervously. "Sir, this letter is dated only several days ago. His Lordship states, and I quote: 'What is our plan? Without one, we cannot succeed. My present undertaking sits heavy on my mind. I have experienced the distresses and dangers of marching some hundreds of miles, in a country chiefly hostile, without one active or useful friend, without intelligence, and without communication with any part of the country. I am tired of marching about the country in quest of adventures.'"

"In quest of adventures?!" screams Sir Henry. "In quest of adventures?! Is that what he has written?"

"It is, sir," replies Dawkins. "And he goes on. 'If we mean an offensive war in America, we must abandon New York and bring our whole force into Virginia. A successful battle may give us America. If our plan is defensive, mixed with desultory expeditions, let us quit the Carolinas and stick to our salt pork at New York, sending now and then a detachment to steal tobacco, etc.'"

"This is insolence!" shouts Sir Henry. "Insolence!"

"Sir," says Captain Dawkins, "I beg to report that it gets worse. This second letter was written from a site in Virginia. His Lordship is marching north to join with General Phillips. He states that he must destroy Virginia's manufacturing centers and break up her government."

"What?" yells Sir Henry. "What? Virginia? Phillips is to hold Virginia. Washington cannot stop them without a naval presence. Cornwallis is to hold the Carolinas. I gave no orders for Cornwallis to move into Virginia. Did you issue such orders without my knowledge?"

"Indeed, I did not, sir," responds Dawkins.

"Did you, Gurwood?" snaps Clinton to his other aide, who is standing meekly in a corner.

"Of course not, sir," replies Gurwood. "Perhaps His Lordship received approval from Lord Germain, again."

"Blast it all to hell! I can never, never be cordial with such a man as Cornwallis!" screams Sir Henry, flushed red with rage. "He marches into Virginia without consulting me?! I might as well not be here. The insolence! The insolence! I shall resign immediately! I shall resign!"

Sir Henry then turns, abruptly leaves the room, and marches down the hall. "Make duplicate copies of those letters for the files," he screams to his aides as he stomps up the staircase. "We shall preserve a record of this impertinence."

When Clinton reaches the top of the stairs, he goes into his room and slams the door behind him. Then, while furiously talking to himself, he pulls out his ornate chamber pot, drops his pants, and relieves himself. Afterward, he covers the pot, sets it outside his door, and yells for his servants to come upstairs and attend to it. Then he slams the door and stays in his room for hours by himself—brooding, fuming, and pouting.

◆   ◆   ◆

Sir Henry Clinton and Lord Earl Cornwallis had a long history of contention. As a matter of fact, they hated each other. Cornwallis didn't want to communicate with Clinton—and Clinton begged to be relieved from working with Cornwallis. In 1779, a year after having been given military command in the American colonies, Clinton submitted his resignation following Cornwallis's return from England with a promotion but without reinforcements (as Clinton had requested). King George III, however, refused to allow his most experienced general to resign.

Again, in 1780 (shortly before the fall of Charleston), Clinton asked to be relieved of his command largely because he could not get along with Cornwallis. This time, as part of his resignation, Sir Henry recommended Cornwallis as his replacement. Delighted, Cornwallis assumed he would shortly be the supreme commander and began to act as though Clinton was already gone—which thoroughly angered Sir Henry. But when the king again refused to accept Clinton's resignation, Cornwallis withdrew into a shell of self-pity and depression. After that, almost all communications between the two commanders were reduced to formal, frigid memorandums.

In addition to their personal dislike for each other, the two generals had very different philosophies about how to conduct the war in America. In the wake of his victory at Charleston, Clinton was content to conduct a stalemate. After all, he reasoned, with limited land forces and a strong Navy, the British had been able to secure a stranglehold over the major lucrative port cities along the Atlantic seaboard. Only a few, such as Boston and Philadelphia, were not in their control. Part of Clinton's plan was to establish one base in the Chesapeake Bay from which he could control Virginia and launch a drive against Pennsylvania. Being in command of the American economy through shipping, he believed, would eventually squeeze the life out of the rebellion. And if Cornwallis could hold the Carolinas, Great Britain would be in perfect position to take advantage of the Vergennes plan.

But Cornwallis, who knew nothing of the French minister's strategy, viewed Clinton's conservative policy as negative and lacking in imagination. A slow strangulation, or a virtual stalemate, was unthinkable. To him, it was no plan at all. He wanted a strategy that would lead to all-out victory. These upstart colonists, he thought, must be taught to respect their masters. To anyone who would listen, Cornwallis advocated that Virginia was the key to victory. Not only was it the most populous of the thirteen colonies, but the entire American army was dependent on Virginia for shipments of salt, arms, and gunpowder. Also, Virginia's tobacco trade, being international in scope, was a source of revenue and commercial credit for the colonies. Cornwallis wanted control of it all, and he wanted it fast. By marching into Virginia, he hoped to force the issue—believing that Sir Henry Clinton would have no other choice but to join him with troops from New York.

Lord Cornwallis had good reason to think he could get away with this strategy. For months, he had been carrying on a quiet correspondence with Colonial Secretary Lord George Germain in London. Because of this close relationship, Cornwallis believed he could ignore Clinton. With the particulars of Minister Vergennes's strategy, however, Germain had chosen to observe the proper chain of military command by communicating directly with Clinton. But when Cornwallis did not follow orders, Sir Henry, understandably, became quite upset. Despite his rage, though, he was afraid to take any action that might be damaging to him after the war was over.

Unfortunately, Clinton's insecure personality quickly descended into paranoia. He began to believe that Cornwallis was conspiring against him. And his rage was vented on those around him—his staff and his mistress. He was, however, careful not to let this anger filter over into his written communications. Rather, he would often lock himself away in his room for hours, even days, until he had regained his composure. Then he would compose letters to Cornwallis that were anything but direct orders. His wording was usually suggestive or advisory so that, should anything go wrong, Cornwallis would have to suffer the blame.

◆   ◆   ◆

It is late evening of the same day. Captains Dawkins and Gurwood are lounging in the downstairs study—Dawkins leaning against the wall near the door, Gurwood slouched down in the general's chair behind his huge extravagant desk. Suddenly,

Dawkins hears Sir Henry's familiar gait approaching and bolts upright. "Pssst! He's coming."

Both aides snap to attention when Clinton walks in.

"Gurwood, we have two letters to write," *says Sir Henry, matter-of-factly.*

"Yes, sir," *responds the aide taking a seat on the other side of the general's desk and pulling out pen and paper.*

"Dawkins, I would like a cup of tea."

"Yes, sir," *says Captain Dawkins, who steps into the hall and has a word with a nearby black servant. Then he steps back into the study.*

"To His Lordship Earl Cornwallis," *begins Clinton.* "Sir, I have the honor of receiving your letters of the fifteenth and twenty-fourth relating your past skirmish in Carolina and your recent march into Virginia. I am of the opinion that operations in the Chesapeake are attended with great risk unless we are sure of a permanent superiority at sea. I tremble for the fatal consequences that may ensue. As much as I fear a strong French Navy in the Chesapeake, I am also concerned of the prospects for a summer campaign in that fever-ridden zone."

At this moment, a black servant brings in a tray with a tea service on it. He sets it on the desk and withdraws. Captain Dawkins pours tea into Sir Henry's cup. The general ignores Dawkins and continues his letter.

"Given the situation of your presence now being in Virginia, I propose that you either move your army north into the region of the Delaware River, where our two armies may join, or that you withdraw the majority of your army by sea to New York for operations against Washington and Rochambeau, which are certain to occur soon.

"Furthermore, as Your Lordship is now so near, it will not be necessary for you to send your dispatches to Minister Germain. You will therefore be so good as to send them to me in the future."

"Have you got that, Gurwood?"

"Yes, sir."

"Good. That is all I have to say to Cornwallis. Please prepare the letter for my signature. Also, I wish you to draft an order for Generals Phillips and Arnold to cooperate with His Lordship fully and without reservation once he reaches Petersburg—which is where I presume he will end up."

"Yes, sir," *responds Gurwood.*

"May we be of any other service this evening, General?" *asks Captain Dawkins.*

Clinton pauses and stares out the window. "My wonder at this move of Lord Cornwallis will never cease," *he says.* "I think this Virginia campaign pointless. I would have preferred that he stay in the Carolinas. By his actions, he has now made both the Carolinas and New York secondary considerations rather than primary. But he has *made the move, and we shall say no more but, instead, make the best of it. He and Lord Germaine will have to bear the responsibility for its consequences."*

Clinton then abruptly turns and leaves the room. "Be sure to make two copies of those letters, Gurwood," he says as he walks out.

"Yes, sir," responds Captain Gurwood.

Captain Dawkins pokes his head out the door and watches the general march down the hall.

"I don't understand," says Gurwood quietly. "He asks His Lordship to march to the Delaware—but tells us he would rather have Cornwallis in the Carolinas. Next he orders Phillips and Arnold to cooperate with His Lordship in Virginia!"

"He is very inconsistent," agrees Dawkins.

"When will he make up his mind?"

"He does so often—every time the winds change direction."

"Why doesn't he simply tell Cornwallis about the Vergennes plan and order him back to the Carolinas instead of suggesting he go north to Delaware or New York? That certainly would make more sense."

"Perhaps he doesn't want to risk that dispatch being intercepted. But is it a good idea," says Dawkins, with a smile. "Why don't you mention that to Sir Henry? I'm sure he'll be glad to receive your advice."

"My dear Captain," says Gurwood, with muted sarcasm, "when did Sir Henry ever ask either of us for our advice?"

Both men shake their heads and chuckle.

Dawkins pauses, looks at the desk, and shakes his head. "He didn't even drink his tea."

8

Major General Marquis de Lafayette's Camp
Head of Elk, Maryland
Mid-April 1781

Behind his tent, the Marquis de Lafayette is pacing back and forth. He is tense—his head down, his hands wringing nervously. He has just received orders from General Washington instructing him to return south and place his army under the command of Nathanael Greene in the Carolinas. Less than an hour ago, he had dispatched his aide to inform the troops of these new orders.

It had been a long, tough march down from New York for Lafayette's ragtag band of 1,200. Two hundred miles in less than seven days—more than thirty-four miles a day. It had been brutal. Then they had all been loaded on boats, transported eighty miles down the Chesapeake, and disembarked at Annapolis. When the French fleet was unable to rendezvous with them, they were all reloaded on the boats, transported back up the Chesapeake, and disembarked right back where they started.

Now they have been waiting for nearly a month—without reinforcements, without supplies, without food. Morale is not good. Most of the men want to go home. Lafayette is worried what their reactions will be upon hearing the new orders. So he is pacing—back and forth, back and forth.

Suddenly he hears a voice outside the front of the tent. "Mon general! Mon general!" yells Captain Michel du Chesnoy.

Lafayette runs around the side of the tent and up to his aide. "Michel," he says. "Ques que ce? What is it?"

"Sir, the troops are upset. They are gathering. Some men from the northern colonies have already deserted. I fear a mutiny, sir."

"Mon Dieu!" exclaims the marquis who immediately starts running to the main camp where the soldiers are gathering. The closer he gets, the more he hears his men shouting and cursing in anger. Finally, the young general arrives on the scene followed closely by du Chesnoy. They push their way to the center of the melee.

"General Lafayette," shouts a sergeant, "the men do not want to go south again. They are fed up! And I cannot blame them."

"General Lafayette," yells another soldier, "how much must men endure? We have no uniforms. We must forage for every scrap of food!"

"And no pay!" yells another. All the others quickly join in the shouting and complaining.

Lafayette steps on a tree stump so all can see him. "Mes amis! My friends!" he shouts. "Ecoute! Listen! Si vous plait! Please!"

Finally the crowd (which numbers nearly 1,000) becomes quiet enough for Lafayette to speak. "You have every right to complain, every right. You have endured unimaginable hardships."

"Good men can take only so much!" a man yells.

"It is true," continues Lafayette. "And you are good men, one and all!"

"Why should we march south? Why?"

"I will not lie to you," continues the marquis. "Going south through Virginia will not be easy. Governor Jefferson tells us that we can expect scant support in his state, where there are mild laws and the people are not used to prompt obedience. I have written to both General Washington and the Congress in Philadelphia about the issue of your pay. They understand the seriousness of our situation and, I hope, are taking actions to correct it—even though the U.S. Treasury is empty. But we shall not march south empty-handed. Soon we shall have all an army needs to be successful. When I was last in Baltimore, I arranged to receive supplies enough for all. In a day or so, we will have hats, shoes, pants—and shirts made from fine linen that are being made by the women of Baltimore. We will also be receiving arms and food aplenty."

"How could that be, General, when the Treasury is without funds?" asks a soldier.

"I raised money by borrowing on my estate," responds Lafayette.

Suddenly, all the whispering, murmuring, and whining stops. Every man is quiet now, listening intently. "I promised the citizens of Baltimore that I would make good on all the food, materials, and labor—and that I would repay them with interest."

"But how?" asks a soldier.

"You have heard the rumors that I come from a wealthy family in France, have you not?" asks Lafayette.

"Yes, we have."

"Well, it is true—and it was confirmed by bankers in Baltimore. So I have pledged my word and signature that it will be done."

"You would use your own money to feed, clothe, and arm us, even though we are not your countrymen? Why?"

"Uncommon dangers require uncommon remedies," Lafayette replies. "And even though we are not from the same country, we are surely brothers. Have I not marched with you and slept with you along the long roads we have traveled together?"

"Yes!"

"Indeed, you have!"

"He has!"

"And are we not fighting for the same thing? Are we not fighting for our families, for our brothers and sisters, for our freedom?"

All eyes are fixed on Lafayette. There are no responses this time, though they hear his every word.

"It is true that we will be met by an experienced British army. But we will not engage unless forced. We will stalk them, harass them, prick them. Along with our new supplies, we have our artillery. But more than that, we have each other. All good men, all fighting for a common cause, a noble cause. And I will ask no man to do what I would not do myself. I will be with you every step of the way. But I will not force any man to go. I will take with me only those who are resolved to defend their country—and die for it, if necessary. I have made my choice. Now you must make yours."

The young general pauses for a moment and looks around at his troops. "So who will come with me?" he finally asks. "Who is willing to fight for their own liberty, for that of their families, and their countrymen?"

A change of mood falls across the crowd. Men look at each other. Some look down at the ground, some up to the sky. They mutter back and forth. One or two men step forward and say they will go. Others begin to raise their hands in agreement. An elderly sergeant, sick and barely able to stand, rises and holds his crutch high. "I beg of you, my general," he says, "take me. Take me even if I have to be carried into Virginia on a cart!"

There is a loud "hurrah" and more shouting from the troops. Lafayette steps down from his perch. He hugs the sergeant, hugs and slaps on the back some of the other men, looks over at Captain du Chesnoy, and breathes a deep sigh of relief.

◆　　　◆　　　◆

A little more than a week later, Lafayette received a dispatch from Nathanael Greene relating the alarming news that Lord Cornwallis had marched out of Carolina to join with Generals Phillips and Arnold in Virginia. With this letter, Greene also awarded Lafayette independent command of his army and encouraged him to move against the British forces in Virginia to prevent them from uniting with Cornwallis.

The young marquis immediately called his three regimental commanders together to inform them of the news. Colonel Joseph Vose of Massachusetts,

Lieutenant Colonel Francis Barber of New Jersey, and French Colonel Jean-Joseph Chevalier de Gimat all agreed with their general that they should rapidly march south and try to reach Richmond before Lord Cornwallis.

Now properly supplied, with new energy and inspiration, Lafayette's small army began the 140-mile march from Annapolis to Richmond. Oxen pulled many of the wagons due to a shortage of horses. Men marched during daylight hours, sometimes at a double trot. Few rest breaks were taken, and troops ate on the move. Two days later, near Alexandria, Virginia, they crossed the Potomac River amid wind-raised whitecaps and continued on their dash toward Richmond.

Petersburg/Richmond, Virginia
Late April 1781

One hundred twenty-five miles south, British Major General William Phillips joined forces with Benedict Arnold and attacked Petersburg. With superior artillery and a force numbering nearly 4,000 British troops, they quickly overpowered 1,000 members of the Virginia Militia and forced them to withdraw. Then they burned much of Petersburg and its surrounding villages—with a special emphasis on destroying tobacco crops and the ships that transported them.

The British generals now began formulating plans to move twenty-five miles north to take Richmond. Once that objective was accomplished, they planned to await the arrival of Lord Cornwallis and next move to seize the entire state of Virginia.

On April 29, 1781, General Phillips began the movement of his army toward Richmond. But on the evening of that same day, Lafayette's forces reached the city and joined with the Virginia Militia, which was under the direction of its commander, Thomas Nelson Jr. They were, in turn, quickly reinforced by an unlikely ally, Major General Von Steuben, and his contingent of militia.

Major General Friedrich Wilhelm Augustus Henry Ferdinand, Baron Von Steuben was another volunteer from the European continent. A former captain in the army of Frederick the Great, this colorful Prussian had arrived in America in early 1778 posing as a lieutenant general. He wore a scarlet red coat decorated with shiny medals and was accompanied by three French aides. At age fifty, he was rotund, muscular, and ruddy-faced.

Mired down for the winter at Valley Forge, Washington had brought Von Steuben in to train his dispirited troops. Speaking no English, the Prussian worked through interpreters to accomplish his task.

Often, he would bellow orders and swear profanities in three different languages—which brought both respect and laughter from the ill-clothed and starving American soldiers.

Von Steuben, in turn, had gained new respect for the young Americans when he realized that almost all of them were unpaid volunteers. In a letter to a military friend in Europe, he had written: "The genius of this nation is not in the least to be compared with that of the Prussians, Austrians, or French. You say to your soldier, 'Do this,' and he does it. But I am obliged to say, 'This is the reason why you ought to do that,' and then he does it."

Baron Von Steuben could also be quick-tempered, quarrelsome, and scornful of timidity. Having been sent to Virginia earlier in the year by General Washington with orders to organize an army of militia, he had frightened off many prospective volunteers with his harsh demeanor. The haughty Prussian, however, refused to accept any personal responsibility and blamed what he described as an arrogant populace. "I am not less tired of this state than they are of me," he wrote to a superior. "I shall always regret that circumstances induced me to undertake the defense of a country where Caesar and Hannibal would have lost their reputations, and where every farmer is a general, but where nobody wishes to be a soldier."

Despite his gruff personality, Von Steuben had still managed to raise and train an army of militia that now numbered six hundred. That brought Lafayette's makeshift force to nearly 3,000—his own 1,200 troops, a little more than 1,000 militia under Nelson, Von Steuben's 600, forty cavalrymen, and a small contingent manning six pieces of artillery.

This largely untrained patchwork army was large enough, however, to discourage the British from attacking Richmond. Phillips and Arnold were less than ten miles from the city when their scouts informed them of Lafayette's arrival. Rather than risk a loss, General Phillips, who had fallen ill with swamp fever (malaria), elected to retreat to the outskirts of Petersburg and await the arrival of Lord Cornwallis.

General Benedict Arnold's Headquarters
Petersburg, Virginia
May 20, 1781

It is mid-afternoon. A soft spring breeze rustles the British Union Jack atop the makeshift flagpole in front of General Benedict Arnold's headquarters in Petersburg. All the trees and flowers are in full bloom now. The pastures are green. The sun is shining. A few wispy clouds hang high in the sky.

The advance guard of General Lord Cornwallis's army has already appeared on scene to alert the command of His Lordship's imminent arrival. General Arnold has changed into his finest British dress uniform. After having worn American blue for so many years, his red coat still feels uncomfortable, not quite right. He has assembled his staff outside to greet Cornwallis who is approaching on horseback surrounded by a contingent of smartly dressed officers.

The man who is second in command of all British forces in America slowly rides up and dismounts. General Arnold and his staff snap to attention and offer a salute. Cornwallis returns the salute. Arnold speaks first and introduces himself. "General Cornwallis, sir. I am Benedict Arnold. Welcome."

"General Arnold," Cornwallis states in a formal manner, casting his eyes about. "Where is General Phillips?"

"I beg to inform Your Lordship, with much sorrow, sir, that General Phillips died five days ago. He had suffered greatly from the swamp fever. The end came quietly, sir."

Cornwallis looks stunned. He has known Phillips for years. They were friends. "My God, what a loss," he says quietly. "What bad news this is."

"Would you like to come inside, General?" asks Arnold, beckoning toward the headquarters building. "We have prepared a light meal, sir."

"Very well," replies Cornwallis.

The two generals walk inside followed closely by Lieutenant Colonel George Chewton and Major Alexander Ross, Cornwallis's aides-de-camp, and the officers of General Arnold's staff. Cornwallis and Arnold sit down at a table laid out with a variety of food.

"Would you like some tea, General?" asks one of Arnold's aides.

Cornwallis nods, and the aide pours him some tea. Then he moves around and fills Arnold's cup. "Tell me of our troop strength, General Arnold," says Cornwallis.

"Sir, we have just received a contingent from General Clinton in New York."

"Clinton has sent us help?" Cornwallis asks sarcastically. "Will wonders never cease? How many?"

"Fifteen hundred, sir. Hessians."

"And how many men are currently under your command, General?"

"Nearly 4,000, sir, not including the Hessians," replies Arnold. "But many are ill with the fever and not fit for duty."

"I see," says Cornwallis. "With my 1,500, that gives me an army of 7,000. Good. That is a formidable force with which to begin."

"*Begin, sir?*" *inquires General Arnold.*

"*Yes, General, I mean to reduce Virginia to complete subservience to the Crown. And we will start with that young Frenchman. Where is he now?*"

"*Lafayette is in Richmond, sir—about twenty-five miles north. We estimate his strength to be between 2,500 and 3,000. More than half are untrained militia.*"

"*Good! He shall be no match for us, then,*" *states Cornwallis, as he sips some tea and begins to eat.*

During this pause in the conversation, Benedict Arnold sits back in his chair and looks over his new superior. This is the first time he has actually met personally with Lord Charles Earl Cornwallis, First Marquis of Cornwallis, lieutenant general in the British army. Of course, he knows the man's history. Born to an aristocratic family of privilege, wealth, and royalty, Cornwallis had been educated in Cambridge, served for years in the military, and upon the death of his father, had assumed his birthright—a seat in the House of Lords. Interestingly, Cornwallis had been one of the few members who had consistently opposed British policies that led to the American Revolution. He had argued eloquently for a repeal of the Stamp Act and had denounced Britain's right to tax the American colonies at all. Yet, at the outbreak of war, Cornwallis willingly went to fight on American soil after receiving a promotion to major general. He had beaten George Washington at the battle of Long Island in 1776, lost to the American general at Princeton, and beat him again at Brandywine Creek and Germantown in 1777. Cornwallis had also been second in command to Sir Henry Clinton when Charleston fell in 1780.

Arnold is aware of the deep rift between Cornwallis and Clinton, which may have begun back in 1776 when His Lordship refused to attack Washington at Long Island announcing he would "bag the fox" in the morning. Of course, that next morning, the American general escaped after an all-night evacuation by water. When Clinton heard of the episode, he charged Cornwallis with "the most consummate ignorance I ever heard of in any officer above the rank of corporal."

Now sitting opposite him, Arnold sees a forty-three-year-old man—tall, ungainly, heavyset. Overall, Cornwallis appears rather dull to him.

"*Well,*" *says Cornwallis, abruptly breaking the silence.* "*What are your plans, General Arnold?*"

"*My plans, sir?*"

"*Yes, your plans. Your plans,*" *repeats Cornwallis.* "*Surely you realize there is no need for you here now that I have arrived to assume command.*"

Benedict Arnold's face flushes red. He does not respond.

"*Have you received any orders from His Majesty on high?*" *inquires Cornwallis.*

"*If you mean General Clinton, sir, no I have not.*"

"Well, then, I think it best for you to make plans forthwith to return to New York and put yourself at his disposal."

Rising sharply to his feet, Arnold bows. "By your leave, sir," he says to Cornwallis. Then he turns and, followed by his staff, quickly leaves the room.

After a pause, the general takes a sip of tea and looks at his aide. "Can you believe that man?" he says. "Did he really think I was going to keep a traitor under my command?"

"Unbelievable, sir," replies Colonel Chewton.

"Indeed," agrees Major Ross.

"Well, Major," says Cornwallis in an authoritative tone. "I would like you to prepare several orders on my behalf for tomorrow morning."

"Yes, sir," responds Ross pulling out a pen and paper. "The subject, sir?"

"I am fed up with the shocking excesses of our troops when it comes to these hundreds of women camp followers. I will issue orders—on a daily basis, if necessary—to control this lurid behavior. Make sure you put wording to the effect that I demand that the men, especially the officers, put a stop to their licentious conduct. I will no longer tolerate it. Do you hear me?"

"We do, sir," says Chewton. "We'll see to it."

"You do that. You do that."

"Anything else, Your Lordship?" inquires Ross.

"Indeed, there is," replies Cornwallis. "We will issue orders for our troops to begin preparations for a march north to Richmond. We will commence operations within the week. I intend to capture Lafayette and his inferior little army. The boy cannot escape me."

The Virginia Countryside
Late May 1781

On May 24, 1781, Lord Cornwallis and his legion of 7,000 crossed the James River and advanced north toward Richmond. The young Marquis de Lafayette, on his very first independent command and outnumbered more than two to one, kept a cool head and a calm demeanor. He recognized that it would be foolish, almost suicidal, to engage the British head on. Figuring it was his main army that Cornwallis was after, Lafayette decided to lighten his number by sending Von Steuben, with his 600 militiamen, down the James to guard American supplies. Then he took the rest of his small army and headed north hoping to join up with General Anthony Wayne's New Jersey Continentals who, according to recent dispatches, were headed south to reinforce him.

Lafayette's main strategy was to avoid major confrontation but remain within striking distance of the British. Central to this tactic was to keep himself between Cornwallis and a line of communications to the north, which would ensure that he would eventually meet up with Wayne. Interestingly enough, one of Cornwallis's strategies was to try and get behind "the boy's" northern line of communication to prevent that from happening.

Over the next ten days, with Cornwallis in hot pursuit, Lafayette's band crossed the South Anna River, the North Anna, passed through Fredericksburg, and moved to Ely's Ford on the Rapidan. During the chase, Lord Cornwallis ordered Colonel Banastre Tarleton and his 250 dragoons (newly reformed since the battle of Cowpens) to raid Charlottesville and capture Governor Thomas Jefferson and the state legislature.

Dashing more than seventy miles across country in less than twenty-four hours, Tarleton narrowly missed capturing Jefferson at his home in Monticello and most of the assembly members in Charlottesville. They had been warned only minutes in advance and had escaped west to Staunton. Tarleton, however, was successful in capturing seven legislators and destroying army supplies of powder, clothing, and muskets.

Lafayette, meanwhile, was showing signs of weakening. It was difficult to keep his men motivated and fed while constantly on the run. They had run out of flour, soap, candles—and their remaining supplies of meat were barely edible.

"I have been guarding against my own warmth," the young marquis wrote to General Washington. "When one is twenty-three, has an army to command, and Lord Cornwallis to oppose, the time that is left is none too long for sleep. Were I to fight a battle, I'd be cut to pieces, the militia dispersed, and the arms lost. Were I to decline fighting, the country would think herself given up. I am therefore determined to skirmish. I am not strong enough to even get beaten."

Sir Henry Clinton's Headquarters
Harlem Heights, New York
Early June 1781

Captain Dawkins rushes into the back study where Sir Henry Clinton is dictating a letter to Captain Gurwood. "General Clinton, sir," says Dawkins excitedly, "we have just received a pouch of intercepted dispatches bound to Philadelphia from General Washington."

"Excellent!" replies Clinton. "How many dispatches are there?"

"Three sir—two to the Congress and one to a Dr. John Baker."

"Let me see the one to the doctor," says a curious Clinton. "It is most probably of a personal nature."

"I wonder what the great American hero would think now if he knew you were opening one of his private communiqués this instant, sir," comments Captain Gurwood as Clinton opens the envelope.

"It is dated New Windsor, May 29, 1781," Sir Henry reads out loud. "Sir: A day or two ago, I requested Colonel Harrison to apply to you for a pair of pincers to fasten the wires of my teeth. I hope you furnished him with them.'"

"Why, it is for his dentist!" remarks Dawkins with a grin.

Clinton continues. "I now wish you would send me one of your scrapers, as my teeth stand in need of cleaning, and I have little prospect of being in Philadelphia soon. It will come very safe by the post and, in return, the money shall be sent as soon as I know the cost of it. I am your very humble servant, G. Washington."

As Clinton finishes reading, he looks at his two aides, who have big grins on their faces and are obviously trying to keep from laughing out loud. Finally, Clinton smiles and then bursts into uproarious laughter. Dawkins and Gurwood quickly join in. Other aides and servants rush in to see what all the ruckus is about.

"What is it that has you all laughing so hard?" inquires one officer. "Good news from the field?"

"Why the great General Washington is having problems with his teeth," shouts Sir Henry with merriment. "They are in need of cleaning!"

"Yes," laughs Gurwood, "and he needs new pincers to wire his false teeth together!"

"Well," says Dawkins, "as we have this letter to his dentist, he'll not be receiving them anytime soon. I guess that means he'll be eating mush for another few weeks."

The laughter gets louder at this joke. Finally, Sir Henry calms down and hands the document over to Captain Gurwood. "Let us make more copies of this than usual," he says. "Send the extras to our commanders in the field with instructions to pass the information among the troops. They will get a good laugh from it, as we did."

"Yes, sir," replies Gurwood. "And it will also make General Washington a laughing stock."

Sir Henry smirks and nods affirmatively.

9

Home of Joseph Webb
Wethersfield, Connecticut
May 22, 1781

It is mid-morning. Outside this pastoral, three-and-a-half-story, reddish brown house, the Count de Rochambeau and his aides dismount their horses and walk toward the main entrance. Their boots slop in the ever-present mud of the late-coming spring season.

George Washington steps down from the front porch to greet his French counterpart. "General Rochambeau," he says with a handshake and bow, "I trust Stillman's Tavern provided suitable accommodations for you last night."

"Oui, General, tres bien," responds the count. "Tres bien."

The two men step up onto the porch followed by Rochambeau's aides.

"Looks like rain," notices Washington, pointing to the east. "Dark clouds on the horizon."

Rochambeau utters something in French that the American cannot understand.

"My general asks if these gray skies in New England ever go away, sir," notes Major General Francois Jean, Chevalier de Chastellux, Rochambeau's designated interpreter.

"Yes, they do," replies Washington with a smile. "Spring comes later here than in Virginia, where I'm from. There, the blue skies are already abundant. Soon, it will be that way here also."

Chastellux translates for Rochambeau as the men wipe their feet on the doormat and move into the interior of the house.

Ten days earlier, Washington had received a dispatch from Rochambeau in Newport reporting that his son, the Viscount de Rochambeau, had just returned from France with important information. "I have seen enough to perceive that it is indispensable that we should have a conference as soon as possible," he had written. Washington immediately responded by setting a date and time for this meeting. The small community of Wethersfield, Connecticut, only six miles south of Hartford, was a convenient halfway point. A Washington acquaintance, Mr. Joseph Webb, had offered up his residence as a meeting place.

Into the main sitting room stride the two commanders, Chastellux, and Washington's contingent of Alexander Hamilton, Brigadier General Louis Duportail (chief engineer), and General Henry Knox. The table there is large enough for them to spread out—to view maps, take notes, and get down to business. Chastellux translates every word spoken between the two generals.

"Your son is well, I presume," remarks Washington as everyone takes their seats.

"Oui, merci," responds Rochambeau politely. "But I'm afraid the news he has brought us is not good, my dear general."

"No?" asks Washington.

Shaking his head, Rochambeau begins to explain. "Prime Minister Vergennes convinced the king to disband the main body of troops that had been promised to me. I'm afraid we can expect only a few hundred."

"How many hundred?" asks Washington.

"Six hundred at the most."

General Washington takes a deep breath, cocks his head, and stares out the window.

"There is more I have to tell you," says Rochambeau. "My son has also brought news of Minister Vergennes's plan to end the war. The final settlement is to be based on the status quo as of 1781. Britain has agreed. France controls the votes of Russia, Sweden, and Austrio-Hungary. It will not be good for America."

"Did he say when this summit is to convene?" asks Washington.

"Winter. Perhaps late autumn."

"We have received a captured letter from the British minister of war, Lord Germain," states Washington. "He has ordered Sir Henry Clinton to drive our armies north of the Hudson River."

"This is most certainly in preparation for Vergennes's conference," replies Rochambeau.

"I think so. They want to gain control from New York to the Carolinas—leaving us only Boston and to the north."

"Oui. Oui. Of course."

"Well, at least that order will be delayed before it reaches Clinton," notes Washington.

"I think there is no time to lose," says Rochambeau matter-of-factly. "We must act."

"Agreed," says Washington.

"It does appear," continues Rochambeau, "that our French fleet under Admiral de Grasse will be operating in the West Indies all during the summer months."

Washington's eyes dart back to the count. "Oh?" he asks.

"Oui, c'est vrai. It is true."

"In what manner is the fleet to be employed?" inquires Washington. *"Might we expect the fleet's presence on this coast?"*

Rochambeau wavers. *"Um, de Grasse is acting in the West Indies on orders from France,"* he replies evasively. *"I suppose, however, that he may, at his own discretion, have some flexibility."*

Washington pauses and looks for a long time into the French general's eyes. He leans back in his chair and takes another deep breath. *"Well, perhaps we should address what plan of action we might embark upon for this year's offensive. What do you recommend, sir?"*

"I believe our best hope lies to the south in Virginia," says Rochambeau. *"As Phillips, Arnold, and Cornwallis are now in Virginia, we may be presented with a great opportunity. If we can control the Chesapeake, we can command shipping and the tobacco trade."*

"Yes, that is certainly a possibility," says Washington, *"but we most certainly cannot control anything without a superior naval force. Rather than Virginia, I would much prefer a siege of New York, as we have previously discussed. Henry Clinton has 14,500 troops there, compared to only 7,000 in Virginia. Should the West India fleet arrive at Sandy Hook, we may cut off any reinforcements and supplies by sea. At the same time, if we concentrate our forces around the city and lay siege, we will be most capable of striking a deathblow to British domination in America. I dare say it would end the war altogether."*

"Oui, it may, it may," replies Rochambeau. *"Let me ask you a hypothetical question, sir. Should the French fleet sail from the West Indies to these seas, what operations would you envision?'*

"The French fleet is of essential importance in any offensive operation," replies Washington, *"and indispensable to stop the progress of the enemy's arms to the south. Should the fleet arrive upon the Atlantic coast, the French and American forces thus combined may either proceed in operations against New York or may be directed against the enemy in some other quarter, as circumstances dictate."*

"Oui, I agree," states Rochambeau, *"but we must determine what destination we are to recommend Admiral de Grasse sail, if he can come. The Chesapeake is only half the distance to New York for de Grasse."*

"True enough, of course," retorts Washington, *"but a major movement of our land troops in that direction this summer will not work. It will be too hot—and our New England troops are already disinclined for such a march south. It would lead to abundant desertion and, I believe, sickness. And of course, the expense would be exorbitant if not altogether prohibitive."*

"I see," says Rochambeau. "The summer would be difficult. Of course, if the fleet were to wait until autumn, de Grasse will also have to contend with the hurricane season. I must also point out that the waters off Sandy Hook may not be deep enough to accommodate our ships' low hulls."

"Yes, that would certainly be of concern," agrees Washington.

"Also, I believe we may not have sufficient troop numbers to conduct a proper siege of the city," states Rochambeau.

"You have conducted many sieges before," notes Washington. "How many more troops would we need?"

"Um, I would estimate another 8,000—but I have not the detailed knowledge of the landscape."

Washington sighs deeply. "Perhaps we should make a reconnaissance of the area to see for ourselves," he says. "I would also propose that we join our forces on the outskirts of New York. Our presence there will surely frighten Clinton."

"Oui," agrees Rochambeau. "He is a very cautious man."

"Yes," says Washington, "and he will react emotionally when it comes to saving his own skin. He'll probably recall troops from Virginia to fortify his position."

"I agree with such a consolidation of our forces," says Rochambeau. "We must march past New York even if we elect to head south. But what of the artillery?"

"I believe it is immoral to engage the British without using heavy artillery," replies Washington.

"Indeed so. We cannot conduct an adequate siege without it. That is why we transported the guns 3,000 miles from France. As a matter of realism, however, they all must be transported from Newport by water. Far too heavy to do otherwise."

"We should bring some of the artillery to New York early," states Washington. "The rest should stay in a safe place. Boston, I would suggest, with Admiral de Barras, who may later transport it south."

"Oui, I agree."

"I have already given the order to assemble available American artillery for a possible siege of New York," interrupts General Knox, with a smile.

"Tres bien," responds Rochambeau. "And of course, we must coordinate with Admiral de Grasse."

"If he were to add a body of land forces to his naval armament, it would help greatly," suggests Washington.

"Of course, I will recommend it," replies Rochambeau.

General Washington then summarizes the decisions made. "Very well. An operation against New York seems to be the preference as opposed to sending a force to Virginia.

"The French army will march south and form a junction with American troops on the North River. Admiral de Barras and his fleet shall sail to Boston with the siege artillery. A force of 200 will be left behind for the security and, along with 500 militia, should be sufficient to guard the works. Are you in agreement with this, General?"

"Oui," replies Rochambeau, "I agree."

"Letters shall be sent to Admiral de Grasse requesting that he bring the West Indies fleet to the Atlantic coast. The force thus combined may either proceed in the operation against New York, or may be directed against the enemy in some other quarter to the south as circumstances shall dictate. That final decision shall rest largely upon where Admiral de Grasse decides to go when and if he departs the West Indies."

Generals Washington and Rochambeau subsequently sign a document agreeing to the plan. The conference quickly ends with Rochambeau returning to Newport and Washington to New Windsor. Both groups ride through driving rainstorms on the way back.

General Washington's Headquarters
New Windsor, New York
May–June 1781

When Washington arrived in New Windsor, a letter from John Laurens was waiting for him. The young officer reported that he had spent six weeks in Paris appealing to Minister de Vergennes for a loan of twenty-five million livres. He had been so persistent that the American emissary to France, Benjamin Franklin, actually cautioned him to slow down. "Even the best friends may be wearied by too frequent and unexpected demands," warned Franklin.

Unable to make any headway with the French minister, Laurens audaciously went to King Louis XVI in Versailles and pleaded for help. The king, who, according to Laurens, had "an exalted opinion of George Washington," agreed to provide a gift of six million livres to the Americans. Now armed with the king's support, Laurens was able to secure an additional loan of ten million livres from Holland, guaranteed by the French government.

Rejoicing at this good news, Washington at once began laying the groundwork for a major siege of New York City. He started by writing a series of letters designed to alert key people and gain their support about the upcoming summer campaign.

To the Chevalier de la Luzerne (French Minister to the United States) in Philadelphia, Washington wrote: "Our object is New York. The Count de Rochambeau and the Chevalier de Chastellux agree perfectly in sentiment with me that the West Indies fleet should run immediately to Sandy Hook where it may be joined by Count de Barras."

Washington also sent an update to Lafayette in Virginia. "My dear Marquis," he wrote, "I have just returned from Wethersfield at which I have met the Count de Rochambeau. Upon a full consideration of our affairs in every point of view, an attempt upon New York was deemed preferable to a southern operation. The French troops are to march this way as soon as circumstances permit."

The American commander then began working out logistics for the movement of troops and armaments. He sent circulars to the states urging a step-up in recruiting and enlistments. He arranged for additional gunpowder, arms, and stores to be sent from Massachusetts to New York. And he created a plan to provide Admiral de Barras with dozens of additional boats to use for the transportation of artillery and troops from Newport to Boston and, eventually, to New York.

George Washington's quickness at taking steps for a siege of New York was countered by Count de Rochambeau's sluggishness. Although the French commander had consented to the New York plan, he really believed it would only lead to a stalemate. Rather than conducting a costly siege of a well-fortified, well-mannered enemy position, Rochambeau preferred the opportunity that a campaign in Virginia afforded. Quick movements to the south to engage a smaller enemy force, he believed, could very well result in a low-risk battlefield victory. The French commander, therefore, was in no hurry to commence preparations for a siege of New York. And he certainly was not going to encourage Admiral de Grasse to bring his fleet to Sandy Hook.

Rochambeau began a letter to de Grasse on May 28, five days after the Wethersfield Conference. On and off over the next two weeks, he added to the message. But he delayed sending it until he clearly understood the status of the West Indies fleet. Finally, on June 11, Rochambeau received a dispatch from de Grasse relating that the fleet could be in American waters by mid-July. Meanwhile, the admiral requested information about plans for the summer campaign. Depending on the determined destination, de Grasse asked that expert sea pilots be sent to him.

At this point, Rochambeau finalized his letter. He first discussed the plan to converge the two armies, but with a twist as to the reason for doing so. "I am going to join General Washington," he wrote, "and try, by threatening New York with him, to create a diversion for the benefit of Virginia."

Rochambeau next recommended that de Grasse sail first to the Chesapeake. "The southwesterly winds and the distressed state of Virginia will probably lead you to prefer the Chesapeake Bay," he wrote. "It is there that we think you can render the greatest service. You can achieve much against the enemy that will be there," he states. "Afterward, the wind may bring you to New York in two days."

Rochambeau also told de Grasse that, in order to accomplish the mission, there was a great need for additional troops and money. "It is of the utmost importance that you take on board as many soldiers as you can—four or five thousand men would not be too many. I also do not have enough money to pay our troops beyond this summer. Therefore, it would be of great help if you could secure a loan of no less than 1.2 million livres from the French colonies of the Caribbean."

Before Rochambeau sent his letter to de Grasse, he forwarded it to George Washington for review. Understandably upset because the French commander had recommended that the fleet first sail to Virginia, Washington immediately wrote a note (dated June 13) to Rochambeau requesting that his preference also be sent to de Grasse.

"Please recollect that New York was looked upon by us as the only practicable object under present circumstances," he stated. "Instead of advising de Grasse to run immediately to the Chesapeake, will it not be best to leave him to judge which will be the most advantageous quarter for him to make his appearance in? Sandy Hook has been mentioned as the most desirable point. By coming up suddenly there, he would certainly block up any fleet that might be within the harbor. He would even have a very good chance of forcing an entrance before dispositions could be made to oppose him. Should the British fleet not be there, he could follow them to the Chesapeake, which is always accessible to a superior force."

One week later, on June 20, 1781, the French frigate *Concorde* sailed from Newport for the West Indies. On board were seven New York coastal pilots and more than twenty pilots from the Chesapeake Bay. Rochambeau's dispatch to de Grasse was also on board—but it did not include General Washington' counter opinion about first heading to New York. Rather, Rochambeau wrote a letter to Washington stating his regret that the American general's communication had arrived too late to include his statement to de Grasse. "The *Concorde* has already sailed," said Rochambeau, "but I will send your sentiments with the next ship."

◆   ◆   ◆

While feverishly working on the logistics for the upcoming siege of New York, General Washington received a visit from Rochambeau's dashing leader of the

French cavalry. Armand-Louis de Gontaut-Biron, Duke de Lauzun, had ridden at a furious pace from Newport to New Windsor to relate news that a French council of war had convened as soon as Rochambeau returned from Wethersfield. Unfortunately, Admiral de Barras and the other officers opposed moving the small French fleet from Newport to Boston. It was too much of a gamble, they believed, to risk being intercepted by the nearby British fleet. Therefore, the cavalryman begged to report that Rochambeau had bowed to the wishes of his officers. The fleet would stay in Newport.

De Lauzun later noted that this news "threw Washington into such a rage that he would not give me an answer." Finally, after three days, "and then only out of regard for me," the American general provided a written response to be taken back to Newport.

"I take the liberty still to recommend removal of the fleet to Boston," wrote Washington to Rochambeau. "That aside, I must adhere to my opinion and to the plan fixed at Wethersfield."

10

Sir Henry Clinton's Headquarters
Harlem Heights, New York
June 1781

During the early evening hours, just before the sun has set completely, a dozen riders gallop up to the front of the headquarters mansion. Hearing all the commotion, Sir Henry Clinton opens the front door and steps onto the porch, Captains Gurwood and Dawkins following close behind. A high-ranking British officer carrying a leather pouch jumps off his horse, runs up to the porch, and salutes the general. "What is the news, Colonel?" says Clinton, returning the salute. "You have many riders with you, and I anticipate it must be important."

"Yes, sir. We thought it best for protection, sir. An American rider was intercepted yesterday with dispatches bound for Philadelphia and Virginia, sir. Our intelligence officers relate that it is of the utmost urgency that these be delivered directly into your hands, sir."

"Very well, Colonel," replies Clinton who takes the pouch, then abruptly turns and walks back into the mansion. "Dawkins! Gurwood! Take this and review them," orders Clinton. "I will be right with you."

"Yes, sir."

"Yes, sir."

By the time Sir Henry arrives in the back study ten minutes later, the two officers have scattered the contents of the pouch on the desk and are busy reading. "Well, what have we got," asks Clinton, "another letter to Washington's dentist?"

"No sir, far from it," responds Captain Dawkins. "Among other miscellaneous letters, there are at least three documents of major significance. This first one is a copy of an agreement reached between Washington and Rochambeau for the upcoming summer campaign, sir. It is marked "Confidential" and dated last week, sir—apparently the result of a conference between the two commanders at a place called Wethersfield. Wethersfield is south of Hartford, sir."

"Yes, yes, I know where Wethersfield is," says Sir Henry impatiently. "What does it say? What does it say?"

"The French troops are to march south from Newport to form a junction with the Americans on the Hudson, sir. French Admiral de Grasse is to be ordered to sail from the West Indies for Sandy Hook. A plan is set to lay siege to New York, sir."

"Is that what it says?" asks Sir Henry in disbelief. "Let me see it."

While Clinton is reviewing the document, Captain Gurwood waves another letter in the air. "Sir, this one is from Washington to Lafayette. May I read it, sir?"

"Yes, yes, read, read."

"'My dear Marquis: I have just returned from Wethersfield at which I met the Count de Rochambeau. Upon full consideration of our affairs in every point of view, an attempt upon New York was deemed preferable to a southern operation as we had not the command of the water. The reasons which induced this determination were the danger of the approaching heats, the inevitable dissipation and loss of men by so long a march, and the difficulty of transportation; but above all, it was thought that we had a tolerable prospect of expelling the enemy or obliging them to withdraw part of their force from the southward. The French troops are to march as soon as certain circumstances will admit, leaving about 200 men at Providence with the heavy stores and 500 militia upon Rhode Island to secure the works. I am endeavoring upon the states to fill up their battalions for the campaign.'"

Sir Henry sits down and stares at Gurwood for the longest time. Finally, he speaks. "It is possible that this may be a ruse—false information planted by Washington."

"Well, certainly, we know him to have done so before," replies Gurwood.

"I think not, sir," interrupts Captain Dawkins. "Here is a letter from the Chevalier de Chastellux to the French representative to the American Congress. It is written in French, General, but I am well enough versed to make out its meaning."

"Yes?" asks Clinton.

"Well, sir, Chastellux is boasting of having artfully brought Rochambeau around to the opinion of Washington, who apparently favored an attack on New York. He says that orders have been sent on to Admiral de Grasse to come with his fleet and force his way over the bar at Sandy Hook to the mouth of the harbor at New York. 'A siege of the island has been determined upon,' he writes, 'and our two armies are on the march for that city.'"

"I do not think the Chevalier would be writing a letter boasting of such a thing if it were not true," says Sir Henry.

"I think not, sir," replies Dawkins.

"That would surely not be part of a deception," says Gurwood. "It must be true, then. We are to be attacked this summer!"

"Yes! Yes!" shouts Sir Henry, rising to his feet. "An attack is imminent. We must take all preventive measures as soon as possible. This means, of course, that we must

fortify our position. We must call for more Hessians. It also means that we shall not need to make a strong push in Virginia. That Washington is wise and crafty. He infers from our field movements that we are planning a major campaign in Virginia, so he proposes one bold stroke to lay siege to New York and end the war. I knew Lord Cornwallis's unwise maneuvers would get us into trouble. Well, we will just have to outsmart General Buckskin. Gurwood, prepare to write a letter to His Lordship."

"Yes, sir," responds Gurwood, who quickly pulls out pen and paper.

"Lord Cornwallis," begins Clinton, now pacing back and forth. "I have just received significant copies of secret American dispatches which I enclose for your review. As they indicate, an attack on my position here in New York is planned along with an American de-emphasis on the southern theater. Accordingly, it is necessary to implement new strategy.

"Regarding your position, I have no reason to suppose the Continentals under Lafayette can exceed 1,000. With the addition of troops under General Wayne, Your Lordship may possibly have opposed to you from 1,500 to 2,000 Continentals and a small body of militia. As the enclosed dispatches indicate, the enemy appears for the present to have no intention of sending further reinforcements. On the other hand, I am threatened with a siege at this post. My present effective force is only 10,931. The enemy here may amount to at least 20,000—including French reinforcements and numerous militias of the five neighboring provinces. As you can see, the sooner I concentrate my forces, the better.

"Have you got all that, Gurwood?"

"Yes, sir. Please continue."

"As soon as you have finished the active operations you may now be engaged in, you are to abandon any plan to subdue Virginia. Instead, you are to take a defensive station in any healthy situation you choose along the coast, be it Williamsburg or Yorktown. After reserving to yourself such troops as you may judge to be necessary for an ample defensive station, the following corps may be sent to me in succession as you can spare them: two battalions of light infantry; the 43rd Regiment; the 76th or 80th Regiment; two battalions of Anspach infantry; the Queen's Rangers, cavalry and infantry; remains of the detachment of the Seventeenth light cavalry; such proportion of artillery as can be spared, particularly men; four vessels; twenty-four boats having platforms for cannon; your military engineer, Lieutenant Alexander Sutherland; and as many entrenching tools, horses, and wagons as you can spare.

"That will do, Gurwood. Prepare it immediately for my signature," says Clinton as he exits the room. "I wish it to go out tonight."

"Yes, sir," responds the captain, who turns to Dawkins and says, "I wonder how His Lordship will react to sending nearly 3,000 of his men northward."

"He will be apoplectic," replies Dawkins. "This is perhaps the first time I have heard Sir Henry give a direct order."

"Yes, it can be interpreted no other way."

◆   ◆   ◆

One week later, Sir Henry Clinton dictated another letter requesting that Lord Cornwallis move into the vicinity of the Delaware River or, if he preferred, to New York City, itself. When Dawkins pointed out that they had as of yet not received a reply to their last letter to Cornwallis, Clinton screamed at him to do his job and not question his superior.

Another four days went by and, increasingly worried and frustrated at still not having heard from Cornwallis, Clinton dictated yet another letter demanding action from his southern commander. This time, neither Dawkins nor Gurwood said a word to Sir Henry—but listened attentively as the general departed the room talking to himself: "Where is the bastard? Why hasn't he responded? What is he doing?"

Lord Cornwallis's Encampment
Williamsburg, Virginia
Late June 1781

Lord Cornwallis stopped his army about six miles north of Williamsburg on the evening of June 25, 1781. The next morning, he ordered Major John Graves Simcoe and his cavalry "Rangers" to collect cattle and destroy stores at nearby Spencer's Ordinary. They were met, however, by a cavalry contingent of Lafayette's army that had ridden all night to conduct a surprise attack. During this brief but fierce battle, the mounted troops fought hand-to-hand until both sides retreated from the field. The British suffered thirty-three casualties and the Americans, thirty-one.

Cornwallis was stunned by the engagement. He thought he had slipped away from Lafayette's army a week earlier and left them a hundred miles back in Virginia's interior. Even with the dire conditions of Lafayette's force, Cornwallis had been unable to outflank the young Frenchman and cut off his communications. As a matter of fact, Lafayette had been so swift and nimble that the British general was unable to get close to the American army, let alone "catch the boy." Running low on supplies, Cornwallis finally abandoned the chase and began a deliberate march to the Chesapeake. His plan was to rest and resupply his troops and then consolidate the British position at a strong base along the coast of Virginia where the Royal Navy could provide ample protection. From there, he would devise a new offensive plan against the Americans for the upcoming summer campaign.

On this day, engaging Lafayette had been the furthest thing from his mind. Now, with the attack at Spencer's Ordinary, Cornwallis would have to reevaluate his situation. Not wanting to engage in a major battle, he sent out scouts to determine the enemy's strength and position while he rode into Williamsburg with the main body of his army.

Waiting for Cornwallis at British headquarters were two of the three letters written by Sir Henry Clinton. Clinton's first letter had been intercepted by an American patrol along the way. Therefore, Cornwallis did not receive copies of the Wethersfield Plan or Washington and Chastellux's letters.

After reading the two dispatches, Cornwallis groused to his aide, Major Alexander Ross. "In his first letter, Sir Henry inflates the number of troops mobilizing against him and deflates the size of the force Lafayette has against me. Then he orders me to send nearly half my army to him. Can you imagine? And rather than begin an offensive campaign, he orders me to take a defensive position at either Williamsburg or Yorktown. In his second letter, written only four days after the first, he suggests I move the entire army up to Philadelphia or New York."

"This is unusual, even for Sir Henry," commented Ross.

"Yes," agreed Cornwallis. "It seems he has overreacted to the threat of the Americans and French joining forces to attack him. He is afraid for his own skin. He is also impatient. That is why he wrote the second letter without allowing me enough time to respond to the first. Yet a siege on New York is impractical. I do not believe Washington and Rochambeau together have enough men for such a siege. I wonder if it is a ruse. Hmmm."

"What will you do with these two conflicting orders, My Lord?" inquired Ross.

"Well, as the first letter is in the form of an order, whereas the second is only a suggestion—and since I am already in Williamsburg, and it is utterly impractical for me to move north—I will obey orders."

Over the next several days, Cornwallis rode the twelve miles to Yorktown and personally surveyed the location's suitability for a defensive station, as per Clinton's direction. Accompanying him were Major Simcoe along with fifty of his Rangers and a Hessian Field-Jager detachment commanded by Captain Johann Ewald.

Yorktown was a small town with four principal streets and about two hundred buildings. It was located on the southern shore of the York River. Here the river narrowed such that the northern shore at Gloucester Point was a little more than half a mile away. Farther eastward, the river widened significantly until it opened into the Chesapeake Bay just a few miles downstream.

Lord Cornwallis and his contingent approached Yorktown from the west along the Williamsburg Road preceded by local scouts who relayed word of their approach. As soon as the British were in sight, the local Virginia Militia manning a small battery at Gloucester Point began a wild and haphazard bombardment which did little to slow the redcoats, but frightened the town's residents considerably.

After a half-day's reconnaissance of the area, an unimpressed Cornwallis headed back to Williamsburg. The day he returned, on June 30, 1781, Lord Cornwallis penned a letter of response to Sir Henry Clinton.

"Upon viewing Yorktown," he wrote, "I was clearly of the opinion that it far exceeds our power, consistent with your plans, to make safe defensive posts there and at Gloucester Point, both of which would be necessary for the protection of shipping. In practicality, the site is unsuitable for a naval station because of its inevitable susceptibility to an enemy naval attack.

"For your defensive post, I will cross the James River and move to Portsmouth which is, under my judgment, much more appropriate and suitable for establishing a post consistent with your wishes. From there, I will embark to New York the troops and supplies you have requested.

"Lafayette has begun to mount a considerable force, including many reinforcements of militia, 800 Continentals under General Anthony Wayne, and about 800 Virginia and North Carolina mountain riflemen. He keeps his main body about eighteen or twenty miles from us; his advanced corps about ten or twelve—probably with an intention of harassing our rear guard when we pass the James River."

Marquis de Lafayette's Encampment
Southeastern Virginia Countryside
Late June 1781

The Marquis de Lafayette was camped twenty miles northwest of Williamsburg at Tyree's Plantation. He had kept his army constantly on the move, not allowing them a moment's rest as Cornwallis began his march to the Virginia coast. When the Americans passed through Richmond, smoke was still billowing from houses and stores burned by the British less than twenty-four hours earlier. And as Cornwallis moved to cross the James in his drive to Portsmouth, Lafayette followed again, only not quite as cautiously as before.

Buoyed by the fact that they were no longer running for their lives, the Americans almost overtook the British before they reached the James. Morale was also running high because Baron Von Steuben and General Anthony Wayne had arrived with reinforcements. Wayne brought with him more than 800 seasoned Continental soldiers drawn mainly from the Pennsylvania regiments he had reorganized after the New Jersey mutiny. At age thirty-six, Anthony Wayne was a five-year veteran of the war and had distinguished himself under George Washington at Valley Forge, Brandywine, Germantown, and Monmouth. Known for his high energy, his bursts of passion, and an uncommon generosity with his enormous wealth, "Mad" Anthony had earned his nickname at the battle of Stony Point, New York, when he offered $500 cash prizes to the first five men who entered the British-occupied fort. After taking Stony Point, he wrote General Washington that, "Our officers and men behaved like men who are determined to be free."

Also uplifting spirits in the American camp was the unexpected arrival of General Daniel Morgan with a large contingent of Virginia Militia from the Shenandoah Valley. After his brilliant victory at Cowpens, Morgan had returned home to recuperate from crippling arthritis. Now feeling better, he had recruited a new group of light infantry, outfitted them all with frocks and linen overalls, and trained them for battle.

Morgan also brought news of a change in the government of Virginia. Thomas Jefferson's term had expired on June 4, and he had been succeeded by Thomas Nelson Jr. of Yorktown. The state legislature immediately granted their new governor special emergency powers, which Nelson used aggressively to recruit new volunteers and to commandeer food, munitions, and clothing for the troops. General Morgan reported that Governor Nelson would join Lafayette at the earliest opportunity.

With the addition of Anthony Wayne's 800 Continentals and nearly 3,000 militiamen under Von Steuben and Morgan, Lafayette's once meager army now outnumbered that of Lord Cornwallis. So it is not surprising that when the British marched toward Portsmouth, the young marquis hovered closely—hoping to find just the right opportunity to turn the tables and, for the first time, engage the enemy head on.

In a letter to General Washington, Lafayette described his new strength and informed the commander in chief of Cornwallis's movements. He also marveled at the fortitude of the mountain marksmen from the Shenandoah Valley.

"*Mon Dieu*! What a people!" he wrote. "The riflemen ran the whole day in front of my horse without eating or resting."

11

Dobb's Ferry, New York
Late June 1781

The summer heat has finally set in. Many of the American troops sweat profusely as they line up to receive General Rochambeau's army. The French force of 4,000 has just completed its march down from Newport to this place on the Hudson, barely a dozen miles north of Manhattan. They had moved 220 miles in eleven days—across Rhode Island, Connecticut, and into New York. Not bad for a band of Europeans unaccustomed to American summers.

The Continental troops, nearly 3,000 strong, line up on one side of the dusty road leading to the encampment. Excited to see their allies, they pack next to each other, two to three deep for nearly half a mile, without much regard for organization by regiment. They are a ragtag lot. Some of the officers are dressed in faded or torn buff and blue uniforms. But most have no uniforms at all. They are clad in whatever they have been able to find: hunting shirts, old linen jackets, short tattered knickers without socks. Some are without shirts. Many are barefoot. Most wear shabby three-cornered hats with holes in them. Others have on only the lids of hats, because the rims have worn away. Hundreds have nothing on their heads—except tousled, dirty hair.

Twenty-seven-year-old, five foot six inch Dr. James Thacher of Boston stands about halfway down the line intermingled with a group of Virginians. It has been six years since he volunteered for service in the Continental Army. Nearly all his friends advised him not to do it. He would be committing treason, they told him—condemning his head to the gallows. Since signing up, he has traveled with the army as needed—at Saratoga, at Long Island, at Trenton, Brandywine, Germantown, and Valley Forge. He has tended to the wounded, the sick, and the infirmed. He has seen many men, young and old, die fighting for freedom. He is a keen observer and keeps a meticulous diary.

As the procession begins, Dr. Thacher and the American soldiers first hear music. They see a large French military band with many instruments and a large drums corps. Next come the regiments. At the head of each are officers mounted on noble steeds. Almost all officers are noblemen—princes, counts, viscounts, marquis, chevaliers, barons, and dukes. They are dressed in immaculate, brightly colored uniforms adorned with medals, gold braids, and plumes. Each officer is followed by his personal contingent of servants and baggage.

Following the officers are the regimental standards, the battle flags. Each has a white background emblazoned with fleur-de-lis—the golden lilies of France. A cross divides each flag into quarters—and each quarter, in turn, reflects the individual regiment.

From head to toe, all the soldiers are immaculately dressed. Everyone wears crisp black, three-cornered felt hats. Shoes are low-cut, stockings clean and bright. The infantry wears short white embroidered jackets. The sergeants have white plumes stuck in their hats and carry gold-knobbed canes that are the symbols of their specialties. Grenadiers wear red plumes in their hats. Chasseurs, the French light infantry, wear green.

Every soldier's uniform is base white with regiments distinguished by different colors on lapels, coat collars, and buttons. The Bourbonnais wear crimson lapels, pink collars, and white buttons. The Soissonais have rose-colored lapels, sky blue collars, and yellow buttons. The Auxone Battalion and Metz Regiment, the artillery companies, are clad in deep blue waistcoats and iron gray breeches trimmed with red velvet. The Royal Deux-Ponts and the Saintonge Regiment, led by Rochambeau's son, the Viscount de Rochambeau, are equally adorned in their own brilliant colors. But perhaps the most dazzling of all are the dragoons of the Duke de Lauzun's Cavalry Legion. All are mounted on beautiful horses with saddlecloths made of tiger skin. Their uniforms are adorned in bold shades of red, green, and blue. Officers wear scarlet breeches and pale blue coats, and the Polish hussars all have handlebar mustaches and carry lances and sabers with curved blades. The Legionnaires wear tall fur hats with brightly colored plumes.

Every brigade is followed by several pieces of cannon and mortars accompanied by ammunition carriages. In the rear of the long line are wives and children of some of the soldiers. They, in turn, are followed by a great number of caissons and wagons pulled by horses or oxen—each loaded with tents, provisions, and other baggage.

The Americans view all this with admiration and awe. They wave their arms and cheer wildly for their new allies, which seems to please members of the French army, many of whom smile and wave back.

Dr. Thacher is amazed at the contrast between the elegantly dressed French and the slapdash American lot. But the Continentals, though poorly dressed, hold their heads high, with pride and self-confidence. They have withstood the fire and trial of the previous six years and are not easily humbled or impressed.

A Virginia officer standing nearby says that the French are not the fops he had expected. "Finer troops I never saw," he admits.

"Now we greet them as friends and allies," responds Dr. Thacher, *"and they seem determined to act in unison with us against the enemy."*

◆　　　◆　　　◆

Later that day, and in the days and weeks that followed, the curious Americans walked through the French encampment that General Washington had staked out next to their own between White Plains on the east and Dobb's Ferry on the west. They shook hands with their new colleagues, swapped tokens, and sang and danced together.

The Europeans purchased fresh food and invited the Americans to dine with them. They laid out a myriad of courses prepared by their skilled chefs—special soups, roast beef or chicken served in French wine sauce, and delectable desserts. Language was often a barrier in communicating, because few Americans spoke French, German, Prussian, or Polish. And most of the Europeans were not fluent in English. But good cheer, a common desire to get along, and flowing rum and wine easily made up for the inability to engage in personal conversations.

Many of the Americans scraped together what they could to return the entertainment. But barely able to avoid starvation themselves, they usually delivered only freshly killed game to the French encampment with apologies that they could not do more.

◆　　　◆　　　◆

Late one night, after enjoying a hearty meal with their American guests, several French officers sit around a table near a campfire. The Chevalier de Chastellux, the Count de Deux-Ponts, the Viscount de Noailles (the Marquis de Lafayette's brother-in-law) of the Soissonais Regiment, and Baron Ludwig Von Closen (aide to General Rochambeau) sip wine and speak quietly in French.

"They told us at Newport that the American army had 10,000 men," says Deux-Ponts, *"but it is not possible. I count only four small regiments from New York, New Jersey, and Rhode Island."*

"They also have a small Canadian regiment, a little more than 200 artillerymen, a handful of engineers, sappers, and miners, and about one hundred cavalrymen," adds Chastellux.

"Washington can have no more than 2,500 or 3,000 men," concludes Deux-Ponts. *"He has concealed his numbers not only from the enemy, but from his own troops. Now we all see how he does it. With this small number, he forms a spacious*

camp and spreads a large number of tents. It appears much more numerous than it really is."

"I admire these American troops tremendously," interjects Baron Von Closen excitedly. "It is incredible that soldiers composed of men of every age—of whites and blacks, hundreds of old men, even children of fifteen—almost naked, unpaid, and rather poorly fed can march so well and withstand fire so steadfastly."

"One must remember that these men are survivors of six years of misery and deprivation," says Chastellux. "They sleep three or four to an odorous tent, without so much as a mattress. They lay on branches covered with dirty blankets and have virtually no baggage. None!"

"Yes, it is amazing," says Noailles, "and despite all this, they are a cheerful lot. With such meager supplies, they are, for the most part, lean and slender—quite healthy and handsome in appearance."

"Their marching is indifferent," states Deux-Ponts. "I think it is because they choose their own leaders and pay no attention to discipline."

"But one should not think that this American army can be compared to a motley crew of farmers," remarks Chastellux. "I was greatly surprised that, during drills, the men are not in close formation, arm to arm, but consistently leave a place for a man between every two men—which is a very good thing in penetrating a thick wood or underbrush with entire battalions."

"And have you noticed how they keep their muskets clean and shining?" asks Noailles. "They are excellent and dangerous shots!"

"Speaking of excellence," says Von Closen, "did you see the Rhode Island regiment? Mon Dieu, they are the best-uniformed, best-trained, most competent troops General Washington has."

"Yes," agrees Chastellux, "and they are three-quarters black. I have seen them march and perform several mountings of the guard. There is nothing to criticize. The men are complete masters of their legs, carry their weapons well, hold their heads straight, faced right without moving an eye, and wheel so excellently that the regiment looks like it is dressed in line with a string!"

"Yes, they are brilliant," agrees Deux-Ponts. "And I'm forced to admit that nearly all these Americans have a quality I have rarely seen in a large group of soldiers. It is their proud bearing. They have the look of men who will not be easily overcome."

"That is because they are fighting for their freedom," says Chastellux.

"Yes, and also because they hate the British more than we do."

"Indeed! Do you notice how they refuse to wear the color red? It is to that degree they hate the British."

All the officers laugh at this comment. Then there is a pause.

Baron Von Closen draws a deep breath, and preparing to retire, rises from his chair. "With what soldiers in the world could one do what has been done by these men—who go about nearly naked and in the greatest deprivation?" he asks. "If you deny the best-disciplined soldiers of Europe what is due them, they will run away in droves—and the general will soon be alone. But from this brave group of soldiers, everyone can see what can be done with a common bond. A bond they unashamedly call 'Liberty!'"

"Well, said!" responds Chastellux. "But I can tell you that General Washington will never be left alone. I have spent much time with him. The proud bearing of the army springs directly from him."

Deux-Ponts frowns. "Perhaps," he says, "but I do not see it as so obvious. Look at the informality of Washington's headquarters. Thirty people sit at his table most evenings. The food is fairly abundant, but the coffee is weak, and the salad is served with only vinegar. And since we are given only one plate, we have to slosh all the foods together. Then they expect us to wash it all down with beer and rum."

"Come, come, mon amis," says Noailles, with a wink and a smile, "where are they to obtain fine wine?"

"It is interesting how long they sit at the table after the meal," says Von Closen, still standing. "Washington and his fellow American officers crack hickory nuts by the hour, engage in free and agreeable conversation, and offer toast after toast into the night."

"Such open and carefree conversations would never happen during a French general's dinner," states Deux-Ponts. "Never!"

"Perhaps that is one reason his officers revere him so?" stated Von Closen. "He gives liberty in his daily life. His men have the freedom to speak their minds, to be themselves."

There is another pause in the conversation as the officers reflect on this comment.

"And yet Washington, himself, does not drink to excess," notes Noailles. "He has no reason for prolonging the meal other than pure enjoyment of the company."

"Indeed," agrees Chastellux. "His conviviality is an emotional release from the problems that forever besiege him. But I also believe he works hard to build bonds with his officers and with us, his new allies. These long gatherings provide an opportunity for him to do so. And do you notice how his conversation is always cheerful, his demeanor affable? How can anyone not be impressed?"

"I liked very much his formal welcome speech to us," says Von Closen. "He complimented officers and men alike. It resounded down the lines in a most positive manner."

"I tell you," concludes Chastellux, rising from his chair, "it will be said of General Washington at the end of this long war that he had done nothing with which he could reproach himself."

With that final comment, the French officers bid each other good night and retire to their quarters.

General Washington's Headquarters
Dobb's Ferry, New York
Mid-July 1781

Less than a week after the French army joined with the Americans, Alexander Hamilton arrived at headquarters. He had been with Washington at Wethersfield, but their relations had again become cold and tense—so much so that Hamilton had stayed at Stillman's Tavern. And as soon as the conference ended, he had ridden directly home to Albany. After speaking with his wife, he had written a formal letter of resignation to the American commander and began making plans to serve as a civilian assistant to Robert Morris in Philadelphia. Hamilton was fed up with not having been given a command of his own and, since John Laurens was returning to the general's staff and could act as a French interpreter, he believed it was a good time to resign.

But Tench Tilghman sent a letter urging him to return to headquarters, because General Washington said he would see to it personally that an appointment as near as possible to Hamilton's wishes would be found. That opportunity came when Washington ordered the formation of a special corps of light infantry under the command of Colonel Alexander Scammel, formerly the Continental Army's adjutant general. This corps would consist of the most active and professional young men and officers available. Their mission would be to march in advance of the main army, the most dangerous point.

Colonel Scammel had been given the freedom by General Washington to choose his own officers and personnel. He wanted only the best for his regiment. For his chief army surgeon, he selected Dr. James Thacher. And to command his battalion of New York troops, he chose Alexander Hamilton, who had been given a strong recommendation by General Washington, himself.

Hamilton was now both energized and delighted. He knew Scammel quite well and thought highly of his leadership abilities. Despite his wife's wish that he return to civilian life, Hamilton told her that his honor obliged him to accept the new post.

◆　　　◆　　　◆

Tench Tilghman strides into General Washington's study at headquarters. "A message from the Congress in Philadelphia, General," says Tilghman with some apprehension. "I'm afraid it will disturb you."

"Go ahead, Colonel."

"Well, sir, it seems that a commission has been formed to handle future peace negotiations—this according to the wishes of French Minister de Vergennes, who has threatened to cut off all aid from his government if Congress does not cooperate fully with his plans to end the war."

"My God," Washington says quietly.

"Worse yet, sir," continues Tilghman. "Congress has instructed the commission to insist only on recognition of American independence. The French are to determine division of the states and ports, sir."

Washington rises from his chair and looks out the window. He lowers his head and shakes it negatively. He says nothing.

After a long silence, Tilghman interrupts. "Sir, Colonel Hamilton is outside. He wishes a word with you."

"Is he not pleased with his new command?" asks the general.

"I believe he is very pleased, sir. I do not know to what this is in regard."

"Very well. Send him in."

Tilghman opens the door and motions for Hamilton, who has been standing in the hall, to enter.

"General, sir," greets Hamilton, offering a smile and a crisp salute.

"Colonel Hamilton," says Washington returning the salute. "It is good to see you."

"Thank you, sir. And you, as well. I have an important request, sir."

"Yes?"

"General, my men need shoes. The quartermaster general refuses to allocate the funds necessary. He says, sir, that it is the state of New York's problem. I submit, sir, that the article of shoes for the army's advance guard is absolutely indispensable. My request, sir, is that you order the funds to be released immediately, sir."

Washington looks directly into the eyes of his former aide-de-camp. Hamilton does not lose eye contact or change expression. There is a slight pause.

"Very well, Colonel," Washington says, at last. "Your men will have their shoes."

12

Green Spring Plantation, Virginia
July 6, 1781

On the very same morning that the French army was staging a grand parade for the Americans up in New York, Lord Cornwallis was down in Virginia laying a trap for the Marquis de Lafayette. At a ferry near Jamestown Island, British forces were preparing to spend two days crossing the James River on their way to Portsmouth. Cornwallis knew that Lafayette's army was nearby at Green Spring Plantation and anticipated that "the boy" might try to attack him during this vulnerable moment. So the British commander positioned a few cavalry and outpost formations such that they appeared to be a rear guard, and next sent some of his troops to the other side of the river—all to deceive the young marquis into believing he had a golden opportunity to attack. Cornwallis then hid the bulk of his army in the woods just north of the ferry crossing—and waited.

At about three o'clock in the afternoon, Lafayette took the bait. He ordered General Anthony Wayne to advance on the British position with 500 men, including two bodies of riflemen, a light infantry regiment, and a small cavalry contingent.

Wayne opened fire when he encountered what he believed to be the enemy's rear guard. Over the next few hours, the Americans skirmished mostly with Banastre Tarleton's cavalry dragoons. Tarleton slowly and cleverly made it look as if he were getting the worst of the skirmish. As he drew back toward the river, Wayne's forces slowly advanced—getting closer and closer to Cornwallis who waited in ambush.

At about five o'clock, as the skirmishing continued, Lafayette galloped down to a position on the James River where he could have a good view of the entire battlefield. From a high vantage point, he was able to see the British army in hiding. Realizing the true situation, Lafayette immediately galloped back to warn General Wayne. But he arrived too late. The redcoats had already burst from the woods and attacked in force.

Surrounded on three sides and outnumbered more than ten to one, Wayne refused to either retreat or surrender. Instead, "Mad" Anthony closed his columns and ordered a full charge into the face of the oncoming British troops. This audacious move stunned the redcoats and temporarily blunted their advance. But due to the overwhelming size of the enemy force, the Americans soon began to wither. Every officer lost his horse and men began to drop from grapeshot and musket fire.

In a stunning display of courage, the Marquis de Lafayette rode right into the middle of the fray and had two horses shot out from under him while rallying the troops. The Americans finally broke through a hole in the British line and, keeping compact and close together, ran until they were out of the range of enemy fire. Wayne rallied his troops near a farmhouse, and Lafayette quickly ordered his main force to advance.

Lord Cornwallis considered a full-scale engagement, but the sun was setting rapidly, and he realized it would be dark before a proper line of battle could be organized. So he ordered a cease-fire and began ferrying his troops across the river.

The British trap had almost worked. Unable for months to "catch the boy," Cornwallis had taken advantage of Lafayette's youth and enthusiasm and almost dealt the American cause a mortal blow. The young Frenchman lost 140 men killed or wounded—more than he had lost in all his other skirmishes combined. British casualties, on the other hand, were lower than normal—only seventy-five.

Over the next two days, Cornwallis crossed the James River and marched his force to Portsmouth, Virginia. The Marquis de Lafayette's army followed—but at a much more respectful distance.

Lord Cornwallis's Headquarters
Portsmouth, Virginia
July 8, 1781

Major Alexander Ross hands Lord Cornwallis a letter. "Just received from a dispatch rider, My Lord," he says. "It is from General Clinton."

Cornwallis opens the envelope and begins to read. "This is dated June 28," he says to Ross. "Therefore, Sir Henry had not yet received my letter of June 30."

"He writes again without giving you a chance to respond," comments the major. "Sir Henry is so impatient and impulsive. Does he not know you are fighting a war down here while he sips Madeira at his mansion in Harlem Heights?"

Cornwallis just shakes his head and begins to read. "'If Your Lordship has not already embarked the reinforcements I called for in my letters of the 8th, 11th, 15th, and 19th, and should not be engaged in some very important move, you will be pleased as soon as possible to order an embarkation of the troops specified below'—and then he lists his specific requests again."

"I do not believe we received a letter dated June 8, sir," notes Ross.

"No, we did not," replies Cornwallis. "It must have been intercepted."

"Is there anything new, sir?" asks Ross.

"Yes. Sir Henry states: 'When Admiral de Grasse hears that we have taken possession of the York River before him, I think it most likely he will come to Rhode Island from the West Indies.' Then Sir Henry asserts the need, once again, for a defensive station."

"Shall we respond now, sir?" asks Major Ross.

"Yes, I think we must."

As Ross pulls out a pen and paper, Cornwallis begins to dictate. "'Sir Henry: Your communication of June 28 is now received. Two days ago, on July 6, we engaged the enemy.' Major, you will write a synopsis of the battle. Be sure to mention our current position and our intention to embark the requested troops."

"Yes, sir," Ross responds.

"Regarding your direction, I must again take the liberty of calling Your Excellency's serious attention to the question of establishing a defensive post in this country. Such a post cannot have the smallest influence on the war in Carolina. It will only give us a few acres of an unhealthy swamp. Most important, however, is that it is forever liable to become prey to a foreign enemy with a temporary superiority at sea.

"It is my opinion that desultory expeditions in the Chesapeake may be undertaken from New York with as much safety, whenever there is reason to suppose that our naval force is likely to be superior for two or three months. As you have more than enough troops at your station, I will be pleased to return to Charleston, if Your Excellency wishes, and leave no post in Virginia."

"That should get Sir Henry's attention," comments Ross. "Anything else, sir?"

"No, that will do. Please prepare the letter for my signature—then send a special rider with an escort to carry it with all possible speed. These communication delays and crisscrossing letters are harming us."

Sir Henry Clinton's Headquarters
Harlem Heights, New York
Mid-July 1781

On July 8, the same day Cornwallis penned this most recent communiqué, his previous letter of June 30 reached Sir Henry Clinton in New York. Now miffed to learn that Cornwallis was heading to Portsmouth rather than Yorktown, and unhappy that the reinforcements he had asked for a month earlier had not yet arrived, Clinton shot off another angry letter.

"I cannot but be concerned," he wrote Cornwallis, "that Your Lordship should so suddenly lose sight of Yorktown, pass over the James River, and retire with your army to the sickly post of Portsmouth. If you do go there, I am convinced that the Marquis de Lafayette will promptly seize Yorktown for his own benefit."

Within a few days of sending this agitated letter, Clinton received a dispatch from Lord Germain in London stating that "Lord Cornwallis's opinion entirely coincided with my own of the great importance of pushing the war on the side of Virginia with all the force that can be spared, until that province is reduced." Sir Henry had been overruled by his superior, thanks to the higher social standing of his subordinate. But with General Phillips dead, it would have to be Cornwallis who seized control of Virginia. Now forced to reverse his strategy from defensive to offensive operations in Virginia, Clinton sought the advice of Rear Admiral Thomas Graves who had recently taken over command of the Royal fleet at Sandy Hook.

Graves expressed the opinion that it was imperative to seize control of a port where his ships could be anchored "with the greatest security" and he would "be capable of acting with most effect against the enemy." His preference, he told Clinton, was Old Point Comfort (a small battery near Hampton Roads) and Yorktown because it "will deprive the rebels of using the two best settled rivers (the James and the York) of the Chesapeake." Clinton agreed and asked Graves to write a letter to Cornwallis stating this recommendation.

Clinton then wrote yet another letter, dated July 11, to Lord Cornwallis. Sir Henry advised his southern commander of the new situation and ordered him to "hold a station in the Chesapeake for ships of the line." He also wrote that it was his opinion that Yorktown "might give security to the works at Old Point Comfort" which Cornwallis was to "examine and refortify." Finally, Clinton told the southern commander that, if he had not already crossed the James River, he was to "continue on the Williamsburg neck" until he received further orders.

Four days later, on July 15, Sir Henry received Cornwallis's letter of July 8 notifying him of the results of the battle at Green Spring, of the fact that he had already crossed the James River, and of the dangers of taking a defensive position in Virginia. Clinton became flushed with anger when he read the sarcastic comments about "desultory expeditions" being conducted in the Chesapeake from New York, and Cornwallis offering to take his army to Charleston.

Totally ignoring the victory at Green Spring, Clinton vented his frustration in another harshly worded letter. "I had flattered myself you would, at least, have waited for a line from me," he fumed to Cornwallis, "before you finally determined upon so serious and mortifying a move as repassing the James River and retiring with your army to Portsmouth."

Then, despite the fact that he had already agreed to conduct an offensive campaign in Virginia, Sir Henry stubbornly argued with his subordinate. "I cannot but suppose," he wrote, "that a defensive station in the Chesapeake, with a corps of at least 4,000 regular troops for its protection and water movements during the summer months, would have the most beneficial effects. Nor do I recollect that I have suggested an idea that there was a probability of the enemy's having a naval superiority in these seas for any length of time—much less for so long as one or two or three months."

Sir Henry also stated matter-of-factly that Cornwallis "must take possession of the Chesapeake and not relinquish it." There could be no reinforcements from New York, Clinton informed him. Therefore, he now was given "full liberty to detain any part, or even the whole of the troops" Clinton had originally asked for.

San Domingo, West Indies
Mid-July 1781

On July 16, 1781, the French fleet pulled into port at the Caribbean island nation of San Domingo (present-day Haiti and the Dominican Republic). It was a magnificent sight: twenty-eight tall ships of the line armed with 1,700 guns and manned by 19,000 sailors. Also present were some 150 small merchant vessels the fleet had been accumulating over the past month as it raided various islands across the Caribbean. The sheer size of the fleet had been too daunting to be challenged by the West Indies British naval fleet commanded by Admiral Samuel Hood, whose ships seemed always in the distance so as to monitor the French position.

In his flagship, the *Ville de Paris*, the largest and most elegant warship ever built, Admiral Paul de Grasse sat at a desk in his polished wood-paneled cabin. Handsome, tall, and energetic, but prone to frequent asthma attacks, de Grasse was reviewing several letters he'd just received from Count de Rochambeau. The French frigate *Concorde* had slipped the British blockade at Newport and arrived in San Domingo a few days earlier with the letter from Rochambeau and the American boat pilots.

De Grasse thought it odd that one of the letters was written in code and the others not. While his aide decoded that document, de Grasse read Rochambeau's letter relating that the French and American troops were to converge on New York "to create a diversion for the benefit of Virginia—and recommending that he first sail to the Chesapeake Bay with four or five thousand more troops and 1.2 million livres." Included with this letter was a copy of the formal agreement that both Washington and Rochambeau had signed at Wethersfield.

Once the other letter was decoded, de Grasse was surprised to read that Rochambeau was urging him to completely ignore the official Wethersfield document and, again, telling him to sail directly to the Chesapeake Bay. Rochambeau would see to it that the combined American and French armies would meet de Grasse there.

Then the French general relayed a frank message about the Americans. "I must not conceal from you that the people here are at the end of their resources," he wrote. "Washington, though he is hiding it, has less than 6,000 men. Lafayette has not a thousand regulars with the militia to defend Virginia."

Finally, Rochambeau told de Grasse that only he and the French fleet could save the cause of freedom in North America. "That is the state of affairs and the very grave crisis in which America finds herself at this particular time," he concluded. "The arrival of the Count de Grasse would save this situation. It is needless to write you the important service you will render if you are able to bring here a body of troops and your ships. The decision is in your hands."

After reading this letter, Admiral de Grasse did not hesitate. He knew full well that Rochambeau would receive no more troops from France, and that the only way to win the war was for the French fleet to sail north. So he immediately began preparations to secure the required loan from local banks—and an infantry brigade from the governor of San Domingo. He issued an order for the entire fleet to prepare to set sail. Then de Grasse sent the *Concorde* back to Rochambeau with a message:

"Though this whole expedition will be concerted only on your order and without warning to the ministries of France and Spain, I believe myself authorized to take some responsibility on my own shoulders for the common cause. I will sail to the Chesapeake and expect to arrive by September 2. But I must depart by October 15 and head back for the West Indies. Please make the most of our fleet's presence on American shores."

New York City
Mid-July 1781

No sooner had Sir Henry Clinton sent out his July 15 letter to Cornwallis than he received intelligence that more than 9,000 combined French and American troops had moved south from Dobb's Ferry and amassed overnight at Kingsbridge Heights on the other side of the Harlem River. Other disturbing news was also reported that rebel boats were being deployed up and down the Hudson, that French engineers were laying out plans for a new battery, and that there were rumors of a large French fleet headed to New York.

While the number of troops in this intelligence was greatly exaggerated, Generals Washington and Rochambeau had, indeed, moved a force of some 5,000 to Kingsbridge to provide a screen for them to perform a reconnaissance of Manhattan. Accompanied by Chief Engineer Louis Duportail, his team, and a guard of 150 Continental soldiers, the two generals rode all around the edges of the island—from the New Jersey shore on the east to Throg's Neck on the west. Their mission was to make a complete study of British positions and determine the feasibility of a siege of New York.

Meanwhile, an alarmed Sir Henry Clinton rode out to the Harlem River battery before dawn to observe the situation firsthand. At sunrise on July 22, the view to the east toward Kingsbridge revealed that the Americans had, indeed, dug into the heights. But the British were surprised when General Washington, on his white horse, rode out into plain view to survey the situation. Sir Henry immediately ordered the artillery to open fire, and the resulting bombardment caused hundreds of rebel soldiers to scurry from their sheltered positions. While the members of Washington's detachment also scrambled to safety, the general himself simply sat on his horse and stared back across the river at the British guns. Five minutes later, after repeated requests from his staff, Washington finally rode off.

Later that same day, around sunset, the two commanders were a full ten miles away at Throg's Neck. As their engineers conducted surveys, Washington and Rochambeau, who had received no sleep the night before, went off and took a nap behind a hedge. But when they awoke several hours later, they found that the tide had come in and completely surrounded them with water. Laughing at themselves, and somewhat embarrassed by the situation, the generals were quickly rescued by a couple of small boats.

After this comprehensive three-day reconnaissance, Washington and Rochambeau estimated the British force to be comprised of approximately 14,000 troops, solidly dug in with numerous fortifications and armed with a large amount of artillery. The added presence of a strong British fleet made a full-scale siege of Manhattan Island nearly unthinkable. Louis Duportail's engineering assessment affirmed that even the combined American and French armies simply did not have the required number of troops, artillery, or ships to achieve success.

After reflecting on the reality of the situation, Washington wrote in his diary on August 1, 1781, that he "could scarce see a ground upon which to continue my preparations against New York. Therefore, I turned my view more seriously than I had before done to an operation to the southward."

That very day, the general began contingency plans for a move to the Chesapeake—including logistics and possible routes. He sent out inquiries about available shipping for transporting troops across the Delaware River and through the Chesapeake Bay. He wrote to Robert Morris stating that the planned allied siege of the British in New York "must be laid aside" and requesting assistance in obtaining and paying for merchant services.

Washington also dashed off a letter to the Marquis de Lafayette, whom he had not heard from in more than a month. He did not know, for instance, that Cornwallis had moved to the Tidewater region of Virginia. At first, the general expressed concern for his friend. "I fear some of your letters have been intercepted because, knowing your usual punctuality, you must have written recently," he wrote. "But be assured, my dear Marquis, that my anxiety to hear from you is increased by my sincere regard for you and by the interest I take in everything which concerns you."

Then the American commander got down to business. "You will not regret your stay in Virginia," he stated. "We have already effected one part of the Wethersfield plan, and I shall shortly have occasion to communicate matters of very great importance to you."

In the meantime, Washington directed Lafayette to "draw together as respectable a body of Continental troops" as he possibly could, augment his cavalry, and open chains of communication to the north and to the Virginia coast. Then the American commander used his very close relationship with the young Frenchman to send a message shrouded in secrecy. Without ever mentioning so specifically, he let Lafayette know that the entire Franco-American army might soon be marching south.

"There is a danger of my letters falling among those clouds of light troops that surround Lord Cornwallis's army," wrote Washington. "You must be prepared if we should transport a part of this army to the southward should the operation against New York be declined. I wish to send a confidential person to you to explain what I have so distantly hinted. However, I hope I have spoken plain enough to be understood by you."

Despite his contingency preparations, General Washington delayed a final decision for a march to Virginia. He still held out hope that Count de Grasse would sail to New York, and he wished to remain flexible. Even if his forces were unable to conduct a full-scale siege of the city, he knew that an overwhelming French fleet could seriously damage the British cause in America if it were able to take over the harbor.

Washington was also emotionally and stubbornly holding on to his original plan. He had lost New York City back in 1776 when his entire force was nearly captured by Lord Cornwallis. And his heart was set on getting it back.

Lord Cornwallis's Headquarters
Portsmouth, Virginia
Early August 1781

Right about the time that George Washington was moving his troops to the heights overlooking Kingsbridge, Lord Cornwallis was awakened from a deep sleep at one o'clock in the morning. "My Lord, we have just received a dispatch pouch," whispers Lieutenant Colonel Chewton. "In it there are three letters from General Clinton and one from Admiral Graves. You asked to be awakened, sir."

"Yes, yes," replies Cornwallis fumbling around for his reading glasses. "Only three letters from Sir Henry? We have not heard from him in nearly two weeks. That would give him time to issue at least a dozen conflicting orders. Give me the one from Graves, first. It is likely coherent."

Chewton hands over the Graves letter and, while Cornwallis reads, he peruses Clinton's July 8 letter. "This first note is very short, My Lord," says Chewton. "Sir Henry just whines about hearing that we have come to what he calls the 'sickly post of Portsmouth.'"

"Graves states that a letter has been received from Lord Germain instructing us to conduct an offensive campaign in Virginia," says Cornwallis with a smile.

"Good news, indeed, sir," responds Ross. "Sir Henry is reversed."

"The admiral also asks that we occupy and fortify either Old Point Comfort or Yorktown so that he may have a secure station for his large ships."

"Good!" shouts Cornwallis. "Good! This means that our navy will soon be here, and this defensive station nonsense is at an end. At last! At last!"

"My Lord," says Chewton, "Sir Henry's second letter, written on July 11, states the same regarding Old Point Comfort or Yorktown. He does not mention Lord Ger-

main, but he does order you to 'continue on the Williamsburg neck' if you have not already crossed the James."

Cornwallis and Ross both laugh at this comment.

"I suppose he had not yet received Your Lordship's letter after Green Spring, sir."

"I suppose not," agrees Cornwallis opening the last letter from Clinton. "But that is probably in this one."

"What does he say?" Chewton asks as the general reads. "What does he say?"

"He does not mention our efforts at Green Spring at all," says Cornwallis, shaking his head in disgust. "Rather, he again assails me for coming to Portsmouth. He also argues about my warning to him of conducting a defensive campaign down here."

"This is petty, Your Lordship," says Chewton.

"Yes, but let us not forget we have won the argument," Cornwallis reminds his aide. "Sir Henry is just grousing, because he has lost. Look here, it says that we must now 'take possession of the Chesapeake and not relinquish it.' And to do that, he has rescinded his call for our 3,000 troops if I determine we need them."

"But, My Lord, they are all on the ships and are to embark at daylight."

"Well, let's get them off," responds Cornwallis. "Then we shall take one of the ships and the engineers and go have a closer look at Old Point Comfort."

"Right away, sir," says Chewton who quickly exits.

◆   ◆   ◆

After several days of inspecting and comparing the works at both Yorktown and Old Point Comfort, Cornwallis sat down and penned letters to both Graves and Clinton. "Upon receiving your letter, I immediately went with our engineers to inspect Old Point Comfort," he wrote politely to Graves. "It is our unanimous opinion that it will not answer the purpose of your wishes. Therefore, I shall immediately seize and fortify the posts at Yorktown and Gloucester Point."

To Clinton, Cornwallis was more biting and abrupt. "Your criticisms of my moves in Virginia are as unexpected as they are undeserved," he stated. "It is the opinion of the captains of the navy, the engineers, and myself that Old Point Comfort might be easily destroyed by a fleet and will not answer the purpose intended. Therefore, in obedience to the spirit of Your Excellency's orders, I shall take measures to seize the York River, as it is the only harbor in which we can hope to be able to give effectual protection to line-of-battle ships."

And in one final dig, Cornwallis informed Clinton that he was going to keep his 3,000 troops in Virginia. "I was prepared to send them until I received your most recent letter," he wrote. "But superiority in the field, foraging for supplies, and carrying on our work without interruption dictates that the troops you originally requested will all stay with me."

13

Yorktown, Virginia
August 2, 1781

It is midsummer in the Tidewater region of Virginia. The heat is oppressive, the air heavy and unbearably humid. With no wind, it is like standing in a brick oven.

Four British small ships sail up the York River and anchor between Yorktown and Gloucester Point. Lord Cornwallis and his staff are rowed to the Yorktown shore. In addition to Lieutenant Colonel Chewton and Major Ross, present are Major John Despart (deputy adjutant general), and Lieutenant Alexander Sutherland (chief engineer).

Stepping off the boat, the officers walk up a rather steep hill and along the northern perimeter of the village. Upon reaching the east side, they pause for a rest. The men complain about the stifling heat and mop sweat from their foreheads with white handkerchiefs. Their heavy, woolen uniforms have made the short hike almost unbearable.

"I believe this broad plain will be the best place for a permanent encampment," says Cornwallis. "Do you agree, Lieutenant?"

"Yes, my lord," replies Sutherland. "It will also provide a good staging area for us to erect fortifications."

"Before we begin erecting defenses here, though, I believe it will be necessary to work on those at Gloucester Point across the river," remarks Cornwallis.

"Yes, sir," affirms Major Despart. "Both stations must be held to make this base secure."

"But Gloucester Point is key to maintaining control of the river," notes Chewton. "If we do not fortify it immediately, the enemy could establish a strong point from which to threaten our operations."

"It will also serve us well as a base for foraging through the rich countryside," remarks Despart.

"Yes," agrees Chewton, "along with providing a secondary means of evacuation, if necessary."

"Lieutenant Sutherland, you will immediately begin designing a plan of defense," orders Cornwallis. "Your first priority will be Gloucester Point."

"Yes, My Lord," replies Sutherland.

"We should be secure here as long as the Royal Navy controls the seas," says Cornwallis. "Our ships will be able to protect, supply, and reinforce us. It ought to provide a good base for offensive operations. But the Chesapeake is key."

"Agreed, sir," responds Chewton.

"Major Ross, send out the confirmation directives to have all our forces converge on this place."

"Yes, My Lord."

"Now let us find a suitable place to locate our headquarters," says Cornwallis, pulling his collar away from his neck. "A place with a breeze, if at all possible."

The officers then walk down into the small village.

◆   ◆   ◆

Yorktown and Gloucester Point had been secured the day before when the horsemen of Colonel John Simcoe's Queen's Rangers and the British 43rd infantry regiment arrived in force. Many of the town's inhabitants quickly fled—along with some 300 members of the Virginia Militia who never even fired a shot. A few civilians remained, however, including Yorktown's leading citizen, Secretary Thomas Nelson, a retired Colonial official and uncle of Virginia's newly elected governor. The remaining residents, although loyal to the American cause, were both suspicious and cordial toward the British occupying force.

Over the next three weeks, the normally quiet area around Yorktown and Gloucester Point came alive. Nearly all Southern forces reporting to Lord Cornwallis began arriving by both land and sea—more than 9,000 men in total. These were some of the best military troops in the world, including: the 17th, 23rd, 33rd, 43rd, 71st, 76th, and 80th infantry regiments; the 17th, 23rd, and 82nd light companies; Tarleton's cavalry legion; Simcoe's Queen's Rangers; four German mercenary contingents, including the Fusilier, Musketeer, Jagers, and Anspach regiments; and hundreds of artillerymen and naval gunners.

More than 3,000 slaves also flooded into the area. They came from all over the Virginia countryside—fleeing their masters and hoping for a fair shake from the British. Cornwallis promised freedom to all those who cooperated with him. Then he put them to work constructing defenses and fortifications. Because they were used to performing manual labor in the summertime, the slaves ended up doing the vast majority of work. As British soldiers withered in the hot sun, slaves built a long palisade to protect Gloucester Point, then a line of earthworks along the bluff, and finally a triangular fort to surround the small battery. And they went about their work singing happily—believing all along that they would be delivered from the bonds of slavery.

Marquis de Lafayette's Encampment
Portsmouth, Virginia
Early August 1781

On the same day Lord Cornwallis arrived at Yorktown, a thirty-three-year-old black man of medium height walks up to the Marquis de Lafayette's headquarters tent. When Lafayette sees the man, he smiles and reaches out his hand.

"General Lafayette, sir," says the black man, with a salute. Then he shakes the marquis' hand.

"Good to see you, James," says Lafayette. "What news have you?"

"Sir, yesterday morning 750 infantry and cavalry sailed up the York and landed at Gloucester Point. Another 600 proceeded overland along with 150 horses. His Lordship arrived today."

"Hmmm, this is a significant movement," Lafayette remarks.

"I think so, sir. The British officers say Portsmouth is a sickly place. They have determined that their expeditions in Central Virginia have been a success and wish now to take command of the coast."

"These English are mad!" snaps Lafayette. "They march through a country and think they have conquered it!"

"I believe, sir, that Cornwallis has been ordered to make Yorktown a major station."

"Have you seen letters to that effect?" asks Lafayette.

"No, sir. I've overheard this in conversation only. His Lordship is so shy of his papers that I am not able to get at them."

"Well done, James. Thank you."

"General, sir, is there any information you wish me to carry to Lord Cornwallis?"

"Yes," responds Lafayette. "Why don't you tell him that we have been recently joined by another two hundred militia? Say also that we are a bit shy since Green Spring. Say that 'the boy' has new respect for His Lordship."

"Yes, sir," James responds with a grin. "That will reach his ego."

"Good. Let him remain confident and keep him believing he has the upper hand," says Lafayette.

"Yes, General. I will be off now—to Yorktown."

"Travel safe and well, my friend," says Lafayette, again offering a handshake.

"I shall do so," replies James, accepting the general's hand. "But since both the Americans and British believe I am on their side, the only people I need fear are unknown plantation masters."

"Yes, beware of them. And if you have problems, send for me immediately," replies Lafayette. "Au revoir, James."

"Good-bye, sir," responds the black man, who leaves the encampment and starts on his journey to Yorktown.

◆   ◆   ◆

James was a Virginia plantation slave. In mid-July 1781, he had asked his master for approval to serve in the American army under Lafayette. After receiving permission, he enlisted and, for a time, performed menial duties for the French general. But Lafayette soon realized that James was very intelligent and had an exceptional memory. So he proposed that the black man cross over to the British camp and act as a spy, which James agreed to do.

His first duties for the enemy were at Portsmouth where he served as a guide on the road. But within a few weeks, he was given the job of waiter for Lord Cornwallis and his staff. With this new position, James could listen as the officers discussed plans and details of troop movements. And soon, he was reporting these details directly to the Marquis de Lafayette.

Interestingly enough, Lord Cornwallis also noted the black man's intelligence and asked him to cross over to the American encampment on occasion and be a spy for the British. So James became a double agent—solidly entrenched in the British commander's camp, but working for Lafayette and instantly reporting on Lord Cornwallis's every move.

Armed with the new information provided by James, Lafayette quickly moved his army toward Yorktown and sent out a large contingent of scouts to keep tabs on British activities. At first, when it was reported back to him that Cornwallis was fortifying Gloucester Point, Lafayette thought that the British commander was preparing a base of operations for a drive to the north. But gradually, as troops began to arrive at Yorktown, and as James reported more detailed information, he realized the true British strategy.

In a letter written in early August, Lafayette reported all substantive intelligence to General Washington in New York. "There is no doubt," he wrote, "but that the principal post will be at Yorktown. Cornwallis does not push his works with rapidity, and no blunder can be hoped for from him."

And the young marquis quickly summed up to Washington the opportunity that seemed to be presenting itself. "Yorktown is surrounded by the river and a morass," he noted, "and Gloucester Point is a neck of land projected into the river. Both are vulnerable to amphibious attack. The enemy could be surrounded on the landside, while naval supremacy would make escape by water impossible. Should a French fleet now come to the Chesapeake, the British would, I think, be ours."

San Domingo, West Indies
Early August 1781

On August 5, 1781, twenty-eight great ships of the line set sail out of the harbor. Most of the ships were 170 feet long, forty-seven feet wide, and had masts that towered nearly 200 feet into the air. Each ship carried between sixty and 110 guns that hurled a half ton of metal in a single broadside. Following the big ships were seven frigates, two cutters, and fifteen chartered merchant ships. The head of the line was the 110-gun, triple-decker, *Ville de Paris*. Tropical plants and vines running along the railings and between the guns decorated Admiral de Grasse's flagship. A new coat of varnish caused it to glisten brilliantly in the morning sun.

De Grasse had worked hard over the past several weeks and had come through when the chips were down. He had raised more than 1.2 million livres from the government in San Domingo and the Spanish governor of Havana. As security for the loans, he used his own plantation on San Domingo and his chateau in France—both of which far exceeded the amount of the loans. The French admiral also procured nearly the entire French garrison at San Domingo. Led by the Marquis Claude Henry de Saint-Simon, this 3,000-man force included the infantry regiments of Agenais, Gatinois, and Touraine, 100 dragoons, and 350 artillerymen with a train of siege cannon. Upon leaving the harbor, the French flotilla strung out nearly two miles and took nearly half a day to disappear over the northwest horizon.

After learning that the French fleet had left San Domingo, British Admiral Samuel Hood set sail with fourteen ships of the line in an effort to prevent the French from joining with the allies. De Grasse, however, predicted this maneuver. Rather than taking the usual direct route east of the Bahamas, he sailed along the northern coast of Cuba and next headed into the dangerous Bahamas Channel, noted for its reefs and violet storms. No French fleet had ever before dared take this passage, but de Grasse risked it in an effort to hide from the British.

Admiral Hood never did catch sight of the French sails. He took the normal route and sailed so fast that he was nearing the coast of South Carolina by the time de Grasse emerged from the Bahamas. The French admiral then pressed on up the eastern shore of Florida and Georgia capturing every hostile ship in sight.

Fearing the worst, Hood sent word to General Clinton and Admiral Graves in New York. "I shall keep as good a lookout as possible," he wrote. "However, it is entirely likely that the French ships ahead of me are making toward New York. Please take note that de Grasse has taken with him every fighting ship in the West Indies."

Sir Henry Clinton's Headquarters
Harlem Heights, New York
Early August 1781

Upon receiving Hood's dispatch, Admiral Graves turned to Sir Henry Clinton and remarked that "such boldness by the Count de Grasse is beyond imagination. If a British admiral had adopted such a measure, he would have been hung."

Right about this time, Clinton received two conflicting bits of information about enemy movements. First, a letter from Count de Rochambeau to French Minister Luzerne had been intercepted on its way to Philadelphia. It had been dated May 27, 1781, and, because it was in cipher, had to be sent all the way to London for decoding. The translation revealed that New York was to be the main allied objective this summer. The second bit of intelligence, only a day old, was from one of Clinton's field spies who stated that General Washington appeared to be taking preliminary steps in "forming a plan to relieve Virginia by a direct move to the Chesapeake—with all the French land and naval forces."

Sir Henry emotionally discarded the most recent message. "I cannot credit these reports!" he thundered to his aides. "They must be the result of a heated imagination! I saw Washington myself not ten days ago making a reconnaissance of Manhattan! And according to Hood, de Grasse is headed this way! I am convinced! New York must be their main objective!"

Now extremely frightened for the safety of his own garrison, Clinton quickly sent another letter to Lord Cornwallis. "I do not think you will need a force of 7,000 men or more to defend Yorktown and Gloucester Point," he wrote. "I have spoken with General Benedict Arnold, and he has judged that 2,000 troops would be ample. You are therefore directed to retain that number of men and send the rest to me at once."

General Washington's Headquarters
Dobb's Ferry, New York
August 14, 1781

It's mid-afternoon. A soothing breeze moves in from the Hudson River and eases the recent summer heat wave. Quartermaster General Timothy Pickering and Superintendent of Finances Robert Morris have been conferring about the upcoming summer campaign. They have come to certain conclusions about the necessary number of supplies and finances that will be needed. As they enter headquarters to make their report, they overhear General Washington in conversation with his aides, Tench Tilghman and David Humphreys.

"General, we have just received a dispatch brought to Newport by the French frigate Concorde," reports Tilghman. "It contains a letter from Admiral de Grasse."

"Yes, yes," says Washington eagerly. "What does it say?"

"Sir, the French fleet is under way," responds Tilghman. "It is sailing from San Domingo directly to the Chesapeake Bay and will arrive no later than September third. Admiral de Grasse also states that he will..."

"Blast it all to hell!" screams General Washington. "The Chesapeake?! The Chesapeake?! They are sailing to Virginia?! Not New York?!"

Washington's face flushes red with rage; his eyes water. Tilghman and Humphreys both step back as the commander in chief paces back and forth in an almost blind fury. "How many times must our hopes be dashed?" *he shouts.* "How many times will the French disappoint us? We will never take back New York, now! Never! Our cause is lost! Our country ruined!"

As he paces back and forth, Washington runs his hands through his hair. He takes many deep breaths, as if he were hyperventilating, then places his left hand to his cheek when pain shoots from an aching tooth. He is so emotionally distraught that he does not even notice Pickering and Morris standing at the entrance. Tench Tilghman motions for them to leave, which they quickly do. After a few minutes, the general regains his composure and becomes quiet.

"There is more here, sir," *says Tilghman.* "Shall I continue?"

"Admiral de Grasse states that, in order to honor commitments to the Spaniards, he will only be able to stay until October 15, at which time it will be necessary for him to sail back to the Caribbean. However, he states that he is duly authorized to lend assistance to you and General Rochambeau as you desire, sir. He is bringing with him the following, sir: twenty-nine to thirty-five warships, three regiments of regular troops numbering a total of 3,000 men, 100 dragoons, 100 artillerists, ten field pieces, and various siege cannon and mortars. Finally, sir, the admiral recommends that in order *to make the most effective use of the French fleet, a formidable land force should be on the Chesapeake by the time he arrives."*

There is a long pause. Tilghman and Humphreys wait for a reply. But Washington does not speak. He walks over to a window and stares out toward the woods, his right hand tightly gripping his mouth and chin.

"Sir, more communications have just been received," interrupts David Humphreys.

Washington does not respond. He keeps staring outside as if in a trance.

"Our scouts report that Sir Henry Clinton yesterday received reinforcements of between 2,500 and 3,000 Hessian reinforcements. This brings the British garrison in New York to well over 17,000, sir."

Again, Washington says nothing. After another pause, Humphreys reports that he has also received a dispatch from Lafayette in Virginia. "General, sir, the marquis reports that Lord Cornwallis has proceeded up the York River, has landed at Gloucester Point and Yorktown, and is consolidating his entire force at that station."

Humphreys begins reading from the dispatch. "'Yorktown is surrounded by the river and a morass,' states Lafayette, 'and Gloucester Point is a neck of land projected into the river. Both are vulnerable to amphibious attack. The enemy could be surrounded on the landside, while naval supremacy would make escape by water impossible. Should a French fleet now come to the Chesapeake, the British would, I think, be ours.'"

Humphreys and Tilghman glance at their general—still at the window, still staring out toward the woods. They notice Washington's jaw clench. His eyes squint as if focusing on something of great importance outside. Otherwise, he does not move an inch.

Another long pause ensues. Finally, the general speaks. "Gentlemen," he says, "I wish to be alone."

Tilghman and Humphreys quickly step outside, but Washington still does not move. He continues to stand, his right hand holding his chin or occasionally running through his hair.

For the longest time, Washington stares out at the woods—for five, ten, fifteen minutes. Every now and then he shifts his weight from one leg to the other. Sometimes his hands go behind his back, he clears his throat and, as he thinks, his head moves slightly. His bluish gray eyes rarely blink. He squints, fixes his stare, sometimes brings down his eyelids for a brief rest—but he does not blink.

At last, Washington stands erect, with equal weight given to both legs. He clenches his hands behind his back and finally takes his view away from the woods. He stares at the floor for a few moments, then shakes his head affirmatively, as if he has come to a conclusion.

Washington walks to the door and calls for his aides to return.

"Gentlemen," he says, "matters have now come to a head. From the shortness of Count de Grasse's promised stay on this coast, from the apparent disinclination of French officers to force operations northward, and due to the fact that our states have not come through with their enlistment quotas, we must give up all idea of attacking New York.

"Our affairs up to this point have often been in the most ruinous train imaginable. But now, a new course is as clear to my view as a ray of light. The American and French armies must march immediately south to Virginia. We must cooperate with the naval force from the West Indies for a major operation against the British force at Yorktown. If we arrive in time, and if de Grasse can gain control of the sea approaches, Lord Cornwallis will be trapped and overwhelmed."

"That could end the war!" says an electrified Tench Tilghman.

"Indeed, it could," agrees Washington. "But such an operation will have great risks. We must march 450 miles in a very short period of time. We must arrange for transports, for supplies, money for the troops. Everything must be in perfect readiness to commence our operations at the very moment de Grasse arrives in the Chesapeake."

"It can be done, sir!" states David Humphreys, matter-of-factly.

"Yes, General," agrees Tilghman. "Once our troops hear the news, everyone will respond well."

"But we must conduct our plans and the first part of our movements with the strictest secrecy," says Washington. "If Clinton or Cornwallis gets wise, they can easily thwart us."

"Where shall we begin, sir?" asks Tilghman.

"Robert Morris is in camp, is he not?"

"He is, sir," responds Humphreys. "Actually, he and General Pickering entered headquarters at the very moment we were discussing the admiral's letter."

"Uh, so they saw my unseemly outburst?" asks Washington looking down.

"They did, sir."

"Well, these men are critical to our operation. Please send for them at once."

"Yes, sir," says Humphreys, who quickly turns and exits. He finds Morris and Pickering right outside. When they reenter headquarters, General Washington greets them with a smile and in a much more composed manner.

"Gentlemen, I must apologize for my conduct when you were here earlier," he says. "I had been hoping for so many months to carry out our plans with the French—only to have them thwarted. I wish to God the French would not raise our expectations."

"It is all right, General," replies Morris. "We understand the difficulties you have faced."

"Yes, sir," agrees Pickering. "We understand."

"Thank you," acknowledges Washington. "But now we must determine upon a decisive plan of action. Our new course will be fraught with danger. But if successful, we will make a decisive stroke for the freedom of our nation."

"How can we help, sir?" asks Pickering.

"Yes, General," says Morris. "We are prepared to do anything you request of us."

"Very well," smiles Washington. "Please sit down."

◆   ◆   ◆

Over the next several hours, George Washington spoke to Morris and Pickering about the requirements of a major march to the south. He asked them to make arrangements to transport troops down the Chesapeake Bay. As many wagons, light vessels, small boats, and arms as possible had to be procured. Provisions would be needed—at least 300 barrels of flour and equivalent quantities of salt meat and rum. Not only did the materials have to be obtained from local merchants, but funds were needed to pay for everything. Morris and Pickering immediately accepted the challenge and went to work.

Washington next met with General Rochambeau who was, of course, delighted with the new plan. It was what he wanted all along. Together, they resolved to persuade Admiral Louis Jacques-Melchior (Saint-Laurent), Count de Barras to load his eight ships with all the French siege guns and provisions possible and sail from Newport to the Chesapeake. Rochambeau would handle this task—making sure that de Barras sailed a wide path to avoid British patrol ships and give de Grasse plenty of time to arrive ahead of him. Once in the Chesapeake, de Barras would join with de Grasse thereby making the French fleet that much more formidable.

A special courier was immediately dispatched to Virginia with a letter to the Marquis de Lafayette. The young Frenchman was informed of the march south and instructed to "be in perfect readiness and to take such a position as will best enable you to prevent the sudden retreat of Lord Cornwallis's forces into North Carolina." Keeping the British at Yorktown, Washington believed, was essential if the advantage provided by the French fleet was to be effective. "I presume Lord Cornwallis will attempt to retreat the instant he perceives we are on the move," he wrote to Lafayette.

Louis Duportail, the army's chief engineer and an expert in siege warfare, was asked by Washington to board a French frigate, locate Admiral de Grasse's fleet, and personally give him a letter. "We have determined to remove the whole of the French army and as large a detachment of the American as can be spared to meet Your Excellency in the Chesapeake," the General wrote to de Grasse.

Then he laid out for the French admiral three possible scenarios of action once all the allied forces had converged. If the enemy "should be found with the greater part of their force in Virginia," said Washington, "we should, without loss of time, attack and lay siege to them with our united force." If only a detachment was there, Washington recommended that the enemy be immediately reduced and that the combined forces move south and lay siege to Charleston, South Carolina. If the British force were entirely withdrawn, then Washington wished to "make a solid establishment at Portsmouth in order to render a fleet in the Chesapeake Bay entirely secure."

Finally, de Grasse was asked to "send up to Elk River all your frigates, transports, and vessels for the conveyance of the French and American troops down the bay. We shall endeavor to have as many as can be found in Baltimore and other ports, but we have reason to believe there will be very few."

As Washington continued to make plans and work on details, he was constantly haunted by the uncertainties that lay before him.

Would Clinton detect the American and French troop movements?

Would Cornwallis retreat to a more secure position?

Would the French finally do what they said they were going to do?

Would de Grasse be able to defeat an English fleet if they were to meet at sea?

Would the combined force be able to complete the entire 450-mile march on schedule?

Would his unpaid troops mutiny on the road?

Would everyone—de Grasse, de Barras, Rochambeau, and himself—convene on schedule?

George Washington knew that the risk he was taking was enormous.

If Clinton were to attack General Heath at West Point, the British could effectively seize all of New York. Boston would then surely fall. If the march south did not go well, American and French forces could end up scattered all over Maryland and Virginia. If Cornwallis were to deploy his troops in a more secure manner, he could control all of Virginia. In such a scenario, the British would be master of both the northern and southern states at the very moment the Vergennes peace conference was convening. It was a frightening thought.

But Washington was determined to move forward. After six years of being on the defensive—of running for his life, of playing cat and mouse—he was at last taking a bold offensive stroke. He was putting all his eggs in one basket and taking the risk of his life. It was going to be all or nothing.

"Not a moment's time is to be lost," Washington told his aides as he threw himself into preparations for the march. "We must move on the wing of speed!"

PART III
THE MARCH

14

General Washington's Headquarters
Dobb's Ferry, New York
August 17, 1781

Sunlight shimmers through the glass panes of the small house that is now headquarters for General Washington and his staff. The windows are open, and the morning breeze blows in. There is the feeling of dryness in the nose and throat that indicates it will be another hot summer afternoon.

Sitting in the main room taking coffee and early morning tea are Tench Tilghman, David Humphreys, and one Jonathan Trumbull Jr., newest member of Washington's "family." Trumbull is a thirty-one-year-old valedictorian graduate of Harvard and the son of Connecticut's current governor. All three men rise quickly when the general bounds into the room with unusual enthusiasm. "Good morning, sir," they say almost in unison.

"A good morning it is," he responds with a smile. "Please, as you were."

"Coffee, sir?" asks Trumbull, holding up the hot pot.

"Thank you very much, Colonel."

As Trumbull fills the general's cup, Tilghman and Humphreys cast an odd look at each other. Washington lays a stack of papers on the table and rubs his hands together. "Well, gentlemen," he says, "I have been up nearly all this night laying out plans for the upcoming march. Are you ready to hear them?"

All three men immediately pull out papers and pens. "We are, sir." "Indeed, sir." "Yes, sir."

"I have designated approximately 2,400 of our own troops for the march," begins Washington. "And nearly every able-bodied French soldier, more than 5,000 in total, will be put in motion. We will begin by marching in three columns toward New York. We will cross the Hudson at Kings Ferry and move to Stony Point. Then we will march behind the Palisades of New Jersey through Newark and New Brunswick to Trenton where we will travel by water down the Delaware to Christiana. From there, the combined armies will march through Philadelphia on to Head of Elk and, if necessary, to Annapolis where they will board vessels for transport down the Chesapeake to Williamsburg."

"An ambitious plan, sir," says Tilghman who, like his two colleagues is furiously taking notes. *"We have much work to do, many preparations."*

"Indeed, we do," replies Washington. *"A letter must be sent to General Lincoln explaining that he is to march through New Jersey in two columns. The left column, to be composed of Scammel and Hamilton's light troops, will, on the twenty-fifth, march within three miles of Paramus; on the twenty-sixth, two miles below Acquakenach Bridge; on the twenty-seventh to Springfield. The right column, to consist of the artillery, will march three miles beyond Suffrans on the twenty-fifth; the twenty-sixth, five miles beyond Pompton on the road to the two bridges at the fork of Posaic; on the twenty-seventh behind the mountains to Chatham."*

"I will take care of that letter," states David Humphreys.

"The route of the French army will be accomplished as follows," continues Washington: *"August 19 to North Castle, fourteen miles; August 20 to Kings Ferry, eighteen miles; the 22nd, cross the North River; the 23rd to Suffrans, sixteen miles; the 24th to Pompton Meeting House, fourteen miles; the 25th to Whippany, fifteen miles; the 26th to Bullions Tavern, fifteen miles; the 27th to Somerset Court House, fourteen miles; the 28th to Princeton, fourteen miles; and finally, the 29th to Trenton, twelve miles."*

"I will draft a letter to General Rochambeau to that effect, sir," says Jonathan Trumbull.

"Here also is an additional letter I have prepared for Lincoln," says Washington handing several pages to Tench Tilghman. *"It is quite long, I'm afraid—sixteen paragraphs. He will be in complete charge of all troops sailing down the Chesapeake, so I have made extensive suggestions for him. A few things I have thought of since last night should be added."*

"I'm ready, sir," responds Tilghman, pen in hand.

"Horses and oxen must be collected at strategic points, magazines with flour, beef, and rum must be set up. Wagons for tents must carry tents only. If officers, as is their want, pile their baggage on them, it must be thrown off. Repair roads and bridges well in advance and find boats and small ships to transport the troops down the Chesapeake. The tow ropes ought to be strong and of sufficient length. Otherwise we shall be much plagued with them in the Bay and probably lose many. Oh, that reminds me," continues Washington. *"In order to conceal our actions, we must not amass boats on the Delaware. They will be brought up at the last minute. Horses and oxen must be swum across."*

"Anything else, sir?" asks Tilghman.

"Not for Lincoln," replies Washington. *"But General Knox must be advised to make every necessary arrangement for the transportation of his ordnance and stores. No*

need for sending him much detail. He will know what to do. He has been through it before."

"Yes, sir, his feat at Ticonderoga certainly demonstrates his ability," agrees Humphreys. "I will handle that dispatch."

"And we must send circulars to the governors of Rhode Island, Connecticut, Delaware, Maryland, Pennsylvania, and Virginia requesting salted meat, general provisions, rum, flour—and vessels to transport at all."

"I will take care of it, General," declares Trumbull.

"We must also inform them that, as we have no money to buy supplies, wagons and forage will be commandeered on the march. I do not want the governors complaining to me after the fact."

"Yes, General. I will see it is included."

"Give to them, also, the broadest statement of our plan—and next say this: Should the time of the fleet's arrival prove favorable, and should the enemy under Cornwallis hold their present position in Virginia, we will have the fairest opportunity to reduce the whole British force in the South. Colonel Trumbull, I hesitate to make any mention of our destination to the governors, but it is necessary. You must hold those circulars until the last possible moment so as to preserve secrecy. I will let you know the appropriate time."

"Yes, sir."

"To Robert Morris," says Washington, who pauses until he sees Colonel Humphreys grab another sheet of paper, look up, and nod. "We must secure the vessels and provisions necessary and have them all at Head of Elk at the appointed time. Take all that may be in Baltimore and the upper parts of the bay. I shall direct the quartermaster to take up all the small craft in Delaware for the purpose of transporting the troops from Trenton to Christiana. Please note, my dear friend, that there is great discontent in the line at not having been paid for such a long time. Please pull together some hard cash for them by the time of our arrival in Philadelphia. I have no doubt that it will invest our troops with the proper temperament for the next two months."

"To the Marquis de Lafayette," Washington abruptly states.

"Yes, sir," acknowledges Tilghman, ready to write.

"Please convey as soon as possible information on horses and wagons that will be available for use in Virginia. As soon as Admiral de Grasse arrives in the Chesapeake, you are to assist him in conveying as many vessels and landing craft as can be spared up the bay to provide for transportation of the troops. Future communiqués will provide the necessary details."

"Finally, a letter to General Heath," declares Washington.

"I have that one," replies Trumbull.

"After informing him of the march south, say the following: I am assigning you 2,000 troops for the protection of West Point and the Hudson Valley. You are to observe Sir Henry Clinton and keep the enemy in check until it is too late for reinforcements to be sent southward."

Trumbull looks up and swallows hard at this statement. He knows full well that Clinton has at least 14,000 men at his disposal. How could only 2,000 hold such a force in check, he wonders.

Washington continues: "The enemy's uncertainty as to the movement of our army ought to be increased by every means in your power—and the deception kept up as long as possible. Have you got all that, Colonel Trumbull?"

"Yes, sir."

"Very well. Now, gentlemen, as to the deception of the enemy. It is my intention to misguide and bewilder Sir Henry Clinton in regard to the real object of our march. We will finesse him into thinking we are going to attack New York. I have already worked it out. The path of our march will seem to Sir Henry as though we are positioning the army for an attack on Staten Island. I have calculated that two-thirds of our route to the Delaware is along the same path we would travel if we were to meet the French fleet at Sandy Hook."

Trumbull looks at Washington with amazement. How did he work that out, he marvels.

"We must also send our engineers out to work on the roads and repair the bridges leading to Staten Island," continues Washington, "and then begin preparations for what will look like a major encampment in New Jersey. This activity should include sending out foraging parties and constructing ovens capable of baking thousands of loaves of bread. We must also accumulate as many boats and other landing craft suitable to crossing the isthmus from New Jersey to Staten Island."

"I will prepare orders to that effect, General Washington," states Tilghman.

"Good," replies Washington. "But make certain that those dispatches do not give away our true destination. They must be a series of fictitious communications where our men follow orders and think that we are really going to attack New York."

"But who is to know the truth, sir?"

"Well, certainly, General Lincoln must know. Rochambeau is already informed, and I have spoken to him about the need for secrecy. We must also inform Colonels Scammel and Hamilton as the leaders of the light infantry. But only them. Their troops need not know until the last moment possible. I should think that will be enough for now."

"Sir, what of General Knox?" asks David Humphreys.

Washington pauses a moment. "I think not," he says. "Knox will have his artillery ready, and he will go wherever we send him. He is also capable of turning in an instant."

"But sir," asks Tilghman, "do we not risk the feelings of our own men? Will they not think we do not trust them?"

"That is a valid point, Colonel, and I have thought it through. I believe the troops trust us. They are also intelligent enough to know that if we are to make such a bold move, it must be done in the strictest secrecy. Besides, the fact is that if we do not deceive our own men, we will never deceive the enemy. Once our troops begin moving down the Delaware, they will know our true destination. Then they will reflect on what happened. It is at this point, I believe, that they will clearly understand and accept our actions."

"Very well, sir," replies Tilghman. "We will immediately prepare the appropriate orders, circulars, and dispatches."

"Good," says Washington rising from his chair. "You will please excuse me, gentlemen. I have work to do."

After Washington departs, Tilghman, Humphreys, and Trumbull continue writing their assigned letters.

"I do not understand," says Trumbull.

"What's that?" asks Humphreys.

"How could one man plan so many different things? And the details! How could he think of so much? I have trouble just keeping it straight on paper—and he has it all in his head!"

"Don't feel bad, Jon," says David Humphreys. "There are three of us here, and we can barely keep up with him."

"I do feel uneasy about one thing," replies Trumbull, "but I hesitate to mention it."

"Go ahead," Tilghman encourages.

"Well," says Trumbull sheepishly, "the general did not take one sip of his coffee."

"Oh, he doesn't drink coffee," replies Humphreys with a smile. "Sometimes tea, but never coffee."

Trumbull pauses and just stares. "Then why did he let me pour it for him?"

"He was just trying to be nice to you, Jon," says Tilghman. "He did not want to embarrass you on your first day."

"But why did he not ask for tea, instead?"

"He was not in the mood to drink anything. He was in the mood to work."

"I feel bad," Trumbull says.

"Don't," replies Tilghman. "Once you've been around the general for awhile, you'll know. He is unusually thoughtful—always kind, affable, and courteous. He also works

harder than anybody I've ever met. It's amazing. Did you know that he has been in the field with this army for the entire duration of the war?"

"Oh?" replies Trumbull. "I have heard that. Is it really true?"

"Indeed it is," says Humphreys. "He has not been to his home at Mount Vernon during that entire time. No holidays, no vacations, not even a week off."

"And I have seen men come to him and beg to go home to see their loved ones," says Tilghman.

"And what does he say to them?" asks Trumbull. "Does he cite the fact that he himself has not been home in six years?"

"On the contrary, he almost always obliges them. He understands a man's need to be with his family. I tell you, upon my word, I have never heard him complain about his own sacrifices, never once. Not many people know what we have just told you."

There is a long pause among the three men. Finally, Trumbull remarks that Mount Vernon is on the way to Yorktown. "I wonder if he can be persuaded to ride by and visit for a day or two?"

Tilghman and Humphreys look at each other for a moment and nod in agreement. "I will mention it to him," says Tilghman.

◆   ◆   ◆

On August 18, 1781, Washington issued orders for the march. The next day, more than 7,000 combined American and French troops commenced a southward movement. Leading the way were Scammel and Hamilton's light infantry corps—accompanied by Quartermaster General Timothy Pickering who was ordered to prepare for the speedy transportation of all allied troops across the Hudson River at Kings Ferry. General Lincoln and the rest of the American army followed on a path that would take them near Sing Sing and Haverstraw on their way to the river's crossing point. The French troops, slowed by a shortage of healthy horses, took a different route—through Newcastle and Pinesbridge—while their light field artillery, escorted by de Lauzun's cavalry, moved on a parallel path slightly to the east.

As the march began, General Washington's own movements were intentionally slow, methodical, and designed to give the impression that he, personally, wasn't going anywhere. He continued to handle routine discipline—even going so far as to schedule a general court martial for desertion. He also took General Rochambeau on a leisurely horseback tour of West Point. Behind these public scenes, however, Washington was taking a variety of steps to deceive the British as to his true intentions. He sent a battalion of pioneers, for example, to clear key roads leading into New York City. And he ordered Colonel Moses Hazen's Canadian regiment, along with two New Jersey light regiments, to march down the Jersey shore and take posts between Springfield and Chatham, where the French baking ovens were to be constructed. Washington knew that this movement, which he directed to take place in full view of Sir Henry Clinton's lookouts, would be perceived as a natural preliminary maneuver for a threatened attack on Staten Island.

The general's movements were perplexing to his own troops. Only a handful knew the army's true destination, but many suspected they might not be going to New York City. In the first few days of the march, countless soldiers recorded their thoughts in personal journals. "I cannot make up my mind as to the object of our march," wrote Count Deux-Ponts. "We are all in perfect ignorance whether we are going against New York or whether we are going to Virginia to attack Lord Cornwallis."

Dr. Thacher noted that many of the soldiers were disgruntled "not only because they were marching south, but because they did not know where they were going." Then he made some key observations and speculations that reflected the buzz ruminating through the ranks. "Ostensibly, an investment of New York is in contemplation," he wrote. "But it is well fortified both by land and water—and garrisoned by the best troops of Great Britain. A field for an extensive encampment has been marked out on the Jersey side, and a number of ovens have been erected and fuel provided for the purpose of baking bread for the army. We are led to conclude that part of our force is to occupy this encampment for the purpose of besieging the British garrison on Staten Island. But General Washington possesses a capacious mind, full of resources, and he resolves and matures his great plans and designs under an impenetrable veil of secrecy."

As to the destination of his artillery regiment, Major General Henry Knox simply wrote in a letter to a friend: "We don't know it ourselves." And Alexander Hamilton noted to his wife, Betsy, that because the troops were told to "stay fit for action and free from every encumbrance," they had immediately begun taking bets as to their true destination. Interestingly, the young colonel not only disclosed the army's real destination to Betsy, he also expressed doubts about the potential success of the operation. "It is ten to one that our plans will be thwarted by Cornwallis escaping to South Carolina by land," he wrote. Then Hamilton reassured his wife that he would return to her in October, or November at the latest, in time for the birth of their first child because, as he said, "That is the length of time the French fleet could be counted on to stay in the Chesapeake."

At ten o'clock on the morning of August 20, the head of the American army arrived at King's Ferry and began crossing the Hudson River, moving as fast as possible so as not to delay the French who were thought to be right on their heels. By the end of the next day, all the Americans, with all their baggage, artillery, and supplies, had successfully made the crossing.

Washington, himself, went across early on the afternoon of August 21. French Commissary-General, Claude Blanchard, recorded in his journal that the American commander seemed deeply moved by the event, as though it signified something extraordinarily special. "He pressed my hand with much affection when he left us," Blanchard recalled.

At that moment, Washington's thoughts were drifting back to 1776—to the battle of Long Island where he had made the disastrous mistake of consolidating all his troops in one place. After being cornered by the British, the only thing that had saved his army (and thereby the young revolution) was an all-night mass evacuation by water and an unexpected morning fog that shrouded the retreat. Now crossing the Hudson River, he was doing it again—concentrating all his forces in one place—only this time it would be at Yorktown.

Later in the day, General Rochambeau crossed the river and joined the American commander for dinner at the deserted home of Joshua Smith. This dwelling had quickly become known as the "Treason House," because it was where Benedict Arnold had met secretly the previous year with Major John Andre to plan for the turnover of West Point to the British. As Washington and Rochambeau were just concluding their meal, Commissary-General Blanchard arrived with a confidential dispatch. Washington read the message in silence, took a deep breath and exhaled. He turned and informed Rochambeau that the French forces were behind schedule and would probably take an extra twenty-four hours to cross the Hudson. He then handed the dispatch to Rochambeau.

Over the next several days, while waiting on the French army, Washington rounded up thirty small boats, had them mounted on huge wagons, and ordered that they be made part of the line of march. To make sure this was a conspicuous operation, he equipped all the wagon drivers with large bullwhips to crack over the oxen and even placed a marching band in front of them. This particular move, as Washington later noted, was designed to "deceive the British as to our real movement," at least for a few more days, because it would make the enemy think the boats were going to be used for a crossing at Staten Island.

After taking five full days to cross the Hudson, the French joined the Americans and began weaving their way down through New Jersey in three separate columns. The Americans went through New Brunswick, the French through Morristown, and the artillery by way of Bound Brook. Many officers were confounded by the specific orders surrounding the routes they were to take, especially since the point of their final destination was always left so vague. One of Washington's orders to the artillery (as relayed though General Benjamin Lincoln) was typical: "You will march through the Scotch Plains, Quibble Town, and Bound Brook. On the thirtieth to Princeton. On the thirty-first to Trenton, where you will meet me and receive further instructions. You will keep these orders a perfect secret."

Most of the troops were aroused by drums at 3:00 AM each day and were on the march within an hour. The weather was hot, the food poor and scant. Each man was allotted one pound of flour and one pound of beef per day. They also received only a half pint of salt for each hundred pounds of beef. They drank what water the brooks and streams afforded along the way. At 5:00 AM, they stopped for a brief rest, then marched on until noon when they sometimes ate whatever meal they had left over from the previous evening. From one to five in the afternoon, they marched. At 7:00 PM, cattle would be slaughtered and distributed as fairly as possible (sixty pounds to sixty men). The soldiers boiled the beef in camp kettles, adding a little flour to make soup. The rest of their flour would be mixed with creek water and baked into bread on a stone by the campfire. Next they would eat a supper of the soup and half the bread—saving the remainder for the next day's breakfast and lunch. Conversations before bed usually revolved around making bets on their final destination. Would it be New York or Virginia? Most of the soldiers retired by 9:00 PM—some sleeping in tents, others in the open air—all trying to get as much rest as they could for the next day's march.

After two full days of marching, Washington and Rochambeau halted the allied armies four miles north of Staten Island at Chatham, New Jersey. With specific orders to make as much noise as possible, foraging parties were sent into the countryside to gather materials, as if preparing for a long encampment. Both commanders then made overtly public tours of the entire area—handing out specific instructions left and right. While inspecting the French baking ovens, a member of Washington's Life Guard was shot in the chest by a British sniper. A nineteen-year-old soldier from New Hampshire named Asa Redington helped care for this wounded comrade. "The day was very warm so we had to rest him in the shade quite often and fan him with small bushes," wrote Redington in his journal. "We had high hopes of pulling him through, but he was too severely wounded, and at the last he left with us a sad but hopeful message for his mother in New Jersey telling her that the dawn of American liberty was being assured by the great loss that she and other mothers were suffering. Such scenes made us realize what a dreadful thing war is. We gave him as good a burial as we could."

General Washington's Headquarters Tent
Chatham, New York
Late August 1781

It is late afternoon. Washington is seated at a table outside the entrance to his tent. His hat is on the table; the top two buttons of his jacket are unbuttoned. Tench Tilghman is seated next to him. Humphreys and Trumbull are standing. Tilghman is briefing the general as to the contents of a just-received dispatch.

"Sir, Admiral de Barras has set sail from Newport to rendezvous with Count de Grasse in the Chesapeake," Tilghman relates. "With him are eight ships of the line, four frigates, and six transports carrying the French siege artillery and related heavy equipment."

"Excellent," responds Washington. "De Barras was trying to avoid fighting under the command of de Grasse, who is technically his junior. I was not completely sure he would engage. I am much relieved."

"We've also received a communiqué from Colonel Laurens, sir," says Tilghman with a smile. "He has arrived back in Boston and is on his way at this moment to Philadelphia where he will join us."

"Very good news, indeed," Washington says. "That young man did a great service for us while in France. I am looking forward to thanking him personally. Is there any word about his father?'

"I'm afraid not, sir. It appears he is still in held in the Tower of London."

"Hmmm. Well, perhaps we should take some of that money his son procured from the king of France and put it to good use. Please compose a letter to Robert Morris, as follows."

David Humphreys quickly sits down and begins to write.

"I must entreat you," Washington begins, "to procure one month's pay in coin for the entire American army. The men are grim-faced and grumbling. I fear they will mutiny upon learning that they are marching all the way to Virginia. Many of these troops have not been paid anything for a long time past. Make no doubt that a little hard money will put them in the proper temperament."

"Anything else, sir?" asks Humphreys.

"Not for Morris. But I think a note to Governor Lee of Maryland is also appropriate."

"Yes, sir. Go ahead."

"First explain to him our true destination," says Washington. "And then ask him for…"

"Begging your pardon, General," interrupts Tilghman. *"But is it appropriate to divulge our plan to Governor Lee at this time?"*

"Yes, I believe it is, Colonel. But this communiqué must be delivered personally by a special dispatch rider with an appropriate security detail."

"Very well, sir."

"Tell the governor that all hopes of success against Lord Cornwallis depend on our mutual quick action. Ask him for aid and assistance in the following manner: 'All the water craft suitable for the carriage of our army, its baggage, and stores, from the Head of Elk, down the Chesapeake, all the way to our destination; as much in salted provisions as can possibly be rounded up. Our troops are subsisting on meager rations. All should be ready at Head of Elk by September 8th.'"

Washington pauses for Humphreys, who at last stops writing, looks up, and nods. *"End with this, Colonel,"* Washington states. *"The moment is critical, the opportunity precious, the prospects favorable. I sincerely hope that no lack of exertions on your part will prove the means of our disappointment."*

Just then, a rider comes up in front of the tent and dismounts. Washington and Tilghman rise to greet Colonel Philip Van Cortlandt, commander of the 2nd New York Regiment. Humphreys looks up but keeps on writing.

"General Washington, you sent for me, sir?" says Van Cortlandt, with a crisp salute.

"Indeed, I did, Colonel," replies Washington, returning the salute.

Washington takes Van Cortlandt by the arm and leads him to the side of the headquarters tent where others cannot overhear. He reaches into his jacket and pulls out a piece of paper. *"Colonel, these are written orders for you,"* he says quietly. *"I am entrusting you with the rear guard of our forces. Your moves are of primary importance. As such, I will send a dragoon to you every day for your report of progress on the march. As you know, an army can only move as fast as its slowest regiment. The 2nd New York must not be our slowest regiment. You cannot lag behind. You must push the troops in front of you rather than have them waiting for you to catch up. Do you accept this assignment?"*

"Yes, sir," replies Van Cortlandt. *"I am honored."*

"Very well," says Washington, who grabs the colonel's hand and shakes it enthusiastically. *"Take these orders and remember that for the next three days, we must move with the greatest secrecy. You must not even tell your own men of our true destination. We are going to Trenton to cross the Delaware and then march into Philadelphia. Our destination is Lord Cornwallis at Yorktown."*

"Neither the 2nd New York nor I will let you down, General," says Van Cortlandt, with a crisp salute.

"Thank you, sir," responds Washington. "I don't doubt it for a moment. That is why I selected you. Your boats are to halt overnight at the junctions of roads leading east to Chatham and south to Morristown. This will deceive the enemy a while longer. Once you have passed through Morristown, you must take no more than three days to get to Yorktown—and you must move with the greatest secrecy. You must be moving by daybreak—and march until it gets dark."

"Yes, sir," responds Van Cortlandt.

The two men walk back to the front of the tent. Van Cortlandt mounts his horse and rides off. Washington turns to his aides. "Colonel Tilghman, will you have our horses brought up? I would like you to take a brief ride with me."

"Yes, sir," replies Tilghman, who dashes off to get the horses.

Washington turns and addresses Humphreys and Trumbull. "Gentlemen, please prepare written orders for the following: Send one regiment across the dunes toward Sandy Hook to make preliminary preparations to build artillery batteries. Sir Henry will think we do so to aide the French fleet in an attack on New York. Also, send out some small parties to question local civilians between Newark and Amboy as to the availability of boats. Make sure these civilians, preferably Tories, are left with the impression that the boats are to be used for an attack on Staten Island. I also wish that wagons be prepared to carry all the soldiers' packs, so they may press forward with more ease. And finally, I wish to make a special request that all our intelligence officers provide me with as much information as often as possible as to the movements of Sir Henry Clinton and his forces. Do you have all that, gentlemen?"

"Indeed, sir."

"Yes, sir."

A moment later, Tench Tilghman returns on horseback with Billy, who is leading the general's horse.

"Where are we going, sir?" asks Tilghman, as Washington mounts.

"To lay a false trail," he replies.

Washington then spurs his horse and rides off at nearly a full gallop. Tilghman and Billy follow a few lengths behind trying to keep up. "Criminy! Does he ever trot?" Tilghman asks in frustration.

"Almost never, sir," replies Billy. "The general has always been in a hurry. I don't know why."

◆   ◆   ◆

About two miles down the road to Staten Island, Washington, Tilghman, and Billy come up on a small house set back about one hundred feet from the road. An eld-

erly man is sitting in a rocking chair on the porch. He is smoking a pipe. Washington stops in front of the house, looks down the road, scratches his head, and then looks over at the man. He turns his horse and rides over.

"Good day, sir," says Washington, with a smile.

The old man nods quietly, tapping his pipe against his teeth.

"This is the road to Staten Island, is it not, sir."

The old man nods that it is.

"I make it out to be about two miles to the water," says Washington. "Would you happen to know if there are many obstacles blocking the road?"

"A few, not many," the man says tersely, without ever taking the pipe from his mouth. He is still looking Washington over.

"Would you know anything about the roads on the other side leading into the island?"

"A bit."

"Are they wide?"

"Some."

"Do they go through dense forests or are they mostly in open fields?"

"Almost all forests," says the old man taking his pipe out of his mouth and rising from his chair as though he suddenly recognizes his visitor. "Are you General Washington?"

The general then abruptly pulls his head back with an air of concern that he has said too much. "I am, sir," he responds. "My questions were only idle chitchat. My interest is merely in the Jersey countryside."

"I see," says the man, furrowing his eyebrows slightly.

"Well, good day to you, sir," says Washington as he turns his horse.

"Good day, General."

As they ride slowly back toward Chatham, Tilghman speaks up. "Sir, what was that all about?"

"I have been told that man is a Tory," replies Washington.

Tilghman cocks his head and grins slightly. The moment the small house is out of sight, the general spurs his horse and gallops off. Tilghman and Billy follow a couple of lengths behind.

15

Sir Henry Clinton's Headquarters
Harlem Heights, New York
Late August 1781

Sir Henry Clinton is sitting at the dining table with Rear Admiral Thomas Graves. They have just finished their meals and are sipping an after-dinner wine. Captains Dawkins and Gurwood, along with the admiral's naval aide, stand just outside the room.

"Is there anything new on the American troop movements, Sir Henry?" asks Graves.

"A few days ago, I received intelligence from our spy, code-named Squib," responds Clinton. "I have it right here. Let me read it to you. 'General Washington with about 6,000, including French, is on the march for this neighborhood. It is said they will go against New York, but some circumstances induce me to believe they will go to the Chesapeake. Yet for God's sake, be prepared at all points.'"

"Hmmm, do you think they might be headed all the way to Virginia?" asks Graves.

"No, clearly not," responds Sir Henry. "This afternoon I received a dispatch from another of our spies, Marquand, who reported the enemy has stopped in Chatham where they have laid out an extensive encampment. Washington is also clearing roads and preparing for an assault on Staten Island—and he is transporting small boats overland to be used in the attack. There is no doubt. I have therefore shifted some of our troops in that direction, including the 3,000 Hessians just arrived."

"I see, sir," says Graves. "Yes, that is a good move."

"I also have a new battle plan to propose, Admiral—which is the main reason I invited you here today."

"Yes, Sir Henry?" Graves asks inquisitively, taking another sip of wine.

"I would like to strike the French fleet in Rhode Island," Clinton relates enthusiastically. "If we can disable de Barras, he will not be able to join with de Grasse when the main fleet reaches Sandy Hook. That will severely cripple the enemy's morale and will hamper their attack on this city. Therefore, I have given orders for troops and guns to be made ready. Of course, success of the entire operation rests with you, Admiral. What do you think?"

Graves pauses for a moment. He takes a long sip of wine, then another. Admiral Thomas Graves is one of the few British admirals who gets along well with Sir Henry Clinton. Now fifty-six years old, this former governor of Newfoundland has broad naval experience but has only been on American shores for little more than a year. His penchant for caution to the point of inactivity matches Sir Henry's personality. They also resemble each other physically as Graves is about the same height and heavyset with a broad nose.

"Well, sir, that is an interesting idea," *the admiral responds politely.* "We could certainly take such action. However, several of our ships are in dire need of repairs. The Robust, for instance, is leaky and must go to dry dock. And the Prudent must change one mast, perhaps two."

"How long will these repairs take?" *asks Sir Henry.* "When would the fleet be ready for action?"

"I'm afraid no one knows for sure, sir. It will be quite some time."

Clinton frowns at this response.

"Of course, I will press the engineers for speedy action," *Graves says quickly.* "We must be ready as soon as possible—especially as Hood has recently informed us that he believes the French fleet is headed this way. We must be at full strength to repel a possible naval attack on New York City."

"Of course we must," *agrees Clinton.*

"Tell me, Sir Henry, have you a recommendation as to how many ships we should pull from the defense of this place to attack de Barras in Rhode Island?"

Clinton pauses. He refills both wine glasses, then takes a sip. "Well, certainly, enough to overpower the enemy. But, of course, we must keep as many as needed to provide an adequate naval defense."

"Indeed, sir," *responds Graves.* "Well, with your brilliant moves to fortify our defenses, with 17,000 men, and with our fleet at full strength, I would think the enemy would have very little chance of taking this city."

"I agree. However, one can never be too careful. At any rate, it is abundantly clear that Washington is going to try. But still, it would almost be suicide. I wonder if he may back off when he realizes we are at such strength."

"Very possible, sir," *says Graves.* "Well, if I may, sir, let me get an accurate estimate as to the timing of our repairs. I will have a date for you tomorrow."

"Very well, Admiral. Thank you."

After another hour or so of friendly banter between the two British commanders, Graves departs. Clinton calls his aides into the study.

"Gentlemen, I would like to send a brief letter to Lord Cornwallis," *he says.*

"Yes, sir," *responds Captain Dawkins, who quickly pulls out a pen and paper.*

"Your Lordship," begins Sir Henry. *"American forces are now encamped at Chatham, New Jersey. I cannot well ascertain Mr. Washington's real intentions by this move of his army. But it is possible that he means to suspend his offensive operations against this post and take a defensive position at his old winter quarters at Morristown. From there, he may simply remain for the winter or he may detach to the southward. I will keep you informed."*

HMS Barfleur, *Flagship of Rear Admiral Sir Samuel Hood*
Entrance to the Chesapeake Bay
Virginia Capes, Atlantic Ocean
Late August 1781

It is mid-afternoon. The sun is bright, the sea calm. Admiral Samuel Hood is standing at the railing on the side deck looking out at the water. He has sailed a direct route straight up from the Caribbean Sea in hopes of catching the French fleet. His fourteen ships of the line, with their sleek copper-sheathed hulls, have made excellent time—arriving earlier that morning off the coast of Virginia after less than three weeks at sea. But there is no sign of the enemy's ships. Frankly, Hood is flabbergasted that he has not caught up to Admiral de Grasse. "How could they have moved so fast with twenty-eight wooden-hulled ships?" he wonders. "Where are they?" Several hours ago, he had ordered Rear Admiral Francis S. Drake, aboard the Princessa, *to take several ships, sail into the Chesapeake Bay, and see if he could spot any French ships. Now a small rowboat is making its way from the* Princessa *to the* Barfleur. *When it arrives, Admiral Drake comes aboard the* Barfleur *to confer with Admiral Hood.*

"Sir, the Chesapeake waters are unoccupied by French vessels," reports Drake.

"None?" asks Hood, incredulously.

"Not a one, sir. No."

"My God, de Grasse must have sailed directly to New York, just as we had feared—and with a speed I did not think possible."

"I agree, sir," confirms Drake. *"But de Grasse is the best commander the French have. He is very capable of such sailing, sir."*

"I suppose. But we must leave immediately for New York. Do you concur?"

"Indeed, sir. Both General Clinton and Admiral Graves would expect it. But perhaps we should leave some support for Lord Cornwallis, just in case."

"Very well," agrees Hood. *"We will leave two frigates with orders to sail up the bay and report to Cornwallis."*

Admiral Drake proceeds back to the Princessa. *Within an hour, Admiral Hood gives the order for his fleet to sail north "with all deliberate speed."*

Lord Cornwallis's Headquarters
Yorktown, Virginia
Late August 1781

A tall redbrick house with massive chimneys bakes in the summer sun. It is the home of the uncle of Virginia Governor Thomas Nelson—now serving as headquarters for Lord Earl Cornwallis. All the windows are open. The air is thick with humidity. There is little or no breeze.

Cornwallis is sitting at a table with his aides listening as deputy adjutant general, Major John Despart, reports on his recently completed inventory of food and supplies. Cornwallis uses a white handkerchief to intermittently dry the beads of perspiration that perpetually hang on his forehead. Several mugs of rum sit on the table.

"My Lord, we have bread and flour enough to last fifty days," reads Major Despart from a list. "Beef and pork, sixty-three days; oatmeal, forty days; butter, ninety-two; and rum, fifty-three. Yesterday, the commissary purchased an additional three hundred barrels of flour on your order. Of course, this does not include the numerous stores that General O'Hara brought with him upon his arrival here earlier today."

"We shall see what, if anything, he has brought to feed all the indigents who accompanied him," replies Cornwallis, wiping his brow and taking a swig of rum. "In the meantime, Major, we must issue orders to purchase all the rum that can possibly be procured."

"Yes, sir," replies Despart.

"This climate is absolutely unbearable. It makes me so tired all the time. All I feel like doing is sleeping."

"Yes, My Lord, it is awful," agrees Colonel Chewton. "The heat and humidity are taking a toll on everyone—especially those working on the entrenchments."

"Speaking of that, what is our count on excavation tools?" asks Cornwallis.

"My Lord, the adjutant general reports that we have 992 on hand," responds Despart. "Four hundred spades and shovels; 190 pickaxes; 210 axes; 160 hatchets; and thirty-two wheelbarrows."

"Not nearly enough," says Cornwallis, shaking his head. "Give the order for our foraging expeditions to seize as many entrenching tools as may be available."

"Yes, My Lord," responds Chewton.

"Major Ross, I believe it is time to send another letter to General Clinton."

Ross takes out a fresh piece of paper, dips his pen in the inkwell, and looks up.

"Sir Henry," begins Cornwallis, *"allow me to report that Brigadier General Charles O'Hara arrived here this day with stores and troops. A great number of refugees have accompanied him from the counties of Norfolk and Princess Anne."*

"The engineer has finished his survey and examination of this place and has proposed his plan for fortifying it, which, appearing judicious, I have approved and directed to be executed. The Gloucester Point defenses will take the whole labor force five or six weeks more to complete properly. Those at Yorktown will take equally as long. The hot, humid climate is a consideration in the exertion of the troops, as is our lack of the proper number of entrenching tools. If you can spare them, we are in dire need of hundreds of spades, shovels, and a wide assortment of carpenter supplies for this purpose.

"I will not venture to take any step that might retard the establishment of this position. But I request that Your Excellency decide whether it is most important for your plans that a detachment of 1,000 or 1,200 men (which I think I can spare) should be sent to you, or that the whole of the troops here should continue to be employed in expediting the works.

"That will do, Major."

"Very well, My Lord," responds Major Ross.

"Sir, do you mean to send those troops if Sir Henry asks for them?" asks Colonel Chewton. *"Have you changed your mind?"*

"Of course not, Colonel," responds Cornwallis with a grin. *"He would not dare ask for them, either. I'm just tweaking him a bit."*

"That is a relief to me, My Lord, for I have some concern as to our vulnerability at the moment."

"Come, come, my dear Chewton. There is no need to be worried. All signs indicate that New York is the target of the main American army and, as Admiral Hood informs us, the French fleet, as well. If circumstances should change, Sir Henry will move to reinforce us. Furthermore, our navy is vastly superior to anything the French can offer—including the formidable fleet of Monsieur de Grasse. And finally, the enemy army has not the ability, expertise, or the artillery to maintain an effective siege of this area. Once we complete our fortification, the American's cannonballs will bounce harmlessly away from us. So let General Buckskin come, if he wishes. It will be his funeral. Now if you will excuse me, gentlemen, I am going to take a nap."

As Cornwallis walks out of the room, he notices the slave, James, standing by the main door. James, you are back," says Cornwallis. "Is there anything more about Lafayette?"

"Yes, sir. I have heard that he has called for an additional 200 militiamen," comes the reply. "'The boy' definitely has new respect for Your Lordship since the battle at Green Spring, sir."

At this, Cornwallis smiles. "Keep up the good work, James," he says as he walks upstairs.

◆   ◆   ◆

When Cornwallis arrived at Yorktown in early August, he concentrated first on erecting fortifications across the river at Gloucester Point. Holding this position, he believed, was essential for control of the river. It might also provide an effective escape route in an emergency. The village of Yorktown remained a secondary concern for the moment, because its height above the water provided adequate protection from French ships.

By late August, work had progressed at Gloucester Point to the stage where fortifications at Yorktown could begin. British engineers laid out an extensive plan designed to be a bulwark of defense against both land and naval attack. It called for construction of inner and outer earthwork parallels, trenches, redoubts, redans, and gun emplacement batteries.

As construction began, British troops camped on the beach and the higher plain. They occupied homes and public buildings. Artillery and related equipment were moved from ship to shore. Houses and trees in the line of the parallel were torn down and removed. Nearly everybody was involved in the labor—regular troops, seamen, and Negroes. Still, work moved along quite slowly—partly due to the lethargy of Cornwallis, himself, because he was simply in no hurry—and partly due to the hot, humid weather.

"For six weeks, the heat has been so unbearable that many men have been lost by sunstroke, or their reason has been impaired," wrote Captain Johann Ewald in his private journal. "Everything one has on his body is soaked with constant perspiration. The nights are especially terrible, when there is so little air that one can scarcely breathe. The torment of several billion insects has plagued us day and night."

Banastre Tarleton's cavalry legion began conducting extensive foraging operations through the populated area between Williamsburg and Hampton Roads. Also traversed was the area northeast of Gloucester Point all the way to the Severn River. The British troops rummaged local plantations and took whatever they wanted, especially seizing herds of cattle from the local inhabitants. There would be no shortage of food for British troops during the first month of occupation.

The Marquis de Lafayette sent out small parties to harass Tarleton's foragers, but they were effectively swatted away like annoying flies. This enemy presence did not seem to concern Lord Cornwallis in the slightest. He took great comfort in the belief that the young Frenchman could not surmount the overwhelming British troop strength.

Sir Henry Clinton's Headquarters
Harlem Heights, New York
Late August 1781

It is early evening. A light rain taps against the windowpanes. General Clinton and Admiral Graves are seated at the dinner table having a leisurely conversation. A bottle of wine sits between them. Both glasses are partially filled. They are discussing Sir Henry's idea of an attack on the small French fleet in Rhode Island when, without warning, the main door of the mansion flings open and in stomps a rain-soaked, mud-covered naval officer. Clinton and Graves do not rise but immediately cease their conversation and look toward the entryway.

"Admiral Hood!" *Graves bellows in astonishment.* "What in the world?"

Hood abruptly marches into the dining room, leaving a trail of mud and water behind on the shiny wood floors. "Gentlemen, I have just come from the Chesapeake," *he shouts excitedly.* "The French fleet was not there. I thought they had sailed here. But not seeing them, I left my flagship and our other ships outside the harbor at Sandy Hook so I could depart at a moment's notice. I rowed myself here as fast as I could. De Grasse is on the loose! De Grasse is on the loose!"

Hood had sailed for three days and nights to get to New York as fast as possible. Now the fifty-three-year-old aggressive veteran naval commander knew he had been outfoxed.

"De Grasse must have sailed through the Bahamas Channel on his way up from the West Indies," *he cries.* "There is no other explanation. He deliberately let me get ahead of him so that he could enter the Chesapeake unchallenged. He obviously predicted that I would assume he was sailing all the way to New York."

"Come, come, Samuel," *responds Graves, Hood's superior.* "You are overreacting. There must be some other explanation. We have intelligence that New York is the primary objective. The French fleet is most likely still headed that way. It would be best for us to remain where we are."

"No! No! I know he is headed for the Chesapeake! You have no time to lose! Every moment is precious! You must leave immediately—with every ship you have ready for sea. Wait for nothing!"

As Hood and Graves argue their points, a dispatch rider shows up at the door. Captain Gurwood opens the letter, reads it, and quickly interrupts the commanders in the dining room.

"General Clinton, sir," Gurwood states tersely, "we have just received a dispatch from one of our patrol ships. Admiral de Barras sailed from Newport three days ago. He reportedly has on board his ships all the French siege guns and provisions."

Upon hearing this, both Graves and Clinton rise to their feet. They are clearly alarmed.

"You see, sir," says Hood. "There is not a moment to lose."

"Yes, yes, I agree, Samuel," Graves replies. "I will join you tomorrow, and we will attempt to intercept de Barras. We must prevent him from joining de Grasse. Such a combined fleet would be most formidable. Do you agree, Sir Henry?"

"Indeed, I do," responds Clinton. "But I believe the object is New York. Those siege guns will be used against us, not Cornwallis."

"Perhaps," says Graves. "But as for now, our primary concern must be the capture of de Barras and his small fleet."

"But gentlemen," interrupts Hood. "It has been three days since he left Rhode Island. If New York was the objective, would he not have been here by now? I think the Chesapeake is the more likely target."

Clinton and Graves simply stare at each other.

◆   ◆   ◆

The next day, as Graves takes five ships and joins with Hood's fourteen to sail southward toward Virginia, Sir Henry Clinton receives a hastily scribbled message from his spy, Squib. "The Chesapeake is the object—all in motion," it begins. "Washington apparently is in Trenton and heading south."

Sir Henry frowns. "This flies in the face of all our other intelligence," he wails at Gurwood and Dawkins. "It may be a false communiqué. I will need further confirmation before I believe any part of it."

Then Clinton sits down and calmly composes a letter to Lord Cornwallis at Yorktown. "Mr. Washington's force still remains in the neighborhood of Chatham," he writes, "and I do not hear that he has yet detached to the southward."

16

The Quaker Trail
Between Princeton and Trenton, New Jersey
August 29, 1781

It is early morning—the sky clear, the sun low on the eastern horizon, the air thick and humid. George Washington is galloping on horseback at a brisk pace. Slightly behind him are a myriad of riders, including Tench Tilghman, David Humphreys, and Jonathan Trumbull. General Rochambeau and about a dozen members of his French staff are also mixed in the group. Washington's Life Guards, who constantly protect the American commander in chief, ride around the edges. Billy brings up the rear.

The previous day, allied forces had abandoned their deception of an attack on New York and begun to march openly for Virginia. Rochambeau's group rode an extra fifteen miles to join Washington at Princeton—where all had enjoyed a leisurely dinner and spent the night. Now they were on their way to Philadelphia.

Realizing the other riders are tiring, Washington slows his mount down to a walk and moves next to his French counterpart. "It was right about here where we removed the rags from the wagon wheels and picked up the pace," he says to Rochambeau (with DeChastellux translating).

"When was this?" asks the count.

"January '77. After Trenton, on the way up to Princeton."

"You put rags on the wheels?"

"Yes. We were trying to be quiet. Lord Cornwallis had come down from Princeton after we took Trenton. His troops were everywhere. If they had heard our movements, we would not have been able to get around them."

"We have heard of your crossing of the Delaware on Christmas night, mon general," says Rochambeau, with some curiosity in his voice. "Did it really snow all night long?"

"Snow, sleet, and hail," replies Washington, as the rest of the Frenchmen begin to crowd around. "Immediately after our initial crossing, Cornwallis headed back to Princeton—believing we would retire for the winter. But a few weeks later, we marched nine miles upriver to McKonkey's Ferry where we moved the entire army *back across the river. We stayed behind low hills so as not to be seen by enemy sentries. Our sign/countersign was 'Victory or Death.'"*

"How many men, sir?" asks Baron Von Closen.

"Twenty-four hundred," relates Washington. "It was fearfully cold and raw with a snowstorm setting in. The wind was northeast and beat in the faces of the men. It was a terrible night for the soldiers who had no shoes. Some of them had old rags tied around their feet, but I did not hear a man complain."

"Mon Dieu!" exclaims Rochambeau.

"It took us most of the night to cross—soldiers, horses, and artillery. By the time we reached the other side at four in the morning, the men were soaked through and shivering. Two froze to death."

Washington pauses and swallows hard. Then he continues. "We immediately marched downriver the nine miles to Trenton. You could see blood in the snow from our men's exposed feet. We descended on the garrison and quickly took it. The Hessians had celebrated the night before and were still asleep. They put up little resistance."

"How many captured, sir?" asks Von Closen.

"About a thousand—along with artillery, ammunition, horses, and muskets. And we took everyone and everything back across the river into Pennsylvania."

"But you went on to Princeton."

"Yes. A week later—after Lord Cornwallis had moved his entire 8,000-man force to Trenton. We again moved at night. I ordered four hundred men to stay behind to dig trenches and stoke campfires. This was designed to deceive the British sentries into thinking we were preparing for a major defense. We then crossed the river and began our march in total darkness. We wrapped our artillery caisson wheels in rags to muffle the sound as they rolled over ice and snow. No soldier under the rank of general was allowed to know our true destination."

"Tell us about the battle at Princeton, mon general," says Rochambeau.

"There was only a small protective force left to guard the garrison there," explains Washington. "But they fought hard. We attacked at dawn, and the enemy rushed at us with a full bayonet charge. When General Mercer went down, our men broke and ran."

"What happened next?"

"I galloped to the front. Waving my hat furiously, I shouted for the men to stand their ground. An enemy artillery volley landed near me. My horse reared. Smoke filled the air. After it cleared, I waved the infantry forward. 'Bring up the troops!' I shouted to Colonel Fitzgerald. 'This day is our own!' Our men turned and charged. The enemy broke and ran."

"And you took the garrison?"

"Indeed, we did—along with supplies for Cornwallis's entire army. Then we quickly retired to Morristown for the winter."

"And what of General Mercer?" asks Von Closen.

Washington pauses and again swallows hard. "He was at the very front of the line. When the enemy charged, he pulled out his sword and exalted the men forward. He was overpowered and stabbed to death."

Washington spurs his horse and rides forward, quickly accelerating to a gallop. A startled look comes over the faces of the French staff. Each man spurs his horse to catch up. Their rest break is over.

Philadelphia, Pennsylvania
August 30, 1781

After spending the night in Trenton and crossing the Delaware the next morning, Washington and Rochambeau, along with their entire party, galloped hard to Philadelphia, finally riding into the city at one o'clock in the afternoon. They were met by a cavalry troop of the Pennsylvania Militia and escorted to City Tavern for several rounds of rum punch with city officials and members of Congress.

Afterward, Rochambeau went over to visit French Minister Chevalier de La Luzerne, and Washington rode to the home of Robert Morris to discuss business. Morris reported that he had pleaded with governors of the nearby states to supply boats for 7,000 men. However, they had supplied only enough to transport 2,000. Morris also presented a letter from General Knox to the Board of War in which he requested badly needed supplies for his artillery gunners, including: 300,000 cartridges, 20,000 flints, 1,000 powder horns, and as many cannon, artillery tools, and musket balls that could possibly be procured. News from New York included a report that eighteen British ships of war under the command of Admiral Samuel Hood had appeared off Sandy Hook, and that Sir Henry Clinton had posted thousands of troops on Staten Island and shifted many others to the north side of the mountain.

Washington was disturbed at Hood's presence but elated that Clinton seemed to be falling for the ruse. He quickly sent urgent orders for Van Cortlandt's rear guard to "keep your destination a perfect secret for one or two days at least." The boats Washington was transporting overland were now more important than ever. And he sent a detailed directive to General Benjamin Lincoln to move the entire army to Head of Elk, Maryland. When the troops arrived in Philadelphia, Lincoln was to travel ahead to make preparations for the troop embarkation down the Chesapeake. He and Rochambeau would do the same—ride ahead and attempt to secure more water transports. "Please use every exertion for dispatch in our movement," Washington wrote Lincoln, "as not a moment's time is to be lost."

At three o'clock, the general traveled to the State House where he briefed Congress on his plans. He returned to the Morris house for a dinner later in the evening that would include Rochambeau, La Luzerne, Thomas McKean (president of Congress), and many other Philadelphia notables. During the meal, gunships in the harbor fired cannon salutes while the participants offered numerous formal toasts: to the United States; to the king of France; to the allied armies; to the speedy arrival of Admiral de Grasse in the Chesapeake; to the French and American victory over England. Later, Washington took an after-dinner walk along illuminated city streets where he bowed graciously to many citizens who crowded around to touch and speak with him. There were also many British Loyalists who, though curious to see the general, kept silent.

◆   ◆   ◆

While Washington and Rochambeau moved a day or two in advance, the combined American and French forces were rapidly marching southward en route to Virginia. Excitement and enthusiasm now permeated the ranks. Dr. Thacher wrote in his journal that the troops had marveled at their leader's foresight and ingenuity:

> Our destination can no longer be a secret. The British army under Lord Cornwallis is unquestionably the object of our present expedition. General Washington has executed a masterly piece of generalship. The great secret was a judiciously concerted strategy calculated to alarm Sir Henry Clinton for the safety of his garrison in New York and induce him to recall a part of his troops from Virginia for his own defense. The deception has proved completely successful.
>
> It is now rumored that a French fleet may soon be expected to arrive in Chesapeake Bay to cooperate with the allied army in that quarter. We are now pursuing our route with increased rapidity toward Philadelphia. Wagons have been prepared to carry the soldiers' packs, that they may press forward with greater facility. The Royal army in New York might, without risking a great deal, harass our army on its march and subject us to irreparable injury. To our officers, the British inactivity is truly unaccountable.

On the evening of August 30, all three allied lines converged and encamped for the night on the northeastern bank of the Delaware River next to Trenton. Over the next several days, the entire allied force would cross the Delaware and march nineteen miles to the rolling countryside of Lower Dublin—only seven miles above Philadelphia.

The Southern Beach
Yorktown, Virginia
August 30, 1781

Captain Johann Ewald of the Hessian Field-Jager Corps is wiping perspiration from the brow of his forehead. He is of medium height, slender, thirty-seven years old, very bright, and very serious. His main distinguishing physical characteristic is that he has only one good eye, having lost his left eye in battle nearly twenty years earlier. Ewald speaks English with a thick German accent. This day he has lookout duty. From the beach, he can see far across the Chesapeake Bay toward the Virginia Capes. It is noon—clear and hot as usual.

One of the soldiers sitting next to Ewald on the high slope of a sand dune raises his arm and points toward the water. "Captain! Look!" he exclaims excitedly.

The 28-gun British frigate Guadeloupe, *followed by the sloop* Bonetta, *is sailing at full speed back to Yorktown. Farther in the distance, struggling to keep up, is the smaller picket ship* Loyalist. *All three ships had departed early that morning en route to Charleston with orders to deliver several dispatches and search for the British fleet.*

"What in the world?" mutters Ewald under his breath.

His good eye darts to the right and, in the distance, he observes three very large ships chasing the Guadeloupe, Bonetta, *and* Loyalist. *Suddenly, there is the sound of several cannon blasts. Smoke billows from the deck of one of the large ships. Then the main mast of the* Loyalist *topples over in a heap.*

Captain Ewald grabs his spyglass and takes a closer look. The trailing ships do not look British. They are making unfamiliar signals. He moves his spyglass farther to the right—toward the opening of the Chesapeake Bay, toward the Virginia Capes on the edge of the Atlantic. He squints his right eye and opens his spyglass to get maximum distance. He sees what appears to be dozens of ships.

Ewald quickly stands up, rubs his eye, and looks into the spyglass again. He swallows hard.

"Mein Gott! Mein Gott!" he shouts. "They are French! They are French!"

He turns to a younger soldier. "Corporal, take a man and run to Lord Cornwallis as fast as possible," he orders. "Tell him that the Guadeloupe *and* Bonetta *are being chased back up the river by three French frigates. The* Loyalist *has been damaged. I fear these French vessels may open fire on our defenses. Tell him also that there appears to be several dozen more ships in the far distance—at the opening of the bay. It may be the French fleet."*

The corporal's eyes are large, like saucers. The fear in his face is obvious.

"Run!" shouts Ewald. "At top speed! Do not delay! Hurry! Hurry!"

The corporal turns and sprints off, waving to a comrade to follow him. Ewald again looks through his spyglass, back toward the Virginia Capes again.

"Oh, no," he mutters. "Oh, no."

◆   ◆   ◆

The French fleet had arrived along the coast of Virginia at sunset the previous evening. But due to the onset of darkness and following the advice of the local pilots Rochambeau had sent along for the voyage, Admiral de Grasse had anchored his ships nine miles southeast of the entrance to Chesapeake Bay. First thing the next morning, he ordered three frigates to sail ahead and scout the bay. The French were content to chase the *Guadeloupe* and the *Bonetta* back up the York River and, after shooting away its masts, they towed the *Loyalist* back to Hampton Roads. Once de Grasse received the "all clear" signal (meaning the British fleet was not present), he led his entire armada into the Chesapeake and anchored his flagship, the *Ville de Paris*, at Lynnhaven Bay near Cape Henry. The rest of the ships fanned out from there for several miles in both directions.

De Grasse quickly directed four frigates to sail up the York River and anchor about two miles below the town. He also sent several others up the James River to prevent Cornwallis's escape overland to the south. The British outposts at York-town and Gloucester Point were now officially cut off from the sea.

The French admiral next sent out two dispatches. The first went to General Washington informing the commander of the fleet's safe arrival at the entrance to the Chesapeake. The second went to the Marquis de Lafayette asking that arrangements be made to transport land troops ashore. Over the next several days, more than forty boatloads of French troops rowed up the James River, landed at Jamestown, and marched inland to Williamsburg. In all, 2,400 men under the command of Lieutenant General Claude Anne, Marquis de St. Simon joined with Lafayette's force—nearly doubling the size of the local allied army.

◆   ◆   ◆

After the *Guadeloupe* and *Bonetta* arrived back at Yorktown, Lord Cornwallis sent out scouts who quickly confirmed the presence of enemy vessels in the Chesapeake and the fact that French troops had landed on shore to reinforce Lafayette. This news electrified the British encampment where, immediately, confidence turned to worry—and optimism to pessimism. "This surely will result in heavy desertion among us," noted Captain Ewald in his journal, "for our soldiers must realize by now that everyone will be captured with bag and baggage in the end."

Lord Cornwallis, although greatly concerned, did not panic. He immediately sent two messages to Sir Henry Clinton. One was a traditional dispatch, the other was written in code on American bank notes: "An enemy's fleet within the Capes," it read, "between twenty and forty ships of war, mostly large." The British commander next ordered a complete inventory of his troop strength at Yorktown and made plans to personally inspect each regiment. Then he turned his attention to speeding up the construction of fortifications.

Cornwallis first focused on defending enemy approaches downriver by moving cannon off his ships and placing them in the water batteries at both Yorktown and Gloucester Point. Then he transferred sailors to tents on the beaches and directed them to dig trenches facing the river. The redoubts, redans, and abatements at Gloucester Point were ordered completed as quickly as possible. And on the Yorktown side of the river—the construction of which was seriously behind schedule—Sutherland's design involved both inner (300 yards) and outer (700 yards) lines of earthworks around the town. It took advantage of the two swampy ravines cutting the ground around Yorktown. The raised area between these two ravines (called "the gorge") was crucial to hold, because it was there that the roads from Williamsburg and Hampton converged. Following his approval of Sutherland's plan, Cornwallis ordered round-the-clock operations.

Over the next several days, lumber was confiscated from local plantations and hundreds of trees were cut down along the York and Wormley Creek ravines to provide planks and boards for artillery platforms. Countless tons of dirt were moved by hand to form the fifteen-foot-high mounds of the inner line.

As the activity became almost feverish, the troops began to complain about their commanders. "The earthworks are carried forward day and night without relief," noted Hessian soldier Johann Doehla. "We hardly have time for eating and often have to eat raw meat," stated Corporal Stephan Popp of the Bayreuth German regiment. And Captain Ewald was particularly disparaging of Cornwallis and his engineers. "Now they hastily began to unload all the magazines and guns," he said bitterly. "Through negligence and laziness, all were still on board the ships lying in the York River. But what is the reason? The engineer gets a daily allowance of one pound sterling as long as his work lasts; hence, it is to his advantage if it drags on."

Lord Cornwallis's Headquarters
Yorktown, Virginia
Early September 1781

It is mid-afternoon. Heavy thunderstorms soak Yorktown and slow the building of fortifications. The British encampment has been struck by lightning several times. Inside the Nelson house, Lord Cornwallis sits around the table with Major Ross, Colonel Chewton, and General O'Hara. They are leisurely supping tea when Colonel Banastre Tarleton bursts into the room with his customary quickstep and sense of urgency. He hands Cornwallis a dispatch saying it was received just moments ago. He remains standing while it is read.

Dripping from the heavy rain outside, Tarleton holds his hat at his side. Its jet-black color contrasts sharply with his bright green coat. He is short, redheaded, handsome, and athletic. At 27 years of age, he is also one of the finest horseman and most feared swordsman in the British army. Born to a wealthy family in Liverpool, Tarleton is Oxford-educated, impudent, impetuous, brave, and bold. He disdains Cornwallis's cautiousness but holds a grudging respect for his commander largely due to the fact that Cornwallis refused to accept his resignation after he lost most of his cavalry regiment at the Battle of Cowpens.

Cornwallis nonchalantly drops the dispatch on the table. "It's from one of our spies in New Jersey. He reports that Washington and Rochambeau have turned south and are headed our way."

The others stare straight ahead and say nothing. A clap of thunder sounds outside the window. Cornwallis draws a deep breath and motions for Tarleton to take a seat.

As the young colonel pulls up a chair, he breaks the silence. "Sir, I believe we must take immediate action."

"Oh?" *responds Cornwallis quietly.*

"Yes, sir," continues Tarleton. "Lafayette is moving his entire army to Williamsburg. He will not attack us. He will only harass our foraging operations while he waits for Washington. I recommend an attack on Williamsburg."

"Do we have accurate reports on 'the boy's' strength?" asks General O'Hara.

"Yes, General. Our riders constantly monitor the marquis' condition. His force does not exceed 4,000 fighting men. He has 1,500 Continental regulars, 400 new recruits, and 2,000 ill-trained militia. The full complements under the Count de St. Simon are 800 in each of three regiments (the Agenois, Gatinois, and Touraine). However, many of them are debilitated by scurvy and other illnesses contracted in the West Indies."

"It is true," says Cornwallis. "The troops of St. Simon are raw and sickly. They are undisciplined vagabonds collected from the West Indies. They will fall victim to the Virginia winter."

"But we also have fever and dysentery spread among our men," responds O'Hara. "This past month alone, eight Germans have died in the hospital."

"But, sir," responds Tarleton, "we have more than 6,000 men fit for duty. Our infantry are all good; our field artillery unequalled. The cavalry, to the amount of 400, are in excellent order. Besides our regular force, there are sufficient numbers of marines, seamen, convalescents, and refugees to man the batteries and maintain the works against any action of the French fleet during our absence."

"Colonel Tarleton," interrupts Cornwallis, "I do not believe we have a choice in this matter. We have been ordered to set up a defensive post by General Clinton. We do not have the discretion to abandon this position. I believe also that when Sir Henry hears of these new developments, he will immediately send the British navy—which we all know is vastly superior to the French. Also, Clinton will quickly come with most of his army to reinforce us."

"Sir, I respectfully submit that there is no substantial reason to believe that General Clinton will be able to give serious assistance to the king's troops here in Virginia. He has New York to hold. And the French fleet is superior in numbers to our own. Let me also state, sir, that our current position is untenable. Both the York and James Rivers are blocked by French vessels. We are cut off by sea, and our path to the south is obstructed."

"I understand that, Colonel," responds Cornwallis. "Still, I do not think an attack on Lafayette is wise at this juncture."

Refusing to give up the argument, Tarleton continues his plea. "My Lord, I urge some sort of action. If not an attack on Williamsburg, I suggest the abandonment of our posts at Yorktown and Gloucester Point. We can march overland to either New

York or the Carolinas. Our road of retreat in all land directions is wide open—espe-
cially to the north."

"*Colonel, I believe I just made myself clear on establishing a defensive position*
here."

"*Yes, My Lord,"* says Tarleton quietly, "*but to wait for Washington to arrive and*
surround us would be disastrous. We would be subject to a siege. In that event, a loss
would bring disgrace on the army."

Cornwallis suddenly bolts to his feet and slams his fist on the table. "In that case,
the blame will fall on Sir Henry Clinton and not us!" he screams. "He is the reason we
are here! It is his order we are acting upon!"

◆   ◆   ◆

Later that same day, Cornwallis received a detailed report from Major Despart containing the complete inventory of troop strength he had previously requested. It consisted of the following twenty-two regiments with a total of 9,185 soldiers:

British Units (5,773 soldiers): 1st Battalion (light infantry); 2nd Battalion (light infantry); Brigade of Guards (infantry); 17th Regiment (infantry); 23rd Regiment (infantry); 33rd Regiment (infantry); 43rd Regiment (infantry); 2nd Battalion, 71st Regiment (infantry); 76th Regiment (infantry); 80th Regiment (infantry); Royal Artillery; 17th Light Dragoons; 23rd Light Company; 82nd Light Company; Guides and Pioneers.

German Units (2,241): Von Voit Battalion, Anspach Regiment; Von Seybothen Battalion, Anspach Regiment; Fusilier Regiment Erbprinz (Prince Hereditary; Hessian); Von Bose Regiment; Jager Company; German Artillery.

Provincial Regiments (1,171): Queen's Rangers (infantry and cavalry); British Legion (cavalry); North Carolina Volunteers (light infantry).

Also at Cornwallis's disposal were the following warships and transports of the Royal Navy anchored in the York River (including sailors and marines on board): *Charon* (forty-four guns); *Guadeloupe* (thirty-two guns); *Old Foway* (twenty-four guns); *Bonetta* (sixteen guns); *Defiance*; *Spitfire*; *Formidable*; *Rambler*; *Susannah*; and *Tarleton*.

Over the next few days, as things dried out after the rains, work resumed on the Yorktown fortifications, and Cornwallis made a series of inspections of the various regiments. As he did so, the British commander viewed a myriad of colors, histories, and nationalities.

The 17th and 23rd Regiments of Foot had been formed in England back in 1688. The 71st Regiment was Scottish, replete with bagpipes and kilts. The 76th

Regiment, better known as Lord MacDonald's Highlanders wore deep green jackets with black facings. The 80th Regiment of Foot, formed in Canada in 1779, wore standard redcoats with yellow and black facings. Most of the German regiments had arrived between 1776 and 1778. They wore blue or green jackets with yellow or green trousers. Tarleton's cavalry legion was uniformed in green with black trousers and black hats adorned with large feathered plumes.

Most of the British regiments were dressed in their familiar brick red jackets lined with white wool. Around the average soldier's waist was a belt that supported a bayonet and, sometimes, a short sword. A left shoulder belt supported a cartridge box, and backs were hitched with haversacks and knapsacks. Most soldiers wore the standard cocked hat. Grenadiers, however, distinguished themselves with tall bearskin caps adorned with front metal plates.

Nearly every British regular carried the standard infantry weapon—a fourteen- or fifteen-pound, .75-caliber flintlock rifle called the "Brown Bess." Its effective range was 300 yards, but it was considered accurate up to 100 yards. Everyone also carried a fourteen-inch-long bayonet that weighed about a pound. Ammunition consisted of one-ounce lead bullets and strong paper cartridges.

Lord Cornwallis realized that he had some of the finest, most loyal troops in Great Britain. Still he well knew that his fate rested with Sir Henry Clinton, the British navy, and a rescue operation. And over these first several days in September, he would send two more urgent dispatches (now a total of four) to Sir Henry Clinton in New York.

"Count de Grasse's fleet is within the Capes of the Chesapeake," they both read. "Forty boats with troops went up the James River on the 1st and have landed at James Island. Four ships lie at the entrance of the York River."

Cornwallis sent each dispatch via different routes. He hoped at least one would get through.

17

Sir Henry Clinton's Headquarters
Harlem Heights, New York
September 2, 1781

On the morning of September 2, 1781, Sir Henry Clinton received a flood of dispatches, messages, and letters detailing the moves of the combined American and French armies in New Jersey. George Washington, it was reported, had turned his troops (4,000 French and 2,400 rebel, it was estimated) south, away from New York, had marched them all the way to Trenton, and was now crossing the Delaware. The American commander, himself, was riding ahead of the army and making arrangements for a march through Philadelphia and on to Head of Elk, Maryland. From there they would embark on ships and sail down the Chesapeake to Virginia. The Americans had also circulated a report among governors of various colonies declaring their expectations of a French fleet off the coast of Virginia.

If that news didn't shock Clinton enough, he had only to wait until after lunch when a naval captain named Stanhope arrived at his door to report that the French fleet, under the Count de Grasse was bound for the Chesapeake Bay. Stanhope's ship, HMS *Pegasus*, had sailed up from the West Indies to report the news.

Sir Henry, of course, now realized that he had been hoodwinked by Washington. New York was not going to be the target of a summer offensive. It would be Yorktown, instead. Cornwallis was clearly in grave danger, but Clinton could do little to help him at the moment. He had just sent Benedict Arnold and a small army to Connecticut on a raiding expedition, so they were unavailable. Worse yet, just two days earlier, Thomas Graves and Samuel Hood had sailed south. With a combined nineteen big ships of the line, a few frigates, and some other smaller ships, they hoped to intercept the small flotilla of French Admiral de Barras and prevent its union with de Grasse's large fleet.

Graves and Hood began their voyage still believing that Washington's army was threatening New York and Staten Island, and they had no idea that Cornwallis was in real danger. They were going to sail all the way to the Virginia Capes, if necessary, because it seemed like the logical place to go. Admiral Graves expected to find the Chesapeake Bay empty because, in his mind, Charleston would be de Grasse's more likely destination. Admiral Hood, however, had cautioned his superior otherwise.

Back in New York, Clinton wavered about what to do. Feeling that he could not leave the city defenseless, he decided to be ready when Graves, Hood, and Arnold returned. He ordered 4,000 troops to board ships in the harbor and loaded wagons with three weeks of provisions for 8,000 men. Then he waited. In the meantime, tension filled the streets of New York as British soldiers and civilian Loyalists realized that if the Royal Navy was defeated by the French, Cornwallis might lose his entire army. That, in turn, would result in the Americans winning the revolution.

Acutely aware of that possibility, Sir Henry Clinton sent off the following dispatch to Lord Cornwallis:

> By intelligence that I have this day received, it would seem that Mr. Washington is moving an army to the southward, with an appearance of haste, and gives out that he expects the cooperation of a considerable French armament. Washington, it is said, means to go in vessels by Head of Elk down the Chesapeake. Your Lordship can best judge what time it will require. I should suppose he is at least three weeks from Trenton.
>
> Your Lordship, however, may be assured that I shall either endeavor to reinforce the army under your command by all the means within the compass of my power, or make every possible diversion in your favor. However, as Rear Admiral Graves, after being joined by Sir Samuel Hood, sailed from hence on the thirty-first with a fleet of nineteen sail—some fifty-gun ships—I flatter myself you will have little to fear from the French.

Home of Robert Morris
Philadelphia, Pennsylvania
First Week in September 1781

It is early evening at the house of the superintendent of finances, where Washington and his staff have been staying. Tilghman, Humphreys, and the general are sitting around the dining room table making plans for the army's march through the city to begin the next morning. A tankard of ale rests on the table in front of each man.

"There will be much pomp and circumstance," says Tilghman. "The entire town will turn out. And all of Congress will appear in front of Independence Hall for the review."

"Send out orders to have everyone march in single file—and slowly," says Washington.

"But, sir," says Humphreys, "that will take all day."

Washington takes a swig of ale and wipes his mouth with his shirtsleeve. "Actually, I have calculated it will take two days," he replies. "The Americans on the first day and the French the next. I want to give the impression that we have an enormous force—one that will not be easily defeated."

"Very well, General," affirms Tilghman. "I will see to it."

Just then, Robert Morris enters the house. "Good news, General," he says, as he walks briskly into the dining room. "I have just come from Minister Luzerne's home. He and General Rochambeau are hesitating to provide a loan of $20,000 in hard coin. They say they have only $40,000 in their war chest. But do not worry, I am advancing every shilling of my own. I am borrowing money from my friends, and I have pledged my personal credit. That will provide at least $12,000—all in silver."

"Robert!" exclaims Washington. "That is remarkable!"

"Indeed, sir," agrees Tilghman.

"Here! Here!" states Humphreys, raising his tankard.

Suddenly a big grin comes over Morris's face.

"What is it?" asks Washington. "What?"

"Sir, I have just received word that young Laurens is on his way here with the 16 million livres he obtained from France and Holland."

"Bravo! Bravo!" say Tilghman and Humphreys in unison, both rising to their feet.

Washington quickly stands and embraces Morris. "Good news, Robert," he says, his eyes misting. "Good news, indeed."

"We will now be able to pay the troops in hard coin, as you requested," says Morris proudly. "And we will also be able to secure all the clothing, flour, meat, salt, rum, and other supplies you have requested from our governors, legislators, and businessmen. They have donated some but will surely come up with more now that we can pay them."

Washington hears this and is overcome with emotion. Unable to speak, he simply pats Morris on the shoulder several times. Breaking the silence is a loud, emphatic knock at the front door. Tilghman walks to the entryway and answers it. He returns—reading a new dispatch. There is a pause in the room. Finally, Tilghman looks up.

"Sir, a combined British fleet of twenty ships under Graves and Hood has departed New York and is headed south."

Washington begins to pace back and forth, his hands behind his back. "They are out to intercept de Barras," he says at length. "They may also try to enter the Chesapeake first and bar de Grasse. In such a case, Cornwallis would be freed from the trap."

There is another long pause in the room as Washington continues to pace. "We must act quickly," he states, looking at Tilghman and Humphreys, who immediately pull out paper and pens and sit back down at the table. Morris stands aside. "Send an immediate message to General Lincoln. After the march through Philadelphia, he is to embark as many of his troops as possible down the Delaware. All heavy ordnance and baggage will also be transported by water, lighter pieces by land."

"Yes, sir," says Humphreys, writing quickly.

"Dispatch an officer to Christiana (Delaware) to direct the unloading of ordnance and troops at the creek there, and to repair the road to Head of Elk."

"Sir!" responds Tilghman, affirmatively.

"Send an engineering officer to Williamsburg by way of Baltimore, Georgetown, and Fredericksburg to survey the roads and to request all officials and militia to get them into quick repair."

"Yes, sir."

"Prepare letters to officials in Maryland and Virginia asking them to gather supplies along the route of the march, to furnish more boats, and to improve roads for the passage of artillery."

"Sir!"

"General Rochambeau must be provided with detailed routes and distance for his French wagons going overland."

"I will take care of it, sir."

"Send an urgent request to General Heath at West Point to send down one hundred head of cattle each week for this army."

"Sir!"

Washington pauses.

"Gentlemen, if we move quickly, we will be able to change events before Clinton and Cornwallis can communicate with each other. If we move fast enough, we will effectively make their letters to each other outdated. That will create for them both delay and confusion. De Grasse, wherever he is, will have to handle Graves and Hood. I pray that he will arrive at the Chesapeake before they do."

Washington sits down at the table and looks at Tilghman. "I must send an immediate dispatch to the Marquis de Lafayette," he says.

Tilghman grabs a new sheet of paper. "I am ready, sir."

"My dear Marquis," begins Washington. "The whole of the French army, and the American Corps, are now marching from the north. I am informed that a combined British fleet of twenty ships under Admirals Thomas Graves and Samuel Hood has departed New York and is headed south. You must be on the lookout for them. But my dear Marquis, I am distressed beyond expression to know what has become of Count de Grasse. I am also concerned about Count de Barras, who sailed from Rhode Island several days ago. Should the retreat of Lord Cornwallis by water be cut off by the arrival of either of the French fleets, I am persuaded you will do all in your power to prevent his escape by land."

Washington looks at Tilghman, who finishes writing, looks up, and nods. Then the general continues. "The means for prosecuting a siege with rapidity, energy, and success—and of supplying the troops while they are engaged in that service—have been and continue to be the great objects of my concern and attention. You see how critically important the present moment is. For my own part, I am determined to persist in my present plan. Adieu, my dear Marquis! If you get anything new from any quarter, please send it on the spur of speed, for I am almost all patience and anxiety."

◆　　◆　　◆

At one o'clock on the afternoon of the next day, September 2, 1781, American troops paraded through the city of Philadelphia. The soldiers marched single file, in a slow and solemn step to the sound of drums and fifes. Their line extended nearly two miles in length. The general officers came first. Mounted on horses and dressed in weathered military uniforms, they were followed by their aides, servants, and wagons carrying baggage. Next came the various regiments—filled with soldiers—many barefoot and wearing their tattered shirts and shredded pants. Although unkempt, the Americans marched proudly. Many had powdered their hair to look as good as possible. Some marched straight and tall. Others walked casually and waved to the people along the way. Behind every regiment were several field artillery caissons and ammunition carriages. At the end of the long line were supply wagons loaded with tents, equipment, and provisions.

The citizens of Philadelphia turned out en masse and responded enthusiastically. Thousands lined the streets, cheering loudly until their voices gave out. Ladies waved handkerchiefs from the open windows of nearly every house along the parade route. In front of Independence Hall, General Washington stood for hours with Robert Morris, members of the Continental Congress, and French diplomats.

Because the troops were ordered to march straight through the city without a halt, the parade lasted on into the night. And when it became dark, women placed clusters of glimmering candles in the windows to honor the soldiers.

The next day, September 3, it was the French army's turn. With twice the number of troops, they began in the early morning and marched well into the evening hours. In contrast to the Americans, the French marched in full parade dress uniforms—with shiny boots, sparkling colors, unfolded flags, noble steeds, and military bands playing a variety of music. The American crowds cheered enthusiastically all along the way. Men marveled at the military precision—and women blushed at the ruddy and handsome French officers. On the balcony of the State House standing next to General Washington and Count de Rochambeau were the minister from the Court of France, the Chevalier de la Luzerne, and Thomas McKean, the president of Congress. The full Continental Congress stood below on the steps of Independence Hall.

That evening the entire French army crossed the Schuylkill River on a floating bridge and encamped in a huge green meadow on the riverside. The next day a crowd of 20,000 Philadelphians viewed an extensive military drill staged by the Soissonais Regiment. Dressed in white and rose-colored silk uniforms with pink and white plumes tossing in their hats, the French regiment elicited oohs and aahs, and wild cheers with their precision movements and disciplined drills.

The next day, both armies resumed their march south toward Head of Elk by way of Chester, Pennsylvania, and Wilmington, Delaware. It would take three days to march the entire fifty-five miles. While Rochambeau's staff traveled by boat down the Delaware to view Forts Mifflin and Mercer along the river, Washington and his aides rode ahead of the main army to oversee the securing of boats and supplies for the embarkation down the Chesapeake Bay. The two generals planned to meet at Head of Elk within two days.

The Ville de Paris, *Flagship of Count de Grasse*
Chesapeake Bay, Virginia
September 2, 1781

The French frigate carrying Chief Engineer Louis Duportail, who had been dispatched by Washington in mid-August to locate Admiral de Grasse's fleet, finally found it in the Chesapeake Bay at five o'clock in the morning. The sight of the entire French fleet "makes me forget all the hardships I have experienced," Duportail told de Grasse as he boarded the flagship.

After the French admiral read Washington's letter and learned that the combined army was en route to Virginia, he immediately rescinded his offer to Lafayette to land 1,800 more men for the immediate storming of Yorktown. The American general's first scenario was a better option, he believed. "If the enemy should be found with the greater part of their force in Virginia," Washington had written, "we should, without loss of time, attack and lay siege to them with our united force."

Acting without hesitation, de Grasse dispatched one of his cutters, the *Serpent*, up the bay to Head of Elk with a message to Washington. "The coming armies from the North have changed my plans," he wrote. "My first thought was to join the Marquis de Lafayette and attack Cornwallis at once. I have, however, suspended my plans until your arrival. Upon your orders, I have this day directed eighty transport vessels to the head of the Chesapeake Bay to meet your army."

The Marquis de Lafayette's Headquarters
Williamsburg, Virginia
September 4, 1781

Around noon, the Marquis de Lafayette marched his troops into Williamsburg and encamped on the campus of the College of William and Mary. Over the last several days, he had moved them fifty miles northwest from Portsmouth so he could keep a closer eye on Lord Cornwallis—now only fifteen miles distant. Along the way, General Anthony Wayne had met the Marquis de St. Simon's 3,200 French troops when they landed at Jamestown Island, and then headed inland to join with Lafayette. Thanks to a hefty infusion of nearly 3,000 Virginia militiamen, the young marquis' force had now grown to more than 8,000. Although ready to push closer to Yorktown, he first sent scouts out in all directions to spy on the British.

The first intelligence reports noted that after the French fleet arrived, the British had laid out a line of fortifications in an arc around Yorktown and half of the army was put to work at a pace that went on day and night with great intensity. Colonel Thomas Dundas of the 80th Foot Regiment was placed in charge of the works on Gloucester Point where he conducted regular foraging expeditions to the north. And Banastre Tarleton's cavalry was making daily patrols toward Williamsburg on the Yorktown side. Some of these patrols, it was reported, were more like killing raids where pillaging and the murdering of "rebels" were taking place.

Of particular interest to Lafayette were the intelligence reports of desertion among Cornwallis's troops. Over the past few days, numerous deserters had been punished by being forced to run a gauntlet with more than 300 men flailing away at them with whips and chains. Rumors were rampant in the British camp that Lafayette would soon attack, and that Cornwallis had no strategy to escape from the terrible position in which they found themselves.

Now Lafayette cautiously began to move some of his forces closer to Yorktown. He ordered Brigadier General George Weedon, in command of the Virginia Militia, to move near Gloucester Point and harass the foraging parties there. He carefully placed pickets in areas protected by ravines and creeks along the edges of the York and James Rivers. And concerned that Cornwallis might try to flee to the Carolinas by crossing to the south bank of the James River, Lafayette posted several hundred troops in the vicinity of West Point, Virginia, twenty-five miles above Yorktown. In general, the young French commander's plan was to keep an eye on the British, harass their foraging operations, and wait for Washington and Rochambeau to arrive. If Cornwallis's troops attempted to escape, he planned to quickly throw a barrier of soldiers across the Yorktown peninsula and try to push them back.

As the French marines under the command of the Marquis de St. Simon began to venture out into the field on various patrols, they were shocked to observe some of the savage deeds perpetrated by the British. It was one thing to see fields and pastures littered with the carcasses of slain cattle and horses, but they were truly horrified at what they saw in one particular plantation house. As one soldier noted in his diary: "A pregnant woman had been murdered in her bed from several bayonet stabs. The barbarians had cut open each of her breasts and written above the bed's canopy: 'Thou shalt never give birth to a rebel.'"

Back at the Williamsburg encampment, hundreds of French and American troops had come down with malaria—including St. Simon and Lafayette. Suffering from high fevers and nausea, both commanders were confined to bed for extended periods of time. During this time, a frustrated Lafayette would write to George Washington: "Perhaps I am dying of old age since two days ago I rang in my twenty-fourth birthday."

Even Anthony Wayne, second in command to Lafayette, was knocked out of action by a freak occurrence. After having gone out by himself on a reconnaissance mission, Wayne was making his way back into the encampment at ten o'clock one night when he failed to acknowledge a challenge by a young American sentry. The sentry immediately fired a shot from his rifle and struck General Wayne in the thigh. Fortunately, the bulled only grazed the bone. But Wayne, nonetheless, was confined to a hospital bed for several days where he constantly cursed the young man who shot him and vowed to have him brought before a firing squad. In the end, the sentry was found to have only been doing his duty.

Chester, Pennsylvania
September 5, 1781

George Washington and his staff are riding on horseback three miles south of Chester, Pennsylvania, a small country village on the banks of the Delaware River. It is late morning, a hot, dry day. A few scattered clouds float against a hazy blue sky. Dust rises in the distance. A single rider galloping at full speed rushes up to the group.

"General Washington! General Washington!" *the rider shouts excitedly.* "I have an urgent dispatch from Baltimore, sir."

He takes several letters out of his saddlebag and hands them to the commander in chief. "General Mordecai Gist of the Maryland Militia ordered me to ride day and night to find you, sir. These arrived on the French frigate Serpent yesterday evening."

Washington eagerly reads the dispatches. "De Grasse is here!" *he shouts.* "He has blockaded the Chesapeake with his fleet!"

Washington's aides begin to whoop and holler in excitement.

"Well done, young man!" *the general says to the dispatch rider.* "Well done!"

"Thank you, General," *comes the reply.* "As I was riding out of town, the word had already begun to spread. Muskets were firing in celebration. The city was illuminated. I'm sure the taverns roared with toasts."

"Indeed!" *smiles Washington.* "Ride safely back to Baltimore, son. Tell them I will be there in a few days."

"Yes, sir."

As the young rider turns and heads south, Washington spurs his horse back toward Chester. "We must meet General Rochambeau at the docks and give him this glorious news," *he shouts excitedly. The staff follows.*

"The entire French fleet will certainly prevent Cornwallis from receiving any reinforcements by sea," *yells Tench Tilghman.*

"Lafayette and the troops of St. Simon should be able to hold him at Yorktown," *chirps David Humphreys.*

"Yes," *agrees Washington.* "We only have to hurry our armies to Yorktown to begin the siege."

About an hour later, the general and his party are off their horses and standing at the Chester wharf beside the Delaware River, where they know Rochambeau will soon be arriving. Tilghman spots a boat in the distance. "There they are, General!" he shouts. "There they are!"

Washington runs to the edge of the dock. With his hat in one hand and a white handkerchief in the other, he begins waving his arms in circles over his head. Then he starts jumping up and down.

"De Grasse is here! De Grasse is here!" he shouts. "We are in the Chesapeake! We are in the Chesapeake."

On the boat, the Frenchmen begin pointing toward the dock. Can that be General Washington, they wonder? This tall figure dressed in blue and buff; this man who is normally so stoic, so serious, so noble—now letting out his emotions like a small child? "I never saw a man moved by a greater or more sincere joy," Count Mathieu Dumas would later recall.

When the boat docks, Washington runs up to Rochambeau and gives him a bear hug. "De Grasse and his entire fleet are in the Chesapeake," he says with a broad smile. "St. Simon has landed 3,000 troops and joined Lafayette. We've done it!"

Rochambeau, Von Closen, Dumas, and Deux-Ponts all fling their hats in the air and shout for joy. They hug their American counterparts and slap each other's backs in congratulations.

As they all walk off the dock together, Rochambeau looks at Washington. "This will end the war, mon amis. N'est ce pas?"

"Yes, my friend," replies Washington. "It may very well end our long struggle. It may very well."

◆   ◆   ◆

Word of de Grasse's arrival in the Chesapeake spread quickly among the American and French armies that were strung out for miles along the roads. They began yelling, singing, and stepping up the pace of the march. When word reached Philadelphia, crowds surged into the streets. Guns were fired into the air. Beer and ale flowed generously. Several citizens preached funeral orations for Lord Cornwallis and uttered lamentations on the grief and distress of Tories everywhere. And when French Minister la Luzerne heard the news, he immediately told Robert Morris that a $20,000 loan from his war chest would no longer be a problem.

18

Atlantic Ocean
Off the Coast of Virginia
September 5, 1781

As the morning sunrise breaks over the water, Count de Grasse's flagship, Ville de Paris, *sits quietly in the waters of Lynnhaven Bay, near the entrance to the Chesapeake, its anchor cables clanging lightly back and forth, its varnished sides glistening in the sunlight. At 8:00 AM, a lookout in the crow's nest points toward the open seas. He sees the scouting frigate* Aigrette *flashing signals and raising flags. A few British ships are sighted coming from the north. There appear to be numerous sails behind them in the distance. Admiral de Grasse is informed and immediately initiates action. Flag signals go up, pipes shrill warnings throughout the French fleet, decks are cleared, guns are made ready, and preparations get under way.*

◆　　◆　　◆

At 9:30 AM, *a lookout on HMS* Solebay, *the lead ship in the British fleet of Admirals Graves and Hood, summons his captain. "Sir," he reports, "there appear to be many masts about ten miles ahead inside the Chesapeake Bay."*

"You are mistaken," replies the captain. "It must be the charred pines you see. They burn them for tar and leave the trunks standing."

"No, sir. They are ships."

"Well, then, it must be the small fleet of Admiral de Barras we have been looking for."

"I do not believe so, Captain. There are too many sails."

"Here, let me see that," says the captain as he grabs the lookout's spyglass and peers through it toward the bay. His eyebrows rise. He lowers the spyglass and squints his eyes landward. He looks again. Suddenly a look of incredulity comes over his face.

"My God!" he exclaims. "It's an entire fleet! It must be de Grasse!" The captain orders alarm signal flags raised up the mast. Then he turns his ship and sails back toward the British fleet.

Admiral Thomas Graves is in his flagship HMS London, *eighteen miles northeast when he receives the message. The French fleet has been sighted. They are at anchor in three lines—inside the bay, not outside. It is not de Barras. It is de Grasse. The nineteen ships of the British squadron are strung out in a line more than five miles long, so Graves immediately gives the signal to close the line of battle. Then he leads the fleet forward to see exactly what he is up against.*

◆   ◆   ◆

By 11:30 AM, *de Grasse has maneuvered his ships into a line headed for the ten-mile opening between the Virginia Capes. He orders his swiftest ships into the lead, but they move slowly due to the incoming tide. During this delay, the French admiral determines his plan of action. His mission, he believes, is to prevent the British fleet from rescuing or reinforcing Cornwallis. To be successful, therefore, he does not have to win an all-out victory. He only needs to achieve a draw. De Grasse decides to sail south and lure the enemy away from the Chesapeake. That, in turn, should allow de Barras's smaller squadron to slip into the bay and unload guns and provisions. After several days at sea, de Grasse might next sail away under cover of darkness and join de Barras. The British fleet would then be formidably outnumbered.*

By 12:45 PM, *the* Ville de Paris, *in the center of the French line, clears Cape Henry and heads south into the Atlantic. Graves, meanwhile, has approached cautiously. He sees that his fleet of nineteen ships of the line is both outgunned and outmanned. The French have five more ships and, according to his calculations, 300 more guns and as many as 6,000 more sailors. But the English fleet has the advantage of both wind and tide. And their copper-hulled ships are quicker and more easily maneuvered. Graves hesitates. Rather than attack, he merely sails his line parallel to that of the French. Meanwhile, Admiral Samuel Hood paces back and forth on the deck of his ship, HMS* Barfleur, *seething in anger that his superior has allowed de Grasse to sail unmolested out of the Chesapeake and into the open ocean.*

◆   ◆   ◆

For more than three hours, both fleets drifted southeastward, making various maneuvers and sizing each other up. Finally, at 4:00 PM, Graves put up the signal flag to attack. This order called for the captain of each ship to engage the French vessel directly opposite him. In a disastrous oversight, however, Graves neglected to lower the flag reflecting his previous order to sail ahead in line. While the admiral's flagship, HMS *London*, turned toward the enemy, many of the other captains were confused by the conflicting signals. Admiral Hood, for instance, chose to obey the original signal and kept the entire rear guard in line. As a result, the British fleet became a jumbled mess.

The *London* fired several broadsides that fell short and splashed into the sea. When Graves realized that he was the only one firing, he ran up additional signals in an attempt to restore order. But that only confused his captains even more. At last, he took down his original "line ahead" signal, and the rest of the fleet became engaged. But it was too little too late, as the French fleet quickly took advantage of British disorganization by maneuvering within musket range and opening fire.

The French aimed their cannon high, and a number of masts and mainsails on several British ships were hit hard. The English, however, aimed low to impact the wooden hulls of the French ships. Three or four French ships dropped out of line under heavy fire. At 6:15 PM, after more than two hours of fighting, Admiral Graves gave the signal to disengage. When the British ships ceased fire and de Grasse followed suit, silence fell upon the ocean waters.

The British, by far, got the worst of the battle. Seven ships had suffered serious damage, and Graves calculated that his original disadvantage of five ships was now at least ten. He had also suffered 350 casualties. De Grasse, however, had not sustained any serious ship damage and had sustained 209 casualties, mostly wounded.

By the time the sun went down that night, both fleets were sailing parallel to each other in the same line of battle—on a southerly course, about ten miles southeast of Cape Henry and six miles offshore. French and English gunners remained at their battle stations with matches burning. Lanterns glowed on the decks of all the ships as the two fleets simply sailed along—always in sight of each other.

Sir Henry Clinton's Headquarters
Harlem Heights, New York
September 6, 1781

Captain Dawkins is writing at the desk in the back study as Sir Henry Clinton paces nervously back and forth. The general's words are halting, hesitant, and staccato. His hands wring nervously, alternately clenched in his front and behind his back. He has just received several dispatches from Lord Cornwallis, including the coded message on the back of several Continental bank notes.

"As I find by your communiqués that de Grasse has, ah, er, got into the Chesapeake, and I, um, have no doubt that Washington is moving with at least, er, ah,

6,000 French and rebel troops against you…" Clinton takes a long pause and continues.

"I think the best way to relieve you is to join you, um, as soon as possible, um, with a force that can be spared from here—which is about, um, 4,000 men."

"Have you got all that Dawkins?" asks Clinton.

"Yes, sir. I do."

"Do you have any suggestions for other information I should include, Captain?" asks Clinton.

"Perhaps the news from Europe, sir," responds Dawkins.

"Oh, yes, yes. 'By accounts from Europe, we have every reason to expect Admiral Digby hourly on the coast. He has beaten a superior French fleet at St. Jago and, I believe, is proceeding here.'"

Clinton pauses again. He looks at Dawkins, who finishes writing and merely looks up, not offering any other suggestions. Clinton starts pacing and begins to dictate again.

"I beg Your Lordship to let me know, as soon as possible, your ideas on how the troops being readied for the Chesapeake may be best employed for your relief, according to the state of circumstances when you receive this letter. Uh, um, I shall not, however, wait to receive your answer, should I in the meantime hear that the Chesapeake passage is open.

"That will do, Dawkins," says Clinton, who then promptly walks out of the room.

New London, Connecticut
September 6, 1781

General Benedict Arnold landed 2,000 men and 300 cavalry at the mouth of New London Harbor. Aided by a number of local Tories, his force successfully took Forts Trumbull and Griswold from the small forces and militia posted there. At the conclusion of the battle, several American officers were brutally killed after surrendering which, in turn, sparked a riot that left seventy-five more Americans dead. Arnold then plundered and burned the small town of New London, leaving hundreds homeless and destroying the local economy.

Word of the burning of New London spread rapidly through the colonies, including the rumor that Benedict Arnold had stood in the tallest church belfry and watched with pleasure as the fires raged. From there, it was said, he could see his hometown of Norwich, only twelve miles in the distance. This event cemented Benedict Arnold's name in history as the archetypal traitor to his country. Fearing for his life, Arnold and his wife departed for London (by way of Canada) a short time later.

Head of Elk, Maryland
September 6–8, 1781

When Washington arrived at Head of Elk, the principal point for shipments by water to Williamsburg, Virginia, he immediately rode to the waterfront and surveyed the harbor. To his shock, there were not nearly enough boats to transport the army south. He calculated there were barely enough to handle 2,000 soldiers. Four thousand would have to march to Baltimore or Annapolis and hope that enough boats, including those de Grasse had sent, would be available.

Over the next several days, Washington sent off a flurry of letters to prominent Maryland merchants, asking them to convey "all available crafts and vessels to Baltimore." He pleaded with the governors of Maryland and Virginia to raise enough supplies to feed both the livestock and soldiers headed their way. And he sent a note of congratulations to the Count de Grasse for his successful arrival in the Chesapeake, along with a status update of the march.

As the combined American and French armies began arriving at Head of Elk, they were extremely disappointed to learn of the boat shortage. They had marched 200 miles in fifteen days, and now they would have to march even farther. Washington countered their discontent by doing two things. First, he sent out a circular formally conveying the recent good news. "It is with the highest pleasure and satisfaction," wrote Washington, "that I announce the arrival of Count de Grasse in the Chesapeake with a very formidable naval and land force. As no circumstance could possibly have happened more opportunely at this point in time, no prospect has ever had more promise of success. Nothing but our lack of exertions can blast the pleasing prospects before us. I call upon all the gallant officers and the brave and faithful soldiers I have the honor to command to exert your utmost abilities in the cause of our country—and to share with me the difficulties, dangers, and glory of our present enterprise." Next, the American commander in chief did something that had not been done for the entire six-year duration of the war—he paid all of his men one month's salary in hard coins. Regiment by regiment, the troops were mustered together, and the heads of money kegs were knocked open so that everybody could see the silver half crowns roll out on the ground. Then the money was quickly distributed among the ranks. According to one American officer, these two acts raised the troops' spirits such that there was "scarcely a sick man to be found anywhere."

Washington next began directing the embarkation of troops from Head of Elk. He ordered the advance units under Hamilton and Scammel to crowd aboard open boats and begin their journey down the Chesapeake. The rest of the boats were filled by the Duke de Lauzun's "shock" infantry, French grenadiers and chasseurs, and some artillery and siege tools. Washington then directed the rest of the army to march to Baltimore and Annapolis, where he expected adequate shipping to be present.

After delegating command of the march to General Benjamin Lincoln, Washington and Rochambeau awoke early on the morning of September 8, 1781, and rode ahead of the troops to Baltimore. But the American commander galloped so fast that the French officers quickly fell behind. Only Billy and David Humphreys could keep up for the entire fifty-seven-mile ride.

Just before sundown that evening, a group of local militiamen met the general on the northern outskirts of Baltimore and escorted him into town. As word spread of his arrival, crowds rushed into the streets and local officials quickly assembled to give their leader a formal welcome replete with speeches and artillery salutes. As darkness fell on Baltimore, candles and torches illuminated the city in Washington's honor. Rather than basking in the accolades, however, he spent most of his time speaking with anyone who owned a boat or a ship, begging them to help in the army's transport down the Chesapeake. It was after midnight when Washington finally laid his head down on a pillow at the Fountain Inn.

Atlantic Ocean
South of the Virginia Capes
September 7, 1781

After the battle at sea, French and British fleets continue to sail steadily south, always remaining in sight of each other. Satisfied with the status quo, Count de Grasse will not engage the enemy, and Admiral Graves cannot engage because too many of his ships are damaged. The British commander, instead, uses the time to make emergency repairs. Crews are sent to mend the damaged main topmast of the HMS Intrepid. *The HMS* Terrible *has taken on so much water, it is finally stripped and burned.*

Graves also starts a feud with Admiral Samuel Hood by sending him a written reprimand for his inaction during the battle. When Hood lodges a formal protest, a senior officer conference is called.

"Why didn't you bear down and engage?" Graves demands to know.

"Because you had the signal up for 'line ahead,'" Hood responds defensively.

"That was only to push the ships ahead of me forward," retorts Graves.

"Sir, you were flying contradictory signals!" says Hood.

"The original flag had flown for only five minutes, Admiral! You should have engaged when it was taken down!"

"Your 'line ahead' flag flew for more than an hour, sir!" screams Hood, slamming his fist down on the table. "If you had pulled it down immediately, I would have given the order to engage, we would have gone into close action, and the van of the enemy would have been cut to pieces."

Both commanders become red in the face and have to be calmed by the other officers. Graves at last regains control of himself and asks Hood's opinion about what action to take next. Hood responds that, in his emotional state, he can offer no opinion, but he warns Graves that de Grasse might turn sail and head back to the Chesapeake.

◆   ◆   ◆

Over in the French fleet, Count de Grasse sends out formal letters of appreciation and commendation to all his captains for their conduct during the battle. He, too, calls a conference of his senior offices at which they discuss in detail all options—including getting back to the Chesapeake ahead of the British fleet.

"Whatever we decide in the next few days," says de Grasse at the conclusion of the meeting, "I want you all to direct the squadron under your command as if it were a full fleet attached to my own. We are all in this together."

Eutaw Springs, South Carolina
September 8, 1781

Nathanael Greene's army made a surprise attack on a British force of less than 2,000 men camped on the banks of the Santee River. With an overwhelming force that included seasoned Continentals from Maryland, Delaware, and Virginia, Carolina militiamen, and the cavalry of "Light Horse" Harry Lee's Legion, Greene was on the verge of a major victory when British heroics turn the tide of the battle. The American southern commander was once again forced to withdraw and allow the enemy to occupy the battleground. As in previous fights, however, the British got the worst of it. As a matter of fact, the redcoat losses of 693 killed and wounded were the highest of any army in any battle of the American Revolution.

Badly crippled, the British quickly withdrew to the safety of Charleston, Great Britain's only remaining occupied post in South Carolina and one of only five fortified posts left in America. Nathanael Greene had once again lived up to his mantra: "We fight, get beat, rise, and fight again!"

Mount Vernon, Virginia
September 9, 1781

On Sunday evening, September 9, 1781, an hour after nightfall, three dust-covered riders on horseback turn left off the main road and canter up a narrow, tree-lined pathway. Fallen leaves flutter behind the horses as they move along. A few minutes later, they come upon a huge white house with pillared arcades resting on a high bluff above the Potomac River. They are at Mount Vernon, George Washington's 8,000-acre plantation home located eight miles south of Alexandria, Virginia. General Washington, David Humphreys, and Billy have just completed a vigorous sixty-six-mile ride that began in Baltimore before sunrise. This is the first time Washington has been home in more than six years. He has taken the advice of his aides who suggested that, as it was on the way, he stop here for a few days on his journey south to York-town.

As the three riders pull into the small courtyard and dismount, there is movement at the windows of the house. The front door soon opens. Stepping outside are a small woman and a taller young man. They are followed by a young woman holding a baby and three little girls dressed in nightgowns. Martha Washington, the general's wife, rushes up to her husband. They embrace. She stands on tiptoes to put her arms around his neck. He leans down and kisses her gently on the cheek. Jacky Custis, Martha's son, follows and shakes his stepfather's hand. Jacky's wife, Nelly, trails with her new baby and daughters. These are grandchildren that have been born while Washington has been away at war. He has never before laid eyes on them. The general kisses his daughter-in-law on the forehead and then playfully looks for the girls who are hiding behind their mother's skirt. Jacky Custis greets David Humphreys warmly. They follow Washington, Martha, Nelly, and the children into the house. Billy leads the horses off to the stables. He will sleep in his old bed tonight—over in the slave quarters.

Washington washes up and visits with his family. He begins making plans for the visit of General Rochambeau and his staff who are expected to arrive the next day. He informs Martha that he would like to entertain them with a banquet and invite the neighbors. Mount Vernon's servants are assembled and given appropriate instructions. One of them later writes in his diary that the general's face was noticeably "changed by the storms of campaigns and the mighty burdens during his absence."

Before retiring, Washington asks Humphreys into his study where he dictates a letter to Lieutenant Peter Waggoner of the Fairfax County Militia. "Instead of having the militia march to join Lafayette, I wish that they might be employed in repairing the roads from Georgetown to Occoquan," writes Washington. "The wagons of the French and American armies, the cavalry, and the cattle will proceed by that route in a few days. I have just traveled this road and the wagons, especially, will not be able to pass through easily. To do this without a moment's loss of time is of essential importance."

Then Washington himself pens a brief note to the Marquis de Lafayette stating that he and Rochambeau plan to be at Williamsburg by the fourteenth of September. "I hope you will keep Lord Cornwallis safe, without provisions or forage, until we arrive," writes Washington.

Mount Vernon, Virginia
September 11, 1781

The sun is low on the horizon behind the general's house. The ever-flowing Potomac River below is already in the shadows. It's a quiet evening, pleasant, with a light fall breeze out of the north. Washington is seated on the back portico with Rochambeau, Jacky Custis, and the Chevalier de Chastellux. It's been a long day of festivities, but all the neighbors have now left. The four men are enjoying the view of the river and having an amiable conversation—de Chastellux translating for Rochambeau.

"Monsieur Custis," says Rochambeau, addressing Washington's stepson, "I understand you wish to accompany us to Yorktown."

"Yes, sir," Jacky replies. "I burn to see my country win a victory. I would like to contribute in some way."

"Has your mother given her blessing to this?" asks a surprised Washington.

"She has, sir."

"Very well. But I would like you to stay back of the action, for you have young children who need rearing."

"I understand, Father."

"Perhaps Monsieur Custis may serve on my staff as a captain and aide for the upcoming campaign," offers Rochambeau kindly. "We will look after him."

"I will consent to this arrangement," says Washington. "But there must be no sign of favoritism in any way. And Jacky, you must follow the orders of the count. Is that understood?"

"It is, sir," replies Jacky with delight. "Thank you."

After a pause, Rochambeau looks over at Washington. "Mon general," he says, "I have today been informed by several of your neighbors that you have not been at this place in more than six years."

"Yes, that's true," Washington replies. "I was last here on May 4, 1775, when I rode to Philadelphia to serve in the Congress. When appointed to my present position, I rode directly to Boston to fortify Dorchester Heights."

"Boston was under siege at the time, was it not?" asks Chastellux.

"Yes," replies Washington. "We labored on the fortifications all night long, and when the British awoke the next morning, they thought we had a force of more than 20,000 mounted on the heights. After a few days, they slipped away into the night, afraid they were to be attacked by a superior force."

"Am I to understand that you freed Boston without firing a single shot?" asks Rochambeau.

"Well, I would not phrase it exactly that way. But it is true, there were no major battles fought."

"Might I ask a more personal question, mon amis?" requests Rochambeau.

"Please," replies Washington.

"Well, I'm aware that one of your officers requested a liberty before the commencement of this campaign, and that you granted it. Why do you allow your subordinates to take time off to go home when you, yourself, do not?"

Washington looks out toward the Potomac and draws in a deep breath. "People need to spend time with their families," he replies. "To be away from home is a hardship for most of our soldiers, many of whom have served proudly for six years. If I do not let them go home periodically, they will not stay with the cause. They must see their loved ones and be reassured that all is well with their families."

"But you do not do the same," says Rochambeau. "Do you not think your men have your fortitude?"

"We must make the best of mankind as they are," replies Washington, "since we cannot have them as we wish."

"But why have you been in the field all these years without a respite for yourself?"

"The situation has been daunting and dangerous," replies Washington. "At any moment, the Revolution could have collapsed. I felt it necessary to be in the field so that did not happen. At the same time, our brave soldiers have inspired me. The enemy could have tracked us from White Marsh to Valley Forge by the blood of our men's feet. I simply cannot leave troops so dedicated. I cannot."

Washington pauses a moment, looking alternately down at his feet and up toward the river. "I stay here also because I am committed to this cause," he says. "You have seen Jacky's children—my grandchildren. I want them to grow up and live in a free and independent country, where they have every opportunity for advancement and happiness. I do it for them—and for my fellow citizens who have children of their own. I do it because I care, because someone has to do it—and because it is the right thing to do."

19

Lord Cornwallis's Headquarters
Yorktown, Virginia
September 8, 1781

A whaleboat carrying Sir Henry Clinton's letter of September 2nd slipped unde-tected into the Chesapeake Bay at night and pulled up to the Yorktown docks. This was the first communiqué where, after learning of Washington's move south, Clinton promised to "either reinforce the army under your command by all means within the compass of my power, or make every possible diversion in your favor." The whaleboat did not carry Clinton's more recent and less confi-dent letter of September 6th, written after he learned that the French fleet was in the Chesapeake.

Cornwallis immediately sat down and wrote a reply. He began by pointing out that he had already made several attempts to inform Clinton "that the entire French West Indies fleet under de Grasse had entered the capes on the twenty-ninth." Cornwallis then mentioned that there were only seven French ships in the bay as de Grasse had departed with the majority of his fleet—and that naval gun-fire had been heard off the Capes on the fifth and sixth. "Washington is said to be shortly expected," Cornwallis also wrote, "and his troops are intended to be brought by water from the Head of Elk under protection of French ships. The Marquis de Lafayette is at or near Williamsburg and has been reinforced by St. Simon's troops, said to be 3,800 men." Lord Cornwallis concluded by stating that he was "working very hard at the redoubts of this place," that "the army was not very sickly," and that he had "provisions for six weeks."

◆   ◆   ◆

The next day, shortly after the whaleboat bearing Cornwallis's message to Clinton sailed out of the Chesapeake Bay, the French fleet from Newport sailed in. On the way down from Rhode Island, Count de Barras had circled his ships and sailed far and wide to avoid the British fleet. Now he had seized the opportu-nity of luring Admiral Graves out to sea.

De Barras quickly sailed up the James River and unloaded food provisions, the large guns of the French siege artillery, and an additional 600 French soldiers for Lafayette. Afterward, he sent all the transports he had up the Chesapeake to Baltimore and Annapolis for use in moving Washington's troops south. Then de Barras took his large ships back down into the heart of the Chesapeake to await the return of de Grasse or the British fleet.

Over the next forty-eight hours, daily British cavalry patrols would report to Lord Cornwallis not only the arrival of de Barras, but that Lafayette had been joined by Baron Von Steuben, Virginia Governor Thomas Nelson Jr., and their accompanying regiments of Virginia Militia. Rumors of General Washington's approaching rebel army now swept through the British encampment, and panicked soldiers attempted to flee.

"There was another punishment for desertion early this morning," wrote a German officer in his diary. "The man had to run the gauntlet sixteen times. He was quite pitifully cut and beaten and had to be led all day by two noncommissioned officers because he could not walk."

Atlantic Ocean
Off the Coast of Cape Hatteras, North Carolina
September 9–10, 1781

The French and British fleets had sailed almost 100 miles south of the Chesapeake Bay. They had begun to drift away from each other and were now separated by seven or eight miles of open ocean. The morning had been dark and windy; the afternoon marked by violent thunderstorms. By nightfall, rain was still coming down hard.

On the deck of the *Ville de Paris*, Count de Grasse peered through his spyglass, straining to see any sign of the enemy. He saw no lights through the rain and darkness. Realizing that the British could not see him either, de Grasse seized his opportunity. He gave an order for the French fleet to turn northward and head back to the Chesapeake Bay under full sail. It was a bold move, one that would test the durability of his officers and men. They were going to sail all night long, as fast as they could, through a wind-tossed, wave-ridden storm.

◆   ◆   ◆

At dawn the next morning, Admiral Samuel Hood looked through his own telescope into what were now clear skies and calm waters. But he saw no sign of Grasse. Hood immediately sent a sarcastic note from the HMS *Barfleur* over to

Admiral Graves on the HMS *London.* "I flatter myself you will forgive the liberty I take in asking whether you have any knowledge of where the French fleet is?" wrote Hood. "I am inclined to think the aim of Grasse is the Chesapeake. If he should enter the bay, will he not succeed in providing aid to the rebels?"

Graves responded by quickly calling another conference. Hood, of course, urged that the British fleet head north with all deliberate speed, even though it was probably too late. Graves agreed and turned the fleet around. But believing he really had no chance to beat the French back to the Chesapeake, Graves did not give the order to sail at full speed.

Virginia, Maryland, and the Upper Chesapeake Bay *September 11–12, 1781*

Shortly after sunrise, General Washington and his party (including aides Tilghman and Trumbull, who had finally caught up to their boss) left Mount Vernon. A carriage was provided for Rochambeau and Chastellux so they could travel as comfortably as possible. Jacky Custis rode with them. Early in the morning, the group crossed the Occoquan River by ferry to Woodbridge. Just before Dumfries, they were met by a courier with a dispatch relating that the British fleet had arrived off the Virginia Capes. In response, Count de Grasse had hoisted his sails, left the Chesapeake, and vanished into the ocean. When Washington read this, he experienced a shooting pain from one of his infected teeth and immediately raised his hand to his jaw. He quickly dismounted and, with Tilghman's assistance, wrote several urgent messages. Because of the danger of the enemy sweeping up the bay, he ordered all transports carrying troops not to leave Baltimore or Annapolis until further notice. Those who had already embarked were directed to be recalled until the outcome of the sea battle was known. Washington then sent the courier north, and he and his party continued their journey south.

◆   ◆   ◆

Dr. James Thacher, traveling with Scammel's advance corps, was heading down the Elk River on a small schooner with four officers and sixty men. "We are so deeply laden with cannon, mortars, and other ordnance," noted Thacher in his journal, "that we will be in considerable danger if we encounter rough weather." When the schooner finally reached the town of Annapolis (located at the mouth of the Severn River where it falls into the Chesapeake Bay), a severe rainstorm forced the passengers to spend a night on shore.

By seven the next morning, they were again headed down the Chesapeake. But after sailing only four miles, an express ship ordered them back to Annapolis. "This is in consequence of intelligence of a naval action between the British and French fleets," wrote Thacher. "Our safety requires that we should remain in port until the event of the battle is known. Should the enemy get possession of the Chesapeake, we shall be unable to proceed on our voyage—and our expedition will be entirely defeated."

◆   ◆   ◆

Along the west side of the Chesapeake Bay, 4,000 American and French troops were marching south in Maryland with consistent progress—twenty miles from Bush Town to Lower Ferry on one day; twenty miles from Lower Ferry to White Marsh on the next.

Baron Cromot du Bourg, an aide to General Rochambeau, recorded in his diary that his small party marched "over a country covered with woods and roads that must be very bad in the late fall." A rainstorm set in and a very dark night fell fast. Du Bourg's men took a wrong turn and got lost in the countryside. They saw a distant light, walked toward it, and ended up at the house of a Mr. Wacker, aged forty-five. He was inside with his eighty-year-old mother, two women about thirty years old, and a teenage girl.

"At first we frightened the whole household terribly," wrote du Bourg. "But after we assured them that we were French officers who had lost our way, little by little, their faces assumed their natural expressions. They served us an excellent supper, they gave us excellent beds, and our horses were perfectly well treated. When it came to the question of pay, he would not accept more than five shillings. He was a good American patriot."

Du Bourg and the rest of the French column reached Annapolis in a couple of days. But, due to Washington's orders, they had to wait—taking the extra time to repair shoes and uniforms.

◆   ◆   ◆

Washington and Rochambeau continued their ride through Dumfries, Stafford Courthouse, and across the Rappahannock River to Fredericksburg, Virginia. The next day, September 13, they left before sunrise and rode a full fifty-three miles to Hanover Courthouse where they spent the night. Washington was determined to be in Williamsburg the next day.

Chesapeake Bay
September 13, 1781

As dawn broke over the open ocean, the French fleet sailed into the Chesapeake and joined forces with Admiral de Barras. Count de Grasse strategically positioned his ships so as to provide a solid defense against any possible attack by the British fleet. Scouting vessels were intermittently scattered along the Capes to keep a lookout. The James and York Rivers were blockaded. And in a show of force, de Grasse concentrated the majority of the thirty-five battleships he now commanded in the center of the bay so that Admirals Graves and Hood would see they were hopelessly outnumbered. He hoped that would discourage them from any thoughts of attacking.

◆   ◆   ◆

Late that afternoon, the British fleet arrived off the Virginia Capes, and Admiral Graves saw all the French sails in the bay. Distraught at the situation, he sent a note over to Admiral Hood asking his opinion of what to do now.

"I would be very glad to send an opinion," Hood responded, "but I really don't know what to say in the truly lamentable state to which we have brought ourselves."

As French lookouts watched from a safe distance, Graves called another officer's conference on his flagship. The meeting was short and gloomy. No one even thought about an attack. "It appears that given the position of the enemy," said Graves, "given the present condition of our fleet, and given the fact that it is impractical to think we can give any real aid to Lord Cornwallis, I do not see that we have much choice in this matter."

At this point, neither Graves nor Hood understood the real fix that Cornwallis was in. For all they knew, Washington was still on the outskirts of New York. They were unaware that the combined American and French armies had turned south and were closing in on Yorktown.

Admiral Graves then gave the order for the British fleet "to proceed with all dispatch for New York." And as the sun set over the Virginia countryside, the white masts of the British ships of war slowly disappeared over the northern horizon.

Sir Henry Clinton's Headquarters
Harlem Heights, New York
September 13, 1781

Sir Henry Clinton receives a letter from Admiral Thomas Graves in mid-morning. It has been written and quickly dispatched via a fast British frigate on September 9, 1781, less than twelve hours before de Grasse would turn the entire French fleet north and head back to the Virginia coast. Clinton is shocked to learn that the Battle of the Capes had not gone well for the British, and that Admiral Graves is not optimistic. The French fleet is so large, writes Graves, that "they are absolute masters of navigation" in the region. The British admiral also expresses great concern for the safety of Lord Cornwallis and his entire garrison at Yorktown.

General Clinton pens an immediate response to Graves stating that, even though Washington and his entire allied army have turned south toward Yorktown, Cornwallis has provisions to last him until November and that the garrison "is in no immediate danger." Privately, however, he is very concerned about the outcome of the sea battle. "Before this letter," Clinton says to an aide, "I always took it for granted that our fleet was superior to that of the enemy."

Later that afternoon, Sir Henry convenes a council of war with his executive officers to discuss the situation. He does this mostly for show, because he has already made up his mind that no immediate action is necessary. However, Clinton has not counted on the obstinacy of General James Robertson, the military governor of New York. Robertson is seventy-one years old, a former quartermaster and sergeant who first came to America in 1756. The temperamental Scotsman had commanded a brigade at the Battle of Long Island and, after being appointed military governor in 1780, had set up heavy-handed police courts in place of civil rights.

When the war council is briefed of the new situation regarding Admiral Graves, General Robertson pleads for action. "We must crowd all possible reinforcements aboard what transports we have," he urges, "convoy them south under one warship, and get them all to the Chesapeake as fast as possible."

To counter Robertson, Clinton calls in couriers who have recently been to Yorktown. "We are certain that Lord Cornwallis can hold out for a minimum of three weeks against a siege army of 20,000," one reports. "And of course, it will take weeks, perhaps months, for Washington to arrive and prepare his operations."

Sir Henry reasserts that he has just received a letter from Cornwallis stating that there are enough supplies at Yorktown to last until November. It would be better, he recommends, if they wait until Admiral Robert Digby, who is expected shortly, arrives with his fleet.

As the other officers nod their heads in agreement with Clinton, Robertson contin-
ues to argue. "We cannot count on Digby," he says emphatically. "He may never come.
Doing nothing cannot be an option at this point. If Cornwallis falls, we will lose this
war. We have one chance, and we must take it now. We give up the game if we do not
try right now!"

The other officers shake their heads negatively. In fact, a number of them mock and
laugh at the old man. And Sir Henry Clinton becomes angry that Robertson will not
toe the line like the others. He turns on the Scotsman and accuses him if exhibition-
ism, of not acting as an officer and a gentleman, and of not thinking rationally. Faced
with such a stern reprimand and no support among the rest of the council, Robertson
sits down and remains quiet.

In the end, the British war council votes to await the arrival of Admiral Digby
and his fleet. Of course, at this point, they are unaware that Graves has been driven
from the Chesapeake, that de Barras has joined with de Grasse to create a formidable
armada, and that Washington, himself, will be in Williamsburg the very next day.

20

Williamsburg, Virginia
September 14, 1781

A woman and her young son are standing by the road in front of their modest house on the outskirts of town. They look up and see a group of riders approaching from the northwest. The muffled clip-clop of hooves on the dry road and the occasional whinny and grunt from the horses are becoming louder and louder. The sound of rolling wagon wheels is also heard. As it is four o'clock in the afternoon, the sun hits high on the backs of the horsemen and shines over their shoulders, causing the woman and her son to squint. They cannot quite see the faces or the uniforms of the riders who are getting closer and closer, always moving at a steady trot. The woman sees one tall man at the center, the others fanning out on each side and slightly behind him. She notices that the fronts of their horses, the men's boots, and parts of their uniforms are caked and spattered with mud.

When the lead rider reaches her, she sees quite clearly that it is General Washington. As he passes, his right hand reaches up to his hat. He makes eye contact with her and nods his head. His face displays a wisp of a smile when he looks at the boy. The other riders file quickly by, also tipping their hats as they pass. Finally, the carriage with Rochambeau rolls past, the feathered white plume on his hat blowing in the wind. The woman is stunned but manages to wave back. Then she begins chatting excitedly to her son about who they have just seen.

Washington and his party ride on without speaking. Most of them are tired, having ridden forty-seven miles since sunrise. They approach the French and American military encampments without any pomp or ceremony. They ride past the huts and tents of the Virginia Militia and are barely noticed. They reach the French camp. Several soldiers snap to attention. Washington slows his horse to a walk.

The first person to ride up is Lieutenant Colonel St. George Tucker of the Virginia Militia who has met Washington one time many years earlier. He is surprised when the American commander greets him by name and quickly introduces Rochambeau. As Tucker shakes the Frenchman's hand, he sees three officers galloping in their direction. The lead rider is the Marquis de Lafayette who, although still sick with fever, is riding

179

as fast as he can, with Governor Thomas Nelson Jr. and the Marquis de St. Simon following along closely.

Lafayette rides at full speed into the middle of the group. He throws the bridle on his horse's neck, opens both arms as wide as he can, and catches Washington around his body with a big bear hug. "Mon general! Mon pere!" says Lafayette as he kisses Washington on both cheeks. "You are here! You are here!"

The commander in chief smiles and hugs his young friend back, but before he can speak, Lafayette starts chattering excitedly. "Lord Cornwallis is still at Yorktown. He is working furiously on his fortifications. Colonel Tarleton's cavalry rides the countryside frequently—foraging and spying. Governor Nelson and his militia have arrived, as has Baron Von Steuben. And the troops of St. Simon have added greatly to our strength. But there is not one grain of flour in the camp either for the American or French armies. What we are to do, I know not!"

Washington breaks in anxiously. "Have you heard from de Grasse?"

The pale young marquis shakes his head. "Our scouts report that the fleet has reentered the bay. But we have not yet received a messenger from him."

"And what of the British fleet?"

"They appeared off the coast for a short time, but soon set sail to the north."

"Good news!" exclaims Washington, excitedly. "Good news, indeed." Then realizing that Nelson and St. Simon are waiting behind Lafayette, he quickly regains his countenance and cordially greets them. In turn, they introduce Washington to the other officers who have ridden up.

Drums and bugles sound assembly, and the French troops line up in formation on both sides of the road for a review. Lafayette defers to St. Simon who escorts Generals Washington and Rochambeau through the lines. St. Simon's soldiers stand at rigid attention, their eyes darting toward the riders to catch a glimpse of the American commander they have heard so much about.

The group rides over to the American encampment where the troops are already drawn up for their own review and inspection. When the general arrives, he is greeted with a formal twenty-one-gun salute. After it has sounded, he removes his hat and bows formally to the troops from atop his horse. Then with Lafayette and Rochambeau, he rides up and down the lines, visibly disturbed that many of the men appear pale and fever-ridden.

Washington next leads his party into Williamsburg. He rides by the main buildings of the College of William and Mary where he had obtained his surveyor's license some thirty years earlier. A mile down the road, he passes the old capitol building where he had once served as a member of the Virginia House of Burgesses.

As word of the general's arrival begins to spread, men, women, and children amass and follow the group through town. Finally, Washington arrives at the home of his friend George Wythe, who had also served in the Continental Congress. Wythe had signed the Declaration of Independence while Washington was in the field with the troops. The general will stay at his old friend's home and make it his temporary head-quarters. Rochambeau will reside across the street at the home of Mrs. Peyton Ran-dolph, whose late husband had been the first president of the Continental Congress.

◆   ◆   ◆

Sometime after midnight, Washington was awakened by arrival of a French naval officer reporting that de Grasse had successfully fended off the British fleet, was back in the Chesapeake at full strength, and that Graves and Hood had apparently sailed back to New York. Before going back to sleep, Washington dashed off a series of letters directing that all troops again start moving down the bay from Baltimore and Annapolis. General Lincoln was ordered to land the transports at College Landing on the James River (two miles from Williamsburg). "Every day we lose now is comparatively an age," wrote Washington. "Hurry on with your troops then, my dear general—upon the wing of speed."

Bright and early the next morning, Washington wrote a series of new communiqués. He reported de Grasse's victory to Congress. He asked the Virginia Board of War to provide new uniforms for the militia and to supply as many food provisions as possible, especially flour. He ordered all available transports northward to help in moving troops down the bay. And to prevent Cornwallis from escaping by water, he directed small boats to guard the York River twenty-four hours a day.

Washington next concentrated on shoring up relationships with his commanding officers. He sent a letter of congratulations to Count de Grasse for driving off the British fleet and made a request to visit the admiral aboard his flagship for a planning conference. The American commander next met with Virginia Governor Thomas Nelson Jr. to seek advice and discuss the needs of the Virginia Militia, which, at the moment, comprised nearly one-third of all allied forces in Williamsburg. Washington also conferred privately with Baron Von Steuben, the most knowledgeable and experienced officer in siege warfare. He asked the Prussian's advice on the investment of Yorktown and how best to make preparations for the upcoming siege. At this meeting, Von Steuben informed Washington that he was now completely broke. His uniforms and camp equipment were in shambles. The old man had been forced to sell his last personal possessions to feed one of his aides who was sick with camp fever. Washington responded by reappointing Von

Steuben to the position of inspector general of the army, so that he might at least have a small wage.

That evening, a reception was held for Washington and Rochambeau at the quarters of the Marquis de St. Simon. As all the officers filed in, General Washington stood at the doorway flanked by Anthony Wayne (who made introductions) on one side and Rochambeau on the other. Each officer took his turn paying his respects to the commander in chief. Washington returned every salute, shook every hand, and introduced each officer to Rochambeau. A lavish meal, replete with fine wines, was later served by gourmet French cooks while a French band played in the background. The gathering eventually broke up at ten o'clock.

Lord Cornwallis's Headquarters
Yorktown, Virginia
September 16, 1781

Cornwallis has assembled nine of his key officers for a council of war at the Nelson house. Banastre Tarleton has returned from his reconnaissance mission to Williamsburg with disturbing new information. He stands at the head of the table, leaning over a map and briefing the other officers, who are listening intently. It is about 9:00 AM.

"Lafayette's army has taken ground near the college," says Tarleton pointing to a position on the map. "I estimate a force of around 6,000 men, most of which are militia. Generals Washington and Rochambeau arrived on the afternoon of the 14th. They were alone except for their aides. Rumors abound in the encampment that the rest of the rebel army is headed down the Chesapeake in boats—due to arrive within the week."

"How can you be certain of this?" asks Cornwallis.

"Several of our men sneaked close enough to overhear conversations, My Lord."

"Hmmm," responds Cornwallis, murmuring under his breath that it was still only rumor.

"Our other scouting parties have confirmed that de Grasse has reentered the lower reaches of the bay and has formed a triple line of defense extending from Cape Henry to Cape Charles," relates Tarleton, now pointing to another portion of the map. "Four men-of-war block the channel to our harbor. We have also confirmed that de Barras has sent dozens of small transports up the bay, presumably to be used for troop transport."

There is a long pause as the other officers settle back in their chairs. Finally, General O'Hara leans forward. "Do you believe the enemy encampment is vulnerable, Colonel Tarleton?" he asks.

"I do, indeed, sir," replies Tarleton. "The rebels are exposed on several fronts. If we act now, we should be able to attack them and break through before their reinforcements arrive and the circle becomes too tight. I have laid out a detailed plan that I would like to present, with your permission, My Lord."

Cornwallis clears his throat. "Yes, of course, Colonel. By all means, please."

"Under cover of darkness, we may march the principal part of our infantry, cannon, and the whole of our cavalry along the Williamsburg Road," he says running his index finger along the map. "We would then attack at dawn before the marquis can bring his field artillery to bear."

"Let us not forget that we are now dealing with General Washington as commander, not 'the boy,'" Cornwallis says.

"Yes, My Lord," replies Tarleton. "Of course—before General Washington can bring his field artillery to bear. At the same time, sir, I propose that we send 2,500 men in small boats with six or eight pieces of artillery up the York River to Queen's Creek. We land them in the rear of Williamsburg and strike the enemy from that direction by surprise—or shortly after the main attack at dawn. We should be able to secure victory enough to then march overland to either Baltimore or the Carolinas."

Cornwallis is leaning forward now, elbows on the table, his chin resting in his hand. He says nothing.

"Sir, I believe this plan is reasonable and judicious," says General O'Hara. "It is well thought through and, if properly executed, has every chance of success."

"What do you think, Chewton?" Cornwallis asks of his aide.

"It appears a bit too complex to me, sir," comes the response.

"Ross?" asks Cornwallis of his other aide.

"I agree, it is a dangerous course of action, sir," replies Ross. "The James River is too effectively blocked, preventing us from making a retreat south to the Carolinas. If we could make it through and head north to Baltimore, however, would we not simply encounter the enemy forces moving south? If we get the worst of a battle with Washington, we would then be ripe for an attack out in the open."

"Dangerous it is," says Cornwallis. "However, I believe that a surprise movement against the enemy may be our only recourse at this point." As the war council continues to debate the merits of Tarleton's bold initiative, a dispatch rider arrives at the Nelson house with two letters from Sir Henry Clinton in New York.

Cornwallis opens the first and begins reading it aloud to the group. "This is dated two weeks ago, September 2," says Cornwallis. "Sir Henry writes: 'It would seem that Mr. Washington is moving an army to the southward with an appearance of haste.'"

"Now there's some useful information," says O'Hara, slapping his knee with a laugh.

"Timely, too," smiles Tarleton.

"Sir Henry continues," says Lord Cornwallis, in a serious tone: "However, as Rear Admiral Graves, after being joined by Sir Samuel Hood with fourteen coppered ships of the line, sailed from hence on the thirty-first with a fleet of nineteen sail, besides some fifty-gun ships, I flatter myself that you will have little to fear from the French."

Cornwallis, clearing his throat, sets the letter aside as the other officers simply look at each other and shake their heads in dismay. "This one was written on September 6th, gentlemen. Sir Henry writes: 'I think the best way to relieve you is to join you as soon as possible with all the force that can be spared from hence—which is about 4,000 men.'"

Cornwallis now skips around the second letter, reading brief passages. "These troops are already aboard ships in the harbor...I will proceed the instant I receive information from Admiral Graves or from other intelligence I shall judge sufficient to move upon...By accounts from Europe, we have every reason to expect Admiral Digby hourly on the coast. He has beaten a superior French fleet at St. Jago and, I believe, is proceeding here."

"This is welcome news," remarks Colonel Chewton, with an air of optimism.

"Indeed," agrees Alexander Ross. "Sir Henry is soon to meet with Admiral Graves. If he has not already embarked to our aid, he is sure to move shortly."

"Well, that settles it," says Cornwallis, matter-of-factly.

"Settles what, sir?" asks Tarleton.

"There is no need for an attack on Williamsburg now, Colonel," replies Cornwallis. "We will wait."

"Wait, sir! Wait for what?"

"Did you not hear?" replies Chewton to Tarleton. "We are to be reinforced from New York—with 4,000 additional men and Admiral Digby's fleet added to that of Graves and Hood."

"With all due respect, sir," says Tarleton, directly addressing Cornwallis, "there is no substantial reason to believe that General Clinton will be able to provide serious assistance to His Majesty's troops here at Yorktown. Even if the navy shows up, they will not be able to break the French fleet's blockade. It is simply too strong. Nor will Sir Henry be able to send enough land troops to prevent a siege. Washington has seen to it that the troops headed here will far outnumber us—including the 4,000 troops from New York."

After listening politely, Lord Cornwallis replies calmly. "Colonel Tarleton, I admire both your zeal and the fact that you have prepared a thorough plan. You are to be commended for that. However, Sir Henry is our superior, and he has stated that he is send-

ing reinforcements our way. I'm sure he expects us to be here when he arrives. We really have no choice in the matter."

But Tarleton does not give up. *"Again, sir, with all due respect,"* he continues, *"ten days ago, we could have escaped this place by sea when the French fleet headed out to sea to engage Admirals Graves and Hood. Now we have an opportunity to get away by attacking Williamsburg. As I view the situation, this will be our last plausible opportunity to escape the noose that is slowly tightening around us. We must take it, sir! We must act now! An attack on the enemy is our only chance! Inaction means certain defeat."*

"In your opinion," counters Chewton.

"Yes, in my opinion, sir," Tarleton reaffirms.

All eyes now rest on Cornwallis. At last he stands up. *"Gentlemen,"* he says, *"I have made my decision. We will wait!"*

Tarleton looks around the table hoping for some form of support, some sort of protest. But the other officers say nothing. *"So much for the collective wisdom of a council,"* he thinks.

◆   ◆   ◆

Over the next week, Cornwallis began fortifying his defensive position. He drew all his small ships near the shore and moored them close together. He moved all the guns on land and cut up the sails to use for tents. He sunk ten of the ships between York and Gloucester Point to prevent French vessels from getting too close—and he gave orders to sink, bury, and burn all the rest at the first sign of an attack.

Cornwallis next turned his attention to the earthwork fortifications, which were currently not well enough prepared to fend off a major siege. He ordered the ground in front of the town leveled. All houses on the front lines were torn down to provide his gunners with a clear field of fire. Trees were cut along the York and Wormley Creek ravines and the wood used to build palisades for the inner and outer lines of entrenchments. All roads leading into Yorktown were barricaded with trunks and branches, and mounds with gun emplacements were constructed.

At first, Cornwallis concentrated on the detached outer works, figuring he would be able to hold them while completing the inner line. Then he began focusing on the interior fortifications. Work progressed twenty-four hours a day at a feverish pace. Lanterns burned all night as men dug in the trenches. Wagons constantly moved in and out of the woods carrying logs that would soon be sharpened into abatis and palisades.

As work progressed, many of the soldiers took sick with diarrhea, dysentery, and what they called "the bloody flux." Others caught the "southern land fever" (malaria) common to the Tidewater region of Virginia. The sick men believed that "the great heat" and "little rest day or night" had "decomposed" their blood. Their misery was worsened when the sickest among them were cut and bled in order to get the "bad" blood out of their systems. And nearly everybody complained bitterly about the putrid meat, wormy biscuits, and contaminated drinking water. Lord Cornwallis became so worried about the lack of food and provisions that he ordered the expulsion of all women camp followers, their children, and hundreds of "nonessential" Negroes from the encampment.

◆   ◆   ◆

On September 16, 1781, Cornwallis sat down and wrote an update to General Clinton in New York. He explained that the French fleet had returned to the Chesapeake, and he provided specific details of the layout of all the ships and their activity. He pointed out that Washington had arrived at Williamsburg on the fourteenth and new intelligence reported that some rebel troops had left Head of Elk, and others had arrived by land at Baltimore and Annapolis.

Cornwallis also related Tarleton's abandoned escape plan. "If I had no hopes of relief," he wrote, "I would rather risk an action than defend my half-finished works. But as you say that Digby is expected at any hour and promise every exertion to assist me, I do not think myself justified in putting the fate of the war on so desperate an attempt."

Finally, Lord Cornwallis expressed fear that his cavalry horses would have to be killed due to lack of feed—and that there were, at best, six weeks of provisions for his troops. He closed his letter by stating the bottom line as far as he was concerned. "I am of the opinion," he wrote, "that you can do me no effectual service except to come directly here. This place is in no state of defense. If you cannot relieve me very soon, you must be prepared for the worst."

Sir Henry Clinton's Headquarters
Harlem Heights, New York
September 19, 1781

About mid-morning, Admiral Thomas Graves and his fleet pull into the docks of New York Harbor before a crowd of more than 3,000 worried citizens. The sight of ten heavily damaged ships does not make them feel any better.

Sir Henry Clinton quickly calls another council of war. Graves briefs the other officers on the sea battle referring to it only as "a lively skirmish." Although Samuel Hood remains silent during the meeting, he later privately terms the battle "a feeble action." One thing that both admirals agree on, however, is that the French hold the Chesapeake with such a formidable fleet that nothing can get past them except small boats sailing at night.

Clinton points out that, based on the most recent intelligence, Washington's forces are still weeks away from Yorktown. He also reasserts that, based on recent letters, Lord Cornwallis does not seem to be in a state of panic, and that he has supplies to last more than six weeks. "When General Buckskin shows up at Yorktown," Clinton says optimistically, "I feel certain His Lordship will provide a proper reception." While most of the other officers smile and agree with Sir Henry's statement, the elder General James Robertson looks down and shakes his head in disgust.

"The fleet is in need of major repairs and refitting," Graves informs Clinton, matter-of-factly.

"And how much time will the Navy require to perform this action?" asks Sir Henry.

"I am unable to make an accurate estimate right now," Graves replies. "But I will review the extent of the damages with our engineers and give you an answer tomorrow, sir."

"Very well," Clinton responds. "In the meantime, I will order ashore the troops who are waiting on transports. We will reboard them when the time is set to depart."

Signifying an end to the meeting, Sir Henry stands up and closes with one final statement. "I trust everyone here agrees that we must provide Lord Cornwallis with reinforcements at the first opportunity—certainly before the end of October," he says. "We will wait for Admiral Digby and repair our damaged ships in the meantime. When the two fleets join, we will head to the Chesapeake to protect His Majesty's troops at Yorktown and Gloucester Point. Gentlemen, we must stand or fall together!"

◆　　　◆　　　◆

If Sir Henry Clinton was deluded as to the reality of the situation confronting him, the Loyalist citizens of New York City were not. Early word of the navy's defeat at the hands of a superior French fleet was no longer a rumor now that Graves and Hood had returned. As the news spread quickly through the city, anguished cries of "Poor Cornwallis," could be heard nearly everywhere. Hundreds of families loyal to the British Crown began packing their belongings so they would be prepared to leave at a moment's notice. Others did not wait for what they believed to be the inevitable outcome. They booked passages on the first available ships to England and left America straightaway.

21

Chesapeake Bay
September 17–22, 1781

On the morning of September 17, 1781, General Washington and Count de Roch-
ambeau board the Queen Charlotte, *a captured British cutter dispatched by the*
French Navy, and begin sailing down the James River on a twenty-four hour journey
to meet personally with Admiral de Grasse. Accompanying the commanders and their
staffs are two key officers to be involved in siege operations: Louis Duportail and artil-
lery commander Henry Knox. By late afternoon, the group has reached Hampton
Roads where they are first able to see the French fleet floating at anchor in the Chesa-
peake Bay. Washington has never seen so many warships in one place. Jonathan
Trumbull describes the row upon row of enormous ships as "a grand sight."

By noon of the next day, the Queen Charlotte *pulls alongside the mammoth* Ville
de Paris. *As the American and French guests climb up the ladder onto the foredeck of*
the flagship, cannons fire honorary salutes, and a French band plays a welcome march.
Once on board, they are greeted by a formal ceremony with full military honors. As
Washington stands at attention to receive the welcome, he looks over at his host. From
briefings by Rochambeau, Washington already knows that Admiral Francois Joseph
Paul Count de Grasse-Tilly is fifty-nine years old, well educated, and the product of
wealthy French nobility. He knows that de Grasse is tough, energetic, and
brave—having once been captured and thrown into a British prison. Washington is
also aware that the French admiral likes to think for himself and take advantage of
latitude in orders, but, at times, can be a bit too cautious. Slightly taller than the
American commander, he is much broader in the shoulders and upper body. His uni-
form of blue and scarlet is extravagantly decorated with gold lace, medals, and a
bright red sash across his chest. His large hat is adorned with an enormous white
plume and makes him look even taller. The admiral literally dwarfs the six foot, 300-
pound General Henry Knox who, upon seeing de Grasse thinks that he surely must be
the tallest man in the entire French Navy.

After the last cannon has fired and the formal ceremony has ended, a smiling de
Grasse rushes up to Washington, joyfully embraces him, kisses him on the cheeks, and
says: "Mon petite General! [My little General]."

It is one of the few times that Washington has ever been greeted in such a manner—especially by a much larger man. While Trumbull and Tilghman cover their mouths in an attempt to suppress smiles, Knox laughs out loud so hard that his sides shake.

Washington returns de Grasse's hug with an awkward smile and then steps back and produces a crisp, formal salute. "Admiral de Grasse," he says, "it is my great honor and pleasure to meet you, sir."

De Grasse returns the salute and invites his American and French visitors into his cabin. Washington begins the conference. "Admiral de Grasse, I would like to thank you very kindly for hosting this council," he says. "I would also like to acknowledge that your important and courageous decision to be here in the Chesapeake at this point in time is greatly and deeply appreciated by the American Congress, myself, and all people committed to freedom here and around the world."

After the Chevalier de Chastellux translates Washington's remarks into French, Rochambeau smiles and echoes the compliments. Knox, Tilghman, and Trumbull affirm their general's statements. "Here, here! Indeed, it is so, sir," they say.

De Grasse politely bows his head and thanks Washington. "Merci, beaucoup, mon general. Merci, beaucoup."

"It is my firm belief that peace for Europe and independence for the United States hangs upon our success here at Yorktown," continues Washington. "To that end, sir, I would like to inform you of our tentative plans and seek your advice and counsel."

De Grasse shakes his head positively and indicates for Washington to continue.

"We intend to encircle the British encampment and bombard it with heavy siege guns."

"A full and complete siege will be undertaken," confirms Rochambeau.

"Of course," continues Washington, "success depends very much on the French fleet's continued presence."

"Mais, certainment, mon general," responds de Grasse. "I understand this."

"Can you tell us, sir," Washington asks, "whether you can stay long enough to permit a conventional siege as opposed to a coup de main? To storm the works would be faster but would also cost many lives. This we are committed to do, however, if the French fleet's stay is limited in duration."

De Grasse leans forward in his chair and places his huge forearm on the table. "My instructions fix my departure at the fifteenth of October, sir," he says. "But having already taken much upon myself, I am prepared to do more. Therefore, my vessels will not depart before the first of November. Assuming that you and Count de Rochambeau intend to act swiftly and judiciously, of which I have no doubt whatsoever, you may count upon our fleet for the time needed to conduct a traditional siege."

"Tres bon!" replies Rochambeau, with a slap of the table.

"Very good, sir," says Washington, now smiling. "My most hearty thanks."

De Grasse smiles and bows his head again.

"Will you be able to supply us with more men, cannon, and powder for the siege?" asks Washington.

"Oui, mon general. All you want. All we can spare."

"Very well, sir. Again my thanks. Will you be able to send ships farther up the York River, above Yorktown, so as to improve communications and shut off a possible British escape attempt in that sector?"

Upon hearing this request, de Grasse hesitates. He places his hand to his mouth. "The thing is not impossible," he replies after a lengthy pause. "But I think that our ships are too large to permit maneuvering between Yorktown and Gloucester Point. I have heard also that Cornwallis has scuttled a number of his own transports to block such a move. However, I will suspend my final decision on this question until I can reconnoiter more."

"Certainly, Admiral," responds Washington. "I understand."

"Please know, mon general," says de Grasse with reassurance, "that I will do everything in my power to ensure the successful completion of the reduction of Yorktown."

The conference lasts about two hours as more details of the siege are discussed. De Grasse then takes his guests on a tour of the Ville de Paris. *The Americans are impressed not only by the ship's 110-gun firepower, but also by the beautiful tropical flowers intertwining the cannon. After a lavish dinner, everyone retires for the evening.*

Early the next morning, Washington is anxious to get back to Williamsburg. De Grasse, however, has invited all the officers in the French fleet to see off the American commander. For the next few hours, they climb up and down the sides of the Ville de Paris—*and on and off of Washington's launch—for a salute and a handshake. When Washington and his party finally sail away on the* Queen Charlotte, *thousands of French sailors can be seen on the riggings of the nearby French ships. Upon a signal from de Grasse, they all discharge their muskets in an honor ceremony known as a feu de joie. At the same time, hundreds of cannon fire from below decks and send enormous clouds of pink smoke billowing into the sky.*

Only a few hours into its journey, the Queen Charlotte *is blown aground on a sandbar by a strong wind. After being stuck for the night, the ship at length breaks free, but violent thunderstorms force it to anchor near the shore for another day and night. Finally, on the morning of September 21, an impatient Washington insists that the captain get under way even though the storm has not subsided. After several hours of being battered about by huge waves, the ship again weighs anchor, this time near the mouth of the James River.*

As the storm gradually subsides, Washington and Rochambeau can see dozens of flatboats, schooners, and scows also riding out the storm. These are the transports filled with American and French troops that have embarked from Head of Elk, Baltimore, and Annapolis. Both armies, having completed their overland marches four day earlier, have been boarding vessels ever since. This, in turn, creates a steady stream of transports down the Chesapeake that will last for more than a week. After the storm subsides a bit, the Queen Charlotte, *along with the other stranded vessels, begins to sail up the James River to Williamsburg.*

The next day, Washington and his party abandon the slow-moving cutter, still hampered by contrary winds, and are rowed the final thirty miles to Archer's Hope Harbor in a small boat. After spending a full four days trying to get back to Williamsburg, the general is greatly relieved to find that things have gone smoothly in his absence. The light troops under Scammel and Hamilton have already arrived safely, the wagon train (consisting of 1,500 horses, 800 oxen, and extra supplies) is proceeding on schedule on its overland march and, perhaps most important in Washington's mind, Cornwallis is still dug in at Yorktown.

York River
September 22, 1781

Just after midnight, the British ship *Vulcan*, loaded with sulfur, tar, rosin, and other combustibles, quietly sailed away from the Yorktown docks. Following closely behind were four smaller attack ships similarly loaded. A skeleton crew manned each ship. Their mission was to sail undetected to the mouth of the York River and set fire to the three French warships blocking the channel there. This surprise "fireship" expedition had been ordered by Lord Cornwallis in hopes that it might buy some time and delay the allied attack. Every day gained would provide Clinton and the British fleet another twenty-four ours for their rescue mission.

There was a favorable wind, a high tide, and the night was unusually clear and starlit. By 2:00 AM, the French ships were sighted. But the crew of the *Vulcan* set the ship afire too soon. The blaze was so violent that it could be seen by the main French fleet eight miles out in the Chesapeake. The crews of the three French ships were alert and acted quickly. Drummers immediately signaled a beat to quarters, and gunners opened up a furious cannonade. Fearing for their lives, the

Vulcan's small crew pointed the ship toward the French vessels and, at the last possible moment, jumped in a lifeboat.

Two of the French warships, the *Reflechi* and the *Valiant*, had plenty of time to up their anchors and sail away to safety. However, the *Triton*, closest to the *Vulcan*, was nearly rammed. But a fast current, a sudden change in the wind, and a quick maneuver by the *Triton*'s captain caused the fireship to sail past with only two cable lengths to spare. The fire was so intense, however, that some of the flames flared out to the forward deck of the French ship, wounding seventeen sailors and causing some moderate structural damage.

Although the episode was largely a failure, the *Vulcan*'s crew was hailed as heroes when they returned to the British camp. And Cornwallis was pleased to observe that the French guard vessels had dropped farther down into the bay. At least now, on a dark night, he might be able to slip through some dispatch vessels headed to New York.

Negative rumors, meanwhile, continued to fly through the encampment. "There are reports we are in a very bad situation," recorded one German soldier in his diary. "And hopes are fading that Sir Henry Clinton will arrive in time for our rescue."

Sir Henry Clinton's Headquarters
Harlem Heights, New York
September 24, 1781

Sir Henry Clinton is holding another council of war with his executive officers. In addition to receiving Cornwallis's letter of September 16th, Admiral Robert Digby has just arrived on the scene with King George III's sixteen-year-old son, Prince William Henry. However, Digby has brought with him only three warships—nowhere near the fleet Clinton had expected.

It is mid-afternoon. Outside a rainstorm rages. Sheets of water wash down the sides of the white mansion. Tree branches flap against the windowpanes. Clinton and Graves sit next to each other at one end of the table. Digby, Hood, and Robertson are together at the other end. The rest of the officers are seated in the middle. Everyone has a glass of wine in front of him. Sir Henry reads Cornwallis's letter and places special emphasis on the last paragraph.

"'I am of the opinion,' concludes Lord Cornwallis, 'that you can do me no effectual service except to come directly here. This place is in no state of defense. If you cannot relieve me very soon, you must be prepared for the worst.' Gentlemen," says Clinton,

matter-of-factly, "I am of the opinion that he intends to abandon Yorktown and retreat to safety."

"With all due respect, Sir Henry," says General Robertson, "it is apparent that Lord Cornwallis intends to stay right where he is. Does he not say that he has turned down Tarleton's suggestion to attack Lafayette? Does he also not say that he does not think himself justified in putting the fate of the war in so desperate an attempt?"

"Yes, but he is referring to an attack on Lafayette, not an escape," retorts Clinton.

"I must agree with General Robertson," pipes up Admiral Hood. "When Cornwallis says that you should 'be prepared for the worst,' he is most certainly referring to something more serious than a retreat."

"Sir, we must go forward with our plan to send reinforcements to Yorktown," pleads Robertson. "It is apparent that Cornwallis expects you to do so. The outcome of the entire war rests on this decision."

One by one, other officers around the table concur with Robertson and Hood. Finally, Admiral Graves speaks up.

"Sir Henry, we can surely sail our fleet south and rescue Cornwallis," he says with confidence. "It should prove little trouble. We will turn French superiority of numbers and position to our advantage. If we time our moves correctly, the violent tides of the Chesapeake will sweep de Grasse's ships to one side. We will then slip past them before they can maneuver and sail into the mouth of the York."

Admirals Digby and Hood simply stare at Graves in bewilderment and then look at each other. Finally, Digby speaks up. "Let us suppose that de Grasse is not so sound asleep as to be at the mercy of the tides," he says. "What then?"

"Indeed!" states Hood in agreement. "And even if you could get by the thirty-six French warships at the mouth of the bay, simply taking fresh troops to Cornwallis will not save the king's army."

"What do you mean, sir?" asks Clinton.

"I mean, sir," replies Hood sarcastically, "that there must be a larger, more coordinated plan than simply sailing past the French fleet as they become swayed by the tides."

"We cannot possibly attack de Grasse as long as he is at his current position and strength," states Digby sternly. "All we would be able to do is land troops at some safe point along the coast."

"Very well, very well," says Clinton, pausing to take a sip of wine. "We have already sent a message to Lord Cornwallis stating that we are sailing to his rescue before the end of October. I suggest we commit to leave here by the fifth."

"I think we will not be able to sail that early, Sir Henry," interrupts Graves, also drinking some wine. "Our dockyards have no lumber to repair our ships. I have also *been informed that there is a shortage of combustibles for our fireships. We will need to obtain them through additional foraging operations."*

"When will the navy be ready to sail?" Clinton asks.

"Not before the eighth at the very earliest."

"Sir Henry," says Digby to Clinton, "assuming you do catch de Grasse napping and sail by his entire fleet up to Yorktown to unload reinforcements, how do you intend to get out?"

"Well, I am sure there will be less difficulty getting out of the bay than going in," Clinton replies casually.

Digby looks at Hood, shakes his head, and frowns.

"Sir, your countenance seems to express some doubt," says Clinton.

"Gentlemen," says Digby quietly, "I am just the newcomer. Perhaps, from experience, you know more than I do. As you are aware, I have orders to proceed to Jamaica."

"But Admiral, you are the senior flag officer in charge," remarks Clinton. "If you were to leave with even a portion of the fleet, it would be very detrimental."

"Very well, General Clinton. I will not take with me any ships. Rather, I insist that Admiral Graves retain command of the fleet in its entirety."

Graves smiles at this, but Hood almost chokes. "I think Admiral Graves should sail to the West Indies for the good of the cause," Hood mutters none too discreetly.

"What's that, Admiral Hood?" asks Clinton.

"Nothing, sir."

"Well, that seals it, gentlemen," says Sir Henry. "We wait. We will delay our departure to the Chesapeake until the fleet is completely ready. Until then, Lord Cornwallis will have to use his own judgment."

As the officers stand, Samuel Hood turns his back to Clinton and whispers in General Robertson's ear. "That seals it, all right," he says.

◆   ◆   ◆

That afternoon, Clinton penned a letter to Cornwallis. "At a meeting of the general and flag officers held this day," he began, "it is determined that above 5,000 men, rank and file, shall be embarked on board the king's ships, and the joint exertions of the navy and army made in a few days to relieve you, and afterward cooperate with you."

And then, completely ignoring Graves's warning that the fleet would not be able to sail before the 8th, he stubbornly wrote Cornwallis the following: "The fleet consists of twenty-three sails of the line, three of which are three-deckers—and there is every reason to hope we start from here on the fifth of October."

However, the next day (September 25), Clinton sent another dispatch to Yorktown giving himself an out if the fleet did not sail by the fifth. "The repairs of the British fleet will detain us here to the fifth of October," he wrote, "and Your Lordship must be sensible that unforeseen accidents may lengthen it out a day or two longer." In the meantime, Clinton asked Cornwallis to "lose no time in letting me know your real situation, your opinion of how we can best help you, and the exact strength of the enemy's fleet."

After sending the dispatch, Sir Henry Clinton spent the next several days entertaining the king's son (who would later become King William IV). He conducted formal parades so that Prince William Henry could review the troops. He took the young man on a carriage ride to the front lines at Kingsbridge to see the enemy firsthand. And Clinton also entertained the prince with lavish parties, banquets, and music concerts.

22

Williamsburg, Virginia
September 25–26, 1781

George Washington is holding his regular briefing in the dining room of the George Wythe house. Present are Lafayette, Tilghman, Trumbull, Humphreys, John Laurens (who has finally assumed Alexander Hamilton's old job), and General Benjamin Lincoln (just arrived on one of the Chesapeake transports, and who has been appointed second in command of the American army).

It is early morning. Everyone is seated around the table. Washington sits by the open window, his chair turned slightly so he can see outside. He enjoys the cool autumn breeze, the sound of the fluttering multicolored leaves on the trees, and the chirping birds.

Tench Tilghman holds a piece of paper in his hand. "We have an intercepted letter here from a Lieutenant Colonel Duncan McPherson of the 71st Regiment under Cornwallis," *he says, with a slight grin.*

"Anything useful?" *asks Washington.*

"A couple of things, sir," *continues Tilghman.* "McPherson writes: 'Nothing but hard labor goes on here at present in constructing and making batteries toward the river and redoubts toward the land. The troops are in perfect health and, if our enemies are polite enough to give us three day's grace, we will be ready.' He also describes British troop positions in some detail, General."

"Excellent!" *Washington responds.* "Leave it with me, please. I will study it later. What is the status of the troops, artillery, and supplies?"

"Everyone has disembarked, sir," *relates General Lincoln.* "Those who have not arrived here are currently on the march from Archer's Hope. By tomorrow morning, we will have nearly 18,000 men in the vicinity. Ammunition and related supplies are all unloaded, chiefly at Carter's Grove. All the French and American siege guns now lay secure at Trebell's Landing. Food and other provisions are plentiful; Virginia's farmers on the Eastern Shore have really stepped up—although they demand their payment in silver rather than Continental currency."

"Governor Nelson has really come through for us!" *exclaims Trumbull.*

"Along with the French," *adds Laurens.*

"The wagon train and cavalry are progressing nicely, sir," continues Lincoln. "They were in Georgetown two days ago and should be crossing the Potomac at Alexandria by now. We expect them to be at Colchester tomorrow and Marumsco Creek the next day."

"How is the morale of the army?" asks Washington.

"It is excellent, sir," Lincoln replies. "Many of the men spend their liberty shooting billiards and going to hops put on by local citizens. Most have recovered from the fever. Hundreds exercise regularly in the afternoons. I have never seen the troops in a better frame of mind, sir."

"That is good to hear," replies Washington, who turns to Tilghman. "We must issue preparatory orders for the march to Yorktown."

"Yes, sir," responds Tilghman, starting to take notes.

"Ready the artillery to be moved from the wharves. Place the vanguard on alert. De Lauzun and his legion are to move to Gloucester Point to help Weedon. I have already spoken with Rochambeau about this. He has concurred. We will leave 200 men here in Williamsburg to mind the hospital and stores."

The general pauses for a moment. "A quick letter to the Congress," he says.

Humphreys, with pen in hand, indicates he is ready.

Washington tells Congress that "everything has hitherto succeeded to our wishes." He relates that the "debarkation and movement of the heavy artillery and stores will necessarily occasion some delay, but in a very few days, I hope, the enemy at York till be completely invested...The prospects are as favorable as could possibly have been expected."

Baron Von Closen, Rochambeau's aide, suddenly appears at the door and states he has a dispatch from Count de Grasse. Lafayette leaps to his feet and seizes the letter. As the young marquis reads, the others stare and squirm with anticipation. Still standing, Lafayette soon gives Washington an apprehensive look. "De Grasse says he has news that Digby has arrived in New York with more warships for Graves and the British fleet," says Lafayette.

"Yes, yes," replies Washington, "the same news we received two days ago. And I do not believe Digby can have any influence on our operations while there are thirty-six French ships of the line in the bay. What else?"

"But, sir, the admiral writes that he is most distressed by this news and intends to hoist sail and engage the British in a less disadvantageous position. He states, sir, that, 'It could happen that the course of the battle may drive us leeward and put it beyond our power to return. Therefore, I will have to take with me the troops I had brought. I sail for New York as soon as the wind permits.' Sir," continues Lafayette, "de Grasse

asks your advice and states that he will pause in the middle of the bay and wait for your reply."

With this, General Washington rises to his feet, places both hands on the table in front of him, and lowers his head in anguish. He takes several deep breaths. Finally, he looks up. "Colonel Tilghman, we will write an immediate letter to Admiral de Grasse," he says firmly. "General Lafayette, you will deliver it personally and at once. The rest of you are dismissed."

As the other officers leave, Washington stares out the window and begins to dictate. "I am unable to describe the painful anxiety the reception of your letter brings," he says with a grimace. "The surrender of the British garrison will be so important in itself, that it will go a great way toward ending the war and securing the invaluable objects of victory to our allied forces. If you should withdraw, the enemy would instantly avail itself of the opportunity to escape. If you quit the bay, the consequence will be the disgrace of abandoning a design on which are founded the fairest hopes of the allied forces after a prodigious expense, fatigue, and exertions. The report of a large fleet under Digby may be absolutely false. And in the event such a fleet should appear, it would not be able to defeat Your Excellency's strength and naval talents if you are securely positioned in the Chesapeake.

"The confidence with which I feel myself inspired by the energy of your character leaves me no doubt that, upon a full viewing of all consequences, you will reconsider your thoughts of leaving the bay. I beg of you to consider the good of the common cause. The Marquis de Lafayette, who does me the honor to bear this to you, will explain many peculiarities of our situation which could not well be comprised in a letter."

As Tilghman continues to write, Washington looks up at Lafayette. "I presume you are sufficiently recovered from your illness to take this to de Grasse?"

"Indeed, I am, sir," comes the reply. "What more do you wish me to say to the admiral?"

"I will leave that to you, General," replies Washington. "Better take Baron Von Closen with you. He will represent Rochambeau whom, I am sure, will agree with me on this matter."

◆　　　◆　　　◆

The very next evening, about the time that Lafayette and Von Closen arrived on the *Ville de Paris*, General Washington received a letter from de Grasse who had written that a naval council of war had disapproved of his proposal to leave the bay and, instead, had recommended staying in the Chesapeake as previously agreed. "The plans I had suggested," wrote de Grasse, "do not appear to fulfill the aims we had in view. The fleet will remain in the bay."

Upon being told of this new development, Lafayette and Von Closen immediately turned around and headed back to Williamsburg. As soon as he got back, the frustrated Von Closen wrote about the journey. "The weather was devilish, the sea was rough, and I had two hours of tossing in a bitch of an open launch where I was pretty well soaked by the oarsmen!"

General Washington quickly proceeded to issue orders for the final march to Yorktown. On the twenty-seventh, the entire army would march east of Williamsburg a few miles, where they would assemble in battle order and encamp for the night. At dawn on the twenty-eighth, the troops would begin the twelve-mile march. "Every officer will have his men look as neat and respectable as possible," directed Washington. "The men will take care to be well shaven and the commissary will issue twelve pounds of flour to each regiment for the purpose of powdering their hair." Washington further ordered Scammel and Hamilton's vanguard to lead the march through several heavily wooded areas so as to avoid a surprise attack. American and French troops were to form one column on the left; the militia another on the right. After having proceeded approximately half the distance to Yorktown, the French and Americans would separate into two columns. The French would take the direct road, while the Americans would march toward Murford's Bridge where they would join with the militia and proceed to the final destination. If all went according to plan, the points of the army would arrive at Yorktown by mid to late afternoon.

Williamsburg, Virginia
September 28, 1781

Dawn broke with a clear sky, high humidity, and no breeze. It was going to be a hot and muggy day—which would make for a very unpleasant march. The troops struck camp at five o'clock in the morning. American Continental regiments (5,500 in all) from Pennsylvania, Maryland, New York, and New Jersey led the way and were followed by their own artillery regiments. Behind the Americans were eight regiments of 7,200 elegantly dressed Frenchmen. And two miles off to the right were 3,500 members of the militia, including a Virginia corps of riflemen, light dragoons, and attached field artillery.

The troops passed through tall cypress, pine, and cedar forests that were dense with briar and holly thickets. They marched through uncultivated fields of knee-high grass. On the backwoods roads, they passed through the beautiful Virginia countryside lined with partially harvested fields of tobacco, cotton, and corn. They walked across small creeks and marshes where enormous herons flapped their wings and flew away. When the troops emerged onto the main road, they found it covered with dry sand—ankle-deep in some places. And that sand became hotter and hotter as the day wore on. Soon it was burning the feet of the soldiers who had no boots. And the swirling clouds that were kicked up got in everyone's throats and watered their eyes.

As the troops stretched out for miles, the oppressive heat started to take its toll. Everyone began to slow down. Some men staggered and collapsed. Others were helped along by their comrades. Nearly 800 Frenchmen, unaccustomed to the high heat and humidity, were given permission to rest more frequently and lag behind with the rear guard. A couple of French soldiers died and were buried on the side of the road. At the front of the French column, the Marquis de St. Simon, who had been battling malaria, was placed in a litter and carried along by his staff—still at the front, still determined to lead his men down to Yorktown.

At noon, the army rested for an hour or two. Hundreds of small cooking campfires popped up all along the roads. Some soldiers removed their coats and laid down in the shade. Others stood barefoot in streams and splashed themselves with water. During the break, Washington sent out a warning about British surprise attacks and gave orders to repulse them with bayonets alone. Washington wanted no noise, no warning to Cornwallis that they were coming. When the march resumed, the main column divided. The French stayed on the direct road to Yorktown, and the Americans moved to the right on the White Marsh Road where they soon joined with the militia. There were no British attacks on the lines of march even though several enemy cavalry units were sighted along the way.

Head of the Allied Army
Yorktown, Virginia
September 28, 1781

Near the intersection of the Williamsburg Road and Goosley Road, about two miles northeast of Yorktown, a small British party was cutting down trees for wood to be used in the construction of artillery platforms. Stationed slightly beyond were several light infantry pickets keeping a lookout. At approximately 3:30 in the afternoon, French advance units broke through the woods and began fanning out left and right. The British pickets saw these movements from a distance, warned the laborers, and everyone quickly fell back. The French soon found themselves under fire from small artillery guns several hundred yards away. They retreated to the forest's edge just beyond range of the English cannon. While word of the contact was carried back to General Rochambeau, Colonel Banastre Tarleton scrambled his cavalry legion, arrayed them in three squadrons on the plain, and watched for an opportunity to strike.

Rochambeau quickly ordered forward six four-pound field cannon with fifty mounted French cavalrymen. Once in place, the French artillery opened fire. Several British horsemen were killed and the rest retreated out of range to the vicinity of the Pigeon Hill redoubt, one of Cornwallis's forward-most fortifications that had been completed just a few days before. French grenadiers then moved through the forests and ravines to surround the redoubt. They also scouted out and surrounded the Fusilier's redoubt located on the edge of the York River, protecting the far right of the British line. But the French troops stayed at a safe distance, keeping a cautious watch on enemy movements.

Several miles farther south, between Wormley and York Creeks, Colonel Alexander Hamilton's light infantry regiment approached Yorktown from the southwest. Hamilton, who had been among the first to arrive at Williamsburg, found a letter from his father-in-law waiting. Betsy, five months pregnant, was so worried about Alexander that the doctors were concerned she might suffer a miscarriage. After sending a letter of reassurance to his wife, Hamilton formally requested the honor of taking the point. Scammel agreed and Hamilton now found himself at the head of the entire American army.

Near the intersection with the Mulberry Island Road, Hamilton's squad encountered about twenty mounted enemy dragoons who quickly retreated to warn Cornwallis of the enemy's approach. The British soon moved up several small pieces of artillery and opened fire on the Americans. One of the first shots sheared off a soldier's leg. Caught by surprise, Hamilton immediately ordered a retreat back to the cover of the woods. But about an hour later, American field artillery pushed the British back beyond firing range. American Continentals and militia then moved onto the open plain and headed toward Murford's Bridge to cross a marshy creek. But they were forced to a halt when the bridge was found blown to bits. It had been destroyed the day before on Cornwallis's orders.

During the late afternoon hours, the French army formed a preliminary siege line that extended in an arc from the York River south to the American position. While Washington set his engineers to repairing the Murford Bridge, American sharpshooters fired sporadically on Hessian soldiers. French artillery bombardment also kept the enemy at bay. Three German officers were killed in these exchanges. The French suffered no casualties, the Americans only one.

That night, allied advance pickets placed themselves well out in front of the main body of troops. Behind them the Continentals and militiamen took positions in back of the French line. Everyone encamped in the open air. As the troops searched for drinking water, they found the woods full of wild hogs, and soon the aroma of roasting pork drifted through the forests and fields. Dr. James Thacher noted in his journal that morale was high and the army cheerful. "There is an unbounded confidence in our commanders," he noted.

After giving an order for the men to sleep on their arms that night, General Washington camped out in the open right along with his troops—under a mulberry tree.

Lord Cornwallis's Headquarters
Yorktown, Virginia
September 29, 1781

Lord Cornwallis awakens in the comfort of the Nelson house. He has a light breakfast of tea and pastry served on fine china. By 9:00 AM, he is conducting a staff meeting with General O'Hara, Banastre Tarleton, Major Ross, and Colonel Chewton.

Ross opens with a brief status report. "The enemy has formed a line extending from the Fusilier's redoubt to the southwest at Murford's Bridge," he says. "The French are firmly ensconced on the right. The Americans, behind them and to their left, worked all last night repairing the bridge. Several of our officers estimate the enemy force to exceed 26,000."

"That is preposterous!" snaps Cornwallis. "They cannot possibly have that many men."

"Certainly not," agrees O'Hara. "Our pickets are obviously panicked and reacting with hysteria. Actually, the entire camp is in alarm."

"Have we any casualties, yet?" asks Cornwallis.

"Yes, My Lord," Ross replies. "Three pickets of the Anspach battalion killed by cannon fire, one by rifle fire. We also have one young German shot in the back. The ball was cut from between his shoulder blades. He is recovering in the hospital tent."

"Very well," says Cornwallis, who picks up a recently completed letter. "On another matter, I have responded to Governor Nelson's request that citizens be permitted to leave the community, as such: 'I have not the least objection to any of the inhabitants in this place going out with their families and effects; nor to those who formerly resided here sending for their wives and families. All will be permitted to take their effects with them.'"

"*My Lord, we expect all Loyalists to remain along with our army's own women and children,*" *states Chewton.* "*And the Negro labor force will, of course, remain.*"

"*Of course,*" *replies Cornwallis.* "*We must have them—for the time being.*"

"*What of Secretary Nelson, My Lord?*" *asks O'Hara.*

"*I spoke with him last evening. It is his wish to stay.*"

"*Hmmm, I wonder why?*" *O'Hara speculates.* "*His own nephew is now governor of Virginia and head of its militia. Could he be passing messages out of the camp?*"

"*Indeed, not,*" *responds Cornwallis.* "*I have him watched day and night.*"

"*Very good, sir,*" *O'Hara demurs.*

Cornwallis then abruptly takes over the meeting. "*Gentlemen, here are my orders,*" *he states firmly.* "*Once the enemy invests the town, we will no longer be able to employ the cavalry effectively. Colonel Tarleton, you will therefore move your legion to Gloucester Point. The Erbprinz infantry regiment will accompany you.*"

"*Yes, sir,*" *affirms Tarleton.*

"*It is apparent that the Americans are taking measures that cannot fail to turn our left flank in a short time,*" *continues Cornwallis.* "*I fear that they will then move north toward the river, swing to the west, and attack our outer line from the rear. The French may then apply pressure on the front. We must therefore abandon the outer works.*"

At this statement, Tarleton leaps to his feet and shouts in protest. "*Sir, time will be gained by holding and disputing the ground inch by inch,*" *he says.* "*To give it up is to coop our troops in the unfinished works and hasten the surrender of His Majesty's army.*"

"*No, no, my dear colonel,*" *Cornwallis replies,* "*we are in good shape. Late last night a dispatch boat slipped through the French fleet and arrived in our harbor with a message from Sir Henry Clinton. He states that Admiral Digby has arrived in New York and that twenty-three ships of the line will set sail on October fifth with 5,000 troops. Our rescue is imminent.*"

"*But sir,*" *protests Tarleton,* "*they will not be able to break the French barricade in the Chesapeake. The French have thirty-six ships. And even if they are able to land, 5,000 additional troops alone are not enough to help us penetrate the combined French and American forces.*"

"*I think, sir, that you should have more respect for the capabilities of the Royal Navy and Army,*" *Cornwallis replies scoldingly.* "*Clearly, Sir Henry Clinton, Sir Thomas Graves, Sir Robert Digby, and Admiral Samuel Hood believe they can successful. And so should we, sir!*"

Tarleton does not reply. He simply leans against the wall and looks down at the floor.

Later that evening, Cornwallis writes a brief reply to Sir Henry Clinton.

"I have received your letter of the twenty-fourth, which has given me the greatest satisfaction," he states. *"These last two days, I have had to look General Washington's whole force in the face in position on the outside of my works, and it is clear that the enemy will advance. I shall soon retire within the works and have no doubt, if relief arrives in any reasonable time, Yorktown and Gloucester Point will both be in possession of His Majesty's troops."*

◆   ◆   ◆

That night in the British trenches, an aged Scottish Highland lieutenant drew his sword and shouted toward the American lines: "Come on, Mr. Washington, I'm glad to see you! I've been offered money for my commission, but I could not think of going home without seeing you. Come on, then!"

But he seemed to be in the minority as all that night there was a steady stream of British soldiers deserting their positions and sneaking over to the American and French lines.

American Encampment
Yorktown, Virginia
September 29, 1781

By late Saturday morning the Murford Bridge was fully rebuilt, and the American army crossed over and extended its siege line to the southwest. Their main encampment was set out just east of Beaver Dam Creek, where marshland to the north served as a divide with the French, and a morass to the east provided protection from the British. Now only a mile from Cornwallis's outer works, pickets were sent forward as lookouts while each American brigade dug a short trench for additional protection.

French troops also dug in and consolidated their positions farther to the north. Rochambeau ordered detailed surveys of the entire area. All principal highways and plantation roads leading in and out of Yorktown were closed. And across the river at Gloucester Point, the Duke de Lauzun's cavalry joined with General George Weedon's militia to prevent any escape in that sector.

Sporadic artillery and rifle fire occurred all day long. Hessian snipers picked off about a half-dozen Americans on the front lines, and French artillery killed about eight British soldiers within the fortifications. At about three in the afternoon, British cannon fire wounded three American infantrymen with one cannonball. Dr. Thacher quickly assisted in amputating one of the victim's legs while the young man screamed in agony.

By early evening, the allied armies had enclosed Cornwallis on all sides and sealed any possible avenue of escape by land. As Rochambeau said to Washington, "The enemy are now confined to within pistol-shot of their works."

◆   ◆   ◆

Now that Admiral de Grasse had officially declined to send any ships up the York River above the British position, Washington was ready to formulate a detailed plan of attack. So the American commander, along with Rochambeau and several other officers, spent most of that Saturday reconnoitering the front lines. It was a landscape very familiar to Washington. In his youth, he had surveyed the area and bet on local cockfights. As a matter of fact, Yorktown had been built on property once owned by his ancestors.

At mid-afternoon, the party paused in a sandy area under several enormous poplar trees. Washington pulled out his spyglass and began peering through it, making some broad sweeps of the British lines. Chief Engineer Louis Duportail dismounted, kneeled down, and picked up some dirt. He rubbed it in his hands and remarked that the soil was very loose and would require great quantities of fascines and gabions for the construction of sturdy earthworks. Rochambeau nodded in agreement.

Just as Duportail got back on his mount, a puff of gray smoke appeared from the British line about a mile away. Then a whistling cannon ball looped over the group's heads, knocked a number of branches off the trees, and landed behind them. The horses were all startled, but everyone stayed put. A few moments later, however, a second shot plowed into the earth only a few feet away, spraying up dirt and bushes on several of the officers. Everyone spurred their horses and retreated back a safer distance—everyone, that is, except George Washington, who held steady on his tall white horse, Nelson, and continued peering through his spyglass as if nothing out of the ordinary had happened.

"They're well entrenched," Washington murmured to himself. "We're going to have to blast them out of there."

PART IV
SIEGE PREPARATIONS

23

American/French Encampment
Yorktown, Virginia
September 30, 1781

Sunday morning breaks clear and warm over the front lines. It is unusually quiet. The gentle rustle of several grazing deer in the fields, the gurgling waters of York Creek, and a few chirping birds are all that can be heard.

Several French lookouts stationed near the Pigeon Hill quarter are perplexed by the lack of sound and movement in the two enemy redoubts there. These fortifications are strategic to the British outer line, because they guard Goosley Road and defend the western section of land running between the York and Wormley Creek ravines. Normally, the British go through a series of routine exercises at sunrise. But not this morning. At 7:00 AM, a small party of French light infantry moves forward to investigate. They find both structures empty—no guns, no soldiers, nothing.

About a quarter-mile to the north, several American pickets observe that a British outpost near the Williamsburg Road also appears to be deserted. They notify the field officer of the day, thirty-four-year-old Colonel Alexander Scammel, who rides forward to inspect the area. Scammel makes the mistake of galloping too far ahead of his men and is quickly surrounded by a party of British cavalrymen. One dragoon points a pistol at Scammel while another grabs the reins of his horse. The American officer raises his arms to surrender. Two additional British Legionnaires ride up. As one draws his sword, the other pulls out a pistol and shoots Scammel in the back. The bullet lodges between his hipbone and ribs. The second rider swings his sword wildly at the American officer, but Scammel doubles over in pain and falls off his horse before the sword can hit him. In the distance, American pickets witness the event but are too few in number to retaliate. The British dragoons then take Scammel into Yorktown where English surgeons treat his wound.

◆   ◆   ◆

Word of the British pullback and Scammel shooting quickly spread up and down the allied lines. Generals Washington and Rochambeau quickly rode forward to personally survey the situation. To their amazement, they found that Cornwallis had withdrawn from every one of his outer line fortifications except the Fusilier's Redoubt (on his far right flank) and Redoubts No. 9 and No. 10 (on his far left flank). As a result, the entire center of the battlefield, which included the strategic ravine of Yorktown Creek, was now open to the allied forces. Incredulous at this new development, Washington and Rochambeau immediately gave orders to occupy the new ground.

To the south, the American light infantry, under the temporary command of Alexander Hamilton, formed two battle lines and advanced to take the abandoned batteries near Hampton Road. To the north, the Regiment Bourbonnois quickly swooped down and occupied the Pigeon Hill redoubts and the nearby Long Neck redoubt. All three main roads leading into Yorktown—the Williamsburg Road, the Goosely Road, and the Hampton Road—were sealed off. And the entire allied line advanced nearly a half-mile from its previous position. All this was accomplished before 10:00 AM amid a steady British artillery bombardment of about forty shots per hour. The allies, however, suffered almost no casualties.

Emboldened by their easy advance, American troops attacked British redoubts No. 9 and No. 10. They quickly fell back, however, after being met with heavy and well-aimed artillery fire. At virtually the same moment, 100 French members of the light infantry charged the Fusilier's redoubt. This particular fortification was 800 yards west of the main British line and situated on the edge of a cliff overlooking the York River. It represented the outermost limits of the British right flank and served to protect against incursions from both the river and the Williamsburg Road. Constructed by the 23rd Royal Welch Fusiliers, the redoubt was exceptionally well designed. Shaped like a star, it was surrounded by a huge ditch, reinforced with a double row of abatis and buttresses, and ringed by two circles of fallen trees.

The French had a terrible time making any headway against the Fusilier's redoubt. On the first charge, they advanced to the ditch but were met by a hail of bullets, grapeshot, and blasts from two twelve-pound cannon in the fort. Forced to retreat, the light infantry regrouped and attacked again. This time, however, one of the British ships anchored in the river added to the barrage of cannon fire and drove the French back for good. During the two-hour skirmish, the British suffered thirty men killed or wounded. French casualties were lighter: ten wounded (one officer had his thigh shattered by a cannonball) and one fatality.

General Washington's Headquarters
American Encampment
Yorktown, Virginia
September 30, 1781

It is late afternoon. A cooling breeze blows in from the York River. The sun is halfway down the western horizon and warms the worn, weather-beaten gray tents that Washington had first pitched outside Boston six years earlier. The general usually sleeps on a cot in the smaller attached tent, but the much larger "dining" tent can hold up to fifty officers for dinners and meetings.

Washington has called a senior officer's conference, but this day he has asked that everyone stand in the open air. Rochambeau, Lincoln, Governor Nelson, and all the key leaders are milling around outside the tent. Several aides sit at a small table preparing to take notes and write orders. Washington steps up and calls the conference to order.

"Well, gentlemen," he begins, "it appears we now unexpectedly find ourselves on very advantageous ground."

"Within musket range of the enemy's main works!" exclaims Governor Nelson.

"It is unbelievable," shouts the Marquis de Lafayette.

Washington turns to his French counterpart. "General Rochambeau, sir, may I inquire as to your assessment of this new development?"

"Oui, mon general," replies Rochambeau, his aide interpreting. "The enemy has enabled us to enclose him in a narrower circle. We have shortened our own line considerably by moving the center forward taking their abandoned redoubts. We may now further restrict Cornwallis within the confines of his main works by moving our artillery closer than we had dreamed possible at this juncture. This unwise move of Lord Cornwallis will save us much time and trouble. It provides us with a tremendous advantage for upcoming siege operations."

"We certainly would not have attempted any major engagement before we had advanced our heavy cannon," states Henry Knox.

"Indeed not," agrees Baron Von Steuben. "The enemy would have gained great time by holding and disputing the ground inch by inch—both to complete their fortifications and to delay our operations. I would estimate that the outer works could have delayed an attack upon their inner works for at least a week, perhaps two."

"I agree," states Rochambeau. "The enemy ought to have kept their positions until they were forced to abandon them. It would have compelled us to feel our way, would have held us in doubt. Instead, we are now masters of all the approaches to Yorktown."

"It was not only an unmilitary move," states Anthony Wayne, indignantly, *"but an indication of confusion."*

"Why then, do you think Lord Cornwallis took this action?" Washington asks the group. *"Is General Wayne correct? Was he confused?"*

"He may have feared being assailed in such an extended position," remarks Von Closen. *"Perhaps he feared that we might turn his left flank and interject our troops between his outer and main defenses."*

"There appears to have been some haste in abandoning the outer works," Alexander Hamilton points out. *"There were no attempts to destroy the redoubts."*

"That is valid," agrees Lafayette. *"Cornwallis may have acted prematurely and without all due consideration."*

"Perhaps Cornwallis simply abandoned the outer works because they were not finished, and he did not have the time to complete them," says Lincoln.

At this, Washington raises his hand and speaks up. *"In truth, when we first arrived, I was surprised to see that he had been busy erecting a second line of fortifications outside the inner ring. I would have thought that, given the time he had been here, the second ring would have long been completed."*

"Maybe the enemy simply lacks sufficient numbers to maintain their outer fortifications," speculates Nelson.

"I think not, Governor," Washington replies. *"Our intelligence relates that Cornwallis has over 9,000 men—more than enough to manage a second line. No, I fear that his intention is to attempt a retreat up the York River—there being no ships yet above the town to prevent such a move."*

"Perhaps that is why he still maintains the Star redoubt," says Wayne.

"Or perhaps this pullback constitutes a preparatory move in an elaborate escape plan by which the British would either cross by boat to Gloucester Point and fight their way through," says Hamilton. *"Or maybe he intends to break out somewhere along the right flank and flee up the peninsula toward Richmond."*

"I am far from laughing at the idea of the enemy's making a retreat," says Lafayette. *"It is not very probable; but it is not impossible."*

"Mon general," says Rochambeau, addressing Washington, *"it could be that Cornwallis is expecting relief. He would then, quite reasonably, decide to strengthen his main position by shortening his line. Such concentration would make it more difficult for us to overwhelm him."*

"In other words, he is trading land for time," says Washington.

"I believe that is the case," smiles the French commander.

Washington nods in agreement. "Lord Cornwallis is too good a soldier to have made such a move prematurely or in too much haste. He must be expecting reinforcements from New York. That's got to be it."

At that moment, a young lieutenant rides up to the tent and dismounts. He salutes Washington. "General, sir," he says out of breath, "a British officer under a flag of truce has delivered a letter from Colonel Scammel."

"He's alive!" shouts Hamilton in excitement.

Washington opens the note and reads it. "Colonel Scammel reports that he is being paroled and requests that his clothing be forwarded to the hospital in Williamsburg."

"That is good news, indeed!" states Anthony Wayne. "Scammel is one of the most popular officers in the army. Cornwallis should hang the bastard that shot him in the back!"

"It was a treacherous deed!" shouts Von Steuben.

"Well, it appears Colonel Scammel may recover from his wound," Washington says. "I am glad for that. Colonel Hamilton, will you see to it that our colleague's request is carried out?"

"I will, General—forthwith."

"Very well," replies Washington who turns to the dispatch rider. "Thank you, Lieutenant. Please convey to the British courier that Colonel Scammel's wishes will be carried out."

Washington turns back to the group and asks for an update on the new field of operation.

"Sir, the evacuated positions allow us to see and judge all the land surrounding the town and the enemy's interior defenses," responds General Lincoln. "The approaches are easily accessible to us. There are means of shelter everywhere. Some of the smaller areas are nonetheless commanding."

"We have also carefully examined the evacuated redoubts, sir," interjects Count Deux-Ponts. "They are not solid; the parapets are thin and are made of sandy soil which obliges them to be propped up lest they fall down. But the abatis are excellent, having no other fault but being made of pine and, in consequence, are easy to set on fire. The ravine of York Creek is now unobstructed for nearly its entire length. It is nearly twenty-five feet deep and runs for more than 1,600 yards. The enemy had built abatis around it. This ravine seems to provide excellent protection, and I do not understand why the enemy abandoned it. Not only did it comprise a superior defense, but its stream promises much-needed water for our troops. However, I regret to report, General Washington, that drinking water is now scarce, because Lord Cornwallis has thrown into the wells heads of steers, dead horses, and even the bodies of dead Negroes. The poor creatures probably died of the smallpox."

Washington sighs heavily and looks down at the ground in disgust. A long pause ensues among the officers. Finally, the American commander breaks the silence. "Gentlemen, I think that will do for now. We will alert Admiral de Grasse to be on the lookout for a British fleet. Meanwhile, there is no time to lose. We must reinforce the captured fortifications and begin preparations for our own trenches."

As the conference breaks up, Washington walks over to his aides, still sitting at the outside table. "Orders for tomorrow, Colonel Tilghman," he says.

"I am ready, sir," comes the quick response.

"Regarding sanitation and health: No one is allowed to drink water from wells without senior officer approval. Deserters from the British ranks are to be checked scrupulously to prevent those infected with smallpox from spreading the disease. How many deserters last night?" asks Washington.

"Eight reported, sir," says David Humphreys.

"Very well. See to it that our encampment is kept free of litter. For personal cleanliness among the troops, unit officers will inspect the grounds to make certain that no bones or other filth will be in or near them. In good weather, tents are to be struck and bedding aired daily."

Washington pauses until Tilghman stops writing, looks up, and nods. Then he continues. "Regarding safety: Soldiers not assigned to reconnoitering parties are to refrain from independently inspecting the enemy works. The curiosity of such persons often interrupts the observation of officers particularly charged with this business. All officers and men are strictly forbidden to wear red coats—for obvious reasons."

Washington paces back and forth, hands behind his back. After a few moments, Tilghman asks if there will be anything else.

"Yes," responds the general. "I would like the following to be read to the troops tonight."

As Washington dictates, Tilghman carefully takes down every word.

◆   ◆   ◆

That evening, as the sun was setting, sergeants all across the American and French encampments read aloud General Washington's personal message:

"The advanced season renders it indispensably necessary to conduct the attacks against Yorktown with the utmost rapidity. The passive conduct of the enemy indicates his weakness. The general, therefore, exhorts and requires the officers and soldiers of this army to pursue their duties with the most unabating ardor. The present moment may very well decide our struggle for American independence. Gentlemen, the liberties of America and the honor of the Allied Army are in our hands."

Cheers and shouts erupted from the troops. "Hurrah for General Washington!" they yelled. "Liberty or death!" "Freedom for America!"

Over in the Pennsylvania Regiment, a captain turned to the lieutenant standing next to him. "I'll bet a beaver hat that Lord Cornwallis and his army will be prisoners of war by next Sunday," he said. "Done!" came the response. "And it is a wager I hope to lose."

Sir Henry Clinton's Headquarters
Harlem Heights, New York
September 30, 1781

Sir Henry Clinton walks into the back study followed closely by his aides. He has just returned from another council of war with his admirals and generals. Clinton is sweating; wringing is hands; pacing back and forth anxiously.

"I must write a letter to Lord Cornwallis immediately!" he says.

"Yes, sir," replies Captain Dawkins, who sits down behind the desk and pulls out pen and paper. Captain Gurwood remains standing next to the window.

"Your Lordship may be assured that I am doing everything in my power to relieve you by a direct move," begins Clinton, "and I have reason to hope, from the assurances given me this day by Admiral Graves, that we may pass the bar by the 12th of October, if the winds permit, and no unforeseen accident happens."

Clinton looks down at the floor and shakes his head negatively. He is fully aware that only six days earlier, he had written to Cornwallis telling him that the fleet would sail no later than the 5th. Now he realizes that the vacillation of Admiral Graves may delay the fleet even beyond the 12th of October. Clinton clears his throat and continues. "This, however, is subject to disappointment. I shall persist in my idea of a direct move there even to the middle of November—should it be Your Lordship's opinion that you can hold out so long."

Dawkins finishes writing and looks over at Gurwood, who rolls his eyes and looks out the window.

"But if you tell me that you cannot," continues Clinton, "and I am without hopes of arriving in time to reinforce you by a direct move, I will immediately make an attempt upon Philadelphia by land. If this should draw any part of Washington's force from Yorktown, it may possibly give you an opportunity of doing something to save your army."

Upon Sir Henry's reference to a move on Philadelphia, Captain Gurwood's head snaps back in astonishment. Then Clinton shocks him again by stating that he wants a personal courier to take this dispatch directly to Virginia.

The two aides look at each other as if one of them is expected to volunteer. Finally, Dawkins speaks up. "Sir, Major Charles Cochrane has expressed to me his intense desire to see some action in Virginia."

"Very well," Clinton replies, "but make certain Cochrane understands the danger. By the time he arrives, Lord Cornwallis could be in a very bad situation."

"Of course, Sir Henry. I'll see to it."

After Clinton walks out of the room, Gurwood leans over to Dawkins. "Has he not told us many times before that he will not attack Philadelphia?"

"Yes, of course."

"Well, why would he say such a thing to Cornwallis?"

Dawkins pauses a moment before replying. "I guess he does not know what else to say. He basically tells Cornwallis that there probably won't be any help until November. I sure wouldn't want to be standing next to His Lordship when this letter arrives."

"And what of Major Cochrane?" asks Gurwood. "Has he really said he wants to go to Yorktown?"

"He has said he wants to see some real action, yes."

"Will you tell him the full seriousness of the situation there?"

Dawkins does not respond to this question; he merely smirks.

Sir Henry Clinton, meanwhile, has gone upstairs. In the hallway, he passes his mistress, Mrs. Baddeley, who greets him with a kind word and a smile. Clinton, however, ignores her with a frown. He goes into his bedroom, sits down at his desk, and opens his diary. He sits and stares at his journal for the longest time. Finally, Clinton picks up a pen. But he can bear to scrawl out only one sentence: "I see this situation in so serious a light, so horrible," he writes, "that I dare not look at it."

24

British Encampment
Yorktown, Virginia
October 1, 1781

On his march through the Carolinas and Virginia, Lord Earl Cornwallis had commandeered from the local farmers as many healthy horses as he could lay his hands on. Now bottled up at Yorktown as he was, the army was rapidly running out of both feed and forage. At first, Cornwallis ordered the most weakened of the animals driven out of the British encampment—and for days, American and French troops observed them, gaunt and starving, stumbling around in the mist, or wobbling about on the sandy beaches, heads down.

The previous night, however, Cornwallis had given an order that all horses not in use by the cavalry be rounded up, taken down to the shore, their throats slit, and their bodies dumped in the water. So when the sun came up on October 1, 1781, allied sentries were obliged to report to General Washington the sickening sight of 600 or 700 bloated horse carcasses floating in the York River.

As the day wore on, American and French troops witnessed an even more appalling occurrence. Wandering aimlessly through the woods, individually and in groups, were countless numbers of sick and starving Negroes. It turns out that Cornwallis had also expelled from Yorktown all those slaves that were no longer able to work. He took this action primarily because food supplies were low. But Cornwallis also hoped the Negroes, most of whom were inflicted with smallpox, would filter throughout the rebel plantations and mix with the enemy troops. In all, more than 2,000 of the sick and starving Negroes had been sent out to fend for themselves—and many Americans noted this sad occurrence in their journals. Pennsylvania Lieutenant Ebenezer Denny wrote that, "Negroes lie about, ailing and dying, in every state of the smallpox." And Virginia Militia Colonel St. George Tucker described "an immense number of Negroes" that had "died in the most miserable manner"—many of them with "pieces of burnt Indian corn in their hands and mouths."

Both the slaughter of the horses and the expulsion of the slaves signified the deteriorating mental state of the British army and its leaders. Cornwallis was clearly worried about running low on food and supplies. He had cut rations to his men by one-third in hopes of extending the siege until Sir Henry Clinton could arrive with reinforcements. And he constantly fretted about the unsanitary conditions caused by cooping up more than 9,000 men inside the small confines of Yorktown. Within only a few days of withdrawing from the outer lines, nearly 1,500 of Cornwallis's soldiers had become ill with "swamp fever," smallpox, or some other debilitating affliction. These men, of course, were unable to perform their duties, and their situation gave rise to an increased feeling of hopelessness among the British forces.

Lord Cornwallis, however, continued to work hard at fortifying the British inner defenses. He could no longer send out foraging expeditions on the Yorktown side of the river to cut down trees needed to reinforce his artillery batteries. So the British commander gave orders to dismantle as many houses as necessary to obtain the required lumber. He also kept thousands of men working around the clock—in four-hour shifts, all day and all night.

The British main line of defense ran more than a mile long and covered the perimeter of the town—including streets, businesses, and residences. Parapets (earthwork mounds) ranged from five to fifteen feet high and were ten to twenty feet thick. Forward ditches were approximately eight feet deep and covered by well-constructed abatis. The main line extended in an oblong semicircle around Yorktown and included eight redoubts and ten land batteries.

Beginning on the very northern corner of the town, an artillery battery ran three city blocks along the cliff overlooking the river. This line of artillery (dubbed Battery No. 1) protected the narrow stretch of water between Yorktown and Gloucester Point from French attack. It was manned by seamen from British naval vessels and was filled with twenty-six twelve-pound cannon that came from warships in the river—and land artillery that included: five eighteen-pound cannon, one nine-pounder, and two six-pounders.

From Battery No. 1, the British line ran 1,000 feet southwest across the main road to Williamsburg. Redoubt No. 1, manned by the Hessian Erbprinz Regiment, stood on the northeast side of the road. Battery No. 10 (with four twelve-pound cannon manned by the 23rd Infantry) and Redoubt No. 2 (manned by the 17th Infantry) were on the southwest side. These three works, positioned slightly in front of the main line, were joined by a line of timbers placed upright and firmly lodged in the ground. Both redoubts had significant forward abatis surrounding their front and sides. The main parapet and ditch behind were only five feet high and ten feet thick, because the natural terrain made the location impracticable for an enemy assault. The large Fusilier's Redoubt was detached from the main works and was located out front—a full 2,500 feet farther west along the river's edge. The *Charon* and *Guadeloupe* were moored in the York River between the Fusilier's and Redoubts No. 1 and No. 2. Combined, they provided formidable protection from any body of allied troops approaching along the Williamsburg Road.

From Redoubt No. 2, the British main line extended southeast approximately 2,000 feet in one long line of large earthworks that included three redoubts and three artillery batteries. This part of the line essentially faced Yorktown Creek and looked over all the avenues to the swamp that covered the right side of town. Battery No. 9 (next to Redoubt No. 2) began this line. Two hundred fifty feet to the southeast stood Redoubt No. 3 which, in turn, was flanked by Battery No. 8. Redoubt No. 4 stood another 250 feet away and Battery No. 7 was 600 feet farther down the line. Redoubt No. 5 was 250 more feet to the southeast. Battery No. 9 possessed six 9-pound cannon, Battery No. 8 had four twelve-pounders, and Battery No. 7 contained ten eight-pounders. These three redoubts were manned by the British Brigade of Guards (infantry) and the German Anspach Regiment.

Redoubt No. 5 formed the northern edge of a huge hornwork, which was the crown jewel of the British main line. Constructed on a low ridge, it was situated at the head of Hampton Road—which was the most likely place for a head-on enemy assault. The hornwork was shaped like a rectangle. Its west wing measured 500 feet in length, its south front ran 250 feet, and its east wing was 350 feet long. The hornwork's parapets were fifteen feet high and twenty feet thick with a variety of cannon placed along the line. For extra protection, it also possessed extraordinarily strong abatis out front of its entire length. As a post of honor, the hornwork was manned by the British Light Infantry.

From the hornwork, the British main line ran 1,200 feet west. This part of the battlefield was considered crucial, because it was most suitable for the Americans to construct massive siege parallels. It was here that the earthworks were built to their maximum sizes: fifteen feet high and twenty feet wide. In front was an eight-foot-deep ditch that was seven feet wide on the bottom and sixteen feet wide at the top. Six hundred feet west of the hornwork stood the unusually large Redoubt No. 6 (manned by the 80th Infantry Regiment). Immediately east was Battery No. 6, which contained two twelve-pound cannon and two 8-inch howitzers. Six hundred feet farther west was Redoubt No. 7 manned by the 76th Infantry Regiment. The 43rd Regiment of Infantry was assigned to defend the long line between Redoubts No. 6 and No. 7.

The final portion of the British line ran 1,000 feet due north from Redoubt No. 7 all the way to the beach on the York River. Battery No. 5 (with eight nine-pound cannon) stood next to Redoubt No. 7. Two hundred fifty feet farther north was Redoubt No. 8, a rather small, square structure that was manned by the 71st Infantry Regiment and flanked by Battery No. 4 (seven 9-pounders). From there, earthen parapets ran the final 500 feet to the beach.

Just as the Fusilier's Redoubt was detached from the far northeastern portion of the main line, so were two other not-as-well-finished redoubts on the far southeastern side. Redoubt No. 9 was located about 1,000 feet out in front of the main line. It had a perimeter of 103 yards, contained a moat and abatis, could hold nearly 200 men, and was equipped with two 9-pound cannon. Located 1,000 feet due north was Redoubt No. 10, usually called the "Rock" redoubt by the Americans. On the bluff overlooking the York River, it was 768 feet from the main line and had three gun embrasures for firing on enemy ships in the York River. Redoubts No. 9 and No. 10 were not connected to each other in any way, but each had a narrow ditch running back to the main line of fortifications.

Interior to the main works, the British also mounted two additional artillery batteries (No. 2 and No. 3) along the bluffs facing the York River. A total of sixteen twelve-pound cannon in these batteries were operated by able-bodied seamen. Facing the York River, Cornwallis deployed the 33rd Infantry Regiment and the German Von Bose Regiment.

Several additional works were constructed within the main defenses. A small parapet was put in place just south of Battery No. 3. And there was another trench and earthwork behind Redoubt No. 5 that reached from the large ravine behind Cornwallis's headquarters at the Nelson house south to the hornwork. Behind the Nelson house, Lord Cornwallis had dug a bombproof grotto out of the side of a deep ravine. Equipped with sleeping accommodations and large enough to accommodate his executive officers, he would be able to hold councils of war there when the enemy's siege bombardment began. Finally, a 1,000-foot communications trench ran from Redoubt No. 8, past Redoubt No. 6, and all the way to Battery No. 6. The earth removed from this trench formed a parallel parapet for additional protection.

A total of 9,185 men served under Lord Cornwallis inside the British defenses at Yorktown. General Charles O'Hara commanded the area from the hornwork to the Fusilier's Redoubt on the northeast. Lieutenant Colonel Robert Abercrombie, took charge of the southeastern works, including Redoubts No. 9 and No. 10. In all, there were sixty-five mounted cannon in their works. Only one, however, was larger than an eighteen-pounder.

And so stood the British fortifications at Yorktown as of October 1, 1781.

General Washington's Headquarters Tent
American Encampment
Yorktown, Virginia
October 1, 1781

It is early evening at twilight. There is still light coming into the tent from the open front flaps, but numerous lanterns are also burning on the tables.

Washington is conducting a conference with his aides. He has invited Generals Rochambeau, Lincoln, Von Steuben, Chief Engineer Duportail, and French lead engineer Lieutenant Colonel Wuerenet de la Combe. All are seated around the large dining table. Various maps are spread out, and there is a tankard of ale in front of each officer.

"Sir, we have two dispatches just in from New York," Tench Tilghman reports to Washington. "The first relates that General Benedict Arnold has resigned his commission and gone to Canada."

Washington's face flushes red at the mention of Arnold's name. "After what he has done, especially in his own state of Connecticut," says the general, "there is no place in America he could be safe. But enough of that traitor. What of the second dispatch?"

"Sir, Admiral Digby has arrived in New York," says Tilghman. "But he has brought with him only three ships of the line and one corps of troops."

"Only three ships?" asks Washington. "That will hardly be enough to make a difference against the French fleet."

"Our informant also states that great exertions are being made for an attempt to relieve Cornwallis," continues Tilghman, "and that Digby has brought with him the king's son, Prince William Henry."

"Hmmm. That should cause a delay of at least a few days while Sir Henry entertains the boy," speculates Washington. "But I am concerned that when Cornwallis learns Digby has brought with him only three ships, he will try to make an escape."

"Oui," agrees Rochambeau, "his hopes may be dashed for an effective rescue."

"Perhaps he will attempt an evacuation over to Gloucester Point?" says John Laurens.

"Yes, that would make sense," concurs David Humphreys.

"It is possible," replies Washington. "But I think it more likely that he will overload his shipping and flee up the York where the river is divided into the Pamunkey and Mattapony tributaries. With these guarding each of his flanks, he could then push *his army through a country whose population is too scattered to provide any opposition."*

"Sir, doesn't the slaughter of his horses indicate not only a want of storage but no intention of pushing a march?" asks Laurens.

"Cornwallis made that decision without knowing that Digby has brought with him only three ships," says Washington. "And I fear that we have little hope to starve him into surrender. My greater hope is that he is not well provided with artillery and military stores for a proper defense—not having anticipated being reduced to his current situation."

"I agree with that particular assessment, mon general," states Rochambeau. "However, I do not believe Lord Cornwallis is going to make a run for it. He is working too hard on his entrenchments. I'm sure he thinks he can hold us off for an indefinite period. But His Lordship has not been subjected to a proper siege, at least not one of which I'm aware."

At this point, the American commander turns to Benjamin Lincoln. "General, what is your opinion of the enemy's position?"

"Sir, based on our reconnaissance, the British left seems to possess a field of fire superior to either the right or center of the line," replies Lincoln. "And this sector, too, has the added reinforcement of the two detached redoubts. On the right, several warships are anchored close to the shore where their guns may cover the Yorktown Creek ravine. Beyond this line, of course, are Cornwallis's main defenses. They are both extensive and strong—the result of industrious digging by his soldiers in recent days. The main line is commanded by seven redoubts and at least half a dozen gun batteries."

"Is there an area you would recommend above others for our main approach?" asks Washington.

"Indeed, sir," replies Lincoln. "The obvious place for our trenches is on the east side across the barren, sandy plain. It is covered with hedges, browning grass, and bearpaw cactus. Cornwallis, of course, has anticipated this, as it is here he has placed his hornwork."

Turning to Rochambeau, Washington asks if he agrees. "General Lincoln is correct, sir," states the Frenchman. "That has to be the place for our main line. Major Duportail has already laid out preliminary plans."

"Sir, do you believe we can blast the enemy into submission?"

"Without question," replies Rochambeau. "We have the decisive superiority of both strength and means. Our inevitable victory is, in fact, reduced merely to calculation."

"Very well," says Washington. "Major Duportail, will you show us your preliminary plans, please?"

Louis Duportail rises from his chair and spreads his map in front of Washington and Rochambeau. "General, I have plotted our first parallel here," he says, pointing with his index finger, "600 yards distant from the enemy's main line. To adequately protect the parallel, I propose four infantry redoubts—equidistant along its length—here, here, here, and here. By taking advantage of the topography, our line will stretch from the bank of the river northwest all the way to the York Creek ravine." Duportail continues explaining his plan for a few more minutes and then indicates he is done.

"Very well," says Washington with a glance toward the French commander. "With General Rochambeau's concurrence, you may begin immediately. What specific orders may I direct to help you commence operations?"

"Sir, I would suggest approximately 800 men be dispatched into the forest to collect materials for making fascines, gabions, and saucissons, which will be used to strengthen our earthworks. Another 400 will be needed to work on reinforcement of the enemy's abandoned works."

"Colonel Tilghman, will you see to it that 1,200 men are dispatched tomorrow morning according to the major's wishes?" asks Washington.

"Yes, General," replies Tilghman, scribbling notes on a piece of paper.

"What else, Major?"

"Sir, we will also need to acquire as much oak plank as practicable for the building of artillery platforms," continues Duportail. "They should be two to three inches thick and twelve or eighteen feet in length. As much pine plank from one to three inches will also be needed. This wood is absolutely essential for our operations to be successful."

"I've got that," says David Humphreys, who has been writing furiously.

"Very well, Colonel," replies Washington. "Send that dispatch to General Knox for action first thing tomorrow. Tell him to proceed to Somerset on the eastern shore of Maryland. There he will find ample oak."

"Yes, sir."

"Colonel Tilghman," continues Washington, "based on the arrival of Admiral Digby in New York, I would like our schedule of operations to be accelerated as much as is humanly possible."

"Yes, sir," responds Tilghman.

"Also, I would like to send an urgent dispatch to Admiral de Grasse."

"Yes, General," replies Laurens, who begins addressing the letter in French.

Washington starts dictating: "I anticipate that Lord Cornwallis, when he hears of Admiral Digby's arrival with a meager three ships, may attempt to flee up the river and move overland in a manner that would make it impossible for us to overtake him. Therefore, I once more request that Admiral de Grasse post ships in the river above

Yorktown. Only by this action will the investment of the enemy be complete. Otherwise the British remain masters of the navigation for a distance of twenty-five miles above them, and may by their armed vessels intercept supplies of the greatest value on their way to our camp."

The general pauses a moment, grimaces, and grabs his jaw—another shooting pain from one of his infected teeth. He looks at Rochambeau who, ever so slightly, nods his head negatively. Washington then continues. "If the admiral determines that the recommended action is not workable, I request that he at least take a more menacing position with respect to the enemy on our right. Please note that communication with our forces at Gloucester Point currently involves a roundabout land route of ninety miles. With French naval control of the upper river, the distance would be greatly shortened. Have you got all that, Colonel Laurens?"

"Yes, sir."

"Very well, that is all for now. Colonel Humphreys, would you please have the stewards serve dinner?"

"Yes, sir," replies Humphreys, who rises and leaves the tent.

Louis Duportail also folds his map and stands. "General Washington, General Rochambeau," he says, "please excuse me from the meal. I have much work to do."

"Of course," replies Rochambeau.

"You are welcome to stay, Major," says Washington.

"Thank you, General, but I have many drawings and calculations to make."

"Very well. I appreciate your counsel and advice."

Duportail then bows and leaves the tent.

◆   ◆   ◆

During dinner, Washington quizzed General Rochambeau and Baron Von Steuben about the details of a siege, the classic eighteenth-century method of warfare. The American commander had never actually seen or been part of one. As a matter of fact, neither had anybody else in the American army, with the lone exception of Von Steuben, who had experienced his first siege as a teenager in Prague. Most of the French officers, however, had extensive siege experience. Rochambeau had been present at fourteen sieges in various parts of the world.

To compensate for his lack of knowledge, Washington planned to rely heavily on the experienced officers who surrounded him, and he curiously and enthusiastically took every opportunity to absorb as much detailed information as he possibly could. This dinner was one such occasion—and Washington spent most of his time listening.

Over the course of the next three hours, Rochambeau and Von Steuben discussed various key elements of siege warfare. They began by giving the American general a copy of Vauban's Procedures, a manual governing the rules, principles, and techniques of siege craft. It had been written more than a century before by the Frenchmen Sebastien le Pietre de Vauban and contained fifty-five numbered paragraphs in sequential order.

Both Rochambeau and von Steuben counseled Washington that a successful siege depended on endurance, determination, patience, resourcefulness, and dedication to Vauban's procedures. Every siege, they pointed out, began with an investment of the enemy garrison to prevent communications with the outside and to prohibit the entrance of all external resources. The allied armies had already completed this phase at Yorktown—and had done so in relatively short order and quite efficiently. During investment, professional engineers draw up a detailed plan for encampments, fortifications, battle formations, and artillery emplacements. A dozen qualified military engineers were already hard at work performing these tasks under the supervision of lead engineers Duportail and Combe.

The next phase of the siege plan would be conducted by corps of sappers and miners who would dig a number of initial trenches in zigzag patterns straight toward Yorktown. From the heads of these ditches, they would construct the first parallel at right angles. The purpose of a trench parallel was to establish a solid position against the enemy, provide protection for the troops, and fix a base for production of additional fortifications.

After the first parallel was completed, infantry troops would be employed to construct new redans, redoubts, and gun emplacement batteries. Of course, Cornwallis's abandoned fortifications would be properly converted and incorporated into the first allied parallel. Once these fortifications were completed, the artillery would be set in place, and a major bombardment would commence.

This pattern of parallel construction, fortification, and artillery bombardment would repeat itself during the course of a siege. Usually, two additional parallels would be dug, each one successively closer to the enemy's main works. The siege would end when the substantially weakened enemy line was stormed by an all out frontal troop assault—or when the enemy surrendered. Almost all properly executed sieges, Rochambeau told Washington, ended in the total and unconditional capitulation of the enemy.

A curious Washington next asked about details of the various kinds of fortifications. Redans were small detached works, explained Von Steuben. They are formed of two earthen parapets, each up to 200 feet long, placed to make a ninety-degree angle facing the enemy position. Open at the gorge, redans serve to cover approaches through ravines, along rivers and causeways, and across bridges.

Redoubts are larger and stronger than redans. They secure advantageous ground and, when placed along a parallel, guard its length and protect its supply depots from enemy sorties. Most redoubts are square, pentagonal, or triangular. Larger, more elaborate ones can be hexagonal, circular, or star-shaped like the British Fusilier's Redoubt. Every redoubt consists of five main parts: 1) a parapet, 2) a surrounding ditch, 3) a rampart (the base), 4) a banquette (a perch that enables the troops to fire over the parapet), 5) a scarp (the exterior sharp-angled slope that makes it difficult for an enemy approach). As a matter of routine, all redoubts are occupied by members of the infantry. Rochambeau also cautioned Washington that proper construction of redoubts was laborious work and took time—at least three days to do a proper job.

Finally, both European generals emphasized the importance of the artillery. It was the artillery's firepower, and the artillery's firepower alone, that would result in the vanquishment of the enemy. Therefore, judicious time had to be spent constructing batteries properly and with unquestioned strength. Only then could the enemy be battered and blasted into submission.

◆   ◆   ◆

After dinner is over and the French and American officers have departed, Washington grabs the arm of Tench Tilghman and pulls him over to a corner of the tent. The general turns his back to the opening, so that nobody will be able to overhear the conversation. Looking down and careful to speak in a low tone, he leans toward his aide. "Tench," whispers Washington, "what is a gabion?"

Tilghman shakes his head negatively. "Beats the hell out of me, sir," he responds.

Washington shakes his head and frowns. "Well, I guess we will find out soon enough," he says.

Both men nod affirmatively.

American Lines
Yorktown, Virginia
October 2, 1781

At dawn, troops of the allied army began swarming over the terrain surrounding Yorktown. Four hundred members of the American infantry armed with spades, shovels, and pickaxes worked on abandoned fortifications along the Hampton and Goosely Roads. The vacant battery there was converted into a strong redoubt. An equal number of French troops also began altering the redoubts at Pigeon Hill by filling in the British openings and cutting new ones in the opposite walls. The industrious French broke ground, as well, for new redans and redoubts along the Wormley Creek ravine.

Also that morning, 800 American infantry troops were joined by 1,200 members of the militia in the woods more than a mile beyond the British main line. Equipped with axes and hatchets, they cut down huge trees, slashed endless branches from the trunks, and hacked down thousands of saplings. Once they had enough raw materials, the troops broke into groups and began construction of the following seven component materials that would be used to strengthen earthwork fortifications:

1) Gabions were bottomless wicker baskets that usually measured about three feet high by one foot in diameter. They were fashioned by driving saplings into the dirt in small circles, which were then woven together with pliable branches and brush. When completed, the baskets were filled with soil and placed in the sides of the trenches and fortifications to enhance strength and absorb enemy cannon fire. To provide effective shields against enemy bullets, extra-large gabions stuffed with wood were often rolled ahead of trench sappers as they dug straight toward the enemy works.

2) Saucissons were fifteen-foot-long wicker cylinders of tied-together tree branches. They were generally stacked in ascending rows on the insides of artillery batteries, which required greater strength than trenches or redoubts.

3) Pickets were nothing more than pointed sticks used for staking down saucissons (six pickets per saucisson) and other component materials.

4) Fascines were smaller saucissons that measured anywhere from three to six feet long, six to eight inches in diameter. Fascines were usually staked in layers along the interior of earthworks to strengthen the slopes.

5) Hurdles were rectangular mats formed by interwoven tree branches. They usually measured three feet long by five feet wide and were used to stabilize slopes in redoubts and batteries.

6) Fraises and palisades were ten-foot-long, four-or five-inch thick trees or tree branches that were sharpened into points at one end. Used to impede an enemy advance, they were planted three to four feet deep in the exterior slope of a work with their points projecting outward toward the enemy at a forty-five-to sixty-degree angle.

7) Abatis were fallen trees that were used to ring fortifications beyond the surround ditches. They were usually put in place with stripped and sharpened branches facing the enemy.

By the end of the day, these various component materials began to pile high in the woods and along the roadsides. And over the next week to ten days, thousands and thousands of them would be used in both French and American trenches and fortifications.

◆   ◆   ◆

As allied forces converted the abandoned redoubts, British artillery attempted to disrupt operations by unleashing a cannonade that amounted to about forty shots per hour—with breaks of only five minutes or less at a time. One New York soldier noted in his diary that this artillery fire did have an impact. "After having wounded several of our men," he wrote, "we adopted a precaution to establish men in different places on the work who would watch for the flash of the enemy's guns. When we immediately cried out 'a shot,' each man took care of himself by jumping off the works into the trenches. At one point, the enemy fired two eight-inch shells. One burst over our heads, the pieces of which flew among us but did no harm. The other struck the ground and burst fifty yards in our rear." Upon seeing the reactions of the Americans, British gunners often simulated fire by flashing powder charges at their muzzles—and watched the rebels dive for cover.

As the cannonade wore on, a few casualties began to mount. One Maryland soldier's hand was shot off. A corporal died after a nine-pound iron shot passed through his abdomen. Four members of the Pennsylvania Regiment were killed by the same cannonball. And a foolish militiamen clambered on top of a parapet and kept running back and forth taunting British gunners. He finally drew enough attention that shots were repeatedly fired in his direction. "Damn my soul if I'll dodge for these buggers!" he shouted. Then he began swinging his spade at every cannonball that flew by him. The British eventually hit him with a direct shot, flinging his mangled body into the trench.

General Washington Headquarters Tent
Yorktown, Virginia
October 2, 1781

Late in the evening, as Washington was sitting in his small private tent writing a few letters, Tench Tilghman delivered to him a note from the Marquis de Lafayette marked "personal." After Tilghman excused himself, Washington read the message.

Lafayette, in no uncertain terms, asked his commander in chief to transfer General Benjamin Lincoln to the Gloucester Point side of the river. The young marquis would then be left in charge of the entire American wing on the Yorktown side. For a supporting reason, Lafayette noted that Lincoln had already established a reputation, and that the upcoming battle offered him an opportunity to establish one of his own.

Washington furrowed his eyebrows and set the letter down on his writing table. He leaned back in his chair, closed his eyes, and thought about his second in command.

General Benjamin Lincoln, a forty-eight-year-old veteran from Massachusetts, had played a vital role in the American victory at Saratoga. It had taken him ten months to recuperate from the leg wound he suffered there—the wound that would leave him with a limp for the rest of his life. More recently, Lincoln had suffered the trauma of being in command during the worst American loss of the Revolution. He had been defeated by Lord Cornwallis during a siege and had surrendered more than 5,000 troops and the city of Charleston, South Carolina. After the surrender, Cornwallis proceeded to humiliate Lincoln by not according him the full honors of war. After months in confinement, Lincoln was released in a prisoner of war exchange and had promptly reported for duty.

After a few moments, Washington opened his eyes and proceeded to write a brief note back to Lafayette. Kindly, but firmly, Washington refused the young marquis' request. General Benjamin Lincoln would stay on the Yorktown side and remain second in command.

25

Nelson House
Headquarters of Lord Cornwallis
Yorktown, Virginia
October 2, 1781

Lord Cornwallis is sitting at the head of the dining room table. Also seated are General Charles O'Hara, Lieutenant Colonel Robert Abercrombie, Colonel Chewton, Navy Captain Thomas Symonds, and Major Ross. They have just finished the evening meal and are sipping wine.

"Well, we certainly greatly increased the volume of cannon fire today," notes Cornwallis.

"Indeed, My Lord," responds O'Hara, "we must have fired 2,000 rounds."

"What reports have we on impact?"

"At least ten Americans killed and wounded, My Lord," says Abercrombie. "One gunner reported that one of his shots killed four out of five men in an American patrol."

"During the afternoon, one Pennsylvanian crossed over and surrendered to us," states Chewton.

"Good," replies Cornwallis. "Let us be sure to interrogate him thoroughly."

"Perhaps he can tell us why Washington has not returned a single shot in response to our barrage," says Major Ross.

"Come, come, Major," replies Cornwallis. "He is simply waiting, biding their time. He will hold fire until his fortifications are completed, all his cannon are in place, and then he will unleash his cannonade in tandem. The best we can hope to do at the moment is delay the enemy's work on the fortifications—and hope Sir Henry Clinton gets here in time. General O'Hara, what is your opinion of the state of our defenses?"

"Nearly all the main fortifications have been completed, sir," replies O'Hara. "Our efforts are turned to improving the surrounding stockade and establishing communication routes from the redoubt to the hornwork."

"Unfortunately, we are now out of wood, sir," says Abercrombie. "We have pulled down every wooden house in town. There are none left."

Cornwallis rises from the table, walks over to a nearby credenza, and begins writing on a piece of paper. "Well, we need more wood," *he states.* "Colonel Tarleton must move across to Gloucester Point tonight and begin new foraging operations. No more delays. Major Ross, take this order to him immediately. He is to make the crossing late this evening. We will provide him cover with artillery fire."

"Yes, My Lord," *responds Ross, who quickly takes the note and departs.*

"I assume, Captain Symonds, that our ships are prepared to convey Tarleton's troops and provide proper protection."

"Of course, My Lord," *replies Symonds.* "We have ships stretched across the channel of the river in a most formidable manner. Five of them are fireships chained to each other. There will be no interference from de Grasse."

Just then, Major Ross returns. On his way out of the house, he has met a courier. "Sir, we have just received a dispatch from General Clinton," *he says, handing it over.* "A guard boat slipped through the bay undetected again."

Cornwallis eagerly opens the letter and notes it is dated September 25. Unfortunately for the British commander, this is not Clinton's most recent letter, written on September 30, in which he stated that he would not leave until October 12 at the earliest and that, if he had no hopes of arriving in time, he would make a direct move on Philadelphia.

After reading for a moment, Cornwallis turns to the others in the room. "Sir Henry writes that his fleet consists of twenty-three sails of the line, three of which are three-deckers—and there is every reason to hope he will start from New York on the 5th of October. Sir Henry also asks us to let him know our real situation, our opinion of how he can best help us, and the exact strength of the enemy's fleet."

"Good!" *declares General O'Hara.* "That means the fleet will be leaving three days from now and should be here by next week."

"Yes," *exclaims Lieutenant Colonel Abercrombie.* "We can certainly hold out that long."

Cornwallis pauses. "It will be close, I think," *he says quietly.* "Sir Henry and the fleet should arrive about the same time Washington completes his first parallel and opens fire on us. That will be all, gentlemen. I must compose a reply immediately."

As the others excuse themselves, Colonel Chewton pulls out pen and paper. Cornwallis strides back and forth in the room and begins to dictate. "Sir Henry, I have received your letter of the 25th of September," *he begins.* "The enemy are encamped about two miles from us. They broke ground on the night of the 30th of September and are laboring industriously to complete their fortifications.

"Our accounts of the strength of the French fleet are thirty-five or thirty-six sails of the line. They have frequently changed their position. Two ships of the line and one *frigate lie at the mouth of this river, and our last accounts were that the body of the fleet lay between the tail of the Horseshoe and York split. I see little chance of my being able to send troops to wait for you at the Capes, but I will do so, if possible."*

Chewton looks up. Cornwallis pauses and takes a deep breath. Finally, he continues. "We are surrounded. But our works are in a better state of defense than we had reason to hope."

◆   ◆   ◆

At ten o'clock that night, British ships anchored in the river began a heavy cannonade aimed toward the American and French lines. Designed only as cover fire, the barrage lasted approximately one hour, long enough for transport ships to move Colonel Banastre Tarleton and his entire cavalry legion (including horses) across the York and disembark them on the Gloucester Point side.

Trebell's Landing, Virginia
October 3, 1781

The French siege artillery had finally arrived at this remote landing spot on the south side of the James River. And General Rochambeau, awakened in the middle of the night with the news, had galloped the seven-mile distance to oversee the swift and safe unloading of this unusually heavy cargo. With sixty-four sloops and schooners anchored in the river, Rochambeau scrambled to gather as many flatboats and scows as possible—all of which would be used to transport the cannon from ship to shore. When overenthusiastic soldiers began to liberally borrow from locals, stern warnings were issued that a court-martial would be in order for anyone stealing from or otherwise maltreating citizens. Compounding the logistically challenging situation was the fact that the allied supply train, completing its 400-mile journey from New York, had also arrived the day before. Now, all of a sudden, thousands of much-needed supplies, including food, muskets, bayonets, flints, and entrenching tools, were available.

Washington quickly ordered that all wagons of the supply train be unloaded as fast as possible and moved to Trebell's Landing to be used for the movement of artillery and supplies. He also dispatched his personal wagons and horses so that "the heavy artillery may be brought up without a moment's loss of time." Other officers followed the general's lead, and the road between the James River and Yorktown soon became crowded with soldiers, horses, and wagons traveling in both directions.

Ordnance supplies such as cannonballs, shells, barrels of gunpowder, fuses, rammers, and sponges were easily loaded onto wagons and moved without delay. But transportation of the heavy guns was another story. Even though Rochambeau now had use of the newly arrived huge horses (from the equipage) which were used exclusively for moving artillery, the work proceeded excruciatingly slow. Horses hitched two to a cannon sometimes did not provide enough strength to move multiton pieces of artillery. So the troops were often forced to help push and pull guns uphill and over particularly rough terrain. By day's end, however, a steady stream of artillery and supplies were arriving at the American and French lines at Yorktown—and that flow would continue twenty-four hours a day for nearly a week.

American Lines
Yorktown, Virginia
October 3, 1781

With the arrival of the siege artillery, optimism soared and the entire allied line buzzed with activity. Troops dug in for a long stay. Kitchens, latrines, and hospitals were constructed. Tents and brush shelters were set up all across the American encampment, which was laid out with precision, order, and consistency. Sergeants and privates set up their tents and shelters in rows two feet apart. Junior officers placed their tents twenty feet behind; senior officers, thirty feet still father behind. Next came the kitchens (forty feet farther), then the horses and wagons. Finally, support officers (surgeons, paymasters, and quartermasters) were situated well to the rear. Camp guards were posted approximately 900 feet to the front and rear of each regiment.

The Americans occupied the right wing of the allied encampment, viewed and approved as the "position of honor" by the French. Farthest to the right was Lafayette's Light Infantry Division—with Governor Nelson's Virginia Militia directly behind. Immediately to Lafayette's left were General Lincoln's forces, which included the New York, New Jersey, and Rhode Island regiments—and the Corps of Sappers and Miners. Next came Baron Von Steuben's division with General Wayne's Pennsylvanians and the regiments from Virginia and Maryland. Directly behind Von Steuben were Henry Knox's artillery regiments and the quartermaster facilities. Three-quarters of a mile west and behind the artillery regiment was General Washington's headquarters tent—surrounded, of course, by Washington's Life Guard.

The left wing of the allied encampment was occupied by the entire French army. Starting with the French artillery park, where the cannons from Trebell's Landing were being assembled, the encampment ran in a continuous parallel arc from south to north. The Bourbonnois and Deux-Ponts Regiments were located next to the artillery park; then came the Regiments Soissonnais and Santongue—all these troops being under the command of Major General Antoine-Charles du Houx, Baron de Viomenil, who reported directly to Count de Rochambeau. The Marquis de St. Simon guarded the Williamsburg Road with the Genois and Gatinois Regiments. And finally, the Regiment Touraine, situated a safe distance from the Fusilier's Redoubt, held the far left side of the allied lines. General Rochambeau's headquarters were set up only 400 yards east of Washington's tent.

Closer to the front lines, meanwhile, allied forces worked on the approaches and revamped captured fortifications. British forces continued to do everything they could to disrupt their work. When the sun went down, for instance, Cornwallis sent small patrols forward to harass the enemy, so the incessant rattle of musket fire could be heard throughout the battlefield area. In addition, Cornwallis kept up a moderate but relentless cannonade that consistently slowed allied operations.

Late in the day, General Washington ventured out with a small party on reconnaissance. He stopped near some members of Scammel's Light Infantry Corps to take a closer look at enemy fortifications. Standing nearby was Dr. James Thacher and the regimental chaplain, the Rev. Israel Evans. A British gunner must have seen Washington sitting atop his white horse and thought him an inviting target, so he aimed a shot in that direction. The cannonball plowed into the ground about twenty yards in front of the group and kicked up enough earth to shower the chaplain's hat with sand. Washington barely reacted to the shot. But Evans, frightened and a bit agitated, took off his hat, looked at the sand, and exclaimed: "Now, see here, General!"

"Mr. Evans," replied Washington calmly, "you had better carry that home and show it to your wife and children."

Outside the British Fortifications
Gloucester Point, Virginia
October 3, 1781

At dawn on Wednesday morning, with the weather turned cool and cloudy, Lieutenant Colonel Thomas Dundas led detachments from his garrison out to forage in the countryside several miles north of Gloucester Point. After more than three hours of confiscation, commandeering, and what locals viewed as outright thievery, hundreds of farm animals were tied to wagons loaded with corn, wood, and other loot. As the foraging train headed back to Gloucester Point, it was protected in front by Colonel John Simcoe and his Queen's Rangers riding with British infantry regiments. Newly arrived Colonel Banastre Tarleton's Cavalry Legion made up most of the rear guard. Dundas had taken plenty of men and planned for a rather large haul, because he knew this would be one of the last foraging expeditions before his garrison would be completely surrounded by allied forces.

During the month of September, the British had maintained full control of Gloucester Point and its northern surroundings. Washington had earlier dispatched the American militia there, and its commander, General George Weedon, had slowly formed a ring around the British, but at a distance of some fifteen miles. The Duke de Lauzun, who had been ordered to help in the region with his cavalry, was shocked to see Weedon so far from the enemy. He quickly wrote a scathing letter to Rochambeau and Washington complaining that Weedon "detested fighting," was "terribly afraid of gunshot," and appeared "frightened to death."

The allied commanders responded by dispatching Brigadier General Claude Gabriel de Choisy to Gloucester Point along with 800 marines supplied by Admiral de Grasse. When de Choisy, a violent-tempered man known for his tirades, arrived on October 1st, he accused Weedon of using "cowardly tactics" and ordered the 1,200 militiamen to march south toward Gloucester Point. On Tuesday night, October 2, they were camped less than five miles from the British garrison. And on the morning of October 3rd, de Choisy gave an order for his entire command to move even closer to Gloucester Point. As a result, nearly 2,000 allied troops, led by 350 of the Duke de Lauzun's cavalry, were marching along a country lane directly toward Dundas's 300-man foraging expedition.

At about 10:00 AM, the last of the wagon train had just entered the forest north of Gloucester Point when a British cavalryman spotted several enemy horsemen and a column of dust in the distance. He immediately reported to Colonel Tarleton that the riders had noticed him and quickly galloped away. Tarleton, who had no idea that de Choisy's reinforcements had arrived, wrongly assumed that the riders were just a small contingent of Duke de Lauzun's cavalry. After ordering his legion and the infantry to form a line just inside the edge of the forest and prepare for battle, Tarleton rode forward with a few officers to investigate. About a quarter of a mile down the lane, they came to a small farmhouse.

And upon hearing the horsemen ride up, a young woman opened the door and peered outside.

"Good day, madam," said the commander, tipping his hat, "I am Colonel Banastre Tarleton of His Majesty's Legion."

"Good day, sir."

"Can you tell me if you have seen any French or American horsemen in the last few minutes?"

"Indeed, I have, sir," the woman replied with a smile. "Just a few, though—riding rapidly in the other direction. I believe they are part of the Duke de Lauzun's regiment, who are often in the region."

"Well, I am very eager to shake hands with the French Duke," replied Tarleton with a smile. Then, taking off his hat and motioning with it in a long graceful bow, the dashing dragoon thanked the woman and rode back toward his own troops.

Meanwhile, after being told of the British foraging expedition, the Duke de Lauzun rapidly led his cavalry forward while the rest of the American militia continued at a slow march. He soon came upon the same little farmhouse and the young woman still standing at the door. In a serious tone, de Lauzun questioned her as to what she had recently seen.

"Why, Colonel Tarleton left here just a moment ago," she said. "He said he was most eager to shake hands with the French Duke."

"*Merci, madam,*" came the reply. "I am the Duke de Lauzun, and I assure you I have come with the purpose of gratifying him."

As the French officer turned to ride away, the woman shook her head negatively, giving de Lauzun the impression that she felt sorry for him having to fight such a formidable opponent as the handsome and wonderful Banastre Tarleton.

Galloping full speed at the head of the French cavalry, de Lauzun caught sight of the British dragoons after only two or three minutes. Tarleton was less than thirty yards from the edge of the forest where his men were waiting when he saw the enemy out of the corner of his eye. Without a moment's delay, Tarleton turned, drew his pistol, and spurred his horse toward the French, his small group of dragoons riding right on his heels. Seeing this, de Lauzun and a few hussars, about twenty yards in front of the main cavalry, called for a full charge and began racing directly toward Tarleton with swords and lances drawn.

Just as the two groups were about to converge, a French hussar threw a lance that narrowly missed Tarleton but plunged into the mount of a dragoon next to him. The wounded horse and its rider fell directly into Tarleton's mount causing it to stumble. The British cavalry leader then tumbled head over heels to the ground. Several British dragoons quickly positioned themselves between Tarleton and the French riders—and hand-to-hand fighting commenced. Upon seeing their leader go down, the entire English legion of green-coated dragoons left the safety of the woods and charged into the fray at full speed. British infantry muskets also began to spray cover fire at the French cavalry.

Now unable to capture Banastre Tarleton, as he had hoped to do, de Lauzun pulled back a short distance and formed his cavalry into a line of battle. Tarleton, meanwhile, mounted another horse and, realizing his men were in a disorganized and vulnerable state, ordered a hasty retreat back to the edge of the forest. After a few minutes, Tarleton, with his legion reformed, and de Lauzun charged each other and again engaged in close-order hand-to-hand fighting. As British infantry fired from the woods, the green dragoons were able to gain some advantage over the white-coated French hussars. But the American militia force soon arrived at the edge of the plain and began firing at the British horsemen. Both cavalry regiments again pulled back to reorganize and regroup. There were two or three more charges and countercharges with neither side gaining any advantage. Colonel Tarleton finally ordered a full retreat, and the British withdrew back to the garrison at Gloucester Point.

In the skirmish, the French had suffered fifteen killed and wounded; British casualties were only twelve. De Lauzun, however, had captured several British legionnaires, including one officer, and, in something of a moral victory, Banastre Tarleton's horse.

◆   ◆   ◆

By mid-afternoon on October 3, British forces had abandoned all outer positions along the Gloucester Point peninsula and retreated into their main line of defenses. These fortifications included four large redoubts extending east-west across the southern tip of Gloucester Point. Three artillery batteries were positioned along the line and contained a total of nineteen cannon. One of the batteries faced southeast looking down the York River while the other two were oriented northwest toward the mainland. Several small redans sat out in front of the main line, and everything was joined together by large wooden stakes planted in the ground which, in turn, were covered by felled trees. A total of 775 British forces manned the works. The right was occupied by Captain Johann Ewald's German Jagers, the center by the 8th British Infantry Regiment, and Lieutenant Colonel Simcoe's Queen's Rangers protected the left. Colonel Thomas Dundas held overall command.

General de Choisy advanced the allied forces to within one and a half miles of the British main line and began erecting his own temporary fortifications. Over the next day or two, he established a semicircle around Dundas, which effectively cut off all British communications to the surrounding countryside. With a force of only 2,000, de Choisy did not possess sufficient military strength to make an all-out assault. But Gloucester Point, just like Yorktown, was now invested—and Lord Cornwallis's foraging operations were at an end.

On an ensuing evening, American militia commander General George Weedon sat down and penned a letter to his good friend Nathanael Greene. "I am all on fire," he wrote. "I think we may all lay down our swords by the last of the year in perfect peace and security. Cornwallis is trapped. We have got him handsomely in a pudding bag."

26

General Washington's Headquarters Tent
Yorktown, Virginia
October 4, 1781

It is Thursday evening, right around sunset. The flaps of the big tent are open. A number of lanterns and candles are flickering. Washington and staff sit around the table. Tilghman, Humphreys, Laurens are all in good moods.

"Did you hear the cheers erupt throughout the camps this afternoon?" asks Washington, with a big grin.

"Indeed, we did, sir," replies a smiling Tilghman. "I went over to our guards to find out what was happening. They were all ecstatic."

"It's not often that the troops receive word before we do on such a development," states Humphreys. "But I guess the couriers simply could not contain themselves."

"Neither would I if I had their news," states Washington. "And when everybody learned that Tarleton had been knocked off his horse, they considered it to be just as important as an overwhelming victory. Our army's morale has been lifted to a new height!"

"I have never seen the men so happy," replies Laurens, with a smile.

"Yes, yes," says Washington, now looking toward Tilghman. "All good news, so far. Now what of our ongoing preparations?"

"General, sir," responds Tilghman, "Admiral de Grasse has agreed to your request for ships farther upstream to menace Cornwallis and discourage an escape. Despite the constant urging from Admiral de Barras to do so, he will not sail past Yorktown. But two ships of the line are at least now in sight just downriver."

"Very well. If we cannot have them upriver from here to deter an escape, at least they will make His Lordship think twice. What else?"

"The making of fascines and gabions goes on unabated," continues Tilghman, with a wink, "from six in the morning until five in the afternoon. And as of this morning, our redoubts are all completed. The engineers have also finished their design for the first parallel. It will be 600 yards from the British main line directly opposite the hornwork—and will run 6,000 feet from the river to the York Creek ravines."

"Marking of the parallel has commenced, has it not?"

"Yes, sir. It started at sunset. In addition to the engineers, General Knox and Colonel d'Aboville are personally marking the spots where their batteries are to be constructed."

"Are we still on schedule to begin construction tomorrow night?"

"Indeed, sir. Six regiments will be ordered to hold themselves in readiness. You will be called upon for the formal opening ceremony sometime before midnight."

"Very well," concludes Washington. "Colonel Laurens, what is the situation with enemy deserters?"

"Sir, as you know, there were an unusually high number that crossed over last night. This was due, we believe, to Baron de Viomenil's orders for patrols to go as far as the enemy entrenchments. Their aggressive approach and constant musketry must have caused apprehension of a general assault. The deserters report that Cornwallis's army has several thousand men in the hospital, that their soldiers complain of scarce ground to live upon, and that two hundred more artillery horses have been killed due to want of forage. The British commander, it is said, refuses to release the horses, because he fears their capture and utilization by us."

"Have we suffered any deserters?" asks Washington.

"Sir, I beg leave to report that two French soldiers and one American went over to the enemy over the past two days," responds David Humphreys.

General Washington now stands and begins pacing. "Orders for tomorrow morning," he says.

Tilghman and Humphreys immediately grab pens and paper.

"First, every deserter from the American troops, after this public notice is given, who shall be found within the enemy's lines at Yorktown, if the place falls, will be instantly hanged."

"Second, a public word of congratulations for de Lauzun. Please convey the key details of Tarleton's defeat yesterday. Then say this: I congratulate the army upon the brilliant success of the allied troops near Gloucester Point. I request the Duke de Lauzun to accept my particular thanks for the decisive vigor with which he charged the enemy. Please communicate my warmest acknowledgments to your gallant officers and men. Do you have that, gentlemen?"

"Yes, sir," replies Tilghman.

"Yes, General," confirms Humphreys.

"And let's keep up the morale, shall we, gentlemen?" continues Washington, with a bit of a wry smile. "Permission may now be granted for the sale of liquors and refreshments to the army under such regulations as the quartermaster general shall establish."

American Front Lines
Yorktown, Virginia
October 5, 1781

Heavy British artillery fire continues all day. Allied soldiers on the front line have lonely and dangerous work. Everything must proceed quietly. One dares not call out to a sentry or a patrol except to give the agreed signal. Fires cannot be made or even tobacco smoked, because they become a possible target for enemy fire, as the smoke can be seen during the day and the light at night.

Several American lives are lost this day. A Pennsylvania sentry walking on one of the converted redoubts is hit by a nine-pound cannonball that carries off part of his hips. He dies a short time later. A New Jersey private is lying down with his knapsack under his head. A cannonball hits the knapsack, knocking it away without touching the man. He dies from the sonic shock—without leaving a mark on his body. After seeing his comrade die in this manner, another soldier curses the fact that the allied forces have not returned a single shot, even though many of the French and American artillery pieces are now lined up neatly behind the lines.

"When are we going to return their fire?" he screams in anguish and frustration. "When?"

"In a day or two," responds an officer standing nearby. "And I expect we shall return the enemy's compliments with interest."

◆   ◆   ◆

The night turns cloudy and rainy, with a cold wind sweeping in from the Chesapeake Bay. While many of the men in the rear camps huddle around their fires, parts of three American regiments move into no-man's-land between the British main line and the proposed American parallel. Their mission is to do nothing more than provide cover fire as the new line is marked. Under the veil of darkness, Louis Duportail and his engineers steadily pound wooden pegs into the ground at regular intervals. Henry Knox and French artillery commander Colonel Francis Marie d'Aboville follow them closely, staking out the artillery batteries. Coming next are members of the sappers and miners unit of the American army laying strips of white pine wood end to end between the stakes.

Around midnight, Sergeant Joseph Martin and his Connecticut sapping regiment are ordered forward to begin digging operations. Shortly after they arrive at the site of the parallel, Louis Duportail meets them. "Sergeant Martin, please remain here while we move along the line," he says. "Do not allow your men to begin digging and be sure not to straggle a foot from this spot while we are gone."

"Yes, sir," responds Martin. "We will wait here."

Not five minutes later, a heavily bundled George Washington comes up alone from behind the lines. Wearing a hood and cape for protection from the rain, his face is shrouded in darkness, and the soldiers do not recognize him. Washington quietly walks toward Sergeant Martin and, towering over everybody, begins to make small talk.

"What regiments are you, men?" he asks stoically.

"Connecticut Regiment of Sappers, sir," replies Martin.

Washington nods his head and looks around. "Cold and wet tonight, isn't it?"

"Freezing my butt off!" replies one of the men.

"My balls are as wet as if they were suspended in a lake!" states another.

A slight smile crosses Washington's lips. "I think we've all been wetter and colder," he says.

"Colder, maybe," comes a reply. "At Valley Forge. I don't believe wetter, though."

"Well, if we do our jobs well here, there will be no more Valley Forges," responds Washington. "Tell me, Sergeant, where are the engineering officers?"

"Up the line a bit, sir. They left here only a few minutes ago."

"Very well," says Washington taking a few steps in that direction. But then he turns and stops. "Men, if you are taken prisoner, remember that you are in no instance to tell the enemy what regiment you are from. Is that clear?"

"It is, sir," replies Sergeant Martin.

After Washington walks out of sight, one of the soldiers pipes up, "Who the hell was that, anyway?"

"Don't know. Some officer, I guess," replies Martin. "But he certainly didn't need to remind us of that."

"Hell, no! He knows as well as we do that sappers and miners are given no quarter under the laws of warfare. We'd be fools to tell the British. They'd hang us instantly!"

"No matter," says Martin. "I don't think we're in any danger of being captured tonight."

Ten minutes later, Duportail, Knox, d'Aboville, and Washington come walking back along with a number of engineering officers. The closer they get, the more easily Martin and his men overhear the conversation.

"So you do not wish to break ground tonight?" asks Washington.

"We do not, General," responds Duportail. "We simply need more time to make certain the batteries are marked in accordance with our calculations."

"Are you in concurrence with this, Henry?"

"I am, General," replies Knox. *"We would do well to wait one more night."*

"If this weather holds, mon general," says d'Aboville, *"it will be perfect for digging the trench parallel. I could not imagine better conditions than rain and wind. The enemy will never suspect us, and they will definitely not be able to see or hear us."*

"Are you certain that the entire parallel can be constructed in one night?"

"Mais, certainment," replies d'Aboville.

"Of course, Your Excellency," says Duportail.

"Very well, gentlemen," states Washington, who turns toward Martin as he walks by. *"Sergeant, there is nothing for you to do this evening. We will begin the work tomorrow night. For now, you and your men may go back to your tents where you can warm your butts and dry your balls."*

Sergeant Martin snaps to attention and crisply salutes. *"Yes, sir,"* he responds.

The sappers and miners watch silently as the officers walk out of sight. Finally, the men begin whispering to each other.

"That was General Washington!"

"How could we not have recognized him?"

"It's so dark!"

"I didn't recognize him, either. None of us did."

As Sergeant Martin begins leading his men back to their tents, he looks up in Washington's direction and cocks his head.

"Damn!" he says. *"Damn! Damn! Damn!"*

Lord Cornwallis's Headquarters
Yorktown, Virginia
October 5, 1781

It is late night at the Nelson house. Cornwallis and his aides confer around the dining room table. Lanterns burn brightly. The wind whips rain against the windowpanes.

"Guard boats are now posted below the village to sound the alarm if French ships move closer, are they not?" asks Cornwallis.

"Yes, My Lord, they are in place," responds Major Ross. *"We have also prepared three fireships for such an event. Also, in accordance with your orders, ten of our twelve remaining merchant ships have been successfully sunk just off the beach. Wood piles have been placed in their fronts. Should the French ships move closer, they will have great difficulty disembarking any troops."*

"Good. That is good work," responds Cornwallis. *"Do we possess enough transports to cross our troops to Gloucester Point in one night—should we choose to evacuate this position?"*

"Yes, My Lord, we do. But just barely."

"Good. Now tell me of the interrogation of the deserters. What have they said?"

"My Lord, the most recent deserters—one American and two Frenchmen—have given only vague information as to Washington's troop strength," states Colonel Chewton. "They all have stated, however, that he intends to build further approaches—though they do not know exactly where or when."

"Well, we certainly know that General Washington will be constructing a first parallel," replies Cornwallis, glancing toward the window. "But with this weather, it will not be anytime soon."

"All three deserters have also stated emphatically that through the allied armies spirits are running high—perhaps higher than at any time during the long war."

Cornwallis pauses at this remark. After a few moments of silence, he instructs Major Ross to include in the next day's orders the following statements: "According to our recent intelligence, the Americans are lacking in siege artillery and have only small field ordnance to use against us. That is why we have not received any fire from them. Also, the French vessels lingering in the distance of the river seek only tobacco from the nearby fields and will soon leave the area. Regarding preparations in New York for our relief, General Clinton and Admirals Graves, Hood, and Digby are all in agreement. They are willing to sail—and confident of success."

Upon hearing this, Chewton and Ross glance at each other and then look apprehensively toward their leader. "Recent intelligence, sir?" asks Ross.

"James reported back in a few hours ago and provided the information regarding the lack of siege artillery," responds Cornwallis. "As for the French seeking only tobacco, and Clinton being confident of success—well, we must keep up the men's morale. That is all for this evening, gentlemen."

Sir Henry Clinton's Headquarters
Harlem Heights, New York
October 5, 1781

In the afternoon, Sir Henry Clinton received a disturbing letter from Admiral Thomas Graves, who wrote that there would be another delay in launching the fleet toward Virginia, because he had discovered that there was no gunpowder fit for use aboard his flagship, HMS *London*. Furthermore, Graves questioned Clinton's authority over the 69th Regiment, claiming that it rightfully belonged to the Navy's marine force rather than the army. "The resolution of this reporting structure must be resolved," wrote Graves, "before the fleet can sail."

At the same time, Admiral Samuel Hood was venting his frustration about Graves in letters to associates. "I know he is a cunning and theoretical man," said Hood, "but he is certainly a bad practical one—and most certainly proved himself on the 5th of last month to be unequal to the conducting of a great squadron. We should already have been in the Chesapeake. We are going to be too late to give relief to Lord Cornwallis."

American Front Lines
Yorktown, Virginia
October 6, 1781

By sunrise on Saturday morning, several regiments were already busy making additional gabions, fascines, saucissons, sand bags, and other materials to be used to fortify the first parallel. By noon, scores of soldiers and wagons were carrying up all this material as close as possible to the intended line. General Washington had already issued formal orders for 4,300 men to be ready for duty after dark—1,500 of them to dig, 2,800 to stand guard. He also released a lengthy document titled "Regulations for the Service of the Siege," which had been translated from a French publication (based on Vauban's Procedures) used for siege operations in Europe. But because it ran fifty-five numbered paragraphs long, nearly all the American troops refused to read it or even listen to it being read aloud. Some of the regulations included:

18. The trenches shall be relieved every twenty-four hours unless there is a particular order to the contrary by the general.

28. The officers will cause each soldier to work in his place to enlarge the trench and strengthen the epaulment.

29. No honor is to be rendered in the trenches when the commander in chief and general officers of the trenches visit them.

34. Gabions are to be three feet high and two feet and a half in diameter.

39. Each soldier going to the trenches shall take with him a fascine.

43. The fatigue men are to march near each other and observe the greatest silence when the engineers place them.

48.   In the batteries and other places adjacent to the deposit of powder, no sol-
      dier is permitted to smoke.

In addition to the fifty-five siege regulations, Washington's morning orders
included several paragraphs devoted to General Nathanael Greene's fight against
the British at Eutaw Springs in South Carolina. Even though the battle had taken
place nearly a month earlier, word had reached the American commander only
the previous day. To keep morale high, Washington wanted to make sure the
news made it through to the troops as fast as possible. He reported that Greene
had taken five hundred prisoners, that the British had "not less than six hundred"
killed and wounded, and that the enemy had withdrawn to the safety of Charleston. "The commander in chief conveys his warmest acknowledgments to General
Greene for his admirable plan of operations and the exemplary vigor with which
he conducted the battle," read the directive. "He requests the general to congratulate his gallant officers and soldiers grateful esteem for their honorable conduct
on the 8th of September. Each individual soldier is entitled to the thanks of his
country."

Washington spent most of the morning and afternoon with his engineers and
artillery officers, watching final tracings for the parallel being made and guns and
trenching materials moved toward the front. All the while, he and the other officers kept a cautious eye on the weather, hoping that the cloudy skies and intermittent wind and rain would continue throughout the day and well into the night.
By mid-afternoon, all preliminary work had been completed and, at 6:00 PM,
portions of six American regiments (4,300 men total) began to gather on the
plain in preparation for the night's operations. A short time later and a bit farther
to the left, four regiments of the French Bourbonnois and of Soissonais (about
250 men) also assembled to construct their smaller portion of the first parallel.

Preparations that evening, however, were marred by news from Williamsburg
that Colonel Alexander Scammel had taken a turn for the worse and, at five
o'clock that afternoon, had died of his wounds. Universally respected and well
liked, Scammel's death both saddened and angered the allied troops. Soldiers
recounted the fact that he had been shot in the back after surrendering—and that
the barbaric British should be punished accordingly. Washington expressed sincere, heartfelt sadness at the loss—and then immediately named John Laurens to
take over command of Scammel's light infantry regiment.

At about 8:00 PM, under cover of darkness and with rain still falling, the 2,800
men detailed to guard and provide cover for the trench workers, moved into
place about one hundred yards beyond the proposed parallel. From there, small

squads advanced another fifty to one hundred yards closer to the enemy with orders to sound the alarm and drive back any surprise British patrols. Next, the 1,500 sappers and miners (trailed by wagons loaded with sandbags) marched forward onto the open plain carrying knapsacks, guns, spades, shovels, pickaxes, fascines, and gabions. They lined up about three feet apart in back of the white pine strips that stretched for hundreds of yards along the ground. Gabion wicker baskets were placed directly on top of the pine strips—the knapsacks, muskets, and fascines a few feet behind each man.

Sergeant Joseph Martin and his Connecticut regiment had lined up in nearly the same place as the night before. As they waited for the order to begin digging, General Washington and a few members of his staff came up to their position. Martin immediately ordered his men to attention, saluted, and said: "Good evening, General, sir."

As soon as Washington walked by, he returned the salute, but said, "No special honor to be rendered, Sergeant." Recognizing Martin form the night before, Washington flashed him a smile. Then he grabbed one of the pickaxes, struck a few blows in the ground, and headed back behind the line. One of Martin's men asked why that had been done. "So it could be said that General Washington, with his own hands, first broke ground at the siege of Yorktown," replied the sergeant.

Right about this time, French troops began a diversion near the Fusilier's Redoubt on the extreme left flank. The Regiment Touraine, which had already begun construction of an eight-gun artillery battery on the cliff overlooking the York River, now launched a false attack on the enemy redoubt. As patrols moved quietly forward, British watch dogs began barking. Then a rocket signal from the redoubt was sent skyward, and the British unleashed a furious cannonade against the French position. At the same moment, a group of American guards posted along the swamp near the converted Pigeon Hill redoubts, built large bonfires and walked back and forth in plain view of the enemy, which immediately let loose their artillery guns in that direction. These two diversionary actions, planned well in advance by Washington, not only turned British attention away from the new parallel, but the noise from the enemy's artillery fire drowned out the sound of any digging in the trenches.

Only now was the order given for the allied troops to break ground. The gabion wicker baskets were placed on top of the white pine strips in rows three abreast. Then the sappers and miners (one quarter using pickaxes, three quarters using spades and shovels) threw the light sandy soil into the gabions. Once they were filled, fascines were placed on the sides of the dirt face and anchored with four-foot-long stakes. They, too, were then covered by more earth and sod. Wagons brought forth the sandbags that were placed at the foot and crest of each mound. As the trench progressed and became waist-deep, some of the soldiers in advanced positions drew back and took stations along the unfinished mounds. Others stood guard behind the parallel.

Trench workers were relieved at regular intervals and moved to the rear to get some sleep until their next shift. Periodically during the night the British launched sky rockets in an attempt to detect any operations. These rockets would often be followed by a few cannon blasts in the direction of the parallel, even though the enemy had not observed major movement. As it came his turn to be relieved, nineteen-year-old New Hampshire native Asa Redington laid down in the grass a few dozen yards away. But when a cannonball sailed directly over him and threw off his blanket like a gust of wind, he quickly got up and moved several hundred more yards farther to the rear.

Despite an occasional British cannon firing in that direction, work along the parallel progressed rapidly. The men worked like beavers all through the night, with barely a word or whisper being uttered. All one could hear were the steady sounds of pickaxes and shovels moving earth—and the pitter-patter of light rain on the soldier's backs.

By sunrise the next morning, the allies had completed a mile-long trench, four feet deep and eight to ten feet wide—and broad enough for artillery carriages to move through comfortably. The rampart on the side toward the enemy averaged seven feet in height and included the base foundations of four small redoubts placed equidistant along the line. And this first allied parallel was only 600 yards from the British main line of fortifications.

27

British Main Line
Yorktown, Virginia
October 7, 1781

Morning dawns on Yorktown. There are a few scattered clouds here and there, but no rain. When British sentries peer out across the open fields toward the allied position, the light of the new day reveals the shocking scene of an uninterrupted earthen parapet stretching across the Yorktown plain.

Lord Cornwallis, accompanied by his aides, immediately comes to the hornwork where he raises his spyglass to take a look. The British commander quickly lowers it to his side. Both his eyes are as round as saucers and his head lurches forward as if he can't believe what he is seeing. Slowly, almost hesitantly, Cornwallis brings the spyglass back up to his right eye. He looks first to the far left—to the cliff overlooking the York River. Then he pans slowly to the right—all the way to the York and Wormley Creek ravines.

Unconsciously swallowing hard and intermittently shaking his head negatively, Cornwallis carefully looks over the new parallel. It is more than a mile long. He sees the seven-foot-high mounds, the four redoubts under construction, countless soldiers on sentry duty, the artillery batteries being readied, and what appears to be bustling activity behind the parapets. When his view reaches the far right end of the parallel, he focuses in on what seems to be a narrow support trench that leads to a new battery not far from the Fusilier's Redoubt. From this position, he realizes, allied guns will be able to reach British ships in the river.

Lowering the spyglass to his side, Cornwallis turns to his aide, Colonel Chewton, and shakes his head again. "This is unbelievable," he says. "To do all this in one night in simply unimaginable! I have heard the stories that Washington had done something similar at Dorchester Heights back in '75, but I truly thought the accounts were exaggerated."

"Sir, how could they have done all this in one night—without our having the slightest hint?" asks Chewton.

"And the entire parallel appears to be just barely out of musket range," says Cornwallis.

"They must have many more men than we thought, sir. How else, could they…"

"The movement at the Fusilier's Redoubt and the fires at the marsh—they were only diversions," interrupts Cornwallis. "Our own cannon fire drowned out the noise from their digging. And it was cloudy and rainy all night. Amazing. What a feat!"

"My Lord, should we not hit them with some cannonade?" inquires a frightened looking British artillery officer.

"Yes, of course, Captain," replies Cornwallis. "Lob some cannonballs their way. Of course, they will do little damage, but the enemy will certainly know we are awake. Take your shots sparingly, though, with only a few guns. Aim toward the redoubts and batteries so as to disturb and delay their work.

"Major Ross," continues Cornwallis, "we must now be on the alert for an all-out enemy assault. All troops are now to be on constant alert. If an alarm should sound, all must be ready in the blink of an eye."

"Yes, My Lord," responds Ross. "I will give the order."

As Cornwallis and Chewton go back to their headquarters at the Nelson house, several British gunners open fire at American troops erecting an artillery battery in the middle of the parallel—aiming slightly short so the cannonballs will be sure to bound directly into the rampart. Interestingly, a large English bulldog runs out of the main line and begins playfully chasing the bounding cannonballs. A couple of times, the dog runs all the way to the allied parapet and jumps into the trench and back out again. Amused at the scene, a couple of American officers attempt to catch the bulldog and attach a message to take back to the enemy. But the dog growls and barks so ferociously that they decide against it. So the Americans just keep letting the English bulldog run—back and forth, back and forth—until it finally wears itself out and retreats within its own lines.

First Allied Parallel
Yorktown, Virginia
October 7, 1781

Work in the new parallel went on at a feverish pace all morning. Soldiers were busy digging the trench deeper, shoring up its sides, finishing the redoubts, constructing artillery platforms, stacking cannonballs, readying ammunition, and rushing light field artillery into the parallel as an added deterrent to any attack the enemy might be pondering. The British cannonade, meanwhile, had little impact. No allied soldiers were killed. However, a few French soldiers were wounded, and one American officer had his leg torn off by a cannonball.

Manning and relief of the trenches quickly became a massive and formal operation. Rotating sequences of command were established beginning with Major General Lincoln, who had taken charge the night before. He would be succeeded by the Marquis de Lafayette at noon, followed by Baron Von Steuben the following day. This sequence of command (Lincoln, Lafayette, Von Steuben) would remain in place throughout the siege, as would the French sector sequence command of Baron de Viomenil, Chevalier de Chastellux, and Marquis de St. Simon.

Precisely at 11:00 AM, Lafayette and Chastellux's divisions, which included the brigades under Generals Hazen and Muhlenberg and the Regiments Agenois and Saintonge, respectively, began assembling to the far right of the allied line. They were preparing not only to relieve the divisions of Lincoln and Viomenil in the trenches, but also to begin a traditional European ceremony that had been passed down through the centuries—one that formally marked the opening of a siege.

At noon, after arranging their men in order with respect to their assignments, Lafayette and Chastellux led the troops into the trench through the Wormley Creek ravine, so they would not be exposed to British fire. It looked very much like a grand parade—with music playing, drums beating in the front and rear, flags flying, banners unfurled, and muskets in formal carrying positions. Marching to a steady drum beat, the soldiers arrived at their various stations and implanted their flags on top of the parapet. At the same time, and at the other end of the parallel, the Lincoln and Viomenil divisions departed the trenches to the beat of their own drums.

As the ceremony proceeded onward, the British stepped up their artillery barrage until they witnessed an unexpected and audacious sight. Colonel Alexander Hamilton, who was now in command of the second battalion of Hazen's Brigade at the center of the parallel, ordered his entire regiment to mount the parapet to set the American flag in place. Then, as the awestruck British gunners stopped firing and watched, Hamilton led his men through a precise execution of Baron Von Steuben's Manual of Arms—a military drill that included formal soldiery in ordering and grounding of arms. After about ten minutes, Hamilton ordered his men back into the trenches.

The siege of Yorktown had formally begun. And Hamilton wrote to his wife, Betsy: "Thank heaven, our affairs seem to be approaching a happy period. In a week, the enemy must capitulate."

Admiral Thomas Graves's Flagship
HMS London
New York Harbor
October 7, 1781

It is just before noon. Waters in the harbor are calm, although the sky is overcast and there is a light mist falling. Admiral Samuel Hood, along with the other flag officers and several captains, have assembled on board for a meeting called by Admiral Graves. They are all seated around the conference table in the flag cabin. Graves opens the meeting.

"Gentlemen," he begins, "I propose, and wish to reduce to writing, the following question: Whether it is practicable to relieve Lord Cornwallis in the Chesapeake?"

"Admiral Graves, sir," replies an astonished Samuel Hood, "that appears to me an unnecessary and improper question. This subject was maturely discussed on the 24th of last month. The generals and admirals all agreed most unanimously to make the attempt to relieve Lord Cornwallis as soon as possible."

The other officers are clearly stunned at Admiral Hood's vehemence, which seems to border on insolence and insubordination. They remain silent as Graves becomes red in the face and responds in stuttered tones.

"I am aware of that, sir," he states. "Circumstances, however, have changed. It now appears that any relief effort will certainly, in the end, be futile. The French fleet is overpowering in number, and we cannot hope to overcome it, even if we were to reach the Chesapeake before the garrison falls."

Now clearly angry, Hood stands up and pounds his fist on the table. "It is my opinion, sir," he shouts, "and I will give it in writing, that we must try to reach Cornwallis at all costs, and if possible, we must attack the French fleet. Desperate cases require bold remedies, sir. And this is most certainly a desperate case."

Clearly frustrated, Admiral Graves rises from his chair and immediately ends the meeting. After the officers depart, Graves orders his aide to prepare a letter to Sir Henry Clinton. "Sir Henry," he dictates, "I have received your letter informing me of the conference with senior officers you have called for tomorrow morning. Do not hold the meeting for me, sir, as I shall not be there."

American Front Lines
Yorktown, Virginia
October 8, 1781

With a crisp chill in the air, work to refine the parallel continued day and night. Supply troops delivered thousands of gabions, fascines, saucissons, and stakes. Miners and sappers deepened, widened, and strengthened the sides of the trench. The four new redoubts were ditched and palisaded to repel possible enemy assaults. Latrines were dug behind the parallel and screened with new earthen mounds because, as Vauban's siege procedures noted, "you can prevent your people from having to go too far away, from getting themselves killed needlessly, and from infecting the trenches." But now the most crucial and labor-intensive work would involve the construction of eleven artillery batteries and the moving into place of seventy-nine pieces of heavy artillery. While the experienced Colonel Francois Marie d'Aboville supervised on the French end of the parallel, General Henry Knox stepped forward and took the lead on the American side.

Knox was one of George Washington's most trusted and able officers. He had traveled with the American commander throughout the entire war—crossing the Delaware in the same boat, suffering through the disastrous winter at Valley Forge, and helping drive the British out of Boston without firing a shot. In December 1775, Washington had asked Knox to bring desperately needed weapons to Boston from Fort Ticonderoga, New York. In one of the most amazing feats of the entire war, with 2,000 men and 400 oxen, Knox hauled fifty-nine cannon (weighing more than sixty tons) across 300 miles of snow-covered mountainous roads. It took three months, but Knox finally delivered the weapons—and Washington immediately used them to fortify Dorchester Heights in the course of only one night. Two days later, the British sneaked out of Boston under the cover of darkness.

Henry Knox had grown up in Boston, the seventh of ten children. At the age of twelve, when his father died, he was forced to quit school and take a job. He owned his own bookstore by the age of twenty-one, supported the American cause from the very beginning, and had been on the scene at the Boston Massacre, where he attempted to stop British troops from firing on unarmed citizens. Knox was also present at the battle of Lexington as a Massachusetts artillery officer when the first shot of the American Revolution was fired (the famous "Shot Heard Round the World"). After Dorchester Heights, Knox was promoted to brigadier general and given responsibility for the development of the American artillery corps. During the ensuing years, he created four regiments of ten companies each, increased the corps from less than 600 men to more than 2,600, and arranged for hundreds of weapons to be made by iron foundries in eastern Pennsylvania and western Massachusetts. Now at Yorktown, the thirty-one-year-old with an imposing physical presence, a genius for organization, and an unyielding sense of urgency would bring all his skills and abilities to bear.

Over the next couple of days, Henry Knox seemed to be everywhere—overseeing the construction of batteries, supervising the moving forward of siege guns, and inspiring his men, in part, by telling them that their efforts would end the war and win American independence. His ability to speak passing French helped in coordinating artillery operations with his French counterparts who were universally regarded as the finest artillery operators in Europe.

As darkness fell each evening, Knox sent troops out into no-man's-land to guard those who worked in the parallel. Battery positions already had been outlined by engineers who based their calculations on three things: 1) the target in mind; 2) the particular guns that would occupy the battery; and 3) the retaliatory firepower of enemy weapons directly across from them. Workers then outlined with cord the position of every battery parapet. For extra strength, a double row of six-foot gabions was set next to each side of a projected embrasure (gun opening in the parapet) and filled with earth. Powder magazines were built an average of twenty-five to fifty feet (depending on the size of guns in the battery) behind the embrasures. One magazine usually served three guns. All night long, workers hammered away on boards to create heavy wooden artillery platforms needed for each battery. First they rammed the earthen floor to firm the ground. Next they laid six beams (each eighteen feet long and four to seven inches square) lengthwise on the ground with their ends perpendicular to the front of the parapet. The beams were then firmly nailed together. Completed batteries varied in size, design, and number of guns employed. An average battery might run seventy-five feet long with a parapet between fifteen and twenty feet in thickness, seven feet high in front, and five or six feet wide on the exterior sides.

From artillery parks behind the lines, horses and oxen hauled forward the heavy ordnance and wagons loaded with ammunition and gunpowder. The two-wheeled, wooden gun carriages were then pushed and pulled through the trenches to their designated batteries. Next began the backbreaking labor of maneuvering the guns into place. Long lines of men tugged at drag ropes, hammered handspikes into the ground, and used wooden beams as leverage to slowly but steadily position each piece of artillery.

The weight of a cannon varied depending on size, but all were extremely heavy. The smallest, a 4-pound cannon (caliber based on weight of the cannonball), weighed a minimum of 1,200 pounds, while the large twenty-four-pounders tipped the scales at nearly 6,000 pounds. Eight-, twelve-, and sixteen-pounders fell in between at weights of 2,300, 3,500, and 4,600 pounds, respectively. All field and siege cannon were made of either iron or bronze. Most of the French artillery were bronze—more costly, but more durable. They could withstand much more heat than iron cannon which, due to repeated firing during a siege, would often have to sit idle to cool off. Bronze cannon, on the other hand, could keep firing indefinitely.

In general, the various types of cannon at Yorktown fired cannonballs on a relatively flat trajectory. The larger the gun, the farther it could fire. Mortars, on the other hand, with their large truncated bores, were able to fire exploding bombs with deadly precision at very high trajectories. They varied in size from eight-inch (calibrated on the diameter of the barrel) weighing 550 pounds to thirteen-inch weighing 4,500 pounds. Coehorns (which were nothing more than 4.5-inch mortars) were popular because they could easily be moved around by only two men. All mortars fired hollow iron shells (the largest weighing 150 pounds) filled with gunpowder. On bursting, the shells fragmented into a myriad of pieces that destroyed nearly everything in reach. Hand grenades also were fired from mortars. These small, hollow iron shells (sometimes made of tin or papier-mâché) were filled with extra-fine gunpowder and set with a wooden fuse. They were usually thrown by hand when soldiers were in close proximity to the enemy.

The third major piece of artillery used at Yorktown was the howitzer, which looked like a small cannon with a cutoff barrel. Smaller and more mobile than field cannon and mortars, they came in only two sizes (six-inch and eight-inch) and were transported around in short, two-wheeled carriages. The larger howitzer, at 2,600 pounds, was still heavy, but offered a trajectory higher than a cannon, though lower than a mortar. Able to utilize a more diverse line of ammunition (including balls, bombs, canisters, and grapeshot), howitzers were ideal for firing "en ricochet" at lower gun elevations. In such cases, the shells skipped across the ground and bounced over the enemy parapet. This kind of firing often resulted in taking off legs and arms of individual soldiers. It could also be very destructive psychologically, even terrifying, because the shells would often roll around with fuses burning—ready to explode at any moment.

The purpose of the allied artillery batteries during the upcoming siege was simple: batter and breach the enemy parallel and destroy their artillery. Henry Knox and his French counterparts were going to employ several techniques to accomplish this purpose. They would use "direct" fire where the shot struck its target at a twenty-degree angle and then glanced off to strike elsewhere on the line. "Oblique" fire would strike the enemy line at a larger, obtuse angle affording greater destructive impact. They also would fire over the enemy defenses to strike behind the line (called "reverse" fire) and would sweep their cannon fire across the entire length of a face or flank of the parallel (called "enfilading" fire). Of course, the most destructive of all firing techniques was called "joint" or "comrade" fire where two or more gun batteries would fire in unison to create a crossfire effect. The target of this particular technique rarely survived intact.

Slowly, but surely, as the night of October 8th wore on, the allied parallel began to take final shape as the batteries and new redoubts were perfected and the artillery moved into place. Farthest to the north (or left of the line) stood Battery 1A on the edge of the cliff overlooking the York River. It had two parapets meeting at a ninety-degree angle, one facing the river and the other facing the Fusilier's redoubt which stood approximately 1,500 feet due east. This battery possessed two sections. The first consisted of three mortars and four howitzers. The second contained a powerhouse of four twelve-pound cannon and two twenty-four-pounders. Behind the larger cannon was a pit four feet deep and six feet in diameter that was used to heat cannonballs to be fired directly at enemy shipping. Called "hot shot," they would be used to set enemy ships on fire. Other cannonballs were bonded together (two at a time) with either a solid bar or chain. This "bar shot" and "chain shot" could have a particularly devastating impact on a ship's rigging.

Approximately 750 feet south of Battery 1A, bounded on the north by the Williamsburg Road and on the south by the deep ravines, stood the smaller Battery 2A, which contained two mortars. On the other side of the ravines, about 1,000 feet to the southeast, was Battery 3A. French operated, it was on high ground, and its four bronze twenty-four-pound cannon had an unobstructed view of the British main line. Another 750 feet east and just across the Goosely Road stood a powerful complex of four gun batteries and a redoubt (4A through 8A) generally referred to as the Grand French Battery. Battery 4A consisted of eight mortars (three twelve-inch and five eight-inch). 5A (about 500 feet behind 4A) had four bronze twenty-four-pounders mounted in it. Structure 6A, only two hundred feet southeast of Battery 4A, was a square-shaped redoubt that would be filled with infantry troops ready to repel any British attack. Finally, two additional batteries straddled the Hampton Road. Battery 7A, 250 feet behind the redoubt, boasted another four twenty-four-pound bronze cannon. And Battery 8A, the largest in the Grand French Battery, contained eight sixteen-pound cannon, four mortars, and six howitzers.

Nine hundred feet farther southeast along the allied parallel stood Structure 9A, another square redoubt operated by the Americans and designed to protect the artillery parks and supply depots, located immediately to the rear. The rest of the American portion of the parallel, while not containing as much firepower as did the French, nevertheless consisted of formidable strength with three batteries and one redoubt. Battery 10A, located four hundred feet due east of Redoubt 9A, contained four 18-pound cannon. Another 1,500 feet along the line was Structure 11A, a square redoubt that guarded the trench depot and protected the parallel against any possible British assault. Slightly behind and one hundred feet east was a small battery that consisted of four howitzers. Another 1,200 feet farther along, as the parallel swung to the northeast, rested Structure 12A, a combined redoubt and small bomb battery that contained four mortars.

Finally, farthest to the right of the parallel was Structure 13A, also known as the Grand American Battery. Located near the riverbank, it stood 500 feet in front of the main parallel to which it was connected by a lengthy communications trench. The American Grand Battery contained twelve eighteen-pound cannon, two twenty-four-pounders, four mortars, and two howitzers. Interestingly enough, it was in this battery that Henry Knox devised and put to use some specially improvised mortar carriages, which were strengthened to better absorb the direct shock of recoil, more flexible so as to elevate the barrels more effectively, and more easily mobile with the use of "truck-type" wagon wheels. With this new innovation, 8-inch mortars could now lob shells high into the air to fall behind enemy lines, creating even more devastation.

◆   ◆   ◆

Cornwallis kept up a cannonade against the allied lines all night long, primarily to interrupt progress on the gun batteries. In the trenches, as the laborers continued their work, sentinels were posted on parapets all along the parallel. Their job was to watch the British main line. When they saw a match go off from a cannon directly opposite them, they were to fall down in the ditch as a warning to the laborers, who would also duck down. Sometimes, a cannonball would skip along the ground, hit the parapet, and fling a good amount of dirt on the men. This warning system, while crude, was fairly effective, and relatively few soldiers were injured by enemy fire. In another precautionary move, members of the infantry were kept huddled together with muskets in their hands. In case of an enemy attack, they had standing orders to form eight paces to the rear of the trench, wait until the British entered, and then rush forward in a bayonet charge.

As the enemy retreated, the troops were instructed to lie atop the parapet on their stomachs and open fire.

Also in the darkness, Governor Nelson's Virginia Militia moved forth in small patrols to distract the enemy with random sniping and musket fire. Occasionally, they would meet British patrols and skirmish for a short while. But usually they would simply fire, move to another position, fire again, and then retreat. At one point during the night, a couple of Americans ventured forth all the way to the British hornwork and yelled that they wanted to desert. When two enemy officers came forward to escort them behind the lines, the Americans, in retaliation for the killing of Colonel Alexander Scammel, shot them dead.

Allied casualties remained light throughout the night. Only one man was killed—a French worker hit by a cannonball while in the trench. Three allies were wounded, including an American whose arm was blown away by a cannonball as he mounted a battery parapet. Two French officers were also severely wounded. One had his leg shot off by a cannonball while on duty in front of the parallel; another lost his arm in the same manner as he entered the trench.

As dawn approached and the parallel began to wear what some described as "a threatening appearance," emotions among the Americans were mixed. Some were exceedingly optimistic. They believed the British were "embarrassed, confused, and indecisive." Although the allies had not fired a single artillery shot, Cornwallis's cannonade was not particularly heavy. In fact, some thought it "rather feeble" and "randomly done." And anticipation mounted among the Americans, because they knew that General Washington was holding his fire until all of the cannon, mortars, and howitzers were in place and ready to fire in unison.

Despite such optimism, there was doubt that Cornwallis would surrender. In the Pennsylvania Regiment, a captain had to pay his lieutenant the beaver hat he had wagered on a bet that Cornwallis and his army would be prisoners of war by the next Sunday. Now that it was Monday, he had to pay up.

And over in the New Jersey line, a lieutenant made a pessimistic bet with another officer. He wagered a pair of silk stockings "that Cornwallis and his army will not be prisoners of war by this day in two weeks."

PART V
THE SIEGE

28

American Encampment
Yorktown, Virginia
October 9, 1781

It is early afternoon. The sun has just broken through overcast skies. Dr. James Thacher is attending to a patient at the temporary American hospital when he hears the rustle of tent flaps. He turns to see General Washington standing at the front entrance for an unannounced visit. Thacher finishes with his patient and walks up to the American commander.

"Good afternoon, Doctor," says Washington, who towers over the physician.

"Good afternoon, sir," replies a surprised Thacher.

"How are your patients, today?"

There are about twenty sick and wounded soldiers on cots lining the walls of the tent. They will stay for only a day or two. Once stabilized, the wounded will be removed by wagon to Williamsburg. Those who have malaria, however, arrive in a steady stream every day. If their fevers subside in a day or two, they are sent back to their regiments. If not, they are also transported to Williamsburg.

"Two amputations this morning, sir," replies Thacher, motioning toward two cots, each with a man who has lost a leg. "And a wagon just left with about thirty men."

"I see," says Washington, who begins to walk down the line of beds.

"Do not get too close, General," warns the doctor, following along. "Most of these men are contagious."

The American commander continues to walk down the line. He nods his head to those who make eye contact with him. "Do you have everything you need?" he asks Thacher.

"I believe we do, sir."

"And are the accommodations suitable and to your liking?"

"They are, sir."

Washington turns around and heads back to the front of the tent and steps a foot or two outside. He gently pulls Thacher with him, leans down and whispers in his ear. "Doctor, it will not be long now. I expect to open fire on the enemy by tomorrow at the latest. You must prepare for more wounded. To that end, I have ordered an addi-tional tent to be set up and fifty more cots to be brought in."

"Yes, General. We will be ready."

"During the coming bombardment, I expect the enemy to unleash a furious response. Should you need anything—anything at all—you are at liberty to request it from me directly."

"Thank you, sir. I appreciate your concern for the care of our men."

"Very well, Dr. Thacher. And let me say that your conduct, and that of your staff, in the performance of your duties here at Yorktown has been exemplary—as it has been these many years. Should providence be with us these next few weeks, I believe we will end this terrible struggle once and for all."

"Thank you, sir. We pray that it will. God be with you, sir."

"God be with all of us, Dr. Thacher," replies Washington. "God be with all of us."

◆   ◆   ◆

The general leaves the hospital and rides toward the first parallel. He arrives just in time to see the one o'clock troops relieved. General Lincoln's division is moving into the American sector with the same formal ceremony that includes drums beating and flags waving conspicuously. A similar event is occurring over in the French sector as Baron Viomenil's Regiments Bourbonnois and Soissonnais march into the trench there. Washington is alarmed to observe that Von Steuben's men leaving the parallel are met with a furious enemy cannon barrage that causes a number of casualties. He immediately turns and gallops back to his headquarters. On the way, Washington suddenly stops his horse and spits something out into his hand. It is one of his bad loose teeth that has finally broken loose. He slips it into his vest pocket so he can later incor-porate it into one of his bridges of false teeth.

Once back at the headquarters tent, the general summons his aides. "Gentlemen, we must put a halt to these excessive exhibitions when the parallels are relieved," he tells them. "I know they are part of the European tradition, but we are losing too many men. The enemy's attention is too easily drawn in that direction and, because of the consistency of the routine, they can prepare their fire in advance. Henceforth, our parallels must be relieved as quietly as possible and at irregular hours so as to deceive Cornwallis."

"I will put it in tomorrow's general orders, sir," states Tench Tilghman.

"Thank you, Colonel. But I would prefer this change be carried directly to Gener-als Lincoln, Lafayette, and Von Steuben. A written order will not be necessary."

"I'll take care of it right away, sir," replies Humphreys, who quickly exits the tent.

"Has interrogation of this morning's deserters been completed?" asks Washington.

"Indeed, it has, General," replies Tilghman. "One man is an artillerist and very talkative. He relates that Cornwallis has told his troops that they should not fear American forces, because we have no heavy guns, only some field pieces."

Washington cocks his head and just stares back at Tilghman.

"Lord Cornwallis has also told his troops that the French fleet is inferior in battle situations," continues Tilghman, "and that the vessels lingering in the distance seek only some tobacco from the area and will soon set sail."

"Could it really be true British troops do not understand that the entire French fleet has them cut off by water and poses an authentic danger?"

"No, sir," responds Tilghman. "According to the deserter, Cornwallis's soldiers already doubt his word. However, as they rely only on rumor and innuendo, they are not completely certain. Apparently, Cornwallis carefully coordinates all communications to his men."

"Hmmm. So His Lordship is lying to his men in an effort to keep up their morale. If he is willing to do that, he must believe his men are on edge."

"Yes, General," agrees Jonathan Trumbull. "They are also crowded together and may be running low on food and supplies. And as they can no longer forage..."

"They become increasingly worried about their next meal," says Washington, finishing Trumbull's sentence.

"Yes, sir," says Trumbull.

Washington pauses for a moment, walks over to the entrance of the tent, and stares outside. "Tell me, Colonel Tilghman, how are our batteries progressing?"

"Sir, we have just been informed that the French batteries closest to the river are ready," replies Tilghman. "And of course, they are most anxious to open fire on the Star redoubt and enemy ships in the river. The Grand French Battery, and most of the other batteries on the left flank, will not be ready until tomorrow. The American Grand Battery should be ready to open fire later this afternoon—early evening at the latest."

"And the rest of our batteries on the right flank?" asks the general.

"More than half are ready now. The rest tomorrow, for sure. At least that is what was reported this morning."

Washington walks outside the tent for a moment and looks up into the eastern sky. He paces back and forth, hands behind his back, head alternately bowed and looking upward. Finally, he walks back inside.

"Colonel," he says to Tilghman, "I had originally wanted to wait until all guns were in place before opening fire. However, I think it is time to dispel Cornwallis's lies about our capacity to fire upon his troops. We will direct the French artillerists to open

their embrasures and turn their guns toward the enemy. The battery overlooking the river may open fire at three o'clock this afternoon. This order must be taken directly to Count Rochambeau and General Knox. After I receive word from Knox, I will proceed directly to the Grand Battery on the right flank. As soon as it is ready to open fire, we will do so."

"Very well, sir," replies Tilghman. "I will go directly to Count de Rochambeau. Colonel Trumbull, will you go to General Knox?"

"Immediately, sir."

With that, both aides walk briskly out of the tent and head to their horses.

French Battery No. 1A
Yorktown, Virginia
October 9, 1781

At 3:00 PM, with Count de Rochambeau looking on, French forces fired the first artillery shots at the siege of Yorktown. The four twelve-pound cannon, four howitzers, and three mortars contained in Battery 1A opened fire almost simultaneously. Their targets were the Fusilier's Redoubt and the numerous British ships moored near it.

The double abatis surrounding the redoubt were soon set on fire by exploding bombs, and two ships—the frigate *Guadeloupe* and the sloop *Formidable*—quickly pulled anchor and moved farther down river and across to the Gloucester Point side. The attention of British artillerists was immediately drawn to the French battery, but their fire included long intervals of silence and, as a result, was largely ineffective in the midst of the unrelenting French barrage.

American Grand Battery
Yorktown, Virginia
October 9, 1781

It is 5:00 PM, and the sun is low on the western horizon. The rumble of cannon shot from the far left of the battlefield is ever-present. Henry Knox is escorting George Washington along the line of artillery in the battery. Two twenty-four-pounders, two eight-inch mortars, and twelve eighteen-pounders are all primed, loaded, and aimed directly at the British in Yorktown. Three or four men stand next to each gun. Washington nods to them as he walks by.

The two generals stop in the middle of the eighteen-pound cannon line. Knox signals for the American flag to be unfurled and raised over the parapet. Everyone faces the flag, stands at attention, and salutes as the ceremony moves to a steady drumbeat. Knox then picks up a torch, lights it, and hands it to Washington.

A French artillery commander who has been advising the Americans steps up and points in the direction of the town. "Mon general," he says, "this gun will deposit its shot among the second set of houses to the left."

Washington looks toward the houses, nods, and steps up and touches the torch to the lower end of the cannon barrel. The cannon booms forth a shot. And the 18-pound black ball sails through the air, bounces across a couple of rooftops, and disappears.

British-Occupied House on the Lower Side of Town
Yorktown, Virginia
October 9, 1781

Officers of the 76th Regiment (also known as Lord MacDonald's Scottish Highlanders) and their wives are seated around the dining room table enjoying an amiable dinner. The 18-pound cannonball fired by Washington crashes through the wall, tears off the leg of Lieutenant Charles Robertson (quartermaster and adjutant), bounces off the floor, up through the table (scattering dishes and glasses everywhere), and hits Commissary-General Perkins directly in the chest, killing him instantly. Mrs. Perkins, seated at the corner of the table between her husband and Lieutenant Robertson, is not injured.

American Lines
Yorktown, Virginia
October 9, 1781

Immediately following General Washington's first shot, all the other guns in the American Grand Battery opened fire. And then, right down the line in succession, the remaining American batteries (12A, 11A, 10A, and 9A) opened fire as wild cheering swept through the trenches.

Several soldiers recorded their feelings in their journals. "This day, this happy day, we returned the enemy's fire," wrote a Pennsylvanian. A New Englander recorded that he felt "a secret pride swell my heart when I saw the Star Spangled Banner waving majestically in the faces of our adversaries."

Over on the far left side of the battlefield, French Battery 2A joined with its larger counterpart (Battery 1A) in the barrage as both began firing on the town. It took only a few minutes to realize the difference between the French and American artillery. While the French fired with precision and accuracy, the American cannonballs landed haphazardly and often fell far short of their intended targets. In addition, many of the American bombshells failed to explode. "The contrast was humiliating," noted one American. However, a French officer explained that, in contrast to American cannon, the French guns were new, and "the ammunition perfectly suited to their caliber."

Still, Henry Knox was embarrassed and began working diligently to improve performance of the American artillery. Over the next several hours, he brought up more guns, asked the advice of his French counterparts, and sought to adjust and correctly angle his cannons, howitzers, and mortars.

As darkness fell over the battlefield, the allied assault continued at a brisk and steady pace. It wasn't long before many of the enemy gun emplacements were knocked out of commission. But the British aggressively returned fire from three batteries on their right and left fronts. As the night wore on, the heavy cannonade on both sides tapered off a bit. However, while George Washington agreed with the French recommendation to cease direct firing, he ordered ricochet firing to be kept up all night so the British would not be able to repair their damaged batteries.

All through the night, the besieged town was awash in a sea of destruction. French hotshot firing set an English frigate on fire, and it illuminated the darkness. "One could not avoid the horribly many cannonballs, either inside or outside the city," wrote Hessian soldier Johann Conrad Doehla. "I saw bombs fall into the water and lie there for five, six, eight, or more minutes and then explode. Fragments of these bombs flew back and fell on buildings of the city and in our camp where they caused much damage."

General Washington's original purpose for opening artillery fire early had worked well. "The allies deprived us of the suspicion which we formerly had," noted Doehla, "that they possessed only regimental cannon and could bring up no heavy guns."

Sir Henry Clinton's Headquarters
Harlem Heights, New York
October 9, 1781

Sir Henry Clinton is seated at the head of his dining room table along with other senior officers. Notably absent is Admiral Thomas Graves who had sent a terse note the day before stating that he would not attend. After an hour or so of logistical discussion about the intended naval move to relieve Cornwallis, Clinton pulls a map of Virginia toward him.

"And finally, gentlemen," he says, "we must determine a suitable place to land our troops in case the French bar the direct way to Yorktown. After due deliberation, I have concluded that our alternatives will either be Monday's Point on the north bank of the York River, here, or Newport News on the James, here. That will be all for now. This meeting is concluded."

Admiral Samuel Hood and General James Robertson look awkwardly at each other. Hood rolls his eyes. "In case the French bar the direct way to Yorktown?" he whispers. "In order to reach the entrances of both Newport News and Monday's point, one must enter the Chesapeake Bay. How are we going to get past de Grasse's fleet? Aren't we going to talk about that?"

29

Grand French Battery
Allied Lines
Yorktown, Virginia
October 10, 1781

At 9:00 AM, allied forces began the first full day of artillery fire by opening a thunderous assault on Yorktown. General Knox had, the night before, brought up additional weapons to increase the Americans' capacity. While all batteries were not completed and participating in the barrage, the most powerful and devastating onslaught came from the Grand French Battery, which unleashed its entire thirty-gun arsenal (including twenty-four-, eighteen-, sixteen-, and twelve-pound cannons).

At mid-morning, George Washington went out to the Grand French Battery to observe operations. Standing directly behind several of the twenty-four-pounders, he marveled at the skill and accuracy of the shooting. The French were able to fire six consecutive rounds and hit the same small area from up to a half-mile away. And they continuously shifted their weapons in response to key movements by the British. The American commander stood in awe and admiration of the precision, routine, and teamwork that accompanied every shot.

Most of the cannons, especially the larger ones, were made of bronze (in contrast to the American's cast iron). More durable and able to withstand the greater heat generated by multiple firing during a siege, each bronze gun was mounted on a two-wheeled solid oak carriage and handled by a crew of eight to ten men.

One gunner calculated the correct angle of elevation and then several assistants (called matrosses) maneuvered and adjusted the weapon with the aid of handspikes (large wooden crowbars sheathed in iron) and elevating screws or wedges. The matrosses then brought up ammunition from a supply magazine.

Another gunner loaded the cannon's ammunition and propellant into the front end of the bore. A cast iron cannonball was the principal ammunition. The propellant was gunpowder composed of potassium nitrate (saltpeter), charcoal, and sulfur. (The amount of powder varied with calculated distance, but was usually one-third the weight of the cannonball.) The gunpowder was placed in a small cartridge, which was then attached to a sabot, a wooden disc slightly hollowed on one side. The sabot went into the cannon first.

A third gunner pushed the cartridge and sabot down the bore with a rammer (a cylindrical, long-handled wooden tool). Usually made of elm, the rammer had carefully spaced notches marked on it that were used to measure precise seating.

The cannonball was loaded next and it, too, was rammed down the bore.

A fourth gunner primed the vent with either loose powder or a small priming tube.

At that point, the cannon was ready to fire. All the gunners and assistants stood to the side to avoid the recoil. Those who loaded the weapon remained near the front and took care to keep their mouths wide open so that their eardrums would not split from the cannon blast.

A fourth gunner would ignite the charge at the touchhole of the cannon using a match (a three-strand cotton rope that burned at a rate of five inches per hour).

The firing procedure was coordinated by the lead artillery officer who gave the following commands:

Gunners and matrosses! To your posts—march!

Front—face!

Prepare—battery!

To—handspikes!

Enter—handspikes!

From—battery!

To the wedge!

To—sponge! Stop—vent! To—carriage!

Sponge—gun!

Return—sponge! To—rammer!

Cartridge—gun!

Ram—cartridge!

Shot—gun!

Ram—shot!

Return—rammer!

To—handspikes!

Enter—handspikes!

To—battery!

Point—gun!

Lay down—handspikes!

Clear—vent! To—wedge!

March!

Make—ready!

Fire!

After the cannon had been fired, the gunner who handled the rammer took out a wormer (long-handled sponge) and rammed it down the barrel to clean out the cartridge residue. Following ten or twelve firings, however, the barrel had to be cooled to prevent the tube from bending or possibly bursting. This was accomplished when a gunner dipped the sponge into water and passed it up and down the outside of the cannon bore.

The entire firing procedure took about twelve minutes (averaging about five shots per hour). Similar commands and procedures (specific to each gun) were used up and down the allied lines for smaller cannon, mortars, howitzers, and grenades.

General Washington's Headquarters Tent
Yorktown, Virginia
October 10, 1781

It is approximately one o'clock in the afternoon. Washington is having a private lunch with Secretary Thomas Nelson, uncle of the Virginia governor, who has just made an exit from the besieged Yorktown.

At noon, while Washington had still been observing operations at the Grand French Battery, a white flag of truce appeared on the British hornwork. The American commander quickly ordered a halt to all allied firing, because he figured that Cornwallis was responding to an earlier message requesting the release of Nelson for his own safety. Sixty-five years old and suffering from gout, the former Virginia official was living in one of the upstairs rooms of his own house, which Cornwallis had commandeered and made his headquarters. Washington knew it would only be a matter of time before he was killed or injured, because that house was a prime target.

The British commander had readily agreed to the request and, no sooner had the cannon fire ceased across the battlefield, than Nelson came limping out of the enemy fortifications on the arms of two British soldiers. Following closely behind was the slave James, carrying a cloth bundle filled with Nelson family silver. After the secretary was safely delivered to the American parallel, the two British soldiers returned to their own lines, the white flag was lowered, and Washington gave the signal for the resumption of the artillery barrage. For the rest of the day, the allies poured shot and shell into Yorktown. Their primary targets were the hornwork in the center of the battlefield, the Fusilier's Redoubt on the extreme left, and Redoubts No. 9 and No. 10 on the extreme right.

Back at his headquarters tent, Washington was seated at the table with Secretary Nelson, Tench Tilghman, David Humphreys, and Jonathan Trumbull. There was also an empty place setting.

"Secretary Nelson, I'm relieved to find you healthy and in good spirits," says Washington. "I have sent for the governor. He should be joining us soon."

"Thank you, General," came the reply. "I am most relieved to be out of the town. Your artillery fire is having a devastating effect. There are many deaths and injuries. One of my own servants was struck and killed by a cannonball as he was standing in my living room."

"I'm most sorry to hear that," Washington responds.

"I felt it necessary to stay as long as I could," continued Nelson, "so that I might gather as much intelligence as possible."

"Your actions are heroic, sir," replies Washington. "I cannot thank you enough."

Nelson acknowledges the compliment with a nod of the head and begins rattling off information about the condition inside Yorktown. "Most of our citizens have taken refuge below the cliffs of the river. They have been joined by countless enemy soldiers, including officers. There is not a safe spot above ground in all of the city."

"What of Lord Cornwallis?" asks Washington. "Is he not still in your house?"

"Very rarely, General. He mostly shuttles back and forth from there to a grotto in the river bank where he holds meetings with his senior officers."

"I see," responds Washington. "Is there any other useful information you can provide me?"

"Oh, indeed, sir. Tarleton and Simcoe have fallen sick at Gloucester Point and have been incapacitated for days. More than a thousand horses have been destroyed over there due to unavailability of forage. And Lord Cornwallis is increasingly worried that the Duke de Lauzun has been able to completely restrict his movements there."

"How is morale in the enemy encampment?" asks Washington.

"Quite dispirited, sir. They have been much astonished at your capacity to inflict damage. They pretend to have no apprehensions of the garrison's falling. However, it can be easily seen that Lord Cornwallis and the senior officers are exceedingly anxious."

"Good. That is good news, indeed! I want them to feel that way and, hopefully, to panic. It will speed their capitulation."

"One thing, General," says Nelson. "A whaleboat from New York managed to slip through the French fleet this morning. It arrived amidst the bombardment with a British major on board. I have heard that he carries a message from Sir Henry Clinton, but I was not able to glean its contents. There are, however, rumors floating around that Sir Henry is on his way with the British fleet."

"What is your sense of the truth of these rumors?" asks Washington.

"Probably wishful thinking, General," comes the response. "Cornwallis has been too often disappointed by Clinton's promises. Although, I must advise you that it is clearly a possibility that the British navy is going to attempt a rescue operation in some form. Just when, I cannot say."

At that moment, the governor of Virginia enters the tent and rushes over to embrace the old man. "Uncle! I am relieved to see you. Are you well?"

"Yes, yes, I'm fine—thanks to General Washington."

"You have my deep gratitude, sir," says Governor Nelson to Washington.

"Please, sit down, sir," Washington replies. "Join us for the afternoon meal."

Cornwallis's Cave
Bank of the York River
Yorktown, Virginia
October 10, 1781

Cornwallis is sitting at a large table with his aides, Colonel George Chewton, Major Alexander Ross, and the newly arrived Major Charles Cochrane. They are inside a natural grotto in the riverbank that has been excavated to provide safety and room for the British commander to hold extensive meetings. For security purposes, he divides his time between here and the grotto in the ravine near the Nelson house. That way, the allies never know for sure where he is at any time. The walls of this cave are lined with green baize, a coarse woolen cloth usually used as table coverings. Several lanterns and candles are lit to provide light in the back recesses, although some sunlight illuminates the entrance area. Explosions are constantly heard from the allied cannonade. The ground often shakes and, when a shot lands particularly close, dirt from the ceiling loosens and falls down.

"Welcome, Major Cochrane," says Cornwallis affably. "How was your journey? Where is the fleet?"

"Thank you, it is good to be here, Your Lordship," replies Cochrane, with a salute. "I left New York ten days ago, and Admiral Graves had not yet left with His Majesty's navy. My journey was thrilling, sir. When we came in sight of the French fleet, I left our frigate and embarked on a twelve-oared whaleboat. We were able to slip through the blockade only by avoiding the most furious French cannonade. And we arrived here during the midst of the current bombardment."

"Have you not previously been exposed to enemy fire in this manner, Major?" asks Chewton.

"No, sir, I have not," says Cochrane. "I volunteered for this duty and am most anxious to experience it from the front parapets, sir."

"Well, I'm sure we can accommodate you on that point, Major," says Cornwallis. "But tell me, what news have you from Sir Henry Clinton?"

"Your Lordship, I have this letter for you from General Clinton. I do not know its contents, nor has anyone read it since it was placed in my hand."

Cornwallis takes the letter, opens it, and reads in silence. This is Clinton's correspondence of September 30 where he states that he "may pass the bar by the 12th of October." Cornwallis squirms in his seat a bit when he reads this part but continues digesting the entire letter's contents. "This, however, is subject to disappointment. I shall persist in my idea of a direct move there even to the middle of November," the letter reads, "should it be Your Lordship's opinion that you can hold out so long. But if you tell me that you cannot, and I am without hopes of arriving in time to reinforce you by a direct move, I will immediately make an attempt upon Philadelphia by land. If this should draw any part of Washington's force from Yorktown, it may possibly give you an opportunity of doing something to save your army."

After reading the last several sentences, Cornwallis gives a convulsive jerk, rises from his chair, and slams his fist on the table. He sees that the others in the room are shocked at his display, so he quickly gets control of his emotions. "Major Ross, please take Major Cochrane somewhere where he can freshen up, eat, and rest," he says.

"Yes, Your Lordship," replies Ross. "Right away, sir."

After Cochrane and Ross leave the grotto, Cornwallis throws the letter across the table to Chewton and explodes in a torrent of rage. "Here! Read this for yourself!" he screams. "That son of a bitch! Every line describes circumstances that might delay his progress. Not six days earlier, he wrote assuring me that the fleet would sail no later than October 5. It is now the twelfth, and there is no chance it will leave New York until day after tomorrow—and probably not then, either. With the time to traverse the distance of the voyage, and the smaller size of our fleet in contrast to that of the French, our hopes of relief and reinforcement are all but lost."

Chewton finishes reading the letter and looks up in dismay. He is speechless.

"And look at this," shouts Cornwallis. "Clinton requires my opinion regarding any diversion that he might make to cover our retreat. He even mentions attacking Philadelphia to draw Washington away! Philadelphia! Have you ever heard of such ineptness? The man is a complete idiot! An imbecile! And he has lied to me all along. The son of a bitch!"

Cornwallis finally finishes his tirade by slumping down in his chair. He takes the letter from Chewton, reads it again, and shakes his head back and forth. An expression of total despair comes over his face. "George," he says softly to his aide, "we must call a council for tomorrow morning. I will then inform our officers of the contents of Sir Henry's letter, and we will determine a proper course of action."

"Yes, Your Lordship," comes the reply. "I will alert all the senior officers, sir."

Cornwallis holds his head in his hands and shakes it despondently.

"May I ask, Your Lordship, if you might want to inform the officers and men of the contents now rather than later?"

"Why would we do that?" asks Cornwallis.

"Well, sir, there are many rumors being bantered about as to what this letter relates."

"Are the rumors good or bad?"

"Sir, one states that Major Cochrane brought news of the arrival of Admiral Digby in New York with thirty sails of the line, that Clinton has boarded with 5,000 or more reinforcements, and that the fleet has set sail to attack de Grasse and relieve our garrison."

Cornwallis shakes his head in disbelief.

"Another rumor," continues Chewton, "is that our fleet is already in the Chesapeake Bay and preparing to engage, sir."

"George, let us keep this to ourselves until tomorrow morning," replies Cornwallis. "It is best that no one knows for now. It might elicit a panic, and men could desert in droves. It is better to let them have their hopeful rumors."

Behind the British Lines
Yorktown, Virginia
October 10, 1781

All through the day, the allies maintained an artillery barrage that never let up for an instant. So devastating was the cannonade that the tops of the British parapets were blown away, guns had to be withdrawn from embrasures in damaged batteries, and soldiers were forced to re-pitch their tents in the trenches. Eventually, Cornwallis ordered a cessation of return fire, because so many weapons were damaged or it was simply too hazardous to man a battery. The only weapons able to fire were mortars and grenades, which could be launched from below the crest of the parapet.

When the bombardment began, all children and most women were ferried to Gloucester Point for protection. And considerable small boat traffic was maintained back and forth throughout the day. Most of the other residents of the town, including some women, moved to the riverbank and dug in to the sand cliffs. But they were not completely free from harm. Allied shells fell on the waterfront, landing near the huddled citizens and crashing into ships moored near the shore. Some cannonballs flew over the city and landed in the water. Others skipped across the water and wounded soldiers on the Gloucester Point beach, and several of the guns in the French Grand Battery were powerful enough to send their cannonballs all the way to the other side of the river on the fly. Almost no one was safe from the bombardment.

Allied mortar bombs were particularly devastating, because there were so many flying through the air that they could hardly be avoided. The bombshells were made of inch-thick pot metal with large mouths and fuses that caused them to fly in spinning circles on the way to their destinations. The fuses would continue to burn until they reached the body of powder in the center of the bombs. And damage from the eventual explosion could be particularly devastating. When a bombshell fell on a house, it tended to bury itself in the roof shingles before exploding. And when it went off, it literally tore the house to pieces and resulted in a fire. When a bombshell hit the ground, it whirled around and burrowed itself into the earth so deep that, upon exploding, it threw up a wagonload or more of dirt and rubble. People who were standing nearby would be thrown more than twenty feet into the air or blown to bits—fragments of the mangled bodies falling a considerable distance away.

Interestingly enough, when a bombshell hit a hard spot that did not allow it to burrow into the ground, a soldier would often run over and knock off the fuse so it would not explode. Those brave (or foolish) enough to perform such a task were rewarded with a shilling. Mostly though, soldiers behind the British lines ran for cover whenever they heard a cannonball or a bombshell coming near them. There were holes and pits all over the place (some large and some small), portions of which were covered with timber. The men would jump in these pits and squat down until the shell landed. Others huddled with Yorktown citizens on the beaches near the cliffs where the ground rumbled below them like shocks in an earthquake.

Because rations were becoming exceedingly scarce, Cornwallis distributed ample quantities of chocolate that had previously been seized from a captured Dutch ship. And while huddled together, the soldiers would eat chocolate bars or drink hot chocolate four or five times a day just to stay alive.

With the relentless American and French cannonade, however, optimism and hope within the British lines were becoming scarce. And out of shear terror from the slaughter and destruction taking place around them, men began to desert their posts in large numbers.

General Washington's Headquarters Tent
American Encampment
Yorktown, Virginia
October 10, 1781

Washington is in the middle of his meal with Secretary Nelson and Governor Nelson. Tench Tilghman appears at the entrance and beckons the general to come out for a moment, which he does.

"Yes, what is it, Colonel?" he asks.

"General, sir, we have just received word that several flatboats filled with British troops moved up the river to make an attempt on General de Choisy's flank at Gloucester Point. Battery 1A and de Choisy's field guns drove the boats back. The British soldiers were panic-stricken from the cannon shot and bursting mortar shells. They withdrew down the river and splashed ashore in desperate confusion."

Washington puts his hand to his chin and stares blankly into Tilghman's eyes. After a moment or two, he heaves a big sign and starts pacing back and forth. "Time is a problem here, Colonel," he says. "Admiral de Grasse will soon have to return to the West Indies. The arrival this very day of a message from Clinton to Cornwallis is troublesome. We must assume that the British fleet is on the move in this direction. I have no intelligence to indicate otherwise. We must press our advantage. Do you understand?"

"Indeed, sir," replies Tilghman. "Are you referring to the second parallel?"

"Yes," says Washington. "We must move the construction date forward. Have the engineers begin the design of the new siege line. Construction of the approaches may begin as soon as humanly possible. Issue orders for all regiments to build the necessary supplies. I should think 2,000 fascines, 600 gabions, 600 saucissons, and 600 stakes will do for a start. I want all commanders to have a specific quota of materials to be made on a daily basis. For the remainder of the siege, they will be further required to keep that quantity always in readiness by replacing the daily consumption. Von Steuben's men are out of the trench. Direct them to spend the rest of the afternoon on fatigue in the woods."

"Yes, sir, General," responds Tilghman. "Right away."

"Colonel, our work must be grounded in urgency. Make certain everyone understands that. We have no time to lose. The freedom of our nation is at stake."

◆   ◆   ◆

As darkness fell on Yorktown that evening, Count de Rochambeau was determined to ruin any ships Cornwallis might have that would aid him in a possible escape. Accordingly, he directed Battery 1A near the river and the Grand French Battery to launch a major bombardment in the direction of the waterfront using hotshot firing.

At 8:00 PM, Rochambeau gave the order to begin firing with his largest guns—twelve-and twenty-four-pounders. While cannonballs were heated in a pit, gunners rammed a special powder cartridge down the barrel, and then a piece of turf (or water-soaked hay). The barrel was sponged out for cooling and, using tongs, a cannonball was removed from the pit and loaded directly into the gun muzzle. Another gunner then quickly ignited the charge and sent the red hot ball hurtling through the air toward its destination.

Two primary targets were the frigates *Charon* (forty-four guns), most of which had been moved to shore batteries) and *Guadeloupe* (twenty-six guns). Under a torrent of fire, the *Guadeloupe* managed to make a run for it and reach the safety of the York River cliffs on the far right side of the battlefield. The *Charon*, however, was not so fortunate. It was hit by three fireballs and, within only a few minutes, was burning. In all the confusion, the ship collided with a transport and several other small vessels, which also caught fire.

As the fires began to rage, the *Charon* became engulfed in flames. Fire flared through all its portholes. The blaze ran rapidly up the rigging to the tops of the main masts, and the billowing black smoke rose up to merge with the low-hanging clouds. The light from the burning ships reflected back down from dark clouds and lit up the entire Yorktown waterfront. Soldiers and citizens, alike, were awestruck by the sight. Some people climbed up on roofs (at great risk to themselves) to get a better view. One Hessian officer stated in his journal that "the ships were miserably ruined and shot to pieces amid a terrible and sublime spectacle." A senior French officer, in describing the scene, wrote, "Never could a more horrible or more beautiful spectacle be seen."

Amidst the conflagration in the river, the rest of the allied artillery continued its bombardment on the town. Dr. James Thacher sat on the bank of the York River near the American parallel and described the scene:

> Some of our shells, overreaching the town, are seen to fall into the river, and upon bursting, throw up columns of water like the spouting of monsters from the deep. The sky is lit up over the river, and all around there is thunder and lighting from our numerous cannon and mortars. The bombshells from the besiegers and the besieged are incessantly crossing each other's paths in the air. They appear as fiery meteors with blazing tails of fire. Most beautifully brilliant, they ascend majestically from the gun to a certain altitude and gradually

descend to the spot where they are destined to execute their work of destruction.

The entire spectacle continued all night long—with no letup in artillery fire from the allies. The frigate *Charon* drifted across to the Gloucester Point shore, burned down to the water line, and eventually sank. Most of the houses and other buildings in the Yorktown were on fire or torn to pieces.

Before morning dawned, the Americans and French had fired more than 3,600 artillery shots from their complete arsenal of seventy-three guns. It had been an unbelievably powerful and destructive bombardment. And while the British suffered significant numbers of killed and wounded, the allies had virtually no casualties.

30

Cornwallis's Cave
Bank of the York River
Yorktown, Virginia
October 11, 1781

It is mid-morning. Moderate winds blow in from the river. There's a slight chill in the air. The allied cannonade continues, with bombshells and cannonballs whistling through the air, and explosions shaking the earth. Lord Earl Cornwallis is holding a council of war. Colonel Thomas Dundas and Colonel Banastre Tarleton have crossed over from the Gloucester Point shore to attend (Colonel John Simcoe is still too ill to participate). They've sailed past several ships smoldering and steaming in the river. They've seen countless houses reduced to rubble and still burning in the town. And they've trotted along a crater-laden beach dodging bombs and cannonballs along the way.

Also present in the grotto are General O'Hara, Colonel Chewton, Major Ross, Major John Despart, Colonel Alexander Sutherland, Major Charles Cochrane, and several other key officers. Cornwallis has just finished reading aloud the contents of Sir Henry Clinton's most recent letter. The others sit in stunned silence. A bomb explodes nearby, loosening dirt in the roof and rattling lanterns on the table.

General O'Hara finally speaks up. "Your Lordship," *he says to Cornwallis,* "our situation is now extremely disturbing. We are besieged by superior numbers and superior artillery. Every gun is dismounted as soon as it is shown. Powder and iron are growing scarce—not to mention rations. And our casualties number more than 300, with seventy-five killed."

"It now appears that all hopes of relief have totally vanished," *says a pessimistic Colonel Dundas.* "If we are to survive, it must be through our own personal actions. The destruction of His Majesty's army is inevitable if we remain in this position."

"I agree," *states O'Hara, matter-of-factly.* "It would be both honorable and judicious to abandon fortifications that are not tenable and adopt a design that has every probability of success."

"Yes," *confirms Dundas.* "A long defense here is utterly hopeless. We must evacuate these miserable works."

"Of course, that is easier said than done," replies Cornwallis. "Only yesterday morning, we made a run with flatboats up the river, but were quickly repelled by French artillery fire."

"Your Lordship, I agree with General O'Hara and Colonel Dundas, sir," says Banastre Tarleton. "But I do not believe that our route of escape should be on the water."

"Are you suggesting a retreat through Gloucester Point?" asks Cornwallis.

"I am, sir. I had time, while ill with the fever, to give considerable thought to such a plan. I am very familiar with the enemy's defenses and believe, sir, that our tactical military superiority will allow us to easily break through them."

"Very well, Colonel Tarleton. Please relate to the council the details of your proposal."

"Thank you, Your Lordship," Tarleton replies. "The army, exclusive of the navy, has many small boats that could transport 1,200 infantry at a trip—and with the assistance of the navy, above 2,000. We could transport as many troops as possible across to the Gloucester Point shore under cover of darkness."

"What would prevent such preparations from being besieged by Washington's guns?" asks Colonel Chewton.

"The enemy is going to be moving closer by constructing a second parallel—at least, we assume so. In that case, we will have an advantage in that they will not be able to observe our actions. Also, the bank of the river and the shape of the cliffs here are concave. Those two elements combined should allow us to conduct preparations virtually unnoticed. And I expect that we will also be able to clandestinely withdraw, embark, cross the river, and destroy the boats after our passage. The darkness of night should aid us considerably."

"Good points, all," replies Ross.

"Thank you, Major. Once at Gloucester Point, the troops may be supplied with three days provisions to carry on their backs. Upwards of twenty wagons may also be loaded with supplies. The light baggage of the officers might be placed upon horses. Our cavalry is already over there and, I might add, in good order. A body of infantry could be mounted on the spare horses. Our dragoons and infantry might then act together—either to guard the front or rear of the army, or to move rapidly and vigorously upon any emergency."

"But what of General de Choisy's corps and the enemy's defenses?" inquires O'Hara.

"He is in a vulnerable position, sir," replies Tarleton. "Gloucester Point is not besieged, only blockaded. De Choisy's force amounts to only 1,200 militia and 350 of de Lauzun's legion. The main body is encamped on the plain three miles out with a

large detachment advanced to a narrow wood about a mile and a half in their front. I should think that a real attack in the darkness would, in all probability so divide his resolution and that of the undisciplined militia that we would easily break through. There is also a great likelihood that we would destroy most of the French hussars at the outset—and seize a number of their horses. We could not entertain for one moment a supposition that our troops could be beaten back to Gloucester Point.”

“And what then?” asks Colonel Chewton.

“We would march westward for 100 miles,” continues Tarleton. “The country between the Rappahannock and York Rivers is rich and plentiful. It has not been invaded or destroyed and, therefore, abounds with grain, cattle, provisions, and forage. Many hundreds of horses may also be collected. Once we have marched the 100 miles, we may then determine, based on circumstances, whether to march north or south.”

“General Washington would not be idle, sir,” states Chewton.

“Certainly not, sir,” replies Tarleton. “But it would take time to react. There would be councils of war, correspondence with de Grasse, and troop redeployments. I should think it would take at least three days before he could react properly. By then, we would have at least one, maybe two days full march as a head start.”

“And how would you anticipate Washington dividing his combined army in pursuit of us?” asks Cornwallis.

“A division of troops would probably be sent to the head of the Chesapeake Bay,” states Tarleton, “another up the James River, and a third might be ordered to follow us directly.”

“I see,” says Cornwallis. “That is a well-thought-through plan, Colonel Tarleton. We must give some serious consideration to it. For now, let us turn our immediate attention to repairing our works. As soon as they are repaired, let us revisit the escape plan.”

“But, Your Lordship,” interrupts Dundas, “with the enemy’s continued bombardment and a second parallel sure to be commenced, we may never repair our ramparts.”

“Yes, indeed,” Tarleton states. “And if Washington captures even one of our outlying redoubts, this business will be at an end. We must commence our operations immediately, sir. Tonight!”

“I understand your feeling of urgency, Colonel Tarleton,” replies Cornwallis, almost casually. “However, there is still a chance we may hold out long enough for our fleet to arrive. I have not completely let go of that possibility.”

“Your Lordship,” protests Tarleton, “with all due respect, sir...”

“Thank you, gentlemen,” states Cornwallis abruptly. “That will conclude this council of war. I will let you know when we are to assemble again.”

The first officers to leave the grotto are Dundas and Tarleton. They walk along the edge of the cliff back toward their rowboat. "Surely, Cornwallis doesn't think that Clinton and Digby will arrive in time," says Dundas.

"It's preposterous," replies Tarleton. "I do not know what it will take for him to wake up. If he does not make a move in the next day or two, we will surely lose both the battle and the war. I hope he will be able to live with that!"

Back in the cave, Cornwallis asks Chewton and Ross to stay behind. "I would like to begin a letter to Clinton," he says.

"Yes, Your Lordship," replies Ross, pulling out pen and paper.

"Cochrane arrived yesterday," Cornwallis begins. "I have only to repeat what I said in my letter of the third, that nothing but a direct move to York, which includes a successful naval action, can save me. The enemy made their first parallel on the night of the 6th, at a distance of 600 yards, and have perfected it. On the evening of the ninth their batteries opened and have continued firing without intermission. We have lost many men, and our works are considerably damaged. With such works on disadvantageous ground, against so powerful an attack, we cannot hope to make a very long resistance."

Cornwallis looks at Ross. "Have you got that?" he asks.

"Yes, Your Lordship," comes the reply.

"Very well. Let us wait for a day or so to see what Washington's next moves may be—and then we will finish the letter."

General Washington's Headquarters Tent
American Encampment
Yorktown, Virginia
October 11, 1781

Washington and Humphreys are seated at the table when Jonathan Trumbull walks in unexpectedly. "General, sir, I beg to report that Colonel Tilghman has sent me here in his place," states Trumbull. "He has a slight fever and is indisposed."

"Has he gone to see Dr. Thacher?" asks Washington.

"Not as of yet, sir. He is in his tent."

"Well, if he is not better by tomorrow, I would like him to see Thacher," replies the general. "He seems prone to disease and comes down with almost everything that goes around. We must see that he gets well as soon as possible. With Laurens having assumed command of the light infantry, we need Colonel Tilghman here."

"Very well, sir."

"What is the morale of the troops, Colonel?" asks Washington.

"Sir, there is growing optimism that Cornwallis is on the verge of imminent disaster," Trumbull replies. *It is said that, unless the enemy starts making a better defense, the town will soon be too hot for His Lordship and the redcoats."*

"Yes, yes," replies Washington. *"I am happy for the good spirits, but both concerned and puzzled as to why Cornwallis has conducted himself in such a passive manner."*

"Perhaps he is confident that Clinton is on his way to attempt a rescue, sir," offers Humphreys.

"Perhaps. But I think he has either not the means of a good defense, or he intends to reserve his strength until we approach very near him."

Washington rises and walks around the table. He motions for Trumbull to take a seat. *"We can leave nothing to chance when it comes to Lord Cornwallis,"* Washington states. *"Despite the fact that he has inexcusably gotten himself into this situation, we must not forget that he has shown flashes of military brilliance in the past. He was outnumbered two-to-one at Camden and turned that situation into a victory. I do not wish to give him the chance to extricate himself here, though—either by going upriver or over to Gloucester Point. Let us try again to convince Admiral de Grasse to move some ships up the York."*

"According to Count de Rochambeau, both he and Admiral de Barras are still urging such a move," says Trumbull, as he pulls out paper and pen.

In his letter to de Grasse, Washington asks the admiral to consider securing *"General de Choisy's right flank, which is exposed at present, and prevent Cornwallis from crossing to Gloucester Point by deploying two frigates slightly upriver from the town."* Washington also tries to alleviate de Grasse's previous fears by stating that the move would not be as hazardous now that the Charon has been destroyed. *"There remains no other armed vessel of consequence but the Guadeloupe. I am persuaded the frigates may take such a position as will effectually secure them from danger."*

"And finally," says Washington, *"please point out to the admiral that we propose to open the second parallel this evening."*

"Yes, sir," replies Trumbull. *"I have it all."*

"Speaking of the second parallel, sir," interrupts Humphreys, *"we've received word from Colonel Duportail that the first approach will take the shape of a straight line—which, from the west end, will head due east in a straight line. It will then be angled obliquely to protect the sappers from enemy enfilade. The parallel will then proceed in the general direction of the two enemy redoubts on the far right."*

"We will have to stop, I presume, several hundred yards short of No. 9," replies Washington.

"Yes, sir. The engineers are all agreed that the two outposts will have to be stormed and captured before the second parallel can become fully operational."

"Indeed," states Washington. "But first things first. The parallel, then the redoubts."

American Grand Battery
Yorktown, Virginia
October 11, 1781

It is early afternoon. The sky is slightly overcast. Less than an hour earlier, the Marquis de Lafayette's division had assumed duty in the trenches. Artillery continues to boom all along the allied parallel.

Lafayette has invited Governor Thomas Nelson Jr. into the battery to observe Captain Thomas Machin's Second Artillery unit open fire on Yorktown. The young marquis knows that Governor Nelson was one of the original signers of the Declaration of Independence and had vowed to "drive the enemy invaders into the sea." In addition, Lafayette has never forgotten the aid he received from Nelson during his fight in the Virginia countryside against Cornwallis.

Now Lafayette turns to Nelson. "Governor, is there any particular place you would advise us to fire upon?" he asks.

Nelson immediately points to a tall brick house with massive red chimneys. "There. That house," he says. "Now that my uncle's house has been struck, that one is the best in town. It is now likely to be the headquarters of Cornwallis and his staff. Have your men fire there, General."

"Very well, Governor," replies Lafayette, who turns and directs Captain Machin to take aim. "You are certain that is where you wish us to fire?" he asks Nelson again.

"Indeed, I am, sir," comes the reply. "That is my house! And not a particle of the property should be spared."

Lafayette and Machin turn toward the governor in stunned silence. Then Nelson pulls some coins out of his pocket. "I'll give five guineas to the first man to hit it!" he shouts.

Word quickly spread to the gunners in the battery and, within minutes, all of the cannon and mortars were firing toward the brick house with the tall chimneys. Several cannonballs soon struck the roof and plunged downward, shattering several walls.

"Here," says Nelson handing the coins to Lafayette. "You be the judge as to who gets the money. And well done, sir! Well done!"

In the Forest
Behind the American Encampment
Yorktown, Virginia
October 11, 1781

Baron Von Steuben's division is on fatigue duty—collecting materials and fashioning gabions, fascines, and other materials necessary for construction of the second parallel. It is four o'clock in the afternoon when count Deux-Ponts rides up to Von Steuben, General Anthony Wayne, and the other division officers.

After dismounting, Deux-Ponts walks up to the baron and offers a crisp salute. "General, sir," *he says,* "Baron Viomenil has asked me to convey a message to you."

"Yes, what is it?" *inquires Von Steuben.*

"The baron, sir, has observed, while visiting the trenches, that your division is extremely weak. And as it is probable that the enemy will make a sortie tonight, he wishes to reinforce your left wing with from 500 to 800 men—if you should think it necessary, sir."

The old Prussian drillmaster, who has run out of money and been living on camp rations, bristles at this remark. "Count Deux-Ponts," *he snaps,* "I do not think I want any reinforcements! If the enemy should attack, I will be able to hold the battery until the Baron Viomenil can arrive to support me."

"Very well, sir," *says Deux-Ponts.*

"And furthermore," *continues Von Steuben,* "you may say to the baron that, in the event he is attacked, he may rely on me to support him with 800 men in two columns. Is that clear?"

"Indeed, it is, sir," *replies Deux-Ponts.* "Thank you, sir."

After the count mounts his horse and rides off, Anthony Wayne turns to Von Steuben, his superior. "Now, General," *he says quietly,* "you know we only have 1,000 men in this entire division. Why would you make such a statement?"

"No doubt of it, that is my calculation, also," *responds Von Steuben.* "But if it should so happen, I will leave 200 men to defend our line and attack with the remaining 800."

With this, Wayne smiles and cocks his head.

"And if I am guilty of a certain amount of exaggeration with regard the number of my men," *continues Von Steuben,* "then it is for the honor of your country, General Wayne."

A laughing Anthony Wayne shakes Von Steuben's hand and grins at the other officers. "Now, gentlemen," he says loudly, "it is our duty to make good the boast of Baron Von Steuben and to support him just as if he had double the number of troops!"

◆   ◆   ◆

Later that evening, while in the trenches, a cannonball was heard whistling toward Wayne and Von Steuben's position. As the two men ran for cover, they stumbled over each other. The baron went down first, and Wayne fell on top of him as the shot landed about twenty feet away and flung dirt over both of them.

When picking themselves up, Von Steuben grinned at Wayne. "I always knew you were brave, General," he said. "But I did not know you were perfect in every point of duty. You even cover our general's retreat in the best possible manner."

American Lines
Yorktown, Virginia
October 11, 1781

Just after dark, at approximately 8:00 PM, Washington and Rochambeau's forces began construction of the second siege parallel. When completed, this line would extend more than 750 yards from the York Creek ravine on the east in a westward direction to within 300 yards of Redoubt No. 9 on the far right side of the battlefield. Along its length, it would run an average of 1,500 feet north of the first parallel and would lie approximately 300 feet from the British main fortifications—easily within short musket range. Two zigzag approach trenches would be constructed—one on the French side, one on the American.

On the left, French troops were given the task of completing nearly three-quarters of the entire new trench. Nearly 2,000 men moved quietly forward to begin the work—750 from the Regiments Gatenois and Deux-Ponts, several hundred grenadiers and chasseurs of the Regiment Saintonge, and at least 800 night fatigue troops.

On the right side of the battlefield, while Governor Thomas Nelson's Virginia Militia manned the trenches, Von Steuben's division moved into position to begin the American section of the new parallel. Anthony Wayne commanded 400 men from two Pennsylvania regiments that would guard and provide cover fire, if necessary. These men were under strict orders from Von Steuben not to lie down in the night, but to be seated or stand with their muskets in their hands.

Another 600 men, under the direction of Colonel Richard Butler, began their short zigzag approach armed with pickaxes, shovels, hoes, gabions, and fascines.

Once they reached the main line of the parallel—marked by French engineers with white pine strips—the Americans worked in teams of six to dig the trench. A chief sapper led the way by digging a small trench two feet deep and one and a half feet wide. To shield him from musket fire, several men moved along in his front with a specially constructed gabion (five feet in diameter and six or seven feet high) stuffed with fascines and dirt. A second sapper followed closely behind to deepen and widen the trench by another six inches in each direction. The third and fourth sappers proceeded in exactly the same manner—deepening and widening as they went along. A fifth man staked fascines in the sides of the trench as it was being dug while a sixth soldier steadily moved supplies forward. And that's the way it went—Americans and Frenchmen digging at full tilt throughout the night.

On the far left side of the battlefield, St. Simon's division made a decoy attack on the Fusilier's Redoubt. It worked at first, as British guns blazed away at both the French position near the redoubt and the American positions on the first parallel. But by 10:00 PM, members of the Deux-Ponts regiment working on the second parallel heard a volley of musket shots and thought it was the beginning of an all-out British attack. However, this was only one of numerous patrols sent out all night long by Cornwallis in an effort to determine what activities the allies were undertaking.

Of course, as soon as digging on the second parallel was discovered, British gunners opened new embrasures and began a thunderous volley from mortars, howitzers, and muskets on the new activity. This firing did, in fact, interrupt the allied workers. But within minutes, the French unleashed a furious cannonade that sent the British artillery gunners reeling back on their heels. Of consequence, however, was the fact that the French reacted so fast that they neglected to properly adjust their guns. Short-fused bombs were launched forward with very low trajectories—and at least two Americans were killed. As a result, workers on the second parallel found themselves at the center of two cannonades, from both British and French guns.

Once word made it back to the French, they quickly suspended firing to properly adjust their weapons. During that lull in the action, British gunners unleashed a flurry of firing that again halted most digging on the second parallel. However, once the French had completed their modifications, the enemy earthworks started crumbling faster than they could be repaired. As more and more weapons were dismounted and destroyed, the British cannonade slackened to such a degree that it really was not dangerous to the troops working on the new parallel.

On the other hand, conditions inside the besieged town were becoming worse than ever. One British lieutenant described the scene in his daily journal:

> Upwards of a thousand shells were thrown into the works this night, and every spot became dangerous. I held in my hands a piece of an unexploded bomb that weighed more than thirty pounds and was over three inches thick. I saw one man completely blown to pieces by a bomb that fell on him. There were mortally wounded men lying nearly everywhere—and bodies with heads, arms, and legs that had been blown off. The thundering shells going over our heads continued all through the night—as did the distressing cries of the wounded.

31

The Hornwork
British Lines
Yorktown, Virginia
October 12, 1781

At daybreak, when Lord Cornwallis came to the crest of the parapet to view allied progress on their second parallel, he was again stunned at how much had been accomplished. Through his spyglass, the British commander observed the line extending from the morass leading to York Creek, across the Hampton Road, east into the American sector, and terminating several hundred yards from Redoubt No. 9. What he could not see, but knew anyway, was that the new trench was three and a half feet deep, seven feet wide, and artillery was already being moved forward from the first parallel.

Cornwallis now had no illusions as to the gravity of his situation. The noose was becoming ever tighter. And in his mind, the only hope for his army now was to hold off the inevitable as long as possible. To instill some fresh energy into his artillery gunners, he transferred Colonel Dundas and nearly all of the 80th Regiment from Gloucester Point to Yorktown. He also ordered naval personnel to join the light infantry in manning artillery batteries in the hornwork. Meanwhile, the allied artillery kept up a heavy and constant cannonade all day. Within an hour of British naval reinforcements arriving at their new positions, the allies had knocked out three embrasures, dismounted a twelve-pound cannon, knocked off the muzzles of two eighteen-pounders, and rendered fire from the hornwork virtually useless. And worst of all, British casualties continued to climb.

Count de Rochambeau's Headquarters Tent
French Encampment

Yorktown, Virginia
October 12, 1781

Count de Rochambeau has just returned from a meeting with George Washington. He has pulled together some of his senior officers, including Major General Baron Viomenil, Count Deux-Ponts, the Viscount de Rochambeau (his son), and his aides de camp, including Captain Jacky Custis. They are standing outside the entrance to the tent, speaking rapidly in French, although Custis has trouble understanding everything.

"General Washington has assigned us the task of taking Redoubt No. 9 on the right flank," states Rochambeau. "The Americans will lead the attack on No. 10. Baron Viomenil, I would like you to lead our assault. Do you accept?"

"*Oui, mon general*—with gratitude," replies Viomenil.

"In our discussions this morning, all agreed that few advances are possible without the seizure of these two positions," continues the count. "The capture of both will permit the completion of the second parallel all the way to the river. It will also seal off one of the enemy's last possible routes of escape. General Washington has already given the order for American gunners to bombard the palisades, abatis, and other embrasures surrounding the forts."

"May I ask, *mon general*, when the assaults are to take place?" inquires Deux-Ponts.

"At night, two days from now."

"That is too late," states an impatient Viomenil. "That is a useless delay. Our artillery has already softened the abatis enough. We should attack tonight. There is no time to lose."

"Patience does not harm us in this instance," replies Rochambeau calmly. "But you have a point. If they have been properly damaged, we must know now."

"Perhaps a reconnaissance," suggests the Viscount de Rochambeau.

"*Oui*, I think that is in order," agrees the count. "Let us do that now—the two of us!"

"May I accompany you, sir?" requests Custis, in broken French.

"No, sir," replies Rochambeau. "The fewer the better. You and the rest stay here. Count Deux-Ponts, please convey an order to halt our artillery fire for an hour—and ask the Americans to do the same."

"*Oui, mon general*," responds Deux-Ponts. "Immediately."

Rochambeau and his son jump on their horses and ride over to the far right edge of the American first parallel. After dismounting, they set out on foot along the creeks and narrow ravines leading up to Redoubt No. 9. All allied artillery has stopped and, *in an apparent effort to rest and regroup, so has the British cannonade. Staying low and remaining quiet, the two Frenchmen make it all the way to the abatis surrounding the redoubt. After making some careful observations, they return to the American lines. Rochambeau gives the order to resume artillery fire, and then he and his son ride back to his headquarters tent where Viomenil and Deux-Ponts are waiting.*

"The abatis and the palisades are still set in their entirely," states the count. "We must redouble our fire to break them—and to level the parapet. Tomorrow we shall see if the pear is ripe."

General Washington's Headquarters Tent
Yorktown, Virginia
October 12, 1781

Washington and his aides are seated around the table reviewing various lists concerning commodities and supplies for the American troops. "General, sir, we are receiving more and more complaints from the men," says David Humphreys. "They are asking for more clothes, especially shoes and boots."

"Here are requests from our militia commanders," states Jonathan Trumbull, holding several pieces of paper, "stating that they are very low on ammunition and flints."

"We also need firewood, tents, and forage for the horses," continues Humphreys. "Some of the regiments are actually burning fence rails stripped from the fields."

"There is no excuse for running low on firewood," exclaims Washington. "The woods are plentiful. And I do not like this disturbing practice of stealing the Virginia farmers' fence rails. The war we are fighting is as much for them as anybody else. Place in tomorrow's general communication an order to stop it."

"Very well, sir," replies Trumbull.

"Also order a redistribution of tents so that the troops sharing the same danger and fatigue may enjoy equal benefit."

"Yes, sir."

"Governor Nelson has informed me today that he has written to the Virginia delegates in Congress of our plight," states Washington. "He has requested more of everything—ammunition, flints, forage, tents, and especially clothing. The governor showed me his letter. It stated, in part, that the few troops we have now in the field are not fit to be seen and are very naked and getting sickly. I would like one of you to draft a similar letter for the Congress."

"I will take care of it, General," replies Trumbull.

"Speaking of the sick, sir," says Humphreys, "I have Dr. Thacher's report here."

"What doe it say?"

"The doctor is at Williamsburg and reports that there are now more than 400 men (including thirteen officers) who are in the hospital there. He states that the illnesses are caused by the humidity of the peninsula, the hot days and cold nights. Most suffer from swamp fever, but sickness also ranges from the common cold to minor cases of the smallpox, the latter of which he says is under control and not serious among the troops."

"Several deserters have stated that the smallpox is running rampant in the British encampment," states Trumbull. "And our own men report that almost every thicket affords the disagreeable prospects of a wretched Negro's carcass. Cornwallis throws them out of Yorktown to wander and die from disease and starvation."

Washington draws in a deep breath after hearing this last statement. He looks down and shakes his head in disgust. His eyes water. Finally, he speaks. "Well, order the men to stay away from them, because they most likely are contagious with the disease."

American Encampment
Yorktown, Virginia
October 12–13, 1781

Over the next two days, under the protection of a constant cannonade from French and American batteries in the first parallel, the allied forces labored intensely to perfect their second parallel. Thousands of gabions, fascines, saucissons, and wood planks were brought in to fortify the new parapet, five new batteries, and three new redoubts. And then the guns (mortars, howitzers, and heavy cannon) were hauled forward through the zigzag approaches to pound the enemy fortifications unmercifully.

The first battery (1B), situated at the western end of the parallel near the York Creek ravine would contain ten mortars and two howitzers. Next to it would be the first allied redoubt (Structure 2B). Four hundred feet down the line was Battery 3B (with an extraordinarily powerful six twenty-four-pound cannons). It was followed, in turn, by another redoubt (4B) and then by Battery 5B (700 feet away), which contained four twenty-four-pound cannons and two sixteen-pounders. The final two batteries (6B and 8B) would stand at the eastern terminus of the parallel separated by the third redoubt (7B). They would contain six sixteen-pounders and six eighteen-pounders, respectively. Most of the firing from the heavy cannons would be designed to be "en ricochet," where the guns were intentionally aimed low so that cannonballs would skip across the terrain, bounce over the parapets, and roll along the ramparts. Such firing would be particularly devastating, not only to enemy fortifications, but also to troops manning the guns.

During construction of the new batteries and redoubts, unprecedented cooperation took place between the allies. French troops of the Bourbonnois, Soissonais, Gatenois, and Agenois regiments worked with the American divisions of Lincoln, Von Steuben, Lafayette, and Nelson's Virginia Militia. Every man had a spade or shovel. Every second man carried either a gabion, saucisson, or grubbing hoe. They worked side by side digging in the dirt, fashioning the new fortifications, and pulling on heavy ropes to haul in the artillery. The only disagreements that existed were small contests to see who could get the most done. Frenchmen and Americans worked together with a common goal—the knowledge that the war might be ended, and America would gain its freedom.

"I am fully convinced that the siege will not last more than twelve days," said one American.

"As soon as these batteries are completed, I think the enemy will begin to squeak," agreed a Frenchman.

But as the allies went about their work, Cornwallis ordered an escalation in artillery fire. A number of new embrasures were opened all along the British lines. Bombs and grenades were aimed directly at the second parallel with pinpoint precision due to the short range. As a result, allied casualties began to increase rapidly. The French suffered more than half a dozen killed and twenty-nine wounded, and the Americans, about half those numbers. That brought the allied total of killed to sixty-seven (fifteen American, fifty-two French) and wounded to 163 (twenty-nine American, 134 French).

The increased British bombardment brought another furious response from French and American gunners located on the first parallel. In addition to targeting the main British line, Washington and Rochambeau ordered continued bombardment of the abatis and palisades around Redoubts No. 9 and No. 10 to soften them up for the impending attack. The Fusilier's Redoubt was also similarly bombed so that the British would not become aware that this fort was to be excluded from the attack.

For more than twenty-four hours, the allied guns literally rained a hail of shot and fire without any letup whatsoever. For a British soldier, there was no place to hide. "We placed ourselves in position to bombard them by direct, reverse, and cross fire," noted one French gunner. "Our intent was to provide cover for workers in the second parallel by filling the enemy's works with shells and bombs, to throw these into their camp in order to occasion heavy losses—and to instill terror by unremitting fire."

The strategy worked. That night, dozens of redcoats deserted Yorktown and crossed over to the American lines. They told stories of panic and exceedingly low morale in the British encampment. More and more soldiers were being blown to bits. The bodies and body parts could not be removed, because the cannonade was so relentless. And there was a growing resentment against Cornwallis, himself, for having allowed his forces to be placed in such a horrendous situation.

The Hornwork
British Lines
Yorktown, Virginia
October 13, 1781

It is about nine o'clock in the evening. Shells and bombs streak across the night sky. Lord Cornwallis has rushed up to the hornwork followed closely by Major Cochrane, who has been assigned temporary duty as the general's aide-de-camp. They have just received word that the corps of light infantry have refused to perform their duties. Cornwallis must shout to be heard above the booming cannons. "What is the problem here?" he asks.

"Your Lordship, the men absolutely refuse to man the guns any longer," responds the regimental captain in charge. "We have suffered too many deaths and injuries. Nothing I can say will get them to budge."

"Our naval personnel continue to work!" yells Cochrane.

"Yes, sir," replies the captain. "But they have only now arrived from Gloucester Point."

Cornwallis then walks up and down the hornwork exhorting his soldiers to man their guns. "Come, come, men," he bellows amid the incessant roar of guns. "You do not want to let the navy show you up, do you?"

The soldiers scowl or look away from him.

"I know it is difficult," he continues. "You are all brave men. But we do not have long to go, now. Relief is on the way from New York. According to General Clinton's last letter, he and Admiral Graves—along with the entire British fleet—should have sailed past the bar at New York yesterday. Gentlemen, our rescuers are on their way. Our salvation is at hand. It will be only a few more days now. We must stand tall. We must fight together."

"Is it true?" asks some of the men.

"Yes, it is true!" yells Major Cochrane. "I delivered the communiqué myself. The fleet sailed yesterday."

More men begin to stand, but most still look away.

"Come, come, men!" shouts Cornwallis. "You are British soldiers. If you act as such, I will reward you accordingly. I will provide a cask of wine to each corps of the light infantry who stands now and takes their positions." Word of this offer quickly spreads up and down the hornwork. Soon, men begin to move back to their batteries. Guns are readied and firing begins to commence once again.

"Over here, Major Cochrane," says Cornwallis to his aide. "Now is the time to see the effect of ricochet cannonading."

Cornwallis leads Cochrane over to one of the big guns. "Captain, the major has indicated a zeal to fire a weapon and see its effects on the enemy," he says to the lead artillery officer.

"Very well, Your Lordship," comes the response. "This weapon is primed and ready to fire. Now that we have reopened our guns, we must be careful, because the French have taken notice and are directing their cannonade back toward us."

"May I fire this weapon?" asks Cochrane.

"Indeed, Major," replies the artillery officer, handing him the torch. "Stand to the side here and touch the torch to the fire hole. The gun will instantly let off."

"Very well," replies the major excitedly.

Cochrane stands between Cornwallis and the cannon. He lowers the torch, and the cannon instantly fires with a loud, resounding boom. Cochrane then steps up to look over the edge of the parapet. "I want to see its bounding effect," he says.

"Stay as low as possible," shouts the gunner.

Major Cochrane peers over the edge of the parapet to have a look. He is exposed for no more than a couple of seconds when a ricochet cannonball fired by the enemy strikes him directly in the neck and tears off his head.

Lord Cornwallis recoils in shock. He leans on the wall of the parapet and slides down to a sitting position. Cochrane's headless body has fallen right next to him. It is still twitching. The shocked British commander can only stare at the young major's head lying on the ground a few feet away—its face a bloody mess, its eyes wide open.

Sir Henry Clinton's Headquarters
Harlem Heights, New York
October 13, 1781

There is a fierce rainstorm raging outside. It has been this way for two days—wind, rain, hail, and lightning. Captain Dawkins receives a dispatch, reads it, and takes it directly to Sir Henry Clinton.

"Sir, we have just received a note from Admiral Graves," he says. "The Alcide has collided with the Shrewsbury, and both are again in need of repairs. The admiral states that the collision is a result of this freak storm wreaking havoc on the harbor. He mentions, sir, that with this bad luck, combined with our indolent ship workers, the fleet will not be ready to sail until October 17 at the very earliest."

Clinton takes the paper from Dawkins and reads it slowly. Then he looks out the window, the rain pelting against it. He drops his hands to his sides, his shoulders droop. He clenches his jaw and lips—and shakes his head negatively.

32

General Washington's Headquarters Tent
Yorktown, Virginia
October 14, 1781

A meeting is being held to discuss the upcoming attacks on Redoubts No. 9 and No. 10. Present are George Washington and his aides, Jonathan Trumbull, David Humphreys, and Colonel David Cobb (recently appointed to fill the void while Tench Tilghman is sick). Representing the American forces are General Benjamin Lincoln and the Marquis de Lafayette. Count de Rochambeau and Baron Viomenil represent the French command.

It is two o'clock in the afternoon. A cool wind whips through the front entrance of the tent. The senior officers are seated at the table, aides standing behind. Continuous cannon fire can be heard in the distance. Louis Duportail is standing in front, pointing to a map of the redoubts.

"The Rock redoubt, also designated No. 10, is square-shaped, sits on the edge of the cliff overlooking the river, and is barely 180 yards from the closest battery on the enemy front line," says Duportail. "It is occupied by sixty soldiers of the British 71st Regiment of Foot. Approximately 700 feet to the southwest lies the larger Redoubt No. 9. Pentagonal in form, it is occupied by 120 Hessian and British soldiers. According to reports from enemy deserters, the interior of both forts are partitioned by stacked rows of casks filled with dirt and sand. Sandbags also line the tops of the parapets. As we have discussed, both are also surrounded by abundant ditches, abatis, palisades, and fraises."

"Our artillery has been pounding these all morning," states General Lincoln. "What is their condition?"

"According to our scouts, sir," replies Duportail, "the abatis are now sufficiently softened for an attack."

"Very well," says Washington, "but we will continue with the bombardment—both there and on the Star (Fusilier's) redoubt."

"Yes, that is wise, mon general," states Rochambeau. "St. Simon's cannonade has surely created uncertainty in the mind of Lord Cornwallis as to what our true objective will be this evening."

"Based on current conditions, are we all still in agreement to move forward with previous directives?" asks Washington.

"Oui," replies Rochambeau. "The French take Redoubt No. 9, the Americans No. 10."

"With all due respect, sir," interrupts Baron Viomenil, "would it not be more efficient if our French forces handled the attacks on both forts?"

"Surely, sir, you do not mean to infer that our troops are in some way inferior?" responds Lafayette, defensively.

"My dear marquis, it is a matter of substance that our forces are far better trained to bring such attacks to successful completion."

"This is outrageous!" shouts Lafayette. "Our American men deserve the honor of storming this fort. They will perform with precision and honor."

"Clearly, sir," replies Viomenil, "you cannot suggest that your troops are better trained or better prepared than ours for such an offensive operation?"

"Now, see here, sir," says Lafayette. "It is not…"

"Enough!" says General Washington, firmly. "With General Rochambeau's concurrence, the assignments will remain as originally directed. Baron Viomenil will lead the attack on No. 9 with 400, and the Marquis de Lafayette on the Rock redoubt with a like number."

"I am in agreement," replies Rochambeau.

"Major General Viomenil, have you selected your second in command?" asks Washington.

"Oui, mon general. The grenadiers and chasseurs of Regiments Gatenois and Deux-Ponts will be led by Count Deux-Ponts, himself."

"Very well, sir," replies Washington, now turning to Lafayette. "General Lafayette, have you also selected a second in command?"

"Yes, sir. I have chosen the Chevalier Lieutenant Colonel Gimat to lead our troops."

"Good," continues Washington. "I have also given an order for General Wayne to have two battalions at the ready to support either redoubt, if and when necessary. And General Knox will move forward with four field cannon to be utilized upon request."

"To preserve secrecy of the operation, sir," states General Lincoln, "may I suggest that the selected units move apart from the main armies."

"That is an excellent suggestion," replies Rochambeau.

"Then let it be done," states Washington. "We have also given orders for General de Choisy to make a feint at Gloucester Point at seven o'clock this evening. The Regiment Touraine will do likewise against the Star redoubt. That should distract Lord

Cornwallis sufficiently to enable our true objectives to be attacked in complete surprise."

With that, General Washington rises from his chair. "Gentlemen, we have work to
do," he says.

The meeting is at an end.

The Marquis de Lafayette's Tent
American Encampment
Yorktown, Virginia
October 14, 1781

Within half an hour after Washington's meeting ends, Alexander Hamilton, accompanied by his colleague Major Nicholas Fish, appears at the entrance to Lafayette's
tent. "General Lafayette, sir," begins Hamilton, "I have only now heard that you have
appointed Lieutenant Colonel Gimat to lead tonight's charge."

"Yes, that is true," replies Lafayette.

"I believe I have earned the honor of leading the assault on the Rock redoubt," protests Hamilton.

"But Alexander," replies Lafayette calmly, "Gimat and his men have been fighting
the British all summer. Your men have just come from northward. And besides, this is
your very first battlefield command. Gimat is more qualified."

With this, Hamilton patiently pulls out his manual of arms. "General," he says, "it
says right here that a senior officer should not report to his junior. I outrank Monsieur
Gimat. Furthermore, regulations state that such an honor will be offered first to the
duty officer of the day. Today, I am the duty officer. The honor should be mine. May I
also add, my friend, that time is running out for me to achieve any glory on my own.
This may be my very last opportunity—especially if Cornwallis surrenders Yorktown
and the war ends. I beg of you to give me this chance."

Lafayette pauses for a moment. He thinks about his own request of Washington to
have General Lincoln transferred to Gloucester Point, so that he could attain some
glory of his own. "Very well, Alexander," says Lafayette. "However, the decision is not
now mine to make. I have already secured General Washington's approval. He must
concur with this change. I will go to him this instant."

"I must accompany you, sir," replies Hamilton, "to plead my own case."

Lafayette, Hamilton, and Fish ride to Washington's headquarters tent. Fish waits
outside as the other two go in to see the general. A few minutes later, Hamilton, followed by the marquis, excitedly emerges and grabs Fish's hand. "We have it!" he says.
"We have it!"

Within the hour, the three have reassembled back at Lafayette's tent with Gimat and Colonel John Laurens. Lafayette has spoken privately with Gimat and told him of his decision to give overall command of the assault to Hamilton. He has reacted professionally and agrees to make the best of it. Laurens, being a good friend of Hamilton's, also has no objections.

The group plans every detail of the upcoming attack. Sappers and miners are to move forward first. They will clear pathways through the palisades and abatis. Three separate columns will follow. These are to be comprised of five companies from Connecticut and two from Massachusetts. Gimat will lead the main attacking column (comprised mainly of the powerful, and mostly black Rhode Island Regiment) in a direct approach from the south. Hamilton's column will approach from the west along the cliff's edge. A smaller third column (eighty men of the light infantry), commanded by Laurens, will circle around from east to north and block the enemy's escape.

The planning session concludes with some final comments by Lafayette. "General Washington has ordered that the attacks on both redoubts will be silent. Muskets are to be unloaded with bayonets fixed. The element of surprise is crucial. The troops are to be fed early, the columns formed and ready for action by dusk."

Allied Front Lines
Yorktown, Virginia
October 14, 1781

During mid-afternoon, Baron Viomenil met near the eastern terminus of the second parallel with Count William Deux-Ponts, Baron Claude-Amable-Vincent de Roqueplan de L'Estrade (Deux-Ponts's second in command), and two sergeants. Together, they sallied forth to reconnoiter and obtain details of Redoubt No. 9. Then they returned and planned their attack. By dusk, Viomenil's 400 Frenchmen had assembled in the American sector of the first parallel, just to the right of Battery 10A. They ate their dinner of boiled beef and afterward, while waiting for the signal to move forward, either laid down to sleep or have a smoke.

At precisely 6:00 PM, the Marquis de St. Simon led the Regiment Touraine on a false attack of the Fusilier's Redoubt. While a torrent of artillery fire blasted the fort, troops approached on foot—screaming, yelling, and firing their muskets. The ruse worked as British guns from the main parallel redirected their fire to that area. After about ten minutes, the entire French assault team retreated to its lines without sustaining a single casualty. Moments later, General de Choisy initiated a similar operation across the river at Gloucester Point. Again, Cornwallis turned his attention in that direction (fully 180 degrees away from Redoubt No. 9 and No. 10) and ordered his river batteries to fire on enemy positions there.

During these two diversionary maneuvers, Count Deux-Ponts and Baron L'Estrade readied their troops and led them to the debarkation point in the trench. Arrayed in two columns and aligned by platoons, the fifty French miners and sappers led the way. The next fifty men carried fascines to throw into the enemy trenches. Directly behind them were a dozen soldiers carrying ladders that would be used to scale the parapets. Next came the bulk of the troops who would storm the redoubt, including the Regiments Gatinois, Royal Deux-Ponts, Bourbonnois, and Agenois. As these troops moved along, the Americans manning the trench slapped them on the back, hailed them as heroes, and wished them luck. When they reached the exit point, Count de Rochambeau was waiting for them. Walking among his troops, he shouted words of encouragement.

"My children, I have great need of you tonight," he said. "I trust you will not forget that we serve together in this brave army—and that our cause is just."

"We will fight like lions until the last man is killed," responded one soldier.

At virtually the same moment, George Washington was addressing Alexander Hamilton's troops, who had assembled at their exit point near the Grand American Battery. Officers and enlisted men watched the general closely. His knees appeared to shake as he delivered a short, impassioned speech.

"You must be brave and firm this evening," he told the men. "The success of this attack rests with you alone. We must seize the fort. If we do, we will prevent the enemy from escaping Yorktown. And as you all know, this battle may determine the outcome of our long struggle for independence and freedom."

When Washington finished, Yorktown fell silent. The French attack had halted at Gloucester Point, and Cornwallis, while keeping watch in that direction, had ordered his artillery to cease fire so he could listen for any signs of movement. As the sun set below the horizon, a dense fog unexpectedly settled over the battlefield. "Perfect for a surprise attack," thought Washington, who had ridden over to the Grand French Battery to give the order to commence.

At precisely 7:00 PM, on schedule and in utter darkness, six artillery shots were fired in a particular rhythm—first a mortar shell and then five cannon shots. With that, the two allied columns left the trenches and moved toward the enemy redoubts.

Deux-Ponts's men advanced on Redoubt No. 9 in the greatest possible silence. When they were only 120 paces away, a Hessian sentinel on the parapet heard a noise and shouted out. "*Wer da?* [Who goes there?]" The lead French troops did not respond but, instead, hastened their advance pace toward the fort.

A volley of musket fire immediately erupted from the parapet of the redoubt. Deux-Ponts's men were under strict orders not to fire their weapons. As most of them hit the dirt and covered themselves from enemy fire, the lead troops began to chop at the abatis and fraises in a concerted effort to clear a pathway. But the British and Hessian soldiers in the redoubt unleashed an uninterrupted string of heavy musket fire, French soldiers started falling, and, for the moment, Deux-Ponts's forces were pinned down.

Over at Redoubt No. 10, American assault troops moved forward in three columns. While many officers carried espontoons or fixed their bayonets on the ends of slender wooden poles (creating makeshift spears), the enlisted men fixed bayonets on unloaded muskets. Quickly, silently, and with the aid of a thick fog, they advanced up to the abatis without being noticed. But when the sappers and miners began furiously chopping to create pathways through the fraises, British soldiers in the redoubt fired a full body of musketry. In response, Captain Steven Olney and about a dozen of the black Rhode Islanders, jumped up and ran forward, overrunning the troops who were still hacking at the abatis. Squeezing their way through the entanglements, they quickly moved toward the base of the front parapet. As the yellow light from powder explosions flashed all around, Olney observed several of his men fall into shell holes created by the earlier bombardment. But the attacking men rose out of the dense fog and continued moving forward.

When the group reached the ditch at the base of the redoubt, Olney told his men that he had full confidence that they would act as brave soldiers and, if their guns should be shot away on the ensuing charge, they were not to retreat but to take the gun of the first man that might be killed. Then, amid a hail of enemy fire, Olney stood up and called out to the troops beyond the palisades: "Captain Olney's company, form here!"

The Americans yelled and screamed as they charged forward. Gimat's men advanced straight toward the redoubt while Hamilton's battalion circled around to the right. John Laurens took his group of eighty to the left and rushed to the rear of the fort.

At the head of Gimat's line, enemy fire was so heavy that a sergeant dropped down on his knees and began yelling, "Oh God, I am a dead man! I am a dead man!" But the other soldiers charged right over him. And Captain Olney, brandishing one of the makeshift spears, immediately ran up to the top of the parapet. Six or seven British soldiers lunged down at him with bayoneted rifles—stabbing him in the hand, legs, and abdomen. As Olney fell backward, two of his men disobeyed orders by hastily loading and firing their weapons, which drove back the redcoats.

Approaching from the southwest near the cliff's edge, Alexander Hamilton's battalion split into two columns. On the right, Hamilton led the charge over and through the palisades before the sappers and miners could clear a pathway. The British responded by unleashing heavy fire from the redoubt. They fired so many shots and threw so many hand grenades, in fact, that the Americans thought that all the popping was coming from firecrackers. Making it through the palisades and into the ditch, one of Hamilton's officers cried out, "Rush on, boys! The fort is ours!" Hamilton, who was too short to reach the top of the parapet, ordered one of his men to kneel down. Then he jumped on the soldier's back and vaulted onto the rampart. Swinging his sword wildly and yelling for his men to follow, the young colonel jumped down into the enemy redoubt.

A little farther to the left, Major Nicholas Fish led his battalion into the redoubt in much the same manner as did Hamilton. British soldiers manning the redoubt, now faced with an onslaught from three directions, began running away as fast as they could. Several of them actually jumped off the river bluff, fell thirty feet to the beach below, and limped back to Yorktown.

John Laurens, meanwhile, had charged his brigade in from the fort's rear entrance and tried to halt the fleeing redcoats. Although most escaped, Laurens managed to halt the last dozen or so, including the redoubt's senior officer, Major John Campbell of the 71st Foot Regiment. The remaining British soldiers threw down their weapons, dropped to their knees, and begged for mercy. Cheers of celebration then erupted from the American forces.

Dr. James Thacher, who had been waiting just beyond the redoubt, was ordered in to treat the wounded. As he was kneeling down to treat Olney's stab wounds, a captain in the American Light Infantry, who had been a good friend of Colonel Alexander Scammel, approached British Major Campbell. With his sword raised, the captain shouted, "Remember poor Scammel!" But Alexander Hamilton rushed up, grabbed the man's arm, and forced him to lower his sword.

"No, no, Captain," said Hamilton. "This man has surrendered. We are not murderers."

Five minutes later, a captured Irish redcoat came up to Olney as Dr. Thacher was tending to him. The Irishman pulled out a bottle of wine and offered the wounded officer a swig. Olney would later write in his journal that all the British defenders seemed to be drunk that night.

The assault on Redoubt No. 10 lasted only ten minutes. The Americans suffered nine dead and twenty-five wounded. British casualties were only eight killed or wounded, ninety-five escaped, seventeen surrendered.

After the battle, the Marquis de Lafayette rushed into the redoubt. Chatting excitedly, he congratulated Hamilton, Gimat, Olney, and Fish. Then he sent a courier over to Baron de Viomenil with a note. "I am in my redoubt," it read. "Where are you?"

With his troops still pinned down by enemy musket fire, Viomenil responded tersely. "Tell the marquis I am not in mine," he said, "but will be there within five minutes."

When the French sappers had pulled enough abatis and palisades away to create an unobstructed pathway, Count Deux-Ponts immediately stood up and waved his sword. "French grenadiers and chasseurs, charge!" he shouted. "Charge! Charge!" Deux-Ponts led his men in a furious rush through the pathway right up to the redoubt. When he reached the base of the parapet, he was hit in the thigh by an enemy musket ball and stumbled into the ditch—but a young officer helped him up. Ladders were thrown against the walls of the fort, and men began to climb them. The second in command, Baron L'Estrade, fell back into the ditch when a soldier ahead of him lost his foothold and went down. Both men were trampled by a hundred or more onrushing French soldiers. L'Estrade eventually struggled to his feet, cursing his troops as he rose.

The first to reach the top of the rampart was the Chevalier de Lameth. But Hessians in the fort, who had been holding their fire, now unleashed a full hail of shots. Lameth was hit in both knees simultaneously and fell back down the parapet and into the ditch.

As more and more men reached the top of the rampart, Deux-Ponts—wounded but making his way up a ladder—gave an order for everyone to leap into the redoubt. As they did, the Hessians inside made a bayonet charge and wounded or killed several French soldiers. The Hessians quickly pulled back, huddled behind a protective barrier of barrels, and continued to load and fire their muskets.

As more and more Frenchmen climbed the ladders and leaped into the fort, the Hessians and redcoats began to run away in mass numbers. Finally, those left in the redoubt threw down their weapons, held up their hands, and surrendered."

"*Vive le Roi*! [Long live the king!]" yelled Deux-Ponts. "*Vive le Roi*!" responded his men.

And then the Americans and Frenchmen in the trenches behind them echoed the cry. "*Vive le Roi*! *Vive le Roi*!"

It took Deux-Ponts approximately thirty minutes to capture Redoubt No. 9. Enemy casualties were eighteen killed or wounded and fifty captured. The rest escaped back to their main line. The French suffered fifteen dead and seventy-seven wounded.

British Main Lines
Yorktown, Virginia
October 14, 1781

When the American attack on Redoubt No. 10 began, Johann Conrad Doehla (a Hessian private in the Anspach-Bayreuth Regiment) stated that everyone thought the "Wild Hunt" had broken out. "There must have been 3,000 men who under-took the assault," he noted.

Lord Cornwallis sounded the alarm throughout the entire British encamp-ment and ordered all troops onto the ramparts. A full volley of musketry with some artillery was his initial response. But when the French started their attack on Redoubt No. 9, Cornwallis, fearing an all-out allied offensive on the left side of his main line, ordered a furious artillery cannonade in response.

"Such firing never was heard in America," wrote another British soldier in his diary. "You would have thought heaven and earth were coming together." The firing was so dramatic and so haphazard, in fact, that many of Cornwallis's men fleeing the redoubts were killed by their own guns.

Near the Grand French Battery
Yorktown, Virginia
October 14, 1781

George Washington, Benjamin Lincoln, and Henry Knox are standing on a small rise overlooking the assaults on Redoubts No. 9 and No. 10. Their aides stand behind, holding the generals' horses. During the attack, the British main line keeps up an unremitting artillery and musket fire.

As Washington steps forward and looks through this spyglass, Colonel David Cobb, the general's new aide-de-camp, tugs on his sleeve. "Sir, you are too much exposed here," he warns. "Shouldn't you step back a little bit?"

Washington lowers his telescope, turns his head toward Cobb, and looks him straight in the eye. "Colonel Cobb," he says, "if you are afraid, you have the liberty to

*step back." Then he again looks toward the redoubts through his telescope. Cobb steps
back.*

*A few minutes later, an enemy musket ball strikes the cannon next to Washington
and falls at the American commander's feet. An alarmed Henry Knox rushes up to his
leader and grabs his arm. "My dear general," he says, "we cannot spare you just yet!"*

*Washington bends over and picks up the bullet. "See here, Henry," he says showing
it to Knox, "it is a spent ball, and no harm was done."*

*When Washington hears the shouts of "Vive le Roi!" coming from Redoubt No. 9
and being echoed down the lines, he turns to General Knox. "The work is done," he
states. "And well done."*

Washington then turns around. "Billy, hand me my horse," he says.

*Billy brings the general's horse forward. The two mount their steeds and ride back
to headquarters.*

Allied Front Lines
Yorktown, Virginia
October 14, 1781

Rather than storming the British main line as Cornwallis feared, the allies immediately set about extending the second parallel 350 yards east from Battery 8A to
the captured redoubts. As the Regiment Bourbonnois moved into position to
provide cover, nearly a thousand men began digging the new trench and converting the redoubts into allied fortifications, complete with large-caliber cannon.
Construction also commenced on a communications trench, stretching more
than 2,000 feet from Redoubt No. 10 all the way back to the first parallel.

As British guns continued to blaze away, casualties began to mount, especially
among the French. In one blast alone, 27 soldiers were killed and more than 100
were wounded. Count Deux-Ponts, who remained in command at Redoubt No.
9, was called forward by a sentinel who thought a redcoat attack was imminent.
As Deux-Ponts looked over the parapet, a ricocheting cannonball missed his head
by inches, blasting his face with sand and gravel. Now unable to see or hear, and
having already taken a bullet to the thigh, he was whisked off to the hospital in
the back lines.

◆   ◆   ◆

On the far left side of the battlefield, Count de Custine of the Regiment San-
taigne had been ordered to open fire at 7:00 PM as part of the cover fire prior to

the redoubt assaults. Custine, however, got drunk and passed out. When he came to at 8:30 PM (a full hour after the forts had been captured), he had lost all track of time and immediately gave the order to have his men open fire on the enemy. Count de Rochambeau, who was more amused than upset by this episode, placed his subordinate under twenty-four-hour arrest so he could sleep it off. Throughout the rest of the siege, Custine was the butt of jokes among the entire French army.

Over in the American encampment, the cowardly sergeant who had fallen to his knees, yelled that he was a dead man, and subsequently retreated, was tied onto a wooden sword and paraded up and down the lines as a "skulker." Thoroughly humiliated, the sergeant became ill and died a week later.

33

General Washington's Headquarters Tent
Yorktown, Virginia
October 15, 1781

It is 1:00 PM. Washington and his aides are seated around the table reviewing communications. A general staff meeting with Lafayette and Von Steuben is coming up. Tench Tilghman, still ill but recovered enough to get back to work, is reading aloud the general's message to the troops.

"The commander in chief congratulates the allied army on the success of the enterprise last evening against the two important works on the left of the enemy's line," recites Tilghman. "He requests Baron Viomenil and the Marquis de Lafayette to accept his warmest acknowledgements for their gallant conduct, and he begs them to present his thanks to every individual officer and men of their respective commands for the spirit and rapidity of their performance.

"The general reflects with the highest degree of pleasure on the confidence that the troops of the two nations must hereafter have in each other. He is convinced there is no danger they will not cheerfully encounter—no difficulty they will not bravely overcome."

"Very good, Colonel," responds Washington. "Let's begin our letter to the president of Congress."

"Yes, sir," says Tilghman, pulling out pen and paper.

"Here, Colonel, let me take care of this one," jumps in Jonathan Trumbull.

"No, no, Jonathan," replies Tilghman. "I have been absent too long and missed too much. I would like to do the work."

"I have the honor to inform Your Excellency," begins Washington, "that the two redoubts on the left of the enemy's line were taken by assault on the evening of the 14th . Prisoners in both redoubts include: one major, two captains, and sixty-seven privates. These works are of vast importance to us. From them, we will enfilade the enemy's whole line, and I am in hopes we shall be able to command the communication from York to Gloucester Point. I think the batteries of the second parallel will be in sufficient forwardness to begin to play in the next day or two."

There is a rustling of noise outside the tent. David Humphreys walks over to check it out and announces that Lafayette, Von Steuben, and Louis Duportail have arrived for the staff meeting.

Washington looks at Tilghman. "We will conclude this later," *he says.* "But before I forget, please enclose a tally of our casualties up to the present time with a statement that it is much smaller than might have been expected."

"Yes, sir," *replies Tilghman.*

Washington rises and motions for Humphreys to show the others inside. As Lafayette, Von Steuben, and Duportail enter the tent, everyone is all smiles. Tilghman, Trumbull, Humphreys, and David Cobb join the general in congratulating their visitors—shaking hands and slapping backs. The atmosphere is upbeat, almost giddy. Everyone senses that the end is near for Cornwallis.

"Gentlemen, please sit," *beckons Washington.* "Tell us what has happened this morning."

Lafayette speaks first in his typically excited manner. "Sir, we have been busy converting the captured redoubts," *he says.* "We have closed the British entrances and are cutting new ones in the sides facing away from the town. Trenches of the second parallel now reach all the way to the river. This we finished before daylight. His Lordship's left flank is now completely closed off."

"Excellent!" *responds Washington.* "Excellent!"

"It appears now, sir," *says Von Steuben,* "that our guns, once in place, will be able to thoroughly pummel the enemy's position. We should also be able to command British communication lines across the river to Gloucester Point by bombarding both sides of the waterfront."

"I have been advised by Count de Rochambeau that enfilading is the desired bombardment at this stage," *states Washington.*

"Indeed it is, sir," *responds the Prussian siege veteran.* "It is the surest way to keep the besieged from having any cover and to disconcert their batteries."

"And what do our engineers have planned for the completion of the new parallel?" *asks Washington as he turns toward Louis Duportail.*

"Sir, most of this day will be spent in preparing the captured works to receive their designated armaments," *Duportail responds.* "Nearly all of our French artillery platforms will be transported to the new line from the first parallel, which will henceforth serve primarily a supportive function. The American Grand Battery is being dismantled as is Battery 10A. General Knox is currently overseeing all this work, which is why he is not present at this meeting. In addition, sir, four hours ago, members of the Pennsylvania line began construction of a large battery directly opposite Redoubt No. 9. We have designated this structure No. 11B. When completed, it will measure 250 *feet in length and will be armed with ten eighteen-pound cannon, eight mortars, and four howitzers."*

"Good Lord!" snaps Von Steuben. "With such a battery only 200 yards distant, Cornwallis had better beware his head!"

"Yes, indeed," states Washington with a slap of the table. "And what artillery will the converted redoubts contain?"

"Sir, we will place two 10-inch mortars and two howitzers in No. 9. Structure. No. 10 will contain two 18-pound cannon, four howitzers, and three mortars."

"And what of the ground between Battery 8B and No. 9?" asks Washington.

"At 400 yards, it is the longest exposed section of the new parallel," replies Duportail. "This will not be a problem, however, as we are placing six 18-pounders in 8B, and the length of the trench will be reinforced with France's finest infantry regiments."

"That should be sufficient for us to hold the line," interrupts Von Steuben. "But it is so close to the enemy position that nearly every movement draws attention. The position, therefore, is quite dangerous."

"Indeed, General," states Washington, "I received a report shortly before you came in that upon your relief from the trenches, there was a significant burst of enemy fire."

"It is true, yes," responds Von Steuben. "General Lincoln's division under Colonel Van Cortlandt advanced into the redoubt with drums rolling and banners flying. The display drew an incessant shower of bombshells. I immediately directed the colonel to stop his music, which he did, causing an immediate cessation of the enemy cannonade."

"The British obviously took affront to the display," states Tilghman.

"Clearly, that is so," replies Washington. "But I do not understand why such a ceremony was conducted when I have already given explicit orders that they are prohibited."

"Perhaps it was thought that the previous order did not apply as this was the opening of a new parallel," states Lafayette.

Washington looks at the young marquis and frowns.

"It should not have happened," states Von Steuben. "It was foolish. We are attracting enough attention as it is. This morning, one of Captain Vendenburg's fatigue party was killed when struck by a nine-pound cannon ball. It carried off his thigh close to his body. And then one of his sergeants was looking over the embankment when a ball passed so close to his head that the sheer energy killed him, even though it made no physical contact. The sergeant fell back into the trench with his skull fractured to pieces and blood flowing out of his nose and mouth. I am informed that the Marquis de St. Simon was also wounded but would not leave his post until

his duty period was completed. Our current work is exceedingly dangerous—perhaps the most dangerous of the entire siege."

With this statement by Von Steuben, Washington abruptly stands up and calls an end to the meeting. "It is time I visited the captured redoubts," he states. "Colonel Cobb, please inform Billy."

"Yes, sir," replies Cobb, who quickly exits the tent.

"I would like to accompany you, General," states Lafayette.

"Very well," replies Washington.

"Sir, you must be careful," states Von Steuben. "The enemy will surely see you and open fire with musketry and grapeshot."

Washington nods his head affirmatively and smiles. Then he leaves the tent, followed closely by the Marquis de Lafayette.

Cornwallis's Cave
Bank of the York River
Yorktown, Virginia
October 15, 1781

Lord Earl Cornwallis is dictating a letter to Sir Henry Clinton while Major Ross sits at the table and writes. Colonel Chewton stands quietly to the side. As Cornwallis speaks, he walks around the table ringing his hands. He is strangely calm, stern, and businesslike.

"Last evening, the enemy carried my two advance redoubts on the left by storm," he begins, *"and during the night, included them in the second parallel, which they are at present perfecting. My situation now becomes very critical. We dare not show a gun to their old batteries. And I expect their new ones will be open tomorrow morning."*

As Cornwallis pauses, Major Ross looks up. Colonel Chewton stands against the earthen wall with a blank expression on his face—his red coat contrasting sharply with the wall's green bunting. He only stares straight ahead. Cornwallis continues.

"Experience has shown that our fresh earthen works do not resist their powerful artillery, so that we shall soon be exposed to assault in ruined works, in a bad situation, and with weakened numbers."

Cornwallis pauses again, stops walking, and takes a deep breath. "The safety of this place is therefore so precarious," he says, *"that I cannot recommend that the fleet and the army run the great risk of endeavoring to save us."*

Ross shakes his head negatively as he writes. Chewton does not move a muscle. His expression never changes. Cornwallis walks over to the opening of the cave. An allied shell explodes on the beach and showers his uniform with sand.

◆   ◆   ◆

Later that afternoon, the allies launched a furious cannonade from both the artillery that had not yet been moved from the first parallel and the newly emplaced guns in the second parallel. As a matter of fact, the new line was so close to the British main works that when allied shells exploded, some of the shrapnel flew back to the new line causing an unusual cross-fire effect on those in the second parallel.

Despite the fact that this bombardment was primarily meant to protect French and American workers in the new line, the physical and psychological impact in the British encampment was particularly chilling. One mortar shell struck a frigate anchored in the river, caused it to catch fire, and finally explode with a shock that made the earth shake. Another bomb hit a German bake oven and severely killed and wounded those nearby. One Hessian was found in three pieces.

In response, British gunners were only able to answer with light artillery, mortars, and musket fire, largely because that's all they had left. Their parapets were smashed to bits and batteries destroyed as guns were blown off their platforms. Most of the enemy soldiers cowered in the trenches just to survive. They had not expected that the cannonading could possibly have gotten worse than it had previously been.

One German soldier noted in his journal that "the enemy began to fire so fiercely, it seemed as though the heavens would split. It was almost unendurable. And now, for the first time, we saw what was going to happen to us."

That night, a steady and heavy stream of deserters crossed over to the allied lines.

34

Batteries 6B and 8B
Allied Second Parallel
Yorktown, Virginia
October 16, 1781

At four o'clock in the morning, 350 redcoats led by Lieutenant Colonel Robert Abercrombie quietly moved out of the British main works in the vicinity of the hornwork and headed toward the allied position. Their mission was to attack and disable the uncompleted French and American batteries (6B and 8B), which were located directly opposite the left center of the British main line. Moving in two columns, they entered the second allied parallel between Batteries 7B and 8B. To the British good fortune, this part of the trench had no troop protection, because workmen had just been ordered to a different part of the line.

One redcoat column turned east down the trench and headed toward Battery 8B, which was still under construction and occupied by approximately 100 New York Continentals, artillerists, and Virginia militiamen. Upon reaching the edge of the battery, a British officer called out: "What troops?" An American lookout, thinking it was a group of French soldiers coming to provide protection, responded by asking, "French?" The British officer then ordered his men to charge: "Push on, boys, and skin the bastards!" he yelled.

Caught by surprise, nearly all of the battery's occupants, who had deposited their arms in the communications trench behind them, fled into the darkness and escaped. A few, however, were captured or killed on the spot. The redcoats immediately disabled the three 18-pound cannons. This was normally accomplished by driving a nail into the touchhole until it struck the bore of the cannon and spread out like a cotter pin. The head of the nail was then usually knocked off, so that it could not be extracted. Such a procedure almost always rendered a cannon inoperable. This night, however, instead of bringing along the correct steel spikes, the redcoats had brought wheel nails with them—which were too large to fit into the cannon touchholes. Powerless to disable the cannon in the proper manner, several of the redcoats drove their bayonets into the touchholes and snapped them off.

After entering the trench, the second British column turned west, passed through an unoccupied communications trench, and sneaked up to Battery 6B. In another stroke of luck, all the French gunners had left their positions to retrieve two overturned cannon that were being transported from the first parallel. In addition, the soldiers of the Agenois Regiment responsible for guarding the battery were given permission to sleep—and all fifty of them were lying in the adjacent redoubt (7B). So the British raiding party only had to contend with one French sentry, whom they fooled by representing themselves as an American relief party. After killing this guard, the redcoats promptly entered the battery and spiked four sixteen-pound cannons with their bayonets. Lieutenant Colonel Abercrombie then ordered his men to charge over the parapet of the redoubt next door and attack the sleeping Frenchmen. Most of the Agenois soldiers fled in reaction to the surprise attack, but not before many were stabbed as they slept.

All the noise created by the British assaults was heard down the line by the Viscount de Noailles, who immediately led the Regiment Soissonais in a furious charge to retake the batteries. The screaming Frenchmen had no trouble driving off Abercrombie's troops who, because they had already completed their mission to disable the artillery, were more than willing to scamper back to their own lines.

In the end, the allies got the worst of the fight, having suffered thirteen killed and forty wounded, almost all French. The British suffered only eight killed or wounded and six taken prisoner. For the most part, the entire enterprise was judged a failure by both sides. Because the redcoats had neglected to bring the proper nails, the allies were able to remove the spiked bayonets from the cannon touchholes and restore the weapons to working order in just a few hours. Still, this kind of sortie was considered a standard, if not essential, part of siege warfare and was usually conducted near the end of a siege when the besieged were running low on food and supplies. Even the allies believed that Cornwallis was justified in ordering the sortie. If successful, it would have disabled some of the enemy's artillery, delayed the opening of the second parallel, and helped to postpone the inevitable next step—a general storming of the British position by allied troops.

Both the French and American lead officers who were caught, quite literally, napping, accepted responsibility for their poor performance by stating, in part, that they had "hardly dreamed of being attacked that night." But they also pointed out to their superiors that the British seemed to be getting increasingly desperate—not only because of the timing of the attacks, but because most of the redcoats involved in the sortie were apparently drunk. Heavy intoxication was also noted in the taking of Redoubts No. 9 and No. 10 and was a sure sign that British soldiers did not want to fight.

At sunrise, Cornwallis ordered all his still-operational guns to open fire on the enemy position. It was as if he was shouting to the allies, "We're not dead, yet!" But Washington and Rochambeau responded within a few hours by unleashing another devastating cannonade that included heavy fire from the reconstituted guns in Batteries 6B and 8B. "The enemy battered our works so badly," noted Hessian Captain Johann Ewald, "that all our batteries were silenced within a few hours."

Redoubt No. 10
Allied Second Parallel
Yorktown, Virginia
October 16, 1781

Throughout the morning and into the afternoon, French artillerists demonstrate their expertise in ricochet fire, which compounds destruction of the British fortifications and further terrorizes the redcoats. Meanwhile, thousands of American and French soldiers labor to complete the second parallel and move big guns up from behind the lines.

At 4:00 PM, General Henry Knox declares the conversion of Redoubt No. 10 complete and gives the order to open fire on the enemy. American guns all along the line quickly join the bombardment.

Standing nearby, the Marquis de Lafayette takes note of the precision displayed by Knox's artillerists. "You fire better than the French!" he says.

Knox casts a wry look back at Lafayette.

"On my honor, General, it is true!" Lafayette asserts. "Everyone knows the progress of your artillery is one of the wonders of the revolution."

◆　　　◆　　　◆

A few hours later, as the sun sets on the western horizon, a light rain begins to fall. Lafayette has returned to headquarters, and Knox is having a friendly debate with Colonel Alexander Hamilton about the practice of allowing men to yell, "A shell!" whenever an enemy bomb lands in the redoubt.

"It is not necessary!" argues Hamilton.

"Nonsense," replies Knox. "The bombs swirl around before they explode and do great harm. Most of the men are engaged in their duties. Such a warning is not only appropriate but is in the best interests of preserving the men's lives."

"Still, I believe it to be unsoldierly!" says Hamilton. "The men can look out for themselves."

Suddenly, an enemy bomb lands in the redoubt not six feet from where Knox and Hamilton are standing. As it begins whirling on the ground with its fuse spurting out fire, a soldier shouts out, "A shell! A shell!"—and everyone scrambles for cover.

The general leaps behind an earthen barrier followed closely by Hamilton who, as a small man, squats behind and grabs onto the back of the 300-pound Knox for increased protection. The extra weight causes the general to lose his balance, fall down, and, in doing so, accidentally flip Hamilton back out toward the swirling bombshell. Hamilton quickly scrambles back behind Knox. The bomb then explodes, but no one is injured.

As the two men stand up, Knox looks over at Hamilton, whose eyes are as wide as saucers. Knox shakes the dirt from his fat sides and starts to laugh. "And now, Colonel Hamilton, what do you think about crying, 'A shell!'" he says. "And I'll thank you not to make a breastwork of me again!"

◆   ◆   ◆

After this episode, Hamilton sat down in the trench and penned a letter to his wife. "Two nights ago, my Eliza," he wrote, "my duty and my honor obliged me to take a step in which your happiness was too much risked. I commanded an attack upon one of the enemy's redoubts. We carried it in an instant and with little loss. If there should be another occasion, it will not fall to my turn to execute it."

General Washington's Headquarters Tent
Yorktown, Virginia
October 16, 1781

Washington is dictating general orders to be issued the next morning. Jonathan Trumbull is writing. Tench Tilghman is sitting at the table, listening and holding a handkerchief to his face. The general is concentrating on two points regarding troop behavior in the new allied parallel.

"First of all," he says, "I am astounded that the trenches seem to be constantly crowded by spectators. There are to be no spectators in this army! Besides, they prevent the men from working and thereby greatly impede the operations of the siege. So make a statement to the effect that no one, unless on assigned active duty, is to enter the trenches at any time without permission from the major general of the trenches."

"Yes, sir," says Trumbull.

"In addition, let us also reinforce our previous order that relieving troops are not to beat their drums so as to draw the enemy's attention," continues Washington. "Rather, the men are to march into the trenches silently, with trailed arms and colors furled, until they arrive at their posts."

"It will be so noted, sir."

"Good!" states Washington, who turns to Tilghman. "What reports have we from the front?"

"Sir, Count de Rochambeau sends us a note stating that he is outlining actions against the Star redoubt," replies Tilghman, who sneezes and wipes his face. "His engineers are tracing a network of trenches extending forward from our lines between Batteries 1A and 2A. Once the fort is taken, another battery will be erected on the southwest corner straddling the Williamsburg Road. This will effectively cut off the final remaining land route as well as eliminate the enemy's last outer stronghold."

"Very good. What else?"

"Sir, we are informed by General Lincoln that French hotshot and American guns have now destroyed most British shipping in the river. Only the danger of enemy fireships remains to threaten a naval advance up the York."

"I wish de Grasse would move some frigates up there," states Washington, with some frustration. "It would surely prevent Cornwallis from escaping through Gloucester Point. And that now appears to be his last hope. Let us send another letter to the count."

"I am ready, sir," responds Trumbull.

"Sir," begins Washington to de Grasse, "it appears that every objection to the station above the enemy's posts in York River is removed, except the danger of fireships. This, however, can be neutralized by placing a sufficient number of rowboats to guard the front of your ships. To that end, I have ordered the seizure of, and currently expect, a great number of small boats from the upper reaches of the river—as well as all those that can be obtained on the Gloucester Point side."

Washington pauses as his aide writes. "Do you have that, Colonel?" he asks.

"Yes, sir. Please continue."

"From accounts of prisoners and deserters, it is apparent that Lord Cornwallis places all his hopes of survival on a relief expedition from General Clinton and Admi-

ral Digby. It does not appear to me, however, that any port south of the Chesapeake would be chosen for the debarkation of the enemy's troops (on account of the natural difficulties in their march afterward). Rather, I think the relief expedition would land at the mouth of the Piankatank River near Gwyn's Island. From there, enemy troops could march to Gloucester Point without the obstacles or rivers or any other impediments of consequence."

Washington again pauses. He rises from his chair, walks toward the opening of the tent, puts his hand to his chin, and peers outside for a few moments. Then he continues.

"I believe that Lord Cornwallis's only hope is to transport his army across the river to Gloucester Point. As such, the presence of several French frigates upriver would make it all but impossible for him to accomplish this task. If you were able to successfully achieve this maneuver, I think His Lordship would be forced to surrender."

Trumbull finishes writing and looks up. "Is that all, General?" he asks.

"Yes, that is enough. Please have this letter carried to Count de Grasse by special courier."

"Yes, sir," responds Tilghman. "I will take care of it, forthwith."

Cornwallis's Cave
Bank of the York River
Yorktown, Virginia
October 16, 1781

Lord Cornwallis has convened a full council of war. Seated around the table are Colonel Chewton, Major Ross, General O'Hara, Colonel Dundas, Lieutenant Colonel Abercrombie, Major John Despart, and Captain Thomas Symonds, senior naval officer. A number of other young officers are standing, including Lieutenant Colonel Johnson (23rd Regiment and Marines), Captain Aplethorpe (Fusilier's Redoubt), Captain Rochfort, and Lieutenant Sutherland (an engineer). Outside, the sun has nearly set, and a cold steady rain is falling. The British works are being pounded by allied guns. There are intermittent explosions close to the beach and above the cliff. Each time one is felt, some sand sprinkles down from the roof.

"Yorktown is no longer defensible," states an emphatic General O'Hara. "At this time, there is no part of the whole front in which we can show a single gun—and our shells are nearly expended."

"The parapets are tumbling down from the effects of the enemy's ricochet fire," agrees Colonel Dundas. "The fraises are flying apart in small pieces."

Cornwallis listens silently. He is grim, although his face shows no emotion.

"Your Lordship, I believe we are in an untenable position," states O'Hara again. "It is apparent to me that the enemy is preparing an assured route for a full forward movement, so they may take us by storm."

"Yes," says Dundas. "That is the next logical step."

After a long pause, Cornwallis looks around the table and asks one question. "What is my council's recommendation, then?" he inquires.

There is silence. No one sitting wants to make a suggestion. Finally, Captain Rochfort speaks up. "We must evacuate immediately, General Cornwallis!" he says. "The only other option is surrender."

"Agreed! Agreed!" shout a couple of the other officers.

Cornwallis looks at his seated senior officers. "Do you concur, gentlemen?" he asks.

"Yes, Your Lordship," says O'Hara.

The others nod in agreement.

"How then?" asks Cornwallis.

"Colonel Tarleton's escape plan is still viable, sir," states Dundas. "Even though he is at his station across the river, I'm sure I can speak for him."

"Why don't you relate the particulars of the proposed plan to refresh the council's memory, Colonel Dundas," requests Cornwallis.

"Certainly, sir," he replies. "The majority of our troops may cross the river by night. Once there, we will destroy all the boats on the north shore, form a junction with Tarleton's force, and utilize our local artillery and superior numbers to blast a path through de Choisy's troops. Then we will mount captured horses and march one hundred miles inland before Washington can begin a pursuit. Our forces may either move north to New York to join Sir Henry Clinton or south to regain the Carolinas."

"That is a very risky endeavor, Colonel Dundas," replies Cornwallis, with hesitation in his voice. "Many things must go just right if it is to be successful."

"General, sir, it may soon be too late," cautions a younger officer. "The enemy has taken the redoubts on our left flank. We can see they are preparing for a general storming of the main line. And it is logical to assume that Washington and Rochambeau are laying plans to storm the Fusilier's Redoubt, which would cut off our right flank."

"Indeed, sir," states Captain Symonds. "We are also lacking any effective naval force in the river. If the French admiral chooses to move into and up the York, which he can now do at his will, we will no longer have a path of escape through to Gloucester Point."

"I agree, Your Lordship," states Dundas. "It is a wonder that de Grasse has not already made the move."

"And what is the council's estimate as to when Washington might make an attempt on the Fusilier's?" asks Cornwallis.

"They will be able to do so within the next twenty-four hours," replies Captain Aplethorpe, "if they bother with it, that is. It may not be necessary given the condition of our main works."

"Perhaps not," responds Cornwallis, "but knowing General Washington as I do, he will probably insist on it. It will cut off another avenue of escape and, when taken, will provide an additional source of firepower against us. I also understand the council's concern about de Grasse making a move upriver."

"Indeed, sir," interrupts Dundas, "he could move at any time—even this night."

"General, sir," says O'Hara, "I must point out that the morale of our men is extremely tentative. They complain constantly, drink heavily, and each night desert in higher numbers. Everybody easily sees that we cannot hold out much longer if we are not relieved by Sir Henry Clinton and the British navy."

"Sir, I submit that we cannot rely on Sir Henry Clinton to come to our rescue," states Dundas. "We must act on our own volition."

"I certainly agree with you on that point," states Cornwallis. Then turning to the rest of the council, he asks, "Are you all agreed on such a course of action?"

Heads nod all around.

"The army must move or be destroyed," says Dundas.

"I think it is a choice between preparing to surrender tomorrow," replies O'Hara, "or endeavoring to escape with the greatest part of our troops tonight."

"Very well, gentlemen," says Cornwallis. "We will attempt an escape through Gloucester Point. Even if it should prove unsuccessful in its immediate object, it would at the very least delay the enemy in the prosecution of further enterprises against us."

Then Cornwallis turns to his aides, Chewton and Ross. "Please record the following orders, gentlemen." Cornwallis begins to bark out a series of specific directives, and it is obvious to everybody that the British commander has thought through the operation well in advance.

"Sixteen large boats are to be in readiness to receive troops at precisely ten o'clock," he begins. "It is at this time the transportations will begin. Three trips across the river should be sufficient to convey all those fit and ready for duty. Sailors and soldiers are to be dispatched with boats from Gloucester Point to assist the troops in passing across the river. The first embarkation will consist of the light infantry, the greater part of the brigade of guards, and the 23rd Regiment. I will pass with the second embarkation. We will soon forward more specific details as to which regiments will be transported in what order.

"Once the fording is completed and a junction made with Colonel Tarleton, we will charge through the enemy cordon and retreat to the north. I emphasize, gentlemen, that this is all to be done before daybreak. I repeat—before daybreak.

"Commanding officers of regiments are to be acquainted with the intended project. But not the enlisted men—not until the last possible moment. As we expect more desertions in the interim, we cannot tip our hand to the enemy. For the same reason, officers only will be advanced as entries this evening.

"The sick and wounded, most of the stores, and our baggage will have to be left behind. We will leave a small detachment of able-bodied men to capitulate on behalf of the town's people and our sick and wounded.

"I will immediately prepare an order for Colonel Tarleton informing him of our decision. When completed, it will be carried across the river by Colonel Chewton. I will also prepare a letter to General Washington calculated to excite his conscience on behalf of those of us left behind."

Lord Earl Cornwallis rises from the table. In response, the seated officers all stand. "Gentlemen, speed is of the essence," he states. "I know you and your men will perform with excellence and propriety. This meeting is concluded. You are dismissed."

With that, all the officers offer a crisp salute and then leave and descend to the cold, dark, rain-swept beach. Cornwallis, Chewton, and Ross remain behind in the safety of their cave. They prefer it over the grotto near the Nelson house, which is no longer utilized, because it is too close to the guns of the second allied parallel.

The York River
Yorktown, Virginia
October 16, 1781

Promptly at 10:00 PM, more than a thousand members of the British light infantry, Brigade of Guards, and 23rd Regiment began loading into the sixteen waiting transport boats and crossing over to the Gloucester Point shore. At 11:00 PM, German soldiers of the Anspach Regiment, who had been designated by Lord Cornwallis to comprise the skeleton force to remain behind, started relieving British regulars in the trenches. While the redcoats moved down to the river and waited to embark on the next transport, gunners of the Royal Navy manned artillery batteries and kept up a constant fire to distract the allies.

By midnight, the entire first group had landed on the north shore, and the majority of the boats were on the river headed back to pick up the next division. The first two transports that reached the Yorktown shore were immediately loaded and launched back to Gloucester Point.

Up to this point, there had been a constant light rain that helped the British disguise their movements. As soon as the second transports had launched, however, the weather changed dramatically. A violent storm swept in from the Chesapeake and transformed the fairly calm river into a maelstrom of high, white-capped waves, searing winds, and heavy rains accompanied by thunder and violent flashes of lightning. As a result, Lord Cornwallis's smooth escape operation turned into a nightmare.

Most of the empty boats coming back across the river were severely thrashed around by the waves. Several capsized, and all were scattered far downriver. The two boats filled with troops were swept out toward the Chesapeake and captured by French ships. The land-bound British troops could only huddle together on both sides of the river and wait out the storm.

By two in the morning, the tempest had begun to subside. But Lord Cornwallis, who later termed this storm "as severe as any I had ever experienced," realized that there was now no chance to get all of his troops across safely to the Gloucester Point shore before daybreak. By then, the allies would be able to see everything that was happening and would surely open fire on the river. It would be like shooting ducks on a pond. So he dejectedly issued orders to bring back all the troops that had landed at Gloucester Point with whatever boats that could be rounded up. Then he sent out soldiers to repair the existing parapets and batteries.

At first light, with clear skies and no rain, allied guns immediately opened a bombardment on the returning British boats. Although the passage back across the York was extremely dangerous, by mid-morning, nearly all the redcoats had returned safely.

Cornwallis's bold escape attempt had been thwarted by nothing more than a freak thunderstorm. And, as Colonel Banastre Tarleton would later record, "Thus expired the last hope of the British army."

35

General Washington's Headquarters Tent
Yorktown, Virginia
October 17, 1781

It is dawn. General Washington is already up. He hears the cannonade, walks out-
side, and stands looking in the direction of Yorktown. As the sun rises, it reveals clear
blue skies. A soothing breeze blows lightly in his face.

Within a few minutes, Baron Viomenil and the Marquis de Lafayette ride up and
dismount. The two Frenchmen are animated as they brief Washington on the previous
night's enemy activity. The general listens carefully until they've finished. He pauses,
takes two steps in the direction of Yorktown, and clenches his jaw.

"Cornwallis is now desperate," he says. "I want you to open up all the guns. Blast
them hard. Pound the village."

"Oui, mon general," reply Viomenil and Lafayette, almost in unison.

"Go now!" orders Washington. "Quickly! Go! And pass on my order!"

As the two generals mount their horses and race off, Washington turns toward
Jonathan Trumbull and David Humphreys who had arrived during the briefing.
"Send a courier to General de Choisy," he says. "Advise him to tighten up his divisions. Tarleton may now try to escape north by himself. Tell him we will shortly send
reinforcements."

"Yes, sir. Right away."

"Colonel Humphreys, I want you to go directly to Count de Grasse. Tilghman is
already there or en route back. Tell him of Cornwallis's movements last night. He
should act now."

"Surely, he will, sir," agrees Humphreys. "I will be off immediately."

"General, sir," interrupts Trumbull. "Do you know what today is?"

"Hmmm?" wonders Washington.

"Four years ago today, British General Johnny Burgoyne surrendered the entire
British army at Saratoga."

Washington nods. "Perhaps a sign of divine providence," he says. "Perhaps a coincidence."

"Sir, one has to wonder if last night's freak storm was coincidence," states Humphreys. "Just at the time His Lordship was attempting a sneak escape?"

"This is not the first time our cause has been aided by unusual weather," agrees the general. "The freedom of man is of too much importance to remain neutral, gentlemen. I have always believed that God is on our side. And that faith has sustained me these many years."

◆   ◆   ◆

By 7:00 AM, the second parallel was fully operational, and all seventy-three pieces of American and French artillery were smashing into the British defenses at Yorktown. "The whole peninsula trembles," noted Dr. James Thacher in his journal. "We have leveled much of their works and left them in ruins. The enemy has almost ceased firing altogether."

On the British side, Captain Johann Ewald wrote that "the bombardment began again even more horribly than ever before. They fired from all redoubts without stopping. Our detachment, which stood in the hornwork, could scarcely avoid the enemy's bombs, howitzer shot, and cannonballs anymore. One saw nothing but bombs and balls raining on our whole side. They battered our works so badly in the flank and rear that all our batteries were silenced within a few hours. My nerves suffered extremely."

The Hornwork
British Lines
Yorktown, Virginia
October 17, 1781

At dawn, Lord Cornwallis enters the hornwork. He has been up all night. He is tired, out of energy, sullen, depressed.

Amidst the cannon fire, he looks out over the parapet toward the allied lines, which look strong. He sees the enemy guns closer than ever—with one battery of fourteen guns so near the hornwork that one could throw stones into it. Then he looks up and down his own line. The parapets, redoubts, and batteries are in ruins. Out front, the abatis, fraises, and palisades have been blown to bits. There are now easy pathways for the enemy to storm the works.

Cornwallis turns to a Hessian officer. "Why are we not returning the enemy's fire?" he asks.

"Sir, all our major guns are dismounted," the officer replies. "We can only respond with light mortar fire—and we have little more than 100 shells remaining. Some of the men refuse to perform their duties, saying it is far too dangerous."

The Hessian and British soldiers watch Cornwallis closely as he exits the line and heads back to his headquarters. His head is down, his face pale and drawn. He seems to stumble and nearly collapse as he makes his way out. As soon as Cornwallis gets out of sight, a number of angry infantrymen begin slashing their tents to pieces.

Cornwallis's Cave
Bank of the York River
Yorktown, Virginia
October 17, 1781

Within an hour of visiting the hornwork, Lord Cornwallis is back in his cave speaking with General O'Hara, Colonel Abercrombie, Captain Symonds, and his aides. He has elected not to summon the other officers for a full council of war.

Abercrombie, who reached the Gloucester Point shore before the storm hit, is discussing what he saw. "I went into one of the redoubts there," he explains, "and found our men stretched out on the ground like half-dead people. I asked the officer in charge how many troops could be assembled. He advised that Colonel Simcoe, the majority of the Ranger officers, and all the Jager officers were desperately ill with fever. He said he no longer had twelve men who could march a full day."

"What is your opinion of the enemy defenses at Gloucester Point?" asks O'Hara. "Did you have time to either observe or discuss their strengths with the officers there?"

"Yes, sir," replies Abercrombie. "Our officers believe we will never break through there. The enemy has trenches around our entire garrison—and behind them is a cordon of French hussars as far as you can see. Nothing passes in or out."

At this point, Major Alexander Ross tries to be optimistic. "But if we can only get our troops across, we will have sufficient strength to break through," he states. "Perhaps we should try to recross the York this evening under cover of darkness."

"No, Major," responds Cornwallis, glumly. "Washington would be ready for us this time. The element of surprise is gone. It would be suicide."

"Your Lordship, I have received this morning's reports, as you requested," states Colonel Chewton. "They are very pessimistic."

"Go ahead," says Cornwallis. "Let's hear them."

"Our provisions are now almost exhausted, our ammunition near totally gone. And our works are assailable in many places."

"Yes," states Cornwallis. "I just saw it for myself."

"The opinion of the engineer and principal officers of the army," continues Chewton, "is that, by the continuance of enemy fire for a few hours longer, we will be in such a state as to render our situation desperate."

"What is the state of our men?" asks Cornwallis.

"Sir, more men are wounded daily," responds General O'Hara. "Hundreds are ill of fever. We estimate 3,200 still fit for duty on this side, 600 on the Gloucester Point shore. The strength and spirits of the men, however, are much exhausted by the constant enemy bombardment and the unremitting duty. So many men are ill or unwilling to perform their duties that we cannot provide relief in the line."

Cornwallis leans back in his chair and shakes his head. "Gentlemen," he says, "a successful defense is perhaps impossible. The enemy's combined forces number more than 20,000. Their second parallel is completed and in strong condition. I believe that de Grasse will move into the river at any moment. The enemy also has heavy artillery that is well manned and amply furnished with ammunition. Their cannonade will tear into our works, batter an opening, and provide many pathways to storm the garrison, which Washington will undertake without mercy. I think it inhuman to sacrifice the lives of this small body of gallant soldiers."

Cornwallis pauses and looks around the table. "Do you concur, gentlemen, that our situation is hopeless?" he asks.

O'Hara, Abercrombie, Symonds, Chewton, and Ross say nothing. They only nod affirmatively.

"Very well," says Cornwallis. "Then we must negotiate a surrender that will be as advantageous as possible for our command."

"Perhaps, sir, we can negotiate long enough for Sir Henry Clinton and Admiral Digby to arrive," says the ever-optimistic Major Ross. "Perhaps they have already landed somewhere on the coast and are marching here as we speak."

Cornwallis now rises from his chair. "Major, I admire your persistence, but you are naïve," he says quietly. "First of all, Washington will never allow the negotiations to drag out. And second, you must not believe that General Clinton is on the way. Even if he were to arrive on a white charger with 10,000 men, it would make no difference at this point."

Cornwallis then walks toward the entrance to the cave and stares out at the water. A couple of mortar bombs explode on the beach.

"That damned Clinton!" he says, disgustedly. "That bastard!"

Sir Henry Clinton's Headquarters
Harlem Heights, New York
October 17, 1781

In the back study, seated behind his huge extravagant desk, Sir Henry Clinton is sign-
ing two copies of his will. He places a note on one copy with instructions that it be sent
to his family in England. The other he folds and places in his coat pocket. He will give
it to his mistress, Mrs. Mary Baddeley, later today.

    Captain Dawkins rushes into the study. "Sir Henry, a new dispatch from Lord
Cornwallis has just arrived," *states Gurwood.*

    "What is the date?" *asks Clinton.*

    "Only two days ago, sir."

    "Read it!"

    "Yes, sir," *replies Gurwood, who unfolds the dispatch and begins.* "Last evening the
enemy carried my two advance redoubts on the left by storm and during the night
included them in their second parallel, which they are at present perfecting."

    "This would have happened on the fourteenth?" *asks Clinton.*

    "That is correct, sir," *replies Gurwood, who continues to read.* "My situation now
becomes very critical. We dare not show a gun to their old batteries. And I expect their
new ones will be open tomorrow morning. Experience has shown that our fresh
earthen works do not resist their powerful artillery, so that we shall soon be exposed to
assault in ruined works, in a bad situation, and with weakened numbers. The safety
of this place is therefore so precarious that I cannot recommend the fleet and the army
run the great risk of endeavoring to save us."

    "Is that all?" *asks Clinton.*

    "It is, sir."

    "Very well, let us respond immediately."

    Captain Dawkins takes a seat on the other side of Clinton's desk and pulls out pen
and paper.

    "I will let you draft the letter," *says Clinton to Dawkins.* "Tell him that we are
leaving here forthwith. Relate to him the number of men and ships and that our plans
are to land on the Rappahannock River, far up the Chesapeake, north of the York. If
he can hold out for another week, all will be well."

    Dawkins finishes scribbling his notes and looks toward Gurwood. Both aides have
frowns on their faces, and Clinton notices. "What is it?" *he asks.*

    "Well, sir," *replies Gurwood.* "His Lordship has advised us not to attempt a rescue.
His situation sounds desperate."

"Yes, yes, I know," replies Clinton. "But perhaps it is not as bad as he makes it seem. Besides, we must at least attempt to go to his rescue. See to it that this letter is sent ahead with a fast courier. Now we must prepare a letter to Lord Germain."

"Yes, sir," responds Dawkins, who pulls out a clean sheet of paper.

"First relate our intentions and our landing plan as mentioned to Cornwallis," says Clinton. "Then state that we will be leaving 7,000 or 8,000 men here for the protection of New York. Do you have that?"

"Yes, sir," replies Dawkins.

"Next state the following: Should our armies (Lord Cornwallis's and my own) join at York and beat the rebels and French, we stand prepared to improve the advantage by an attack on Philadelphia."

Now standing next to the door, Captain Gurwood looks down at the floor and shakes his head. Clinton does not notice and keeps on dictating. "I still flatter myself that, notwithstanding the rapidity of the enemy's progress and our having been delayed by the necessary repairs of the fleet so far beyond the expected time, it may yet be in the power of our joint exertions to relieve His Lordship."

As Clinton pauses, Dawkins looks up.

"That is all," states Clinton, who rises from his chair. "You will prepare these letters for my signature immediately and dispatch them by special couriers forthwith."

"Yes, sir," replies Dawkins.

Sir Henry then walks out to the foyer, opens the front door, and steps out onto the porch of the white, two-story mansion that sits atop Harlem Heights. It is mid-morning, the sun rising in the October sky. Leaves have fallen off the tall trees. A cold wind whips into the general, and he shivers.

Sir Henry looks down toward New York Harbor and sees the first few frigates straggling out toward Sandy Hook. Clinton will go aboard the HMS London *with Admiral Graves. Admiral Hood will captain his own flagship. Admiral Digby will not make the trip. Over the next two days, nearly 100 vessels, including 35 ships of the line—nearly the entire British fleet—will begin assembling for the voyage down the Atlantic coast to save Lord Cornwallis and his army.*

British and Allied Front Lines
Yorktown, Virginia
October 17, 1781

It is a crisp autumn morning. Skies are blue with a few white, wispy clouds blowing by. The unrelenting allied cannonade deafens the countryside.

Shortly past 10:00 AM, a single red-coated drummer mounts the top of the British hornwork and begins beating a steady "chamade," the signal for a besieged army that wishes to capitulate. At first, he is not heard amid the furious artillery bombardment. But soon an American infantryman spots him and passes the word over to officers manning the artillery. One by one, battery by battery, the French and American guns fall silent.

Dr. Thacher describes the resulting calm as "a solemn stillness." Troops in the second parallel peer over the parapets to see what's going on. They notice the lone redcoat and cup their ears to hear the steady beat emanating from his drum. The French instantly recognize the "chamade" and quickly pass the word of its meaning up and down the lines. A Pennsylvanian in the trenches later describes the drumbeat as "the most delightful music to us all."

As cheers begin to erupt from the allied lines, a British officer waving a white handkerchief joins the drummer. The two move forward, the drummer continuing his steady drumbeat. One American officer runs out of the second parallel and meets the two redcoats. He sends the drummer back to his own lines, ties a white handkerchief around the officer's eyes, and escorts the man forward to the Marquis de Lafayette and Baron Viomenil, who are presiding over the trenches.

General Washington's Headquarters Tent
Yorktown, Virginia
October 17, 1781

Washington is just sitting down to review his morning's correspondence when he hears the guns go silent. He rises and walks outside the tent. Tench Tilghman, David Humphreys, and Jonathan Trumbull stand with him and gaze toward the front lines.

Minutes later, Lafayette and Viomenil come riding up and quickly dismount. The young marquis, beaming ear to tear, hands a letter to Washington. "Sir, a communiqué from Lord Cornwallis," he says, "delivered under a flag of truce accompanied by a 'chamade.'"

Washington opens the letter and silently reads it. He swallows deeply and hands the letter to Tench Tilghman. "Colonel, please read it aloud."

"Yes, sir," responds Tilghman, who begins to recite the contents.
Sir:
I propose a cessation of hostilities for twenty-four hours, and that two officers may be appointed by each side, to meet at Mr. Moore's house, to settle terms for the surrender of the posts of York and Gloucester Point.
I have the honor to be,

Lord Earl Cornwallis

Tilghman raises his head silently and looks at his commander in chief. Humphreys, Trumbull, Lafayette, and Viomenil remain silent, waiting for Washington to speak first.

"Well, gentlemen," says Washington at last, "this comes at an earlier period than my most optimistic hopes and dreams had ever expected."

Then the general puts his hands behind his back, looks over at Lafayette, and nods his head slightly.

He takes a few steps forward and looks in the direction of Yorktown. He hears leaves rustling in the breeze and birds chirping in the background. Washington looks toward the sky. He draws in an extended deep breath and, with a long sigh of relief, slowly exhales.

PART VI
THE SURRENDER

36

General Washington's Headquarters Tent
Yorktown, Virginia
October 17, 1781

It is noon. Washington is standing outside his tent amid a myriad of people, including Rochambeau, de Viomenil, Lafayette, Lincoln, Knox, Governor Nelson, and their various aides. He turns to General Lincoln. "Did the messenger make it back to his lines without incident?" he asks.

"Yes, sir," replies Lincoln. "Men of both armies watched eagerly as the redcoat crossed the open plain. And no sooner had he arrived than we gave the signal to continue the cannonade. That caught the enemy off guard. A number of soldiers on the parapets were killed. Obviously, they had not expected us to reopen fire."

"And we will continue to fire until we know whether or not Cornwallis is serious," says Washington sternly.

"Our lookouts have reported that some of His Lordship's soldiers are busy unloading the few remaining ships in the river," notes Viomenil. "It appears they are to be scuttled."

"This must be for the purpose of preventing Count de Grasse from bringing his ships upriver," states Lafayette. "Or perhaps it is done to delay, to buy more time to allow the British fleet to arrive."

"Have we heard from Grasse, yet?" asks Washington.

"Not as of yet, sir," replies David Cobb.

"Mon general," interrupts Rochambeau, speaking through his interpreter, "it is standard procedure to scuttle any sailable ships prior to the besieged capitulating. It prevents the ships from being used by the enemy. I believe this is a sign that Lord Cornwallis is indeed sincere about surrender."

Washington nods. "General Rochambeau, are you agreeable to His Lordship's request of two officers from each side settling terms for the surrender at the Moore House?" he asks.

"Indeed, I am, sir," replies the count.

Washington turns toward Governor Nelson. "Why do you suppose His Lordship chose this house for negotiation?" he asks.

"It is along the river and well behind our lines," responds Nelson. "Perhaps he selected it because the devastation within the British lines cannot be seen and, therefore, he has hopes of securing better terms. Certainly, it is quiet there. The Moore family left for Richmond shortly before the siege commenced."

"Very well," agrees Washington. "We will use it. As for the terms, however, I am unwilling to suspend hostilities for twenty-four hours."

"I believe His Lordship is already well aware of that fact!" bellows Henry Knox, with a grin.

The officers standing around begin to laugh at Knox's comment. Washington looks down and tries to suppress laughing himself. He smiles and says, "Yes, I suppose he is."

"Perhaps it would be appropriate to request that Lord Cornwallis put his proposed terms in writing prior to the meeting at the Moore House," suggests Rochambeau.

"But he must not be allowed to drag out his response," replies Washington.

"Then give him two hours, mon general," says Rochambeau. "And I would recommend that you show your sincerity by suspending our cannonade for two hours while he works on his proposal."

"I like the recommendation, my friend," says an agreeable Washington, who turns to Jonathan Trumbull. "Colonel, will you please draft a response to Lord Cornwallis accordingly?"

"I will, sir," replies Trumbull. "And we shall soon know whether this is a farce—or if His Lordship is in earnest."

Cornwallis's Cave
Bank of the York River
Yorktown, Virginia
October 17, 1781

It is three o'clock in the afternoon. Cornwallis has been waiting impatiently in his grotto with O'Hara, Abercrombie, Symonds, Dundas, and his aides. Three hours have passed since Washington sent back their messenger. Three hours of incessant artillery bombardment. Three hours of swigging rum and staring at each other.

Finally, the cannonade stops. Major Ross, who does not drink, notices the silence first. He rises from his chair and walks outside. He turns back to the entrance. "Your Lordship," he says. "I believe General Washington has responded."

The others walk outside the cave. In a few moments, a British officer delivers the American message. Cornwallis, slightly inebriated, hands the letter to Colonel Chewton. "Here, George," he says. "Aloud, if you please."

Chewton opens the envelope and begins to read.

My Lord:

I have had the honor of receiving Your Lordship's letter of this date.

An ardent desire to spare the further effusion of blood will readily incline me to listen to such terms for the surrender of your posts and garrisons at York and Gloucester Point, as are admissible.

I wish, previous to the meeting of commissioners, that Your Lordship's proposals may be sent in writing to the American lines; for which purpose a two-hour suspension of hostilities will be granted commencing from the delivery of this letter.

I have the honor to be,

G. Washington

After Chewton finishes reading the message, there is silence as its contents are digested. Finally, Cornwallis speaks. "Well, certainly, a detailed draft of proposals is not possible during the time given."

"Perhaps a short letter of response to Washington would be in order," replies O'Hara. "You might include your key requests."

"Of course, General, that would be appropriate," replies Cornwallis, slurring his words. He pauses for a moment and then addresses the entire group. "Gentlemen, I will ask Washington for the customary honors of surrender. I will also request that our British soldiers be sent to England and the Germans to Germany—with the pledge not to serve against France, America, or their allies until released or regularly exchanged. We will, of course, deliver all arms and public stores."

"I'm sure Washington will allow the usual indulgence of officers retaining their sidearms," states O'Hara, "and private property to both officers and men alike."

"Certainly," replies Cornwallis. "I will also request that we continue the suspension of hostilities. There is no sense in having this continual bombardment. Are you in agreement, gentlemen?"

All heads nod affirmatively.

"Very well," says Cornwallis. "George, you will please draft the reply for my signature."

"Indeed, Your Lordship," replies Chewton. "Right away."

As Chewton and Ross walk back into the cave, Cornwallis looks over at Captain Symonds. "Are we making progress on scuttling the remaining vessels?"

"Yes, sir," states Symonds. "We have towed the Fowey into shallow water. Our carpenters are boring holes into her hull. As soon as the Guadeloupe is completely unloaded of goods and munitions, it will be sunk. We are also in process of sinking and burning all our transports."

"How many do we have left?" asks Cornwallis.

"About thirty, sir."

"Very well, Captain. Let us be done with all this unpleasant business before nightfall. I do not believe we will hear any terms before then from Washington that would prohibit us from taking such actions."

"Better to destroy all the vessels than let them fall into allied hands," says O'Hara.

"Yes, of course," responds the dejected Lord Cornwallis as he takes another swig of rum. "You know this isn't my fault. Clinton promised relief and then delayed and delayed. Besides he should have joined us in Virginia long ago instead of basking in the wealth of his mansion in New York. It is Sir Henry Clinton who will have to bear the burden for this defeat."

O'Hara, Abercrombie, Symonds, and Dundas quickly excuse themselves and leave the cave. As they are walking along the beach near the cliffs, Captain Symonds turns to General O'Hara. "Do you believe that Sir Henry is to blame for all this, sir?" he asks.

O'Hara shakes his head and flashes Symonds a sarcastic smile. "Well, I guess that all depends on your point of view, doesn't it, Captain? I can tell you this, though—it wasn't Clinton who ventured into Virginia on his own. Sir Henry did not order His Lordship to come here. Who is to blame? I think they both share enough responsibility for this catastrophe."

◆   ◆   ◆

Washington had Cornwallis's reply in his hands at 4:30 that afternoon—half an hour before the two-hour deadline. Although he was not about to agree to most of the proposed terms, the quick turnaround persuaded Washington that Cornwallis was sincere about surrendering, and that there would be no great difficulty in fixing the terms. So he sent word back to the British encampment that the cease-fire would be extended through the night and into the next day. Confident that Cornwallis's surrender would shortly take place, Washington then sent a note to Admiral de Grasse asking him to attend the ceremony and sign the formal treaty.

◆   ◆   ◆

At around nine o'clock that night, a number of British artillery soldiers were moving and stacking mortar bombs just in case hostilities resumed the next day. Distressed at the thought of an impending surrender to the upstart Americans, these men had been drinking all day and were falling-down drunk. One of the soldiers carelessly entered a powder magazine carrying a lighted torch, stumbled, and ignited the munitions. The resulting explosion killed thirteen men, some of whom were blown to bits, their body parts flying through the air in pieces.

Front Lines
Yorktown, Virginia
October 18, 1781

As the sun rose over the Chesapeake Bay and the York River, morning's first light was greeted by the pleasing sounds of Scottish bagpipes. Because of the truce, it had been a quiet night—the first in weeks where soldiers on both sides had been able to sleep without fear of being blown to bits at any moment. To celebrate the cease-fire, and to serenade the allies, Scottish bagpipers had risen early, mounted the front parapets, and played one of their favorite tunes. As soon as they finished, the band from the French Regiment Deux-Ponts, the members of which had quickly assembled in the second parallel, returned the favor by playing several lively tunes often heard in Paris music halls.

During this unusual reveille, thousands of British and allied troops awoke, climbed atop the fortifications, and listened to the music. It was the first time most of them were actually able to observe the devastation that surrounded them. The sandy plain between the second allied parallel and the British ramparts looked like the moon—racked with bomb craters at every step. The British parapets, themselves, were a shambles, broken and breached nearly every fifty feet or so. Most of the houses in the town were bombed-out relics of their former structures—entire corners blown away, roofs sagging and filled with holes. In the river, charred remains of sloops and transports that had been burned and sunk the day before were visible close to the shore. And farther out in the channel, the masts of the *Charon* could be seen, rising from the frigate's hull resting on the river bottom. And as the morning wore on, the beach and town became crowded with people walking around for the first time since the siege began.

Meanwhile, George Washington, who had been up since 5:00 AM, sent a messenger across the shell-shocked plain to deliver his counterproposals. "To avoid unnecessary discussions and delays," wrote Washington, "I will at once declare the general basis upon which a definitive treaty and capitulation must take place." He then proceeded to inform Lord Cornwallis that all officers and enlisted men would become prisoners of war, and that the request to send the British to England and the Hessians to Germany was "inadmissible." Rather, wrote Washington, they would all be marched to various parts of America and treated "benevolently." The American commander also rejected Cornwallis's request for the "customary honors of a surrender." Instead, he stated that "the same honors will be granted to the surrendering army as were granted to the garrison of Charleston (South Carolina)." This particular clause referred to the way American troops were treated after the fall of Charleston a year and a half earlier on May 12, 1780. At that time, Sir Henry Clinton had refused to let General Benjamin Lincoln's battered army surrender with full honors. So the Americans were further humiliated by being forced to march out of the city with their flags cased rather than flying proudly.

Continuing his counterproposal letter, Washington agreed to let British officers retain their sidearms and soldiers their baggage. But he stipulated that "any property taken in America would be reclaimed." The American commander also insisted on taking possession of all other British army possessions, including artillery, arms, shipping, money, food, supplies, furniture, and apparel. And finally, Washington gave Lord Cornwallis two hours to "accept or reject" his proposals and appoint two commissions to "digest the articles of capitulation"—or face a "renewal of hostilities."

Cornwallis, who had moved back into Governor Nelson's battered house (with cannonball holes in the roof and walls), grimaced at Washington's reference to Charleston. "That damned Clinton!" he muttered to his aides. "I told him he should have let Lincoln surrender with honor!"

The British commander took the rest of the counterproposal in stride. In reply, he requested a grant of immunity to the British Loyalists who had remained in Yorktown. And he audaciously asked Washington for permission to retain a ship (the *Bonetta*) and its entire fifty-person crew for his own use. "If you choose to proceed to negotiation on these grounds," he concluded, "I will appoint two officers to digest the articles of capitulation."

Right about the time Washington received Cornwallis's reply, an intelligence dispatch from New York arrived in the American encampment warning of "immense preparations" being made by Sir Henry Clinton to attempt a rescue. "A fleet of twenty-eight or twenty-nine ships of the line along with many frigates, fireships, transports, and 5,000 troops aboard," the message read, were due to sail for the Chesapeake on or about the eighteenth of October. Realizing that such a voyage would take at least four or five days, Washington immediately dispatched his two commissioners to the Moore house and sent word to Cornwallis that he should do the same.

Out in the trenches at noon, Baron Von Steuben refused to allow his regiment to be relieved at the appointed time. He cited a European precedent stating that regiments serving in the trenches when negotiations begin must be allowed to stay on duty until the capitulation becomes final. Claiming the same precedent, the French Regiments Bourbonnois and Deux-Ponts refused to leave duty in the second parallel. Also at the noon hour, two French frigates and one schooner sailed up the river past Yorktown, having at long last been dispatched by Admiral de Grasse. In the meantime, Washington gave orders for all allied artillery to be poised and ready to resume the bombardment should negotiations collapse.

The Moore House
Yorktown, Virginia
October 18, 1781

Located about one mile southeast of the British main line, not far from the bank of the York River, rests a two-story, small plantation house. Its wood exterior is painted white, its two masonry chimneys rising high above the dark wood-shingled roof. It is the centerpiece of Temple Farm, a 500-acre estate owned by Mr. Augustine Moore, a local merchant and gentleman farmer. The home is currently deserted, the Moore family having temporarily moved to Richmond just before the siege began. Being out of the line of fire, it has suffered virtually no damage from the two-week bombardment.

Shortly after noon, four British horsemen ride up to the house. They are Lord Cornwallis's chosen commissioners, Colonel Thomas Dundas and Major Alexander Ross. An aide attends each. All four men dismount. The aides stay with the horses as Dundas and Ross walk up to the front door. They are met by Washington's commissioners, Colonel John Laurens and Brigadier General Louis-Marie Viscount de Noailles (selected by Count de Rochambeau). All four men walk inside. The door closes behind them. Several American and French sentries stand guard.

Once inside, Laurens and Noailles escort Dundas and Ross to the parlor where they are to conduct negotiations. There are two windows without curtains in the room. The walls are off-white. Above the small fireplace is a gray-painted mantle. In the center of the room is a circular mahogany table surrounded by four chairs. Several pens and plenty of paper rest on the table. The pendulum of a grandfather clock steadily sways back and forth. The clock's chimes mark the quarter hour, half hour, three-quarter hour, and top of the hour.

Some pleasantries are exchanged among the four negotiators, but not much time is spent on small talk as everyone quickly gets down to business. Laurens and de Noailles present their list of capitulation articles. In response, Dundas and Ross focus on the one with which they have the most trouble—Article III, regarding the surrender ceremony. Under normal circumstances, a defeated army will receive honorable terms, which will allow them to march out of their fortifications with flags flying and their band playing a song of the winning army, symbolizing equal status. In this article, however, the allies are demanding that flags be cased and that a British or German tune be played rather than an American one.

"We find the article denying the British army full honors to be a very harsh one," remarks Colonel Dundas.

"Indeed, it is harsh," replies Laurens.

"But why do you demand it?" asks Major Ross. "It will only serve to humiliate Lord Cornwallis and our soldiers."

"I was present at Charleston," responds Laurens. "General Lincoln and all of his 5,000 men—including me—were humiliated when Sir Henry Clinton refused full honors upon surrender of the garrison."

"But His Lordship was not in command at Charleston," says Ross. "Surely, you're not going to hold him responsible for Sir Henry Clinton's conduct."

"This is not about the individual," Laurens replies. "This is about the nation. Clinton represented Great Britain then; Cornwallis represents Great Britain now."

"But could you at least let us march out with our colors flying rather than cased?" asks Dundas.

"Absolutely not," replies Noailles. "It is not an option."

"Well, perhaps a light American tune with steady drumbeats," begs Ross.

"Perhaps a light tune," replies Laurens, "but either English or German, not American. And certainly not with colors flying. This point cannot be changed in the article. If it is attempted, I will walk out of these deliberations—and then you will be subject to General Washington's absolute rule."

Dundas and Ross look at each other and pause for a long interval. At last, Dundas breaks the silence. "What about this first article?" he says. "We would like to amend it, as Lord Cornwallis had originally suggested—that British soldiers be shipped to Great Britain and Hessian soldiers to Germany on parole and under promise not to fight France or America again."

"That cannot be accepted," replies Noailles. "Neither General Washington nor Count de Rochambeau will allow it."

"But this is not an unreasonable request."

"It will not be allowed!" shouts Laurens emphatically. "Not under any circumstances. I spent six months as a prisoner of war after Charleston. Your troops, too, will become prisoners of war and will stay in this country. That's all there is to it, sir."

"My goodness, Colonel Laurens," replies Dundas in frustration, "is there anything you will give us?"

"Indeed, there is," states Laurens, *calming down a bit. "Article IV allows officers to retain their sidearms—and both officers and men their baggage. Article VI allows Cornwallis, his staff, and senior officers to be paroled to Europe or New York. Article VII allows officers to retain their servants, who will not be considered prisoners of war. And Article XI agrees to provide wagons for your baggage and wounded or sick soldiers."*

"I see," says Dundas quietly. *"That is good and we thank you. What, may I ask, will become of the Loyalists in our encampment? Most of Lieutenant Colonel Simcoe's Queen's Rangers fall into this category. As you are aware, Lord Cornwallis has requested immunity for them."*

"I'm afraid we cannot agree to that," replies Laurens. *"General Washington has only contempt for these individuals. He views them as traitors to their country. Our position is that they fall under the jurisdiction of the government of the United States. As such, they must be taken prisoner and presented to the proper authorities."*

"I see," replies Dundas. *"What, then, of His Lordship's request to have the* Bonetta *placed at his disposal?"*

"General Washington will grant that request," replies Noailles. *"It is provided for in Article VIII. The* Bonetta's *captain and crew will be under the command of Lord Cornwallis from the minute the treaty is signed."*

"We would also like to respectfully request that other officers and men may be taken passenger on the Bonetta, *at His Lordship's discretion,"* states Major Ross, *"and that the ship not be subject to any type of inspection or examination."*

"Agreed," responds Noailles.

◆   ◆   ◆

Over the course of the afternoon and well into the night, Dundas and Ross strung out the negotiations by continually revisiting the terms regarding the surrender ceremony, the disposition of prisoners, and immunity for Loyalists. The four men paused for meals and took numerous breaks. They drafted and redrafted the articles of capitulation, often haggling over every word in the document. Occasionally, during breaks, Laurens would shuttle messengers to and from Washington's headquarters to provide the American commander with status reports and requests for his position on certain issues.

In the end, Laurens and Noailles agreed to leave in language that protected Loyalists in Yorktown. But they warned that neither Washington nor Rochambeau would approve that article. There would be no grant of immunity for Loyalists, even though all four negotiators realized Lord Cornwallis would be able to take every one of them on board the *Bonetta*, which was not subject to search. Regarding the surrender ceremony, a small token was granted to the British. Over at Gloucester Point, where a separate ceremony would take place, Colonel Banastre Tarleton's cavalry legion would be allowed to ride forth with their swords drawn. But none of the regiments at Gloucester Point or Yorktown would be allowed to fly their colors. All flags would have to be cased. The remaining articles of capitulation dealt with standard terms in a major surrender (armaments, materials, ships, relinquished, disposition of the sick and wounded, etc.) and were largely uncontested.

Just as the Moore family's grandfather clock struck midnight, a tentative draft of fourteen articles of capitulation was agreed upon. Dundas and Ross returned to the Nelson house and reported to Cornwallis. Laurens and Noailles rode back to George Washington's headquarters tent where they and the general's aides worked through the night drafting the final formal document.

When Alexander Hamilton received word of the agreement, he immediately sat down and penned Betsy a letter. "Cornwallis and his army are ours," he wrote. "I hope to embrace you in three weeks."

37

Redoubt No. 10
Yorktown, Virginia
October 19, 1781

Shortly before 11:00 AM, Generals Washington and Rochambeau ride up to this former British redoubt, now captured and incorporated into the second allied parallel. The two commanders are accompanied by their aides and a few key officers, including Tilghman, Trumbull, Humphreys, Cobb, Lafayette, Viomenil, Chastellux, Laurens, and Noailles. Captain Jacky Custis, due to attend, has come down with malaria. Already present and waiting in the redoubt is Admiral Louis de Barras who has been sent along by the Count de Grasse as a substitute. De Grasse has come down with an acute attack of asthma and is confined to his cabin.

By seven this morning, Washington had already read the final draft of the articles of capitulation. After most of them, he wrote "Granted." But he refused to approve immunity for Loyalists remaining in the British encampment. Rather, he ordered John Laurens to dispatch the document to the British commissioners with a message stating that he expected Cornwallis to affix his signature and return it to Redoubt No. 10 by 9:00 AM, in plenty of time to allow the British garrison to march out of Yorktown by noon. Cornwallis, however, sent a verbal reply asking for an additional two hours, which the American commander granted.

Now arriving at the Rock redoubt, Washington dismounts, leaves his horse with Billy and, together with Rochambeau, walks up and greets Admiral de Barras. Noting that the signed document has not yet arrived, Washington decides to take a look around while waiting. He climbs to the top of the redoubt's parapet nearest the cliff. Standing there alone, he gazes out over the river and into the Chesapeake Bay. He sees the masts of the tall French ships at anchor. Looking toward Yorktown, he observes countless people milling about on the beaches and in the town.

Within a few minutes, two British soldiers ride up and deliver the formal document of surrender. Washington comes down from the parapet and approaches the small table that has been set up by his aides. Just before he gets there, the general's face cringes. He holds his jaw, walks over to the side, and spits on the ground. Trumbull notices that the spit is blood red. Washington then goes over to the table and reviews the document on one large sheet of paper for possible changes. The first section reads:

> *Settled between his Excellency General Washington, Commander-in-Chief of the combined Forces of America and France; his Excellency the Count de Rocham-beau, Lieutenant-General of the Armies of the King of France, Great Cross of the royal and military Order of St. Louis, commanding the auxiliary Troops of his Most Christian Majesty in America; and his Excellency the Count de Grasse, Lieu-tenant-General of the Naval Armies of his Most Christian Majesty, Commander of the Order of St. Louis, Commander-in-Chief of the Naval Army of France in the Chesapeake, on the one Part;*
>
> *And the Right Honorable Earl Cornwallis, Lieutenant-General of his Britan-nic majesty's Forces, commanding the Garrisons of York and Gloucester; and Tho-mas Symonds, Esquire, commanding his Brittanic Majesty's Naval Forces in York River in Virginia, on the other Part.*

Washington carefully reads each of the following paragraphs: Article I (formal capitulation); Article II (British artillery delivered); Article III (specifics of the surren-der ceremony); Article IV (officers); Article V (soldiers); Article VI (parole); Article VII (servants); Article VIII (Bonetta); Article IX (traders and merchants); Article X (Loyalists and local inhabitants); Article XI (sick and wounded); Article XII (wag-ons); Article XIII (ships and boats); and Article XIV (reprisals).

Washington notes that there have been no major changes made to the document. At the bottom, the British commander has written, "Done at Yorktown, in Virginia, October 19, 1781." He has signed using only his last name, "Cornwallis." And just below is affixed the signature of Captain Thomas Symonds, who has signed as head of the British fleet at Yorktown.

"Does everything meet with your satisfaction, sir?" asks Jonathan Trumbull.

Washington nods.

"Very well, sir," replies Trumbull, who dips a quill pen in an inkwell and offers it to the general.

But Washington pauses. "Before I sign, Colonel, please inscribe the following: 'Done in the trenches before Yorktown, in Virginia, October 19, 1781.'"

Trumbull does so and then hands the pen to the American commander, who takes it, leans over the table, and signs, "G. Washington."

Washington passes the pen to Rochambeau, who also signs. He is followed by Admiral de Barras, who places his signature on the document, specifically noting that it is in place of Count de Grasse.

With these signatures, the siege of Yorktown is formally ended. There is no cheer-ing, however. Washington offers his congratulations by quietly shaking hands with the officers present. Each, in turn, grasps the American commander's hand and nods or bows appreciatively. The last man to be congratulated is the Marquis de Lafayette, who finally breaks the silence.

"What English general will ever think of conquering America now?" he says to George Washington. "The play, sir, is over."

Front Lines
Yorktown, Virginia
October 19, 1781

It is noon. British and German troops lower their flags, evacuate their trenches and parapets, and walk back to their camps. Within the hour, two 100-man allied battalions—one American and one French—march forward from the second parallel with drums beating and colors flying. As the Bourbonnois Regiment enters British Redoubt No. 6, just east of the hornwork, and raises the French flag, the American Light Infantry takes control of Redoubt No. 7, 500 feet farther along the line.

Colonel Richard Butler then orders Major Ebenezer Denny, a tall fellow Pennsylvanian, to take the American flag he has been carrying at the head of the column and plant it on the crest of the parapet. When Denny climbs the rampart, he is closely followed by Baron Von Steuben, who has tagged along with the battalion even though it is not part of his regiment. Then, just as the young officer is about to plant the flag, Von Steuben rudely grabs the staff and plants it himself.

Allied soldiers back in the second parallel cheer at the sight of the American flag flying over the British fortifications. And while Von Steuben smiles and waves to the troops, Major Denny simply steps back and remains quiet. Colonel Butler, on the other hand, can be heard swearing in the background. "That no-good, son-of-a-bitch foreigner!" he screams, trembling with rage. "He is arrogant and ignorant! How dare he humiliate Denny that way! I will not let this go! I will not!"

Once the French and American flags are firmly established, thousands of allied troops swarm over the British earthworks. They plant another flag in the British water battery overlooking the river. They begin to take inventory of Cornwallis's remaining property, artillery, and provisions. Several hundred Pennsylvanians with spades and picks start leveling the trenches and parapets that cross the main road to Yorktown, creating a pathway through which the British and German troops may march out and surrender.

The Nelson House
Yorktown, Virginia
October 19, 1781

It is 1:00 PM. Lord Cornwallis has convened his final officers' conference. Present are General Charles O'Hara, Colonel Robert Abercrombie, Captain Thomas Symonds, Colonel Dundas, Major John Despart, Lieutenant Alexander Sutherland, Colonel George Chewton, and Major Alexander Ross. Everyone is standing round the dining room table. They look solemn, glum. Cornwallis, himself, appears particularly pale. He does not look directly at his officers. Rather, he stares down at the paper he is holding. His hand shakes.

"Gentlemen," *he says quietly,* "I will shortly issue the following communication to our troops." *Then he begins to read.* "I cannot express enough the gratitude due the officers and soldiers of this army for your good performance on every occasion, but especially for your extraordinary courage and resolution in defense of these posts.

"I have done all in my power to obtain a condition for the army to go to Europe. However, this could not be ratified. I have taken pains to procure the best treatment for all of you as long as you are in captivity, and I will repeatedly strive to ensure that you will be provided with all necessities until your freedom is obtained.

"At three o'clock this afternoon, the entire army with martial music will march out in front of the trenches on the left flank, which will be occupied by French and American troops, and will form to the right of the French and left of the Americans, parading in the finest and grandest order. We will march through both armies to the designated field and lay down our arms. We will then march back to our camp along the same trail."

After Cornwallis finishes reading, he hands the communiqué to Colonel Chewton and, without saying another word, walks upstairs to his bedroom. As the other officers begin to file out, Chewton pulls O'Hara aside for a private conversation. "General," *he says,* "I beg leave to inform you that His Lordship is unable to stifle his emotions. He gives himself up entirely to vexation and despair. As such, he will not be present at the surrender."

"What!?" *says the startled O'Hara.* "He will not be present?"

"No, sir. He requests that you state to General Washington that he is indisposed and act accordingly in his absence."

"This is a sad and unbecoming action," *responds O'Hara softly.* "Lord Cornwallis has frequently appeared in splendid triumph at the head of his army, by which he is almost adored. He should also cheerfully participate in their misfortunes and degradations, however humiliating."

Chewton does not speak. He simply looks down at the floor.

After a moment, O'Hara, seeing there will be no response, shakes his head and leaves the Nelson house.

Front Lines
Yorktown, Virginia
October 19, 1781

By 3:00 PM, preparations are completed for the surrender ceremony across the river. General Claude Gabriel de Choisy has already sent forward French and American detachments to raise their standards and occupy the British fortifications. And in an unusual gesture, Colonel Banastre Tarleton has earlier paid a personal visit to de Choisy asking for a copy of the articles of surrender and expressing fear for his own personal safety at the hands of vengeful American militiamen. De Choisy, in response, has reassured the cavalry leader that French and American forces would conduct themselves with honor, and that there is nothing to worry about. Thus reassured, Tarleton has agreed to conduct the ceremony according to allied wishes.

At precisely three o'clock, the Gloucestr Point garrison emerges from its fortifications—drummers beating a British march. Tarleton and his legionnaires, with swords drawn, lead the way on horseback. Although Colonel John Simcoe is still ill with fever and remains behind, his mounted Queen's Rangers follow Tarleton's dragoons. Behind them are the British infantrymen marching with shouldered arms. The redcoats are followed immediately by blue-coated German troops—Hessians first, then the Anspach Regiment. All troops observe allied demands and march with their flags cased.

About a quarter of a mile north of their earthworks, the British and German troops come to a field where, surrounded by 3,000 of the allied forces, soldiers lay down their rifles and cavalrymen their swords. And without further ceremony, the men (now all officially prisoners) return to their encampment.

38

It's about quarter to three in the afternoon. George Washington is standing in his tent. He has put on his dress uniform, which has been used infrequently during the war, mostly for dances and other formal occasions. It looks similar to his field uniform, only crisper and cleaner. His coat is dark blue with buff facings and shiny silver buttons. A silver tasseled epaulette rests on each shoulder. His buff-colored knee pants are tucked into his freshly shined black boots. Standing tall, Washington reaches for his battle sword. He glimpses the "1757" on its silver plate, a reminder of his early years in the British army when he fought in the frontier wars against the French. How ironic, he thinks. Today, the British army is his enemy and the French his ally. The sword rests in a black leather scabbard, which is attached to a thick white belt. He buckles the belt around his waist, picks up his hat, and walks outside the tent where Billy is waiting with his mount. Washington has decided this day to ride his favorite horse, Nelson, a chestnut bay that was given to him years before by current Virginia Governor Thomas Nelson. Billy has brushed and cleaned the horse and adorned him with a newly shined silver harness. He holds the horse while the general mounts. Together, Washington and his horse look magnificent. Billy quickly jumps on his own mount, and the two ride out toward the front lines—Billy about a length behind the general.

Final preparations have been completed, and the stage is set for the formal surrender ceremony. The combined allied armies have, two hours earlier, paraded in the shell-shocked field between the British fortifications and their own second parallel. From there, they have marched along the Hampton Road, forming two parallel lines through which the defeated troops will march. French soldiers line the west side of the road, Americans the east, facing each other, twenty yards apart, three to four men deep. The line extends more than a mile—from the second parallel to the designated field where the British garrison will lay down its arms. Behind the more than 20,000 allied troops are throngs of citizens who have arrived from the surrounding countryside in carriages, wagons, and on horseback to witness the momentous event. French bands are playing a series of tunes to help pass the time. The mood is carnival-like, festive, even giddy with anticipation and excitement.

As Washington nears where the second parallel intersects Hampton Road, he sees the Count de Rochambeau at the head of the French line surrounded by his staff and his other high-ranking officers. They are also wearing dress uniforms and are seated atop their horses. Barons Viomenil and Von Closen, Viscounts de Noailles and Rochambeau, Chevaliers Gimat and de Chastellux, and the others all look splendid. Still suffering from an asthma attack, Admiral de Grasse has declined to attend. In his place, Admiral Louis de Barras seems unusually uncomfortable out of his maritime environment, as though he is unaccustomed to being on a horse. Positioned slightly behind Rochambeau's senior officers are several carriages carrying Count Deux-Ponts and the Marquis de St. Simon, both of whom are wounded and ill with swamp fever but have refused to be left behind. In another carriage is the gaunt and fever-ridden Captain Jacky Custis. Against his doctor's orders, Washington's stepson has traveled all the way from Williamsburg to watch the ceremony.

When General Washington rides up, the other officers salute. The American commander returns a salute and takes his place on the east side of the road opposite Rochambeau. He positions his horse next to General Benjamin Lincoln. Slightly behind and to their right are the mounted members of Washington's staff—Tilghman, Humphreys, Trumbull, and Cobb. The other senior American officers are spread out along the road at the heads of their various brigades. Washington looks up the road. On both sides, American and French flags representing each regiment flutter in the breeze. The temperature is about sixty-five degrees. Skies are blue with a few scattered clouds. Leaves on the trees have begun to turn color. It is a beautiful autumn day.

Washington looks toward the British fortifications. It is 3:00 PM, precisely. He is ready. At this point, Count Guillaume-Mathieu Dumas, designated by Rochambeau to direct the ceremony, signals for the French band to stop playing. Then he rides a few feet toward the British lines, pulls out a white handkerchief, and waves it back and forth high over his head. Inside the British line, General Charles O'Hara has been waiting for the American commander to arrive. When informed that the signal has been given, O'Hara orders the procession to begin.

There is a loud drum roll and, a moment later, the British army emerges onto the plain from its fortifications slightly east of the hornwork. O'Hara leads the way, impeccably dressed and mounted on a magnificent stallion. He is accompanied by a number of senior officers, including Cornwallis's aides Colonel Chewton and Major Ross. Other senior officers march in the procession with their regiments. Immediately following O'Hara is the British fife and drummer corps playing a popular tune of the period titled "The World Turned Upside Down." Next comes the British color guard *carrying regimental flags that are furled and encased in compliance with American demands. They are followed by British infantry regiments, in numerical order, and the British naval contingent. German and Hessian companies bring up the rear.*

As the front of the British column reaches halfway across the plain, Washington flashes a glance across the road to Rochambeau. The Frenchman responds with a puzzled look. Both commanders have noticed that the officer leading the surrender is not Lord Cornwallis. Washington then turns to Benjamin Lincoln. "The procession is being led by General O'Hara," he whispers.

"What has become of Cornwallis?" asks Lincoln.

"Obviously, he is unwilling to participate," replies Washington.

"Most unusual, sir," says Lincoln. "I was very much looking forward to His Lordship's personal capitulation—especially after what happened at Charleston."

Washington pauses for a moment, then speaks. "General Lincoln," he says, "as Lord Cornwallis has elected to have his second in command surrender, I wish that you, as my second in command, accept the sword of surrender."

Lincoln swallows hard. "Yes, sir," he responds.

"You will also lead the prisoners through the lines to the field where they are to ground arms," continues Washington. "And you will give them their directions."

Lincoln, his eyes now watering, looks at his commander in chief and nods.

Across the road, Count Dumas spurs his horse and rides out to meet O'Hara. As he positions himself on the British general's left side, Dumas salutes and introduces himself. O'Hara returns the salute and smiles. "I am General Charles O'Hara," he replies. "Lord Cornwallis is indisposed."

"Very well, General," says Dumas. "I have been appointed by Count de Rochambeau to escort you to the head of the allied line. Once there, it will be appropriate for you to formally surrender. Then, according to the articles of capitulation, you will lead your men through the line to a field where they are to ground their weapons. You will then march them back along the same road."

"I understand," responds O'Hara.

Several minutes later, as they approach the trenches of the second parallel, the British general turns to Count Dumas. "Where is General Rochambeau?" he asks.

"There," points Dumas, "at the head of the French line."

O'Hara spurs his mount and trots forward toward Rochambeau. Realizing, however, that O'Hara might try to surrender to the French commander, Dumas gallops forward and places himself between the two. Realizing the situation, Rochambeau points toward General Washington across the road.

"Sir, you are mistaken," says Dumas. "The commander in chief of our army is on my right."

Escorted by the young count, General O'Hara approaches George Washington. He salutes and removes his hat. "I apologize for the error, General," he says. "I am Major General Charles O'Hara. Lord Cornwallis regrets that he cannot be present. He is indisposed, sir."

As Washington bows his head, O'Hara removes his sword from its scabbard and offers it to the American commander. But Washington politely declines. "Never from such a good hand," he says. Then motioning toward Lincoln, Washington says, "I refer you to Major General Benjamin Lincoln. He will accept your sword and provide directions."

O'Hara bows his head, moves over to Lincoln, and again offers up his sword. General Lincoln takes the sword, holds it for a moment, and then returns it to the British general. "Thank you, sir," responds O'Hara.

"Sir, if you and your army will please follow me," says Lincoln. "We will proceed to the grounding of arms."

O'Hara bows his head and motions for the American general to proceed. Lincoln turns his horse and leads the British column down Hampton Road, through the arrayed lines of American and French troops. At this point, the fifes are not playing, and the procession moves slowly forward to a steady drumbeat.

HMS London
Flagship of Admiral Sir Thomas Graves
Off the Coast of Sandy Hook, New York
October 19, 1781

Sir Henry Clinton and Admiral Graves stand on the deck near the captain's wheel. They have boarded the HMS London only a few hours earlier and have made their way toward the head of the long line of ships assembled over the past several days. A junior officer approaches Graves and informs him that all is in order.

Graves turns toward Clinton. "Sir Henry," he says, "the fleet is ready to set sail. With your permission, I will give the order to hoist sails."

"Very well, Admiral," replies Clinton. "Let's be off. And I pray we are not too late."

With that, Graves gives the order to set sail. Flags are hoisted up the yardarms to signal the other ships of the fleet to proceed. The London's sails are shaken free, and the ship begins to move south. It is followed by a magnificent sight—nearly the entire British naval fleet in America. There are about 100 vessels total, including dozens of frigates, fireships, and transports. But most impressive of all, and leading the way, are thirty-five huge ships of the line—with their sleek copper-lined hulls and shiny wooden sides glistening in the afternoon sun, and their huge masts filled with sails billowing in the wind.

The fleet is carrying more than 7,000 troops, and a powerful array of hundreds of deck-mounted cannon that will provide, if needed, a formidable artillery barrage from ship to shore. As the fleet sails past the bar at Sandy Hook and sails southward into the open Atlantic Ocean, it begins to string out for miles.

Hampton Road
Yorktown, Virginia
October 19, 1781

After Lincoln, O'Hara, and the drum corps pass the allied commanders, the first of the British infantry units pass with arms shouldered. Washington and Rochambeau are both surprised to see the troops dressed immaculately with seemingly brand new uniforms. The Scottish Highlanders look magnificent in their deep green jackets with black facings. And nearly all of the British infantry regiments sport good-looking red jackets with yellow collars and cuffs and white breeches and sashes. The next regiment, consisting of artillerymen, wears blue coats with black-laced hats. Cornwallis had earlier given the order for all these uniforms, previously placed in storage, to be distributed. The soldiers had then spent hours polishing the silver buttons, silver loops, and silver hat cockades, and officers had inspected and reinspected the brigades to make sure that everyone would look as crisp as possible. Bringing up the rear, the German units, as usual, look superb in their blue or green jackets with yellow or green trousers.

As the British garrison proceeds up the Hampton Road, the entire French army stands on their right. At periodic intervals, the flags of each regiment are leaned forward by the standard-bearers so they undulate in the wind just above the heads of the passing troops. Along with the colors of the various regiments, each flag contains a golden fleur-de-lis embroidered on a white silken background. And all the French soldiers are dressed in their grand, multicolored uniforms—the various lapels, collars, and buttons distinguishing them from each other. The Agenois troops wear violet lapels with yellow collars and white buttons, the Bourbonnois crimson lapels with pink collars and white buttons. Royal Deux-Ponts sport blue coats with blue collars and yellow lapels. The Soissonais have red lapels with light blue collars and yellow buttons. Members of the Touraine regiment wear violet lapels and collars with yellow buttons. And all the French soldiers have on black shoes with white stockings.

On the British left, in stark contrast with the French, is the American army. First along the edge of the road stand the regular Continental soldiers wearing their ragged, soiled, uniforms consisting of white, smock-like jackets, tattered shirts, and shredded breeches that have been patched with all sorts of colored cloth. Many men stand bare-foot and wear hats with only lids, no brims or bands. But nearly all maintain a proud stance—standing at attention with hair powdered white and shouldered rifles that are clean and shiny. In the New Jersey regiment, a lieutenant happily hands over a pair of silk stockings to another officer. "I bet you that Cornwallis would not be our prisoner within two weeks. You made it by one day—and I am happy to pay up."

Behind the Continentals stand members of the Virginia Militia who wear the clothes of woodsmen and laborers. Some have fashioned makeshift uniforms of leather hunting shirts and breeches. More than half have no coats, no shoes, no socks. But all stand proudly at attention—beaming with satisfaction at their astonishing victory over the vastly superior army now marching in front of them.

In all, nearly 3,600 members of the British garrison are participating in the sur-render ceremony. Almost the same number have remained back in Yorktown—either wounded or too sick to march. At first, as the soldiers slowly move up the road between the allied troops, the British display respect for the French but contempt for the Amer-icans. The victorious troops, however, maintain a universal silence and respect toward the defeated—the Americans largely because they have been ordered to do so.

However, as the march wears on, the British garrison, crowded only twenty yards between the Americans and French, become intimidated at the sheer numbers that have besieged them. Most had no idea that there were so many allied troops surround-ing Yorktown. "We are just a guard-mounting in comparison to them," whispers one redcoat to another. "Cornwallis never told us, but it is now apparent that we never really had a chance."

Dr. James Thacher, who is positioned near the center of the line, watches the pro-cession from horseback. He notes the supreme irony of General Benjamin Lincoln's position at the front of the column, given the fact that, about a year earlier, Lincoln had surrendered his entire army at Charleston. But the beleaguered British soldiers make the greatest impact on Thacher. "Many of the prisoners appear weary, much in liquor, with their knees trembling," he observes. "Some of the British officers behave like boys who have been whipped at school. Some bite their lips, some pout, and others cry. Those who wear round, wide-brimmed hats, pull them down near their eyes, so their faces cannot be seen."

Thacher also watches the British marching in "a disorderly and unsoldierly" man-ner. "Their step is irregular, their ranks frequently broken, and you cannot see a pla-toon that marches in any order," he notes. The German regiments, on the other hand, "make a much more military appearance—and the conduct of their officers is far more becoming men of fortitude."

On they march—the 3,600 prisoners of war between the 17,000 allied troops—beyond the Pigeon Hill redoubts, through the first parallel, past Generals Lafayette, Von Steuben, Wayne, and the other senior officers sitting proudly atop their mounts in front of their own regiments. Finally, about a mile and a half from the hornwork, General Lincoln reaches the end of the allied twin lines and turns to the right, off the road into a broad cultivated field where the Duke de Lauzun's cavalry hussars are arrayed on their horses in a circle. Lincoln leads O'Hara and the British garrison into the circle and directs the British general, his drummers and fifers, and the color guard to one side. Then he gives the signal for the redcoat troops to move forward and ground their arms.

One by one, the officers of each regiment call out commands to their men. "Present arms! Lay down arms! Put off swords and cartridge boxes!" Many of these officers shout out the orders with tears streaming down their faces. At first, a number of soldiers throw their rifles into the pile so hard that it appears as if they are deliberately trying to break them. With this, General Lincoln rides forward. "Enough of this unsoldierly conduct," he shouts. "You men will stack your weapons in an orderly manner!"

After this scolding, soldiers began laying down their rifles pistols, swords, and cartridge boxes more delicately. Enlisted men are permitted to retain their backpacks, officers their sabers and pistols. Lincoln's admonition, however, does not stop many of the British and German troops from displaying their grief and humiliation at having to surrender to an American army they consider nothing less than "a pack of farmers and shopkeepers." Many enlisted soldiers sob and weep openly. Countless officers bite the tips of their swords and cover their faces. After passing through the circle of French cavalrymen, the surrendering army is directed to stand off to one side of the field. Once all have grounded their arms, the band members move forward and place their drums and fifes in the pile.

The final portion of the ceremony involves delivery of twenty-two cased regimental flags by the combined British and German color guard. But when the regimental standard-bearers advance and are ordered by Count Dumas to hand the flags to American sergeants, they protest. "It is not proper to deliver our regimental standards to noncommissioned officers," one redcoat shouts. At this point, Colonel Alexander Hamilton rides forward. He immediately orders one of his junior officers, an eighteen-year-old lieutenant named Wilson, to receive the regimental colors. Wilson dismounts and receives each regimental flag, one by one, and hands them to the waiting sergeants.

George Washington, Count de Rochambeau, and the other senior allied officers have all ridden forward and are now present at the outer edge of the circle. And as the officers of the color guard, the senior British and German officers, and General

O'Hara pass by to join their troops in the field, Washington, Rochambeau, and the senior allied officers offer their condolences and best wishes.

The entire disarmament lasts just over an hour. General O'Hara then leads his garrison back down Hampton Road, through the combined allied armies who are still holding their places. General Lincoln, however, joins Washington and the other senior officers who ride to their headquarters. As the British regiments march slowly back to Yorktown, the allied troops, at first, remain respectful and silent. However, after years of no pay, of fighting without adequate clothing, food, and supplies, the Americans begin to jeer at the defeated soldiers. And then members of the Virginia Militia, who hate the British because of their atrocities, who detest the color red, and who have never stopped resenting the decade-long attempt by the Crown to take away their freedom, start shouting, yelling, and lunging toward the prisoners. In some places, the militiamen are prevented from crashing through to the road only by members of the regular Continental Army, who stand their ground in front.

By early evening, the entire British garrison is safely back inside its encampment at Yorktown. French guards have taken possession of the earthen fortifications west of Hampton Road, the Americans those on the east. Most of the prisoners lounge around their tents while others wander freely through town and along the beach. That night, there are a few violent outbursts by drunken British soldiers. But, for the most part, the defeated soldiers are quiet—relieved that it is all over. "I had just cause to thank my God, who had preserved my life throughout the siege," writes one Hessian in his journal.

39

General Washington's Headquarters Tent
Yorktown, Virginia
October 19, 1781

It is late afternoon, near dusk. Washington and his aides are gathered around a small table back in the private portion of the tent. Tench Tilghman and Jonathan Trumbull are present, as is John Laurens, who has been asked by Washington to help with translations into French. Humphreys and Cobb are in the large portion of the tent preparing for a grand dinner later in the evening.

Washington has just completed dictating letters of congratulations and thanks to Admiral de Grasse and General de Choisy. "Thank you, Colonel," he says to John Laurens, who has been writing up to this point. "And now, a letter to all the troops—for release tomorrow morning."

"I have that one," responds Jonathan Trumbull, pulling out pen and paper.

Washington, who is standing near the opening to his tent, begins to dictate. "I congratulate the army upon the glorious event of yesterday," he begins. "Upon this occasion, I entreat the Count de Rochambeau to accept my most grateful acknowledgments for his counsels and assistance at all times. I present my warmest thanks to Generals Baron de Viomenil, Chevalier de Chastellux, Marquis de St. Simon, and de Choisy for the illustrious manner in which they have advanced the interest of our common cause. I ask that Count de Rochambeau please pass my personal thanks and congratulations to all the members of the army under his immediate command."

The general pauses for a moment until Trumbull stops writing. "Does that sound all right?" he asks.

"Indeed, it does," responds Trumbull.

"Yes, sir," says Laurens.

"Very appropriate," replies Tilghman.

"My personal thanks also," continues Washington, "to each individual of merit in the whole American army. Bound by affection, duty, and gratitude, I wish to express my personal thanks and congratulations to Generals Lincoln, Lafayette, and Von Steuben for their dispositions in the trenches, and to General Knox and Colonel D'Aberville for their great care and attention in bringing forward the artillery, and

for their judicious and spirited management of them in the parallels, and to all the officers and soldiers of their respective commands."

Washington again pauses, this time staring outside.

"The militia, sir," says Tilghman.

"Yes, yes, of course," replies Washington. "Thank you, Colonel. Similar congratulations and thanks to Governor Nelson for the aid derived from him and from the militia under his command. Anything else, gentlemen? Have I left anyone out?"

"What of our soldiers who are currently in detention, sir? You had spoken previously of granting them a general amnesty," responds Trumbull.

"Yes, add this," replies the general. "All those American soldiers who are under arrest or confinement shall be immediately pardoned and set at liberty without regard to offense."

"Sir, you have also requested that chaplains hold a sacrament of thanksgiving tomorrow," mentions Trumbull.

Washington nods. "A divine service will be performed tomorrow," he continues. "I earnestly recommend that the troops not on duty attend..."

The general pauses and looks outside. After a moment, he continues. "And with seriousness and gratitude of heart, express their thanks for the astonishing intervention of providence."

Just as Washington finishes that sentence, David Humphreys appears at the entrance. The general looks up. "Yes, Colonel Humphreys?"

"Sir, Colonel Richard Butler of the Pennsylvania Regiment has challenged General Von Steuben to a duel. And the Prussian has agreed, sir."

"What!" shouts an astonished John Laurens, rising to his feet.

General Washington, however, cocks his head slightly and smiles. "For what reason?" he asks.

"Well, sir," responds Humphreys, "apparently Butler had ordered Lieutenant Denny to mount the American flag atop the British parapet. Before he could do so, however, the general grabbed the flag away from the young officer and planted it himself."

"Why would he do such a thing?" asks Trumbull.

"I assume he wanted the glory for himself," replies Tilghman.

Washington looks down at the ground, shakes his head back and forth, and begins to chuckle. "Even in this moment of great jubilation, we must deal with our own demons," he says. "Well, gentlemen, I will speak with both men personally. Colonel Humphreys, please send for them one at a time. First Colonel Butler."

"Yes, sir," comes the reply. "One more thing, sir. Dr. Thacher is outside and wishes to have a private word with you."

"Very well. Excuse me for a moment, gentlemen," says Washington, who then passes through the larger portion of the tent where dinner preparations are taking place and walks outside. Thacher comes up, shakes the general's hand, and the two walk away to be by themselves.

"General, sir, I have alarming news," Thacher says.

"Yes, what is it, Doctor?" asks Washington.

"It is about your stepson, Captain Custis, sir. Against our advice, he insisted on traveling from Williamsburg to witness the surrender. I am sorry to report that he has taken a turn for the worse, sir. We have sent him back to Williamsburg where he may receive the best care. But he is in danger, sir. And I am not optimistic."

Washington takes in a long, deep breath. He looks toward the sky. His eyes water. At last he speaks. "Well, I'm very concerned, of course. His mother and wife must be informed immediately."

"I will see to it, sir," replies Thacher.

"Thank you, doctor, I appreciate that. Please inform everyone concerned that I will ride to Williamsburg just as soon as my duties allow me to do so."

Yes, sir. We will do all we can for him, sir."

With that, Dr. Thacher leaves and Washington walks back inside. Although there is a look of concern on his face, he does not mention the condition of his stepson to his aides, and they do not ask about his conversation with Thacher. "Gentlemen," he says, "we must now compose a letter to the president of Congress."

"Yes, General," responds Jonathan Trumbull, pulling out another sheet of paper.

"Colonel Laurens, would you please see to it that the articles of surrender are copied in final form and included in this dispatch for Congress?"

"I will, sir."

"To the president of Congress," begins Washington. "Sir: I have the honor to inform Congress that a reduction of the British army, under the command of Lord Cornwallis, is most happily effected. It occurs at an earlier period than my most sanguine hopes had induced me to expect. The definitive capitulation, which was agreed to and signed on the 19th, is enclosed and, I hope will be satisfactory to the Congress."

Washington pauses and looks toward Trumbull. "Colonel, please include formal praise for the Count de Rochambeau, his officers of every rank, and for all American officers and men."

"Yes, sir," replies Trumbull.

"A special note, also, for engineers and artillerists, and the Count de Grasse and officers of the fleet under his command. Please include special praise for Colonel Laurens and the Viscount de Noiailles, the gentlemen who acted as commissioners for forming and setting the terms of capitulation and surrender."

"Yes, sir," says Trumbull, furiously taking notes.

"My thanks, General," states John Laurens, seated at the far end of the table.

Washington nods and looks around the table. "It would seem to me appropriate for one of you to take this letter to Philadelphia," he says. "Whom shall it be?"

Trumbull, Laurens, and Tilghman look at each other.

"It must be you, Tench," says Laurens. "You have served five years on our general's staff, most of that time without pay. You must do it."

"Absolutely," agrees Trumbull. "You have proven your loyalty and dedication to General Washington. "The honor, Tench, should be yours."

"Thank you, my friends," responds Tilghman. "I accept."

"Very well, Colonel Tilghman," says Washington. "I must inquire, however, whether or not you are up to the journey. You are just recovering from the fever, and I'm obliged to tell you that you still appear weak and flushed."

"I am feeling well enough to go, sir."

"But you will have to travel by transport up the Chesapeake—and then overland by horse to Philadelphia. Such a trip will be taxing. It could cause a relapse. I am concerned for your health."

With this, Tilghman rises from the table. "General, I appreciate your concern," he says earnestly. "But I assure you that I am well enough to make this journey. And I might add, sir, that I most sincerely want to carry this great and glorious news to our American Congress."

"Very well, Colonel," replies Washington, who turns to Trumbull. "Continue the letter, as such: Colonel Tilghman, one of my aides-de-camp, will have the honor to deliver these dispatches and will be able to inform you of every minute detail. His merits, as you maybe aware, are impeccable. Please accept, and convey to the Congress, my congratulations on this happy event. With the highest respect, etcetera."

At the conclusion of the letter, Trumbull, Laurens, and Washington all shake hands with and congratulate Tench Tilghman, who smiles heartily and returns their handshakes with a big smile. "I will be off at the crack of dawn," states Tilghman enthusiastically.

"I will have the letter ready for you well before then," Trumbull says.

"And I will have a flawless copy of the articles for you," adds Laurens.

"Gentlemen," says Washington, moving toward the opening to the larger portion of the headquarters tent, "you will all now please join me in welcoming our French allies and our British adversaries in a celebratory and, I hope, cordial dinner."

Washington and his aides pass by the large dining table. David Humphreys and David Cobb, along with a myriad of French chefs and American cooks, are scurrying around setting things in place. Outside the tent, all the key senior allied officers mill around. French officers present include Count de Rochambeau, Baron de Viomenil, Chevalier de Chastellux, Marquis de St. Simon, General de Choisy, and Admiral de Barras. Mingling with them are Generals Lincoln, Wayne, Knox, the Marquis de Lafayette, Baron Von Steuben, Governor Nelson, and Colonel Alexander Hamilton. When Washington and his aides emerge from the tent, the officers gather around the American commander and begin chatting amiably.

After awhile, the senior English officers arrive. They are led by General O'Hara, because Lord Cornwallis still claims sickness. He is accompanied by Colonel Abercrombie, Captain Symonds, Colonel Dundas, Colonel Tarleton, Colonel Chewton, and Major Ross.

"Welcome, gentlemen," says Washington, greeting them warmly.

"General Washington, sir," replies O'Hara, with a crisp salute. "We thank you for the invitation to dinner."

Washington returns the salute and extends his hand. O'Hara accepts the handshake along with those of the other officers present as he passes into the tent. Washington similarly greets each British officer as he guides them toward the dining table.

Once inside, Washington seats O'Hara on his immediate right, pays him particular attention, and treats all the British officers with the utmost respect. The Frenchmen also are profuse in offering their personal regards and sympathies for the outcome of the siege. In response, O'Hara impresses everyone with his poise, charm, and ability to speak fluent French. As a result of the commanding officers setting the tone, everyone relaxes and settles in to enjoy the meal.

The French chefs serve a myriad of gourmet dishes, including special soups, roast beef and chicken served in wine sauce, and delicious desserts. The food is placed on fine French china. And everyone drinks the best wine available—from bottles that French officers had been saving for just such an occasion. After the meal, everyone sits around the table and cracks hickory nuts, drinks more wine, rum, and coffee, and offers toasts to each other.

All in all, the dinner turns out to be a very pleasant occasion, remarkably free of tension. Jonathan Trumbull would later record that it was "very social and easy." The British chatted with French and American officers "as if they had never been enemies." It was "as if the war had ended long ago, the fighting forgotten."

◆　　　◆　　　◆

Late in the evening, after the dinner is over and everyone else has departed, Washington and his aides sit around the table for a few moments. Tilghman, Hamilton, Laurens, Trumbull, Humphreys, and Cobb are all present. They talk about the siege.

They speculate on what may happen next as a result of this victory. And they discuss what the allied army needs to do in the next few weeks.

As they are conversing, a rider arrives with a dispatch. Tilghman runs outside to receive it. Coming back inside, he opens the letter and reads it.

"It is from Congress, General," he says. "Included are two intercepted letters from Sir Henry Clinton to Lord Cornwallis."

"Where were they written?" asks Washington.

"New York, sir," replies Tilghman.

"And what is the latest date?"

"October 14th, sir."

Washington pauses a moment, raises his hand to his chin, and nods his head. "Well, we can be certain, then, that the British fleet had not yet sailed from New York. I wonder where they are."

"It does not really matter now, does it?" says Alexander Hamilton. "Even if they were to appear off the coast tomorrow morning at dawn, they would be too late."

"Yes, it is true," states John Laurens. "They can now make no difference. Their cause is lost."

"Well, perhaps that is true," replies Washington. "But we had better send word to Admiral de Grasse immediately. If Clinton left on the 15th, he may arrive at any moment and we must be prepared."

"Very well, sir," states Jonathan Trumbull. "I will take care of it."

Rising from his chair, Washington stretches his arms out. "I think I will retire, now, gentlemen," he says. As the other officers rise to take their leave, they shake their leader's hand and congratulate him on the day's events, on the outcome of the siege of Yorktown, and on what may very well be the end of the American Revolution.

Moved by their comments, Washington quietly bows his head and walks alone into his private quarters.

40

After spending most of the previous day pining away in his bedroom, Lord Charles Cornwallis woke up early the next morning and sat down by himself to write a letter to Sir Henry Clinton. It turned out to be a long letter, one with many drafts. As a matter of fact, it was early afternoon before it was finally completed.

"I have the mortification to inform you," began Cornwallis, "that I have been forced to give up the posts of Yorktown and Gloucester Point and surrender the troops under my command (by capitulation on the nineteenth) as prisoners of war to the combined forces of America and France."

After writing down the bad news that had made him physically ill, Cornwallis began setting the stage to fix blame for the surrender squarely at Clinton's feet. "I never saw this post in a very favorable light," he wrote. "But when I found I was to be attacked in so unprepared a state, by so powerful an army and artillery, nothing but the hopes of relief would have induced me to attempt its relief."

Cornwallis explained that, upon General Washington's initial arrival from Williamsburg, he would either have "attacked the enemy in the open field," or attempted an escape "to New York by rapid marches" through the countryside north of Gloucester Point. "But being assured by your letters that every possible means would be tried by the navy and army to relieve us," he wrote, "I could not think myself at liberty to venture upon either of these desperate attempts."

Following several more paragraphs of rambling comments in which he clearly refused to accept any responsibility for losing his garrison, Cornwallis closed by stating that he had made a compassionate and honorable decision. "Under all the circumstances," he wrote, "I thought it would have been wanton and inhuman to sacrifice the lives of this small body of gallant soldiers. I therefore proposed to capitulate."

After writing this letter and sending it by special overland courier, Cornwallis felt better—both physically and emotionally. So he began accepting some of the many dinner invitations that had been extended by senior allied officers. Over the next several days, as Cornwallis socialized extensively with his American and French counterparts, he appeared at times both ill at ease and comfortable.

When with the Count de Rochambeau, for instance, he seemed fine. "His Lordship's appearance gave the impression of nobility and strength of character," the French commander noted. "His manner seemed to say, 'I have nothing with which to reproach myself. I have done my duty, and I held out as long as possible.'"

On the other hand, when with George Washington, Cornwallis was clearly down in the dumps. On one occasion, while standing outside in the evening air, Washington noticed that the British commander was not wearing a hat. "My Lord, you had better be covered from the cold," he said politely.

"Thank you, General," replied Cornwallis. "But it really doesn't matter what happens to my head now."

And later, while having dinner with Lafayette, Cornwallis was both shocked and despondent to find his former black servant, James, serving the dinner as part of the marquis' staff. "Oh, yes, Your Lordship," remarked Lafayette calmly, "James has always been a spy for us."

Front Lines
Yorktown, Virginia
October 21–22, 1781

In the two days immediately following the surrender, allied soldiers kept themselves busy following George Washington's orders. Armed with shovels, pickaxes, and hoes, thousands of men began leveling and destroying the first and second parallels as fast as they had been built. Washington was taking no chances that these fortifications would ever be used by Sir Henry Clinton in the event he arrived with enough troops to turn the tables on Yorktown.

The American commander also occupied his troops by giving orders to clean up the city, which had been devastated by the siege. The allied forces had fired more than 15,000 artillery rounds on Yorktown—an average of more than 1,700 per day. American and French troops described the scene as "a landscape of horrors"—"dreadfully shocking" and "frightfully disturbing." One American chaplain "saw houses riddled by cannon fire, shot through and through in a thousand places, with almost no windowpanes left unbroken—ready to crumble to pieces." Baron Von Closen later wrote that "one could not take three steps without running into some great holes made by bombs—with corpse after corpse lying about, or scattered white or Negro arms or legs, and some bits of uniforms." And Dr. James Thacher noted in his journal that "furniture and books were scattered over the ground" and that "vast heaps of shot and shells" that had not exploded were lying about. "The earth in many places is thrown up into mounds by the force of our shells," Thacher also wrote. "And it is difficult to point to a spot where a person could have resorted for safety. The carcasses of men and horses half-covered the earth."

In addition to gathering and burying the bodies of dead soldiers—and the many horse carcasses that lay rotting in the river and on the beach—American and French troops diligently collected and inventoried captured British ships, guns, munitions, and supplies. The final tally of ships included four ships of war, one fireship, twenty-nine transports, and numerous small boats. Captured guns amounted to 244 artillery weapons (168 cannon, seventy-six mortars and howitzers), 2,867 muskets, and 3,000 swords. Ammunition numbers were an impressive 266,000 musket cartridges, 3,400 flints, 2,000 cannonballs, 600 hand grenades, 120 barrels of gunpowder, and thousands of fuses and powder horns.

Allied forces were not surprised when they found 2,116 pounds in cash. But they were astounded when they discovered an unbelievable amount of food that had, apparently, been withheld from the British and German soldiers. These supplies included 75,000 pounds of pork, 73,000 pounds of flour, 60,000 pounds of bread, 30,000 bushels of peas, 20,000 pounds of pickled beef, 20,000 pounds of butter, 3,000 pounds of cocoa, 3,000 pounds of sugar, 2,500 pounds of coffee, 1,500 pounds of rice, 1,250 gallons of liquor, 1,200 pounds of oatmeal, and 500 bushels of corn.

On Sunday morning, October 21, General Washington rounded up all the American soldiers who had deserted to the British during the siege and had them hanged. Those Americans who served with the British before the siege, however, were set free. Later that same afternoon, the American militia gathered the more than 7,000 British enlisted prisoners of war onto the Williamsburg Road and marched them north, where they were sent to prison camps in either Winchester, Virginia, or Frederick, Maryland. About 1,000 British officers, after agreeing not to fight against the United States, were placed on parole and allowed to leave on their own volition for England or any British port in America.

Final casualty tallies for the battle of Yorktown revealed that the British had suffered a total of 546 (156 killed, 320 wounded, and seventy missing). Allied casualties amounted to 389 (eighty-eight killed, 301 wounded). In addition, more than 1,500 British troops were ill with malaria—as were approximately 2,700 allied soldiers.

Main Street
Yorktown, Virginia
October 21, 1781

It is early evening. As the sun sets low on the western horizon, Colonel Banastre Tarleton and General Charles O'Hara are taking a leisurely ride through town. Their conversation is suddenly interrupted, however, when a middle-aged Virginian, waving a large cane, runs out into the street in front of them.

"Colonel Tarleton, my name is Jonathan Day," *he says in a loud voice.* "I am the overseer of Sir Peyton Skipwith's plantation. The horse you are riding was stolen from us by British troops. It is worth 500 pounds, and I want it back."

"Mr. Day, I'm sure you are mistaken," *responds Tarleton.* "This mount could only have been…"

"Colonel Tarleton, this is not your horse," *interrupts Day, holding his cane as if he is ready to strike a blow.* "Dismount immediately or I will thrash you within an inch of your life! I mean to have my master's property!"

Tarleton looks over at General O'Hara who smiles and says, "You had better give him your horse, Tarleton!"

The dashing colonel jumps off his mount, whereupon Mr. Day leaps into the saddle and quickly gallops away. French and American soldiers standing nearby burst out in hysterical laughter. And Banastre Tarleton heads back to his quarters on foot.

Philadelphia, Pennsylvania
October 24, 1781

At three o'clock in the morning, thirty-six-year-old Tench Tilghman rides into the darkened city, his horse's hooves clip-clopping along the cobblestone streets. Exhausted and shaking with chills and a fever, he makes his way straight for the house of Thomas McKean, the president of Congress.

Tilghman has not slept since disembarking from the ship that transported him up the Chesapeake Bay to Annapolis. He has galloped through the countryside of his native Maryland, shouting to farmhouses as he passes. "Cornwallis is taken! A horse for the Congress." *After being provided with fresh mounts by the locals, he has ridden through southeastern Pennsylvania up to Philadelphia.*

While riding through the streets, Tilghman is stopped by a night watchman on horseback. "Halt! Halt!" shouts the watchman. "Who are you? What is your business at this late hour?"

"Sir, I am Colonel Tilghman, aide-de-camp to General Washington," he replies. "I have just arrived from Yorktown and must see the president of Congress immediately."

The night watchman approaches Tilghman and looks into his tired gray eyes. "But Colonel," he asks, "what can be so important that Mr. McKean should be awakened now rather than waiting until daybreak?"

"Sir, Cornwallis is taken!" replies Tilghman earnestly. "The entire British garrison has surrendered—over 9,000 men with all their armaments and supplies."

"My God! My good God!" shouts the excited watchman. "Follow me, Colonel Tilghman! Follow me! I will lead you to the president's home myself."

Both men spur their horses and gallop through the streets, around corners, and up alleyways—Tilghman riding slightly behind the watchman. In a few minutes, they arrive at McKean's home. The watchman dismounts and rushes up to the front entrance and bangs on the door. "Mr. McKean! Mr. McKean!" he shouts. "Wake up, sir! Wake up! Colonel Tilghman is here—from General Washington's staff! Wake up, sir! Wake up! It is grand news! Grand!"

After a few moments the door opens, and Tilghman is invited inside, whereupon the night watchman mounts his horse and rides back down the cobblestone streets shouting: "Past three o'clock and Cornwallis is taken! Past three o'clock and Cornwallis is taken!"

Soon the entire city comes alive with excitement. Candles are lit in windows of houses. People spill into the streets, shouting in celebration. And bells in the tower of Independence Hall toll until daybreak.

◆   ◆   ◆

At 7:00 AM, a special session of the Congress was convened where McKean read General Washington's dispatch about the surrender of Cornwallis at Yorktown. Members applauded Tench Tilghman for carrying the grand news all the way to Philadelphia and voted to pay for his efforts—including room and board while in the city. When informed, however, that the U.S. Treasury was empty, each congressman gave one dollar to Tilghman and again thanked him for his efforts. They also awarded him a horse, saddle, bridle, and an elegant sword. Then, after declaring an official day of national thanksgiving, all the congressmen walked down the street—past waving flags and banners, amid cheering citizens who fired guns in celebration—to the Lutheran Church where they attended a service ministered by the chaplain of Congress.

   Word of the victory spread like wildfire, and similar celebrations erupted in cities and towns across the country. People fired rockets, lit bonfires, held special dinners, and toasted the American and French armies.

Sir Henry Clinton's Headquarters
Harlem Heights, New York
October 24, 1781

At the large, white two-story mansion atop Harlem Heights, Sir Henry Clinton's two aides, Captains Dawkins and Gurwood (who did not make the naval voyage south), hear cannon fire and wild celebration coming from across the river in New Jersey. They walk out to the front porch of the mansion to take a look.

   "I wonder what that's all about!" Gurwood says to Dawkins.

HMS London
Cape Charles
Virginia Capes, Atlantic Ocean
October 24, 1781

At three o'clock in the morning, the same time Tench Tilghman is being stopped by a night watchman in Philadelphia, the British fleet appears near the entrance to the Chesapeake Bay. Sir Henry Clinton and Admiral Thomas Graves stand on the starboard side of the HMS London, *looking landward through their spyglasses. Clinton leans forward when he sees a scattering of lights in the bay. "There is the French fleet," he says to Graves.*

   "Yes, I see them, Sir Henry," replies the admiral. "There are many ships, and they are formidably positioned in a defensive manner."

   "Well, we had better consider our options," says Clinton. "Either engage the enemy fleet or find an alternative landing place. Don't you agree?"

   "I do, sir. Although it will surely not be an easy task. Meanwhile, we will begin reconnaissance operations immediately. I'll send a number of small boats to cruise the shoreline for information as to the status of His Lordship."

   "That certainly seems appropriate, Admiral," Clinton responds.

Ville de Paris
Chesapeake Bay
October 24, 1781

Admiral de Grasse is awakened from a sound sleep at quarter past three. "Sir, our lead ships are signaling that they have sighted what certainly must be the entire British fleet off the capes," reports his aide.

"How many ships?" asks the Admiral.

"Between thirty-six and forty-four, sir."

"Any sign of an attack?"

"None reported as of yet, sir."

"What is the current direction of the wind?"

"Blowing inland, sir—against us."

De Grasse pauses for a few moments. "Very well, Captain," he says. "Signal the general alarm. All hands to their posts. We will maintain a defensive position but keep a wary eye on the enemy fleet. In the meantime, I will prepare a dispatch for General Washington. Please have a transport ready to carry it to him at once."

"Very well, sir," replies the aide, who then exits.

De Grasse sits down at his desk and begins a note to Washington.

HMS London
Cape Charles
Virginia Capes, Atlantic Ocean
October 24, 1781

At 4:00 AM, three men from a small schooner board the flagship. Cold and drenched, they are immediately taken to Admiral Graves and Sir Henry Clinton. "Who are you men?" asks Graves.

"I am James Robinson, sir, pilot of the HMS Charon,*" one of the men replies. "We left Yorktown on the eighteenth, sir."*

"That was almost a week ago," says Clinton. "Why did you leave? What is the condition of the British garrison?"

"We left, sir, because Lord Cornwallis had given up, and we did not wish to be taken prisoner," replies Robinson.

"Given up?" asks Graves.

"Yes, sir. He proposed terms of capitulation on the 17th and we left the next day."

"You do not know what happened since then?" asks Clinton.

"No, sir, we do not. However, we have heard no artillery fire since."

"Very well," says Graves, who directs that the three men be provided food and fresh clothing. Then he turns to Clinton. "Well, Sir Henry, what do you think?"

"There is now no need to mount an offensive action—having lost the only object that could justify it."

"Agreed, sir," replies Graves. "But we had better seek confirmation of this news. Perhaps Lord Cornwallis did not surrender. Perhaps they are still in a negotiation phase."

"I doubt it, Admiral," says Clinton, pessimistically. "Neither Washington nor Rochambeau would let negotiations drag out this long. And no artillery fire for a week indicates that the garrison has surrendered en masse. But I don't understand why de Grasse is still in the bay."

"He probably had intelligence that we were on the way," responds Graves. "He's been waiting for us."

"Do you think he will attack?" inquires Clinton, noticeably worried.

"I doubt it, General," Graves replies. "If Cornwallis has indeed surrendered, de Grasse will probably keep his defensive position and simply wait for us to go home."

◆   ◆   ◆

Over the next several days, the weather turned gloomy, and a heavy rainstorm pounded the British fleet. Finally, several of the small whaleboats that Graves had sent out in search of information returned with a number of British Loyalists who confirmed that Yorktown had indeed fallen, and that nearly all of Lord Cornwallis's soldiers, now prisoners of war, had already been marched to internment camps in the north.

Shaken and depressed, Sir Henry Clinton and Admiral Graves agreed that to engage the French fleet at this point would be both futile and unnecessary. Accordingly, Graves ordered one of his ships, the HMS *Rattlesnake*, to carry news of the Yorktown defeat to British Prime Minister Lord North in London.

On the morning of October 29, 1781, as the thunderstorms subsided and the sun finally broke through the dark clouds, the British fleet left the coast of Virginia and sailed back to New York.

PART VII
EPILOGUE

Yorktown, Virginia
Early November 1781

After the allied victory at Yorktown, not many people had the will to continue fighting—not the British, not the French, not the American Congress, not the American army. Only George Washington persisted in attempting to mobilize the American and French forces. He realized that Sir Henry Clinton still had at his disposal both the British navy and approximately 30,000 land troops—and that they still occupied all major seaports from Maine to Georgia, with the exception of Boston. Even though Clinton had lost about a quarter of his North American army at Yorktown, Washington well knew that the British commander could reorganize his forces and remain in a formidable position of control and power.

Accordingly, Washington visited Admiral de Grasse on the *Ville de Paris*, personally thanked him for his crucial role in taking Yorktown, and implored him to keep his fleet on the Atlantic coast so that they might join forces in an attack on the key ports of Savannah and Charleston. Washington also tried to persuade Virginia Governor Thomas Nelson (along with the governors of other states) to keep their militias together and work with him in a concerted effort to attack the enemy. And finally, the American commander sent countless letters to Congress asking for extended support and continually warned the government not to fall into a state of "security and relaxation."

Nothing Washington could say or do, however, seemed to make any difference. By early November, Admiral de Grasse, citing previous orders from the French government, sailed back to the Caribbean. The bulk of the American militias, almost all of which were comprised of volunteers, disbanded and went home. And the American Congress, giddy about the victory at Yorktown and certain that British rule in America was at an end, could not be persuaded to take any definitive action whatsoever. Washington, therefore, decided to redistribute his troops. He sent General Anthony Wayne and the regiments from Pennsylvania, Maryland, and Virginia down to the Carolinas to join with General Nathanael Greene's forces. He, himself, decided to move the remaining American troops back to New York and resume the traditional defensive position of keeping a watchful eye on the enemy.

On November 5, one day after the *Bonetta* set sail from Yorktown carrying Lord Cornwallis (along with his senior officers, and more than 200 British Loyalists), George Washington and the American army began their journey north. Staying behind were the Count de Rochambeau and all his French forces. Like de Grasse, Rochambeau rebuffed the American commander's requests to mobilize for an offensive action. Within the month, rather, he would move the majority of the French army up to Williamsburg to await further orders from his own government, leaving behind about 1,000 of his troops and artillery to maintain and defend Yorktown.

On his way north, when Washington arrived in Williamsburg, he immediately went to the military hospital to check on the condition of his stepson. He was told, however, that Jacky Custis had been moved to the home of Martha Washington's brother, Burwell Bassett, near Ruffin's Ferry. The general then spent a couple of hours visiting with wounded and sick soldiers, inquiring as to their condition and thanking them for their service. Later that afternoon, he and his staff began the twenty-three-mile ride up along the banks of the York River to Bassett's house.

Upon arrival, Washington was surprised to be greeted at the door by his wife, Martha, her daughter, and their four grandchildren. Jacky had taken a turn for the worse and was lingering in a coma in one of the upstairs bedrooms. He died later that night, at the age of twenty-seven. "The deep and solemn distress of the mother and wife of this amiable young man requires every comfort in my power to afford them," Washington wrote to a friend the next morning.

Six days later, Washington took his family home to Mount Vernon, stopping along the way to visit his mother in Fredericksburg. He stayed at Mount Vernon until the end of November when he journeyed to Philadelphia to confer with Congress. By April 1782, Washington had established his new headquarters in Newburgh, New York.

London, England
Late November 1781

When the head of the British government, Lord North, was informed of the surrender at Yorktown, according to one witness, he reacted "as though he had taken a musket ball to the chest," and then began pacing back and forth flailing his arms wildly and shouting, "Oh, God! It is all over! It is all over!"

The prime minister now found himself in deep political trouble. First of all, the war had proved extremely costly to prosecute and, as a result, the government had incurred a huge international debt. The expensive prospect of replacing the troops lost at Yorktown would be untenable for most members of Parliament. Second, Spain's recent entry into the war was causing an overwhelming fear that a combined French fleet and Spanish armada might deal a deathblow to the British navy. And finally, public support in England for the war effort had declined drastically.

All this might have been moderated had the prospects of victory in the American colonies looked good. But with Cornwallis's dramatic defeat at Yorktown, calls for an end to the war resounded among the halls of Parliament, and there was nothing anyone could do to stop the momentum.

In March 1782, Lord North resigned, and the British Parliament, in concert with King George III's wishes, passed a resolution declaring that it "would consider as enemies to His Majesty and the country all those who should advise, or by any means attempt, the further prosecution of an offensive war on the continent of North America for the purpose of reducing the revolted colonies to obedience by force." Before the year was out, provisional articles of peace between Great Britain and the United States were signed and, in April 1783, the U.S. Congress officially proclaimed an end to the war. In the wake of these key events, British forces evacuated the ports of Savannah and Charleston. The enlisted ranks of the Continental Army were then furloughed and sent home.

On September 3, 1783, the Treaty of Paris was signed, formally ending the war and recognizing American independence. This document also established official boundaries for the United States, from the Great Lakes on the north to Florida on the south, and from the Atlantic Ocean on the east to the Mississippi River on the west. Two months later, on November 25, 1783, the last remaining British forces in America evacuated New York City and set sail for England.

Just before Christmas 1783, George Washington galloped to Philadelphia and, before a grateful Congress, resigned his commission as commander in chief of the United States military. After congratulating the congressmen on their success at elevating the United States to the rank of an independent nation, and after acknowledging the service and merit of the soldiers with whom he had served, the general bid them "an affectionate farewell."

"Having now finished the work assigned to me," Washington said, his hand shaking as he read from his notes, "I retire from the great theater of action and take leave of all the duties of public life."

◆   ◆   ◆

Dr. James Thacher

After retiring from the army, Dr. James Thacher opened a medical practice in Plymouth, Massachusetts. He also became a writer, publishing books not only related to the field of medicine, but on a variety of general nonfiction subjects. His work, *A Military Journal during the American Revolutionary War*, originally published in 1823, was reissued in 1862 under the title, *Eyewitness to the American Revolution*. It is still in print. Dr. Thacher died in 1844 at the age of 90.

Ebenezer Denny

After the war, Ebenezer Denny stayed in the United States Army and rose to the rank of major. He retired from the service in 1795 and returned to his native Pennsylvania where he took up careers in farming, business, and banking. He was elected the first mayor of Pittsburg after it was incorporated in 1816. Denny died in 1822 at the age of sixty-one.

Johann Ewald

Captain Johann Ewald returned to Germany after Yorktown. Upon being refused for promotion because he was a commoner, Ewald joined the Danish army. He ended his fifty-six-year military career as a Royal Danish lieutenant general. Ewald wrote eight books including *Treatise on Partisan Warfare*, which was praised by Frederick the Great. His personal motto, written in his diary, went as follows: "Honor is like an island, steep and without a shore. They who leave can never return." Ewald died in 1813 at the age of sixty-nine.

Benedict Arnold

In the wake of America's victory in the Revolution, Benedict Arnold escaped the hangman's noose by moving with his family to Canada and then, a few years later, to London, England. Although never fully trusted and generally scorned, Arnold spent the rest of his life trying to justify his treasonous actions. He died in 1801 at the age of sixty and was buried in London's crypt of St. Mary's Church—in the uniform of an American soldier. Today, the name "Benedict Arnold" is a synonym for "traitor."

Samuel Hood

After the war, Admiral Samuel Hood participated in successful naval campaigns against the French and Spanish, including a 1782 victory over the French fleet commanded by Admiral Paul de Grasse. Due in large part to poor relationships with superiors and his sarcastic temper, Hood was never formally made a first-line commander. He was elected to the British Parliament in 1784. At the age of seventy, he retired from active duty and was appointed governor of Greenwich Hospital. Hood died in 1816 at age ninety-two.

Banastre Tarleton

After the surrender at Yorktown, Tarleton was sent back to England on parole. In London, he became a notorious gambler and womanizer and, in 1786, temporarily fled to France to avoid debts. While there he wrote *History of the Campaigns of 1780 and 1781 in the Southern Provinces of North America.* Finally returning to England, Tarleton served for twenty-two years in Parliament as a representative from his native Liverpool; he spent most of his time protecting the interests of the British slave trade. Banastre Tarleton died in 1833 at age seventy-nine.

Sir Thomas Graves

Sir Thomas Graves relinquished command of the British naval fleet in America and soon returned to England. Eventually cleared of any direct responsibility in the loss of the "Battle of the Capes" to the French, Graves was promoted to vice admiral in 1787. During the French revolutionary wars, he was promoted to full admiral and wounded. Forced to retire from active service, Graves was eventually made an Irish baron. He died in 1802 at the age of seventy-seven.

Charles Earl Cornwallis

Lord Cornwallis returned to England in December 1781 after being exchanged for Henry Laurens. At first accused of being "the man who lost America," Cornwallis engaged in a bitter exchange of letters with Sir Henry Clinton justifying his actions. Eventually putting the episode behind him, Cornwallis went on to serve Great Britain as viceroy of Ireland, envoy to the court of Frederick the Great of

Prussia, and governor-general of India. He died in 1805 at age sixty-seven from a fever-related illness and was buried in Ghazipore, India.

Henry Clinton

Soon after the surrender, Sir Henry Clinton was relieved of his command and returned to England. He was eventually reelected to Parliament and appointed governor of Gibraltar. Clinton's remaining years were spent obsessed with blame for the loss at Yorktown. He bitterly indicted Cornwallis, with whom be engaged in a raging series of published papers, and never accepted any responsibility. "I may say with Macbeth," he maintained, "thou canst not say I did it!" He died in 1795 at the age of fifty-seven.

Antoine-Charles du Houx, Baron de Viomenil

Baron de Viomenil returned to France after the American Revolution and became governor of La Rochelle. During the French Revolution, he became an outspoken supporter of King Louis XVI and was named to accompany the monarch on his attempted flight from Paris. Severely wounded in a mob attack on the Tuileries Palace, Viomenil died of complications from his wound in 1792. He was sixty-seven years old.

Armand-Louis de Gontaut-Biron, Duke de Lauzun

De Lauzun left America immediately after the Yorktown surrender to carry the news to King Louis XVI. Later falling out of favor with the king, de Lauzun participated with the rebels during the French Revolution. Serving with the new government, he was promoted to lieutenant general, commanded the Army of Flanders and, later, the Army of the Rhone. Accused of political crimes, de Lauzun was brought before the Revolutionary Council and condemned to death. He went to the guillotine in 1793 at age forty-six.

Jean-Baptiste-Donatien de Vimeur, Count de Rochambeau

Count de Rochambeau returned to France in 1783, was decorated by King Louis XVI, commanded several military districts, and was appointed governor of Picardy. During the French Revolution, he led the Army of the North for the king and, as a result, was imprisoned and put on trial during the Reign of Terror. Spared at the last minute from being guillotined, Rochambeau lived the remainder of his life revered by the French people. He was granted a pension by Napoleon and died, at the age of eighty-two, in retirement on his estate in 1807.

Francois Joseph Paul Count de Grasse-Tilly

Five months after leaving the Chesapeake, de Grasse's fleet was defeated by a larger British navy, commanded by Samuel Hood, off the coast of Jamaica (Battle of the Saintes). Taken prisoner and held for months in London, de Grasse published a letter accusing his captains of insubordination during the battle. After being released and sent home to France, the king snubbed him for his conduct and forced him into retirement. De Grasse died in disgrace at age sixty-five, six years after Yorktown.

Louis Jacques-Melchior (Saint-Laurent), Count de Barras

After the surrender at Yorktown, Count de Barras sailed with his small fleet to participate in French operations in the West Indies. In February 1782, he distinguished himself by capturing the island of Monterrey from the British. The next month, suffering from an undisclosed illness, de Barras set sail back to France. He arrived in April 1783 and retired shortly thereafter. De Barras died in 1800 at the age of eighty-one.

Thomas Nelson Jr.

Within a month of the surrender at Yorktown, Nelson, in failing health, resigned as governor of Virginia. An investigation was convened into his tenure as governor, suggesting that Nelson had exceeded his authority by acting without the approval of the legislative branch. After vigorously defending himself, Nelson was cleared of all wrongdoing. Heavily in debt from spending his family's fortune in the war effort, Nelson retired to a small home in Hanover County. He died there in 1789 at the age of fifty-one. Nelson was the first signer of the Declaration of Independence to die.

Anthony Wayne

After Yorktown, Wayne took his troops south. When the British abandoned Savannah, Wayne marched to South Carolina where he entered Charleston following the British evacuation. He later served as a delegate from Pennsylvania to the Constitutional Convention of 1787. Appointed commander in chief of the U.S. Army by President Washington, he won a decisive battle at Fallen Timbers in Ohio, a victory that opened the American Northwest to settlers. Wayne died in 1796 from a severe attack of gout (arthritis). He was fifty-one.

Nathanael Greene

Nathanael Greene kept his army together until the British evacuated Charleston in December 1782. After the war, he experienced severe financial debt, because he had expended much of his personal fortune to feed and clothe his troops. After being forced to sell his Rhode Island home, the state of Georgia awarded Greene a vast estate north of Savannah. But, refusing to work his new land with slaves, he continued to remain in debt. In 1786, at the age of forty-four, Nathanael Greene suffered a stroke and died. The U.S. Congress eventually paid off his family's debt.

Friedrich Wilhelm Augustus Henry Ferdinand, Baron Von Steuben

After the battle, Von Steuben sold his favorite horse and a set of silver tableware and secured a private loan from George Washington to pay his way north. Congress sent him on a mission to Canada, but, when he returned, they could not pay him his wages. With the U.S. government deeply in debt, New York, Virginia, Pennsylvania, and New Jersey awarded him grants of land, and Congress finally gave him an annual pension. Von Steuben became an American citizen in 1793 and died in Steubenville, N.Y., the next year at age sixty-four.

Benjamin Lincoln

Within two weeks of the surrender at Yorktown, Congress appointed Benjamin Lincoln secretary of war, where he served until 1784. He then became the first major general of the Massachusetts Militia where, in 1787, he led the troops that quelled Shay's Rebellion. Lincoln was later appointed collector of Boston by President Washington. In that post, he supervised the collection of import duties. Also elected lieutenant governor of Massachusetts, Lincoln died at his home in Hingham in 1806. He was seventy-seven.

Henry Knox

After Yorktown, Henry Knox assumed command of West Point, a position he held until the British evacuated New York City in late 1783. In 1785, he was elected secretary of war by Congress and then appointed to the same position when Washington became president. In 1794, Knox retired to his estate in Thomaston, Maine, where he was elected to the state legislature. He also engaged in a variety of businesses, including lumber, cattle, and shipbuilding. He died in 1806 at age fifty-six from an intestinal infection.

Marie Jean Paul Joseph Roch Yves Gilbert du Motier, Marquis de Lafayette

In December 1781, Lafayette returned to France as a hero. When elected to the Assembly, he lobbied for the abolition of slavery, religious tolerance, popular representation, trial by jury, and freedom of the press. During the French Revolution, Lafayette rescued the queen from a mob and risked his life to save many people from the guillotine. As a nobleman, he fled France and was imprisoned in Austria for five years. Lafayette was freed by Napoleon but refused to serve the emperor. He died in Paris at the age of seventy-seven.

Jonathan Trumbull Jr.

Jonathan Trumbull Jr. served as aide to Washington until the Treaty of Paris was signed in 1783. Following the war, he lobbied intensely for ratification of the Constitution. When Washington became the first president, Trumbull ran successfully for the House of Representatives from Connecticut. He became the second Speaker of the House and served there until he was elected to the Senate in 1795. He later became lieutenant governor of Connecticut and was then elected to eleven consecutive terms as governor. Trumbull died in 1809 at the age of sixty-nine.

John Laurens

Following Yorktown, John Laurens returned to his native South Carolina to serve with General Nathanael Greene. He created and operated a network of spies who monitored British operations in and around Charleston. At the Battle of Chehaw Neck near the Combahee River in August 1782, Laurens led a platoon trying to intercept a large British foraging party. He was shot from atop his horse and killed instantly. John Laurens was twenty-seven years old.

David Humphreys

After the Yorktown surrender, David Humphreys delivered the captured British standards to Congress. He remained on Washington's staff until 1784 when appointed secretary to Benjamin Franklin, John Adams, and Thomas Jefferson to aide in negotiating European commercial treaties. As president, Washington appointed Humphreys to become ambassador to Portugal and Spain. Humphreys also served in the Connecticut General Assembly and led the state's militia during the War of 1812. He died in 1818 at the age of sixty-four.

Alexander Hamilton

After Yorktown, Alexander Hamilton headed straight home to be with his wife, Betsy, for the birth of their first child. He became a delegate from New York to the Constitutional Convention and an author of the Federalist Papers. As the first secretary of the Treasury advocating a strong federal government, he established public credit, stock and commodity exchanges, Customs, the U.S. Coast Guard, and the First Bank of the United States. Hamilton was killed in a duel with Aaron Burr on July 12, 1804. He was forty-nine years old.

Tench Tilghman

Tench Tilghman remained with Washington until the British evacuated New York City. Afterward, he moved back to his native Maryland where he formed the Baltimore-based mercantile business, Tilghman & Company. His business partner was Robert Morris, former superintendent of finances during the Revolution. Tilghman did not live to see George Washington become the first president of the United States. Seeming always to be in a state of failing health, Tilghman succumbed to hepatitis in 1786 at the age of forty-one.

George Washington

George Washington stayed in New York and held the American army together until the last British forces left America in late 1783. At one point, he almost single-handedly put down a mutiny against Congress engineered by officers and soldiers who wanted the back pay due them (up to six years in some instances). Washington also refused a proposal that he be made king of the United States, citing the fact that he had just finished fighting a war against a monarch. Washington returned to Mount Vernon where he avoided Virginia politics and concentrated on his private life. Within several years, however, he was joining the chorus calling for a new constitution. "We have a national character to establish," he said. "Let justice be one of its characteristics." In May 1787, he served as presiding officer at Philadelphia's Constitutional Convention. After ratification, Washington was unanimously elected first president of the United States. He served two full terms but declined to run for a third, preferring, rather, to head back home to Mount Vernon.

In his farewell address, Washington related why he had agreed to serve as the nation's first president. "My hope was to gain time for our country to settle and mature," he said, "and to progress without interruption to that degree of strength and consistency which is necessary to give it, humanly speaking, the command of its own fortunes." In December 1799, while inspecting his property at Mount Vernon, Washington was caught in a surprise winter storm of rain and snow. It was the only storm he ever encountered that would get the best of him. The next day, he complained of a sore throat, came down with severe chills, and had extreme difficulty breathing. On December 14, 1799, Washington was taking his own pulse when he died. One of the last things he said was, "I am not afraid to go." Upon his death, as ordered in his will, all of Washington's slaves were freed, including his attendant, Billy. George Washington was buried in the family plot at Mount Vernon. He was sixty-seven years old.

FINALE

General Washington's Headquarters Tent
Yorktown, Virginia
October 19, 1781

It is late in the evening. George Washington has just walked into his private small tent. He has finished dinner with senior British, French, and American officers and said good night to his staff. He is alone.

Washington removes his coat, lays it over the side of a chair, and sits down on the edge of his cot. He takes in a long, deep breath, exhales, and cocks his head. It has been a long six years.

His thoughts begin to drift back. He recalls the trepidations he had on taking the job of commander in chief, in part, because he had never actually been in charge of an entire army. He thinks of all the men who had stayed in the service without pay for years, largely because they believed in him. He thinks of their sufferings, like the hunger and desperation borne by the men of Valley Forge, of whom fully one-quarter died of starvation and disease. He remembers all the other brave lads who had lost their lives, and how it was he who had led most of them to their deaths. For some reason, his thoughts drift back to the two men who died after crossing the Delaware in 1776. They had lain down in the snow to rest and never awakened.

And Washington thinks about having been in the field with his men for the entire six years—traveling with them, living with them, suffering with them. He thinks of his constant discouragement of never having enough money for anything, of the hundreds and hundreds of letters he had written begging for help, of constantly dipping into his own pocket for food and supplies, and of serving, essentially, as a volunteer—having received no salary during the entire war.

He recalls that just six months earlier, news of he impending Vergennes Plan had made things look exceedingly hopeless. He remembers writing to John Laurens stating that "we are at the end of our tether" and that "now or never our deliverance must come." And irony of all ironies, Washington realizes that with this victory at Yorktown, the chord that binds the United States to Great Britain might finally be severed, and that, in a very literal way, he and his countrymen could really be at the end of their tether.

Washington then thinks of his own family—of his wife and children, of the grand-children who had been born at Mount Vernon while he was away. He thinks about how they may now have the opportunity to grow up in a new nation—where justice might be one of the principal characteristics and where the words peace and liberty might no longer be distant dreams.

And then a most unusual thing occurs. George Washington begins to weep. But as he has done so many times over the last six years, he catches himself. He slides off his cot and drops down to one knee. He holds his hands together and lowers his head. And he offers a silent prayer of thanks.

After a few minutes, Washington rises to his feet. He wipes the tears from his eyes and goes over to the table near the tent's open window flap. He sits down in the chair and opens his small leather-covered wooden mess kit. He pulls out a couple of minia-ture brushes, a file, a tin of myrrh, and a folded towel of homespun linen. He sets out the small rectangular mirror and moves the flickering lantern close to his face.

Then Washington grabs his small pair of pliers, carefully unhitches the gold wires that secure his false teeth, and removes the two bridges from his mouth. He takes the small metal file in his right hand, holds his upper lip with his left hand, and begins to clean his teeth—scraping the file back and forth in short strokes. The file touches his inflamed, swollen gums. His head jumps and he groans.

BIBLIOGRAPHY AND NOTES

Barnville, Bricout de. War Diary, May 1780–October 1781. Translated by Herbert Olson from French American Review 3 (October–December, 1950, 217–78). Yorktown, VA: Colonial National Historical Park Library. 1953.

Blanchard, Claude. The Journal of Claude Blanchard, Commissary of the French Auxiliary Army Sent to the United States during the American Revolution, 1780–1783. Translated by William Dunne. Edited by Thomas Balch. Albany, NY. 1786. Yorktown, VA: Colonial National Historical Park Library.

Brooks, Noah. *Henry Knox: A Soldier of the Revolution*. New York: GP Putnam. 1900.

Butler, Richard. General Richard Butler's Journal of the Siege of Yorktown. Historical Magazine 8. March 1864.

Callahan, North. *Henry Knox: General Washington's General*. New York: A.S. Barnes and Co. 1958.

————*George Washington: Soldier and Man*. New York: William Morrow & Company. 1972.

Clark, Harrison. *All Cloudless Glory: The Life of George Washington from Youth to Yorktown*. Washington DC: Regnery Publishing, Inc. 1995.

Clinton, Henry. Observations on Some Parts of the Answer of Earl Cornwallis to Sir Henry Clinton's Narrative. London: John Debrett. 1783.

Clinton, Henry. The Narrative of Lieutenant General Sir Henry Clinton, Relative to His Conduct during Part of His Command of the King's Troops in North America: Particularly to That Which Respects the Unfortunate Issue of the Campaign in 1781. London: John Debrett. 1785.

Cobb, David. "Before Yorktown, Virginia, October 1–November 30, 1781." Proceedings of the Massachusetts Historical Society. 1881–1882.

Commager, Henry Steele. *The Spirit of 'Seventy-Six: The Story of the American Revolution as Told by Participants*. New York: Da Capo Press. 1958.

Cornwallis, Charles. An Answer to that part of the Narrative of Lieutenant General Sir Henry Clinton Which Relates to the Conduct of Lieutenant General Earl Cornwallis, during the Campaign in North America, in the Year 1781. London: John Debrett. 1783.

Custis, G. W. Parke. *Recollections and Private Memoirs of Washington*. New York: Derby and Jackson. 1860.

Davis, Burke. *The Campaign That Won America: The Story of Yorktown*. Eastern National. 1970.

Davis, John. "The Yorktown Campaign: Journal of Captain John Davis of the Pennsylvania Line." *Pennsylvania Magazine of History and Biography*. 1881.

Dawson, Warrington. *The Chevalier D'Ancteville and His Journal of the Chesapeake Campaign*. Paris: Legion D'Honneur. October 1931.

Denny, Ebenezer. *Military Journal of Major Ebenezer Denny, An Officer in the Revolutionary and Indian Wars*. Philadelphia: J.B. Lippincott and Co. 1859.

Deux-Ponts, William de. *My Campaigns in America: A Journal Kept by Count William de Deux-Ponts, 1780–1781*. Translated by Samuel Abbott Green. Boston: J.K. Wiggin and William Parsons Lunt. 1868.

Doehla, Johann Conrad. The Journal of Johann Conrad Doehla, 1777–1785. Translated by Robert J. Tilden. Yorktown, VA: Colonial National Historical Park Library. September 1941.

Du Borg, Cromot. Diary of a French Officer, 1781. *Magazine of American History*. June 1880.

Duncan, James. Diary of Captain James Duncan of Colonel Moses Hazen's Regiment in the Yorktown Campaign, 1781. Pennsylvania Archives. 1890.

Dumas, Mathieu. *Memoirs of His Own Time*. London: Richard Bentley. 1839.

Evans, Emory G. *Thomas Nelson of Yorktown: Revolutionary Virginian*. Williamsburg, VA: The Colonial Williamsburg Foundation. 1975.

Evans, Israel. *A Discourse Delivered Near York in Virginia on the Memorable Occasion of the Surrender of the British Army to the Allied Forces of America and France*. Philadelphia: Francis Bailey. 1782.

Feltman, William. The Journal of Lieutenant William Feltman of the First Pennsylvania Regiment, from May 27, 1781, to April 25, 1782, Embracing the Siege of Yorktown and the Southern Campaign. Yorktown, VA: Colonial National Historical Park Library.

Ferrie, Richard. *The World Turned Upside Down: George Washington and the Battle of Yorktown*. New York: Holiday House. 1999.

Fitzpatrick, John C., editor. *The Diaries of George Washington, 1748–1799*. 4 volumes. Boston and New York: Houghton Mifflin Co. 1925.

Fitzpatrick, John C., editor. *The Writings of George Washington from the Original Manuscript Sources, 1745–1799*. Washington DC: U.S. Government Printing Office. 1937.

Flexner, James Thomas. *George Washington in the American Revolution*. New York: Little, Brown, and Co. 1967.

Flexner, James Thomas. *Washington: The Indispensable Man*. Boston: Little, Brown, and Co. 1969.

Foner, Philip S. *Blacks in the American Revolution*. Westport, CT: Greenwood Press. 1910.

Frey, Sylvia R. *Water from the Rock: Black Resistance in a Revolutionary Age*. Princeton, NJ: Princeton University Press. 1991.

Garden, Alexander. *Anecdotes of the American Revolution*. Charleston, SC. 1828.

Garrison, Webb. *Great Stories of the American Revolution*. Nashville, TN: Rutledge Hill Press. 1990.

Gottshalk, Louis. *Lafayette and the Close of the American Revolution*. Chicago: University of Chicago Press. 1942, 1965.

Graham, James J. *Memoir of General Graham with Notices of the Campaigns in Which He was Engaged from 1779 to 1801*. Edinburgh: R. and R. Clark. 1862.

Greene, Jerome A. Historic Resource Study and Historic Structure Report. "The Allies at Yorktown: A Bicentennial History of the Siege of 1781." Colonial National Historical Park, Yorktown, VA. Denver, Colorado. Denver Service Center, Historic Preservation Division. National Park Service. United States Department of the Interior. November 1976.

Gregory, Mathew. Diary of Mathew Gregory at Yorktown, 1781. Yorktown, VA: Colonial National Historical Park Library.

George Washington Papers, Vols. 183–185. Washington DC: Library of Congress. Yorktown, VA: Colonial National Historical Park Library. September 1941.

Hamilton, John C., editor. *The Works of Alexander Hamilton*. 2 volumes. New York: Charles S. Francis and Co. 1851.

Hood, Samuel. David Hanney, editor. Letters Written from the West Indies by Viscount Sir S. Hood in 1782–2–3 by Extracts from Logs and Public Records. 1895. New York: State Mutual Books. 1987.

Idzerda, Stanley J. *Lafayette in the Age of the American Revolution: Selected Letters and Papers, 1776–1790*. Volume IV, April 1781–December 23, 1781. Ithaca, NY: Cornell University Press. 1981.

Irving, Washington. *The Life of George Washington*. 5 volumes. New York: GP Putnam and Co. 1857.

James, Bartholomew. *Journal of Rear Admiral Bartholomew James, 1752–1828*. New York: GP Putnam and Co. 1857.

Johnston, Henry P. *The Yorktown Campaign and the Surrender of Cornwallis, 1781.* Harper & Brothers. 1881. Eastern National. 1981.

Journal of the Siege of New York in Virginia by a Chaplain of the American Army. Collections of the Massachusetts Historical Society 9. 1804.

Kaplan, Sidney, and Emma Nogady Kaplan. *The Black Presence in the Era of the American Revolution.* Amherst, MA: University of Massachusetts Press. 1989.

Ketchum, Richard M., editor. *The American Heritage Book of the American Revolution.* New York: American Heritage Publishing Co., Inc. 1958.

Knox, Henry. Henry Knox Papers. Yorktown, VA: Colonial National Historical Park Library.

Larrabee, Harold A. *Decision at the Chesapeake.* New York: Bramhall House. 1964.

Lee, Nell Moore. *Patriot Above Profit: A Portrait of Thomas Nelson, Jr.: Who Supported the American Revolution With His Purse and Sword.* Nashville, TN: Rutledge Hill Press. 1988.

Lemkie, Robert. *George Washington's War: The Saga of the American Revolution.* New York: Harper-Perenial. 1992.

Lowell, Edward Jackson. *The Hessians and the Other German Auxiliaries of Great Britain in the Revolutionary War. 1884.* Port Washington: New York University: Kennikat Press. 1965.

Marshall, John. *The Life of George Washington, Commander-in-Chief of the American Forces and First President of the United States.* 5 volumes. London: Richard Phillips. 1805.

Martin, Joseph Plumb, *Private Yankee Doodle: Being a Narrative of Some of the Adventures, Dangers, and Sufferings of a Revolutionary Soldier.* Edited by George E. Scheer. Eastern National. 1962.

Middlekauff, Robert. *The Glorious Cause: The American Revolution, 1763–1789.* New York: Oxford University Press. 1982.

Mitchell, Broadus. *Alexander Hamilton: Youth to Maturity: 1755–1788.* New York: The Macmillan Co. 1957.

Moore, H. N. *Life and Services of General Anthony Wayne.* Philadelphia: Leary, Getz, and Co. 1859.

Morrissey, Brendan. *Yorktown 1781: The World Turned Upside Down.* United Kingdom: Osprey Publishing. 1997.

Orderly Book Kept During the Siege of Yorktown, Virginia, September 26–November 2, 1781. Yorktown, VA: Colonial National Historical Park Library.

Palmer, John McAuley. *General Von Steuben.* New Haven: Yale University Press. 1937.

Pickering, Octavius and C.W. Upham. *The Life of Timothy Pickering*. 4 volumes. Boston: Little, Brown, and Co. 1867–1873.

Popp, Stephan. *A Hessian Soldier in the American Revolution: The Diary of Stephan Popp*. Translated by Reinhard J. Pope. Private printing. 1953.

Purcell, L. Edward and David F. Burg. *The World Almanac of the American Revolution*. New York: World Almanac. 1992.

Randall, Willard Sterne. *Alexander Hamilton: A Life*. New York: HarperCollins Publishers. 2003.

Redington, Asa. Narrative of Asa Redington. Yorktown, VA: Colonial National Historical Park Library.

Reynolds, William. Letterbooks, 1771–1783. Yorktown, VA: Colonial National Historical Park Library.

Rice, Howard C. Jr., editor. *Marquis de Chastellux: Travels in North America in the Years 1780, 1781, and 1782*. 2 volumes. Translated by Howard C. Rice Jr. Chapel Hill, NC: University of North Carolina Press for Institute of Early American History and Culture. 1963.

Rice, Howard C. Jr., and Anne S. K. Brown, editors. *The American Campaigns of Rochambeau's Army, 1780, 1781, 1782, 1783*. 2 volumes. Princeton, NJ, and Providence, RI: Princeton and Brown University Presses. 1972.

Robin, M. L'Abbe. *New Travels Through North America*. Philadelphia: Robert Bell. 1783.

Rochambeau, Jean Baptiste Donatien de Dimeur, Count de. *Memoirs of the Marshall Count de Rochambeau, Relative to the War of Independence of the United States*. Paris: 1838. New York: Arno Press. 1971.

St. George Tucker. Journal Kept by Col. St. George Tucker during the Siege of Yorktown and Surrender of Cornwallis, October 1781. Yorktown, VA: Colonial National Historical Park Library.

Scheer, George F. and Hugh F. Rankin. *Rebels and Redcoats*. New York: The New American Library. 1957.

Selby, John E. *The Revolution in Virginia, 1775–1783*. Williamsburg, VA: The Colonial Williamsburg Foundation. 1988.

Shute, Daniel. *With General Benjamin Lincoln at Yorktown, August 18, 1781–April 28, 1782*. Yorktown, VA: Colonial National Historical Park Library.

Smith, Jacob. "Diary of Jacob Smith, American Born." Charles W. Heathcote, editor. *Pennsylvania Magazine of History and Biography*. July 1932.

Stille, Charles J. *Major General Anthony Wayne and the Pennsylvania Line in the Continental Army*. Philadelphia: J. B. Lippincott Co. 1893.

Stokesbury, James L. *A Short History of the American Revolution*. New York: Quill, William Morrow. 1991.

Stone, Edwin Martin. *Our French Allies*. Providence Press Company, RI. 1884.

Swartwout, Barnadus Jr. "Journal of Barnadus Swartwout, Jr., during the American Revolution from November 1777 to June 1783." 1834. Yorktown, VA: Colonial National Historical Park Library.

Tarleton, Lieutenant Colonel Banastre. *A History of the Campaigns of 1780 and 1781 in the Southern Provinces of North America*. London: 1787. North Stratford, NH: Ayer Co. Publishers, Inc. 2001.

Thacher, James. *Eyewitness to the American Revolution: The Battles and Generals As Seen By an Army Surgeon*. Boston: Cottons and Barnard. 1827. Stamford, CT: Longmeadow Press. 1994.

Tilghman, Oswald. *Memoir of Lieutenant Colonel Tench Tilghman, Secretary and Aide to Washington*. Albany, NY: J. Munsell. 1876.

Thompson, Erwin N. Historic Resource Study. The British Defenses of Yorktown, 1781. Colonial National Historical Park, Virginia. Denver, Colorado. Denver Service Center, Historic Preservation Division. National Park Service. United States Department of the Interior. September 1976.

Trabue, Daniel. "Colonel Daniel Trabue's Description of the Siege of Yorktown. Colonial Men and Times," Lillie Dupuy Harper, editor. Philadelphia: Innes and Sons. 1916.

Trumbull, Jonathan. Minutes of Occurrences Respecting the Siege and Capture of Yorktown. Extracted from The Journal of Colonel Jonathan Trumbull, Secretary to the General, 1781. Massachusetts Historical Society Proceedings. 1875–1876.

Tucker, Glenn. *Mad Anthony Wayne and the New Nation*. Harrisburg, PA: Stackpole Books. 1973.

Tuckerman, J. J., editor. Extracts from Volume IV, Diary of the American War, 1776–1784 by Captain Johan Ewald, Hessian Field-Jager Corps. Translated and edited by Joseph P. Tustin. Yorktown, VA: Colonial National Historical Park Library.

Unger, Harlow Giles. *Lafayette*. New York: John Wiley & Sons. 2002.

Van Cortlandt, Philip. "Autobiography of Philip Van Cortlandt, Brigadier General in the Continental Army." *Magazine of American History*. May 1878.

Von Closen, Ludwig. *The Revolutionary Journal of Baron Ludwig Von Closen, 1780–1783*. Translated and edited by Evelyn M. Acomb. Chapel Hill, NC: The University of North Carolina Press. 1958. (Published for the Institute of Early American History and Culture, Williamsburg, VA).

Wiencek, Henry. *An Imperfect God: George Washington, His Slaves, and the Creation of America.* New York: Alfred A. Knopf. 1964.

Wilcox, William B. *The British Road to Yorktown: A Study in Divided Command.* New York: The Macmillan Co. 1946.

Wilcox, William B. *Portrait of a General: Sir Henry Clinton in the War of Independence.* New York: Alfred A. Knopf. 1964.

Wilcox, William B., editor. *The American Rebellion: Sir Henry Clinton's Narrative of His Campaigns, 1775–1782, With an Appendix of Original Documents.* Hamden, CT: Archon Books. 1971.

Wild, Ebenezer. Journal of Ebenezer Wild. Proceedings of the Massachusetts Historical Society. 1890–1891.

Williams, Catherine R. *Biography of Revolutionary Heroes: Containing the Life of Brigadier General William Barton and Captain Stephen Olney.* Providence, RI: Published by the author. 1839.

PART ONE—PRELUDE
Chapter 1

Circular to governors, 1-5-81, Writings of George Washington, v. 21, p. 61; Letter to Knox, 1-7-81, Writings of George Washington, v. 21, p. 66–68; Letter to president of Congress, 1-6-81, Writings of George Washington, v. 21, p. 64–66; "alarming state of our supplies," Letter to General Heath, 1-13-81, Writings of George Washington, v. 21, p. 96; "absolute want of pay," Letter to Count de Rochambeau, 1-20-81, Writings of George Washington, v. 21, p. 120; "Recruits cannot possibly," Letter to General Lincoln, 1-9-81, Writings of George Washington, v. 20, p. 248.

Chapter 2

Charles Watts letter, 1-21-81, Writings of George Washington, v. 21, p. 123; Letter from Wayne, 1-8-81, Writings of George Washington, v. 21, p. 88; Letter to Jefferson, 2-6-81, Writings of George Washington, v. 21, p. 191; "wretched beyond description," Nathaniel Greene to Joseph Reed, 1-9-81, All Cloudless Glory, p. 4494–495; "remember boys," Great Stories of the American Revolution, p. 264; "and all their music," Letter, Mortan to Greene, The Spirit of 'Seventy-Six, p. 1157; "I wish to congratulate you," Letter to General Greene, Writings of George Washington, v. 21, p. 303–306; "much disguised with liquor," All Cloudless Glory, p. 500; "spirit will spread itself," Letter to John Sullivan, 1-21-81, Writings of George Washington, v. 21, p. 128–129; Letter to New Jersey Congressional Commission, 1-27-81, Writings of George Washington, v. 21, p. 147–148; "We began a contest for liberty," General Orders, 1-30-81, Writings of George Washington, v. 21, p. 157–160.

Chapter 3

"Moment I heard of America," Lafayette to Henry Laurens, The Campaign That Won America, p. 113; "you have kept me waiting," Alexander Hamilton: A Life, p. 223; "please go to Colonel Hamilton in my name," Alexander Hamilton: A Life, p. 224; "I come wholly obedient," The

World Almanac of the American Revolution, p. 258; "Send us troops, ships, and money," Washington: The Indispensable Man, p. 139.

Chapter 4

Washington's twelve points to Laurens, Letter, 1-15-81, Writings of George Washington, v. 21, p. 105–110; "Destouches and his fleet ought to proceed," Letter to Count de Rochambeau, 2-7-81, Writings of George Washington, v. 21, p. 253–256; "you will make appropriate arrangements with respect to the militia," Letter to Gen. Von Steuben, 1-20-81, Writings of George Washington, v. 21, p. 256–258; "put a respectable detachment in motion," Letter to Thomas Jefferson, 2-21-81, Writings of George Washington, v. 21, p. 270–271; "prepare a plan for artillery emplacements," Letter to General Knox, 2-10-81, Writings of George Washington, v. 21, p. 209–210.

Chapter 5

"More naturally and spontaneously polite," George Washington: Soldier and Man, p. 224; "not the imposing pomp," George Washington in the American Revolution, p. 401; "we may be beaten," All Cloudless Glory, p. 512; "rarely ever lay more than two days in a place," Letter, 3-18-81, Greene to Joseph Reed, The Spirit of 'Seventy-Six, p. 1163; "little to eat, less to drink," Letter 3-18-81, Greene to Joseph Reed, The Spirit of 'Seventy-Six, p. 1164.

Chapter 6

"No one who considers the good of the service," Letter, 3-21-81, Writings of George Washington, v. 21, p. 342–344; desertions of Joshua Taylor, John Walker, Nathan Gale, Writings of George Washington, v. 21, p. 232, 458, 459; "the three hundred and eighty pairs of stockings," Letter to Mrs. Dagworthy, 1-9-81, Writings of George Washington, v. 21, p. 77; "troops near Ringwood," Letter to Col. Pickering, 1-21-81, Writings of George Washington, v. 21, p. 126–127; "great dissatisfaction at this time," Letter to president of Congress, 4-8-81, Writings of George Washington, v. 21, p. 429–431; "at my mother's request," Letter to Benjamin Harrison, 3-21-81, Writings of George Washington, v. 21, p. 340–342; "that you should go on board the enemy's vessel," Letter to Lund Washington, 4-30-81, Writings of George Washington, v. 22, p. 14–15; "thanks for your kind invitation," Letter to Philip Schuyler, 1-10-81, Writings of George Washington, v. 21, p. 79–80; "instead of having magazines filled with provisions," entry, May 1781, The Diaries of George Washington; "now or never," Letter to John Laurens, 4-9-81, Writings of George Washington, v. 21, p. 436–440.

PART TWO—THE DECISION
Chapter 7

"An enemy seven times my number," Letter, Cornwallis to Genera; Phillips, 4-10-81, The Spirit of 'Seventy-Six, p. 1201–120; "in quest of adventures," Letter, Cornwallis to General Phillips, 4-10-81, The Spirit of 'Seventy-Six, p. 1201–1201; "can never be cordial," The Campaign That Won America, p. 92; "not be necessary for you to send your dispatches to Minister Germain," Letter, Clinton to Cornwallis, The Campaign That Won America, p. 93–94; "make the best of it," The Campaign That Won America, p. 44.

Chapter 8

Lafayette quells mutiny with own credit, "Letter, Lafayette to Washington, 4-18-81, Writings of George Washington, v. 22, p. 34; "uncommon dangers require uncommon remedies," The Campaign That Won America, p. 114; "The genius of this nation," George Washington's War, p. 442; "less tired of this state," The Campaign That Won America, p. 116; "Were I to fight a battle," Letter, Lafayette to Washington, 5-14-81, The Spirit of 'Seventy-Six, p. 1204; "my teeth stand in need of cleaning," Letter, Washington to Dr. Baker, 5-29-81, Writings of George Washington, v. 22, p. 129.

Chapter 9

"A conference as soon as possible," Letter, Rochambeau to Washington, 5-11-81, and Letter, Washington to Rochambeau, Writings of George Washington, v. 22, p. 86–87; Details of Wethersfield Plan, Letter, Conference With Rochambeau, 5-23-81, Writings of George Washington, v. 22, p. 105–107; "Even the best friends," George Washington's War, p. 635; "I have just returned from Wethersfield," Letter, Washington to Lafayette, 6-11-81, Writings of George Washington, v. 22, p. 143–144; "I am going to join General Washington," Letter, Rochambeau to de Grasse, 5-28-82, Memoirs of the Marshal Count de Rochambeau; "threw Washington into such a rage," The Campaign That Won America, p. 16; "I must adhere to my opinion and to the plan fixed at Wethersfield," Letter, Washington to Count de Rochambeau, 6-4-81, Writings of George Washington, v. 22, p. 156–158.

Chapter 10

"I have just returned from Wethersfield," Letter, Washington to Lafayette, 6-11-81, Writings of George Washington, v. 22, p. 143–144; "our two armies are on the march," "no means to suppose," Letter, Clinton to Cornwallis, 6-11-81, Tarleton's A History of the Campaigns of 1780 and 1781, p. 395–397; "Upon viewing Yorktown," Letter, Cornwallis to Clinton, 6-30-81, Historic Resource Study, The British Defenses of Yorktown, 1781, p. 3; "like men who are determined to be free," Letter, Wayne to Washington, 7-15-81, George Washington in the American Revolution, p. 349; "in front of my horse without eating or sleeping," The Campaign That Won America, p. 125.

Chapter 11

"We greet them as friends and allies," Eyewitness to the American Revolution, p. 266; Conversation among French officers, example: "I admire these American troops," The Revolutionary Journal of Baron Ludwig Von Closen, 1780–1783; "they choose their own leaders," My Campaigns in America: A journal Kept by Count William de Deux-Ponts, 1780–1781; "my men need shoes," Alexander Hamilton: A Life, p. 237.

Chapter 12

"If your Lordship has not already embarked," Letter, Clinton to Cornwallis, 6-28-81, Tarleton's A History of the Campaigns of 1780 and 1781, p. 398–399; "Two days ago, we engaged the enemy," Letter, Cornwallis to Clinton, 7-8-81, Tarleton's A History of the Campaigns of 1780 and 1781, p. 399–401; "I cannot but be concerned," Letter, Cornwallis to Clinton, 7-8-81, Historic Resource Study. The British Defenses of Yorktown, 1781, p. 4; "entirely coincides with my own," Letter, Germain to Clinton, 5-2-81, The Yorktown Campaign and the Surrender of Yorktown, 1781, p. 19; "with the greatest security," Letter, Graves to Cornwallis, 7-12-81, Tarleton's A History of the Campaigns of 1780 and 1781, p. 409; "hold a station in the Chesapeake," Letter, Clinton to Cornwallis, 7-11-81, Historic Resource Study. The British Defenses of Yorktown, 1781, p. 4; "I had flattered myself," Letter, Clinton to Cornwallis, 7-15-81, Tarleton's A History of the Campaigns of

1780 and 1781, p. 404–406; "I must not conceal from you," Letter, Rochambeau to de Grasse, George Washington's War, p. 638; "expedition will be concerted only on your order," Letter, Rochambeau to de Grasse, George Washington's War, p. 639; "could scarce see a ground upon," The Diaries of George Washington, 1748–1799, Entry 8-1-81; "must be laid aside," The Diaries of George Washington, 1748–1799, Entry 8-2-81; "I fear some of your letters have been intercepted," Letter, Washington to Lafayette, 7-30-81, Writings of George Washington, v. 22, p. 432–434; "Old Point Comfort," Letter Clinton to Cornwallis, Tarleton's A History of the Campaigns of 1780 and 1781, p. 404; "It is our unanimous opinion," Letter, Cornwallis to Graves, 7-26-81, Tarleton's A History of the Campaigns of 1780-1781, p. 410; "troops you originally requested will stay with me," Letter, Cornwallis to Clinton, 7-26-81, Historic Resource Study and Historic Structure Report. The Allies at Yorktown: A Bicentennial History of the Siege of 1781, p. 10.

Chapter 13

"These English are mad," The Campaign That Won America, p. 107; "so shy of his papers," The Campaign That Won America, p. 124; "the principal post will be at Yorktown," Historic Resource Study and Historic Structure Report. The Allies at Yorktown: A Bicentennial History of the Siege of 1781, p. 107; "shall keep as good a lookout as possible," Letter, Rodney to Graves, 7-7-81, The Campaign That Won America, p. 64; "such boldness," The Campaign That Won America, p. 60; "I cannot credit these reports," Letter, Clinton to Graves, 8-16-81, The Campaign That Won America, p. 47; "spoken with General Benedict Arnold," Letter, Clinton to Cornwallis, Historic Resource Study. The British Defenses of Yorktown, 1781, Colonial National Historical Park, Virginia, p. 13; "stay until October 15," George Washington's War, p. 639; "surrounded by the river and a morass," George Washington in the American Revolution, 1775–1783, p. 41; "as a ray of light," George Washington in the American Revolution, 1775–1783, p. 439; "without loss of time," Letter, Washington to de Grasse, 8-17-81, Writings of George Washington, v. 23, p. 7–11; "on the wing of speed," Letter, Washington to General Lincoln, 9-15-81, Writings of George Washington, v. 23, p. 119.

PART THREE—THE MARCH
Chapter 14

"He is to march through New Jersey," Letter, Washington to General Lincoln, 8-24-81, Writings of George Washington, v. 23, p. 41–43; "the French army will be accomplished as follows," Letter, Washington to Rochambeau, 8-17-81, Writings of George Washington, v. 23, p. 6; "horses and oxen must be collected," Letter, Washington to General Lincoln, 9-7-81, Writings of George Washington, v. 23, p. 98–101; "Letter to Knox," in Letter to General Lincoln, 8-31-81, Writings of George Washington, v. 23, p. 69–71; "circulars to governors," Writings of George Washington, v. 23, p. 26–28; "We must secure the vessels and provisions necessary," Letter to Robert Morris, 8-17-81, Writings of George Washington, v. 23, p. 11–12; "information on horses and wagons," Letter to Lafayette, 8-21-81, Writings of George Washington, v. 23, p. 33–34; "keep the enemy in check," Letter to Gen. Heath, 8-19-81, Writings of George Washington, v. 23, p. 20–23; "We are all in perfect ignorance," The Campaign That Won America, p. 21; "they did not know where they were going," Eyewitness to the American Revolution, p. 268; "We don't know it ourselves," The Campaign That Won America, p. 21; "it is ten to one that our plans will be thwarted," Alexander Hamilton: A Life, p. 238; "He pressed my hand," The Campaign That Won America, p. 24; "through the Scotch Plains," Letter, Washington to General Lincoln, Writings of George Washington, v. 23, p. 59–60; "high hopes of pulling him through," Narrative of Asa Redington; "procure one month's pay in coin," Letter, Washington to Morris, 8-27-81, Writings of George Washington, v. 23, p. 50–52; "all the water craft suitable," Letter, Washington to Governor Thomas Sim Lee, 8-27-81, Writings of George Washington, v. 23, p. 57–58; "will send a dragoon to you every day," Autobiography of Philip Van Cortlandt, Brigadier General in the Continental Army; Washington's visit to Tory, The Campaign That Won America, p. 29.

Chapter 15

"General Washington with about 6,000," The Campaign That Won America, p. 49; Marquand dispatch, The Campaign That Won America, p. 49; "American forces are now encamped at Chatham," Letter, Clinton to Cornwallis, 8-27-81, The Campaign That Won America, p. 49; Cornwallis report on food and supplies, Historic Resource Study. The British Defenses of Yorktown, 1781. Colonial National Historical park, Virginia, p. 14; "the Engineer has finished his survey," Letter, Cornwallis to Clinton, 8-27-81, Historic Resource Study. The British Defenses of Yorktown, 1781. Colonial National Historical Park, Virginia, p. 17; "the heat has been so unbearable," Extracts from Volume IV, Diary of the American War, 1776–1784 by Captain Johann Ewald, Hessian Field-Jager Corps; "every moment is precious," George Washington's War, p. 643; Squib, "The Chesapeake is the object," The Campaign That Won America, p. 49.

Chapter 16

"This day is our own," George Washington's War, p. 329; "keep your destination a perfect secret for one or two days at least," Letter, Washington to Van Cortlandt, Writings of George Washington, v. 23, p. 61; "not a moment's time is to be lost," Letter, Washington to Gen. Lincoln, 8-31-81, Writings of George Washington, v. 23, p. 69–71; "Our destination can no longer be a secret," Eyewitness to the American Revolution, p. 270; "surely will result in heavy desertion," Extracts from Volume IV, Diary of the American War, 1776–1784 by Captain Johann Ewald, Hessian Field-Jager Corps; "An enemy's fleet within the Capes," Cornwallis to Clinton, 9-1-81, Tarleton's A History of the Campaigns of 1780 and 1781, p. 412; "earthworks are carried forward day and night," The Journal of Johann Conrad Doehla, 1777–1785, p. 412; "We hardly have time for eating," The Campaign That Won America, p. 136; "Now they hastily begin to unload," Extracts from Volume IV, Diary of the American War, 1776–1784 by Captain Johann Ewald, Hessian Field-Jager Corps; Tarleton's urge for action, Tarleton's A History of the Campaigns of 1780 and 1781, p. 366; "The blame will fall on Sir Henry Clinton," The Campaign That Won America, p. 139; Cornwallis report on troops strength, Historic Resource Study, the British Defenses of Yorktown, 1781, p. 26; Description of regimental uniforms, Historic Resource Study. The British Defenses of Yorktown, 1781, p. 27–33; "Forty boats with troops went up the James," Letter, Cornwallis to Clinton, 9-4-81; Tarleton's A History of the Campaigns of 1780 and 1781, p. 415.

Chapter 17

"By intelligence that I have this day received," Letter, Clinton to Cornwallis, 9-2-81, Tarleton's A History of the Campaigns of 1780 and 1781, p. 416–417; "heavy ordnance and baggage will also be transported by water," Letter, Washington to General Lincoln, 8-31-81, Writings of George Washington, v. 23, p. 69–71; "send down one hundred head of cattle each week," Letter, Washington to General Heath, 9-4-81, Writings of George Washington, v. 23, p. 75–78; "makes me forget all the hardships," The Campaign That Won America, p. 66; "if the enemy should be found," Letter, Washington to de Grasse, 8-17-81, Writings of George Washington, v. 23, p. 7–11; "The coming armies from the north have changed my plans," The Campaign That Won America, p. 67; "A pregnant woman had been murdered," The Campaign That Won America, p. 170; "Perhaps I am dying of old age," The Campaign That Won America, p. 172; Washington greeting Rochambeau at Chester, Memoirs of the Marshal Count de Rochambeau, Relative to the War of Independence of the United States.

Chapter 18

"It must be the charred pines you see," George Washington's War, p. 644; "As I find by your communiqués," Letter, Clinton to Cornwallis, 9-6-81, Tarleton's A History of the Campaigns of 1780 and 1781, p. 418; "all available crafts and vessels to Baltimore," Circular to Gentlemen on the Eastern Shore of Maryland, 9-7-81, Writings of George Washington, v. 23, p. 69–71; "it is with the highest pleasure," "General Orders, 9-6-81," Writings of George Washington, v. 23, p. 93–94; "scarcely a sick man," The Campaign That Won America, p. 82; "Why didn't you bear down and engage," The Campaign That Won America, p. 161; "a fleet attached to my own," The Campaign That Won America, p. 162; "instead of having the militia march to join Lafayette," Letter, Washington to Waggoner, 9-9-81, Writings of George Washington, v. 23, p. 109–110; "I hope you will keep Lord Cornwallis safe," Letter, Washington to Lafayette, 9-10-81, Writings of George Washington, v. 23, p. 110; "We must make the best of mankind as they are," Letter, Washington to Gen. Schuyler, 12-24-75, Writings of George Washington, v. 4, p. 178–180; "changed by the storms of campaigns and mighty burdens," George Washington: Soldier and Man, p. 234.

Chapter 19

"Washington is said to be shortly expected," Letter, Cornwallis to Clinton, 9-8-81, Tarleton's A History of the Campaigns of 1780 and 1781, p. 415–416; "another punishment for desertion early this morning," The Journal of Johann Conrad Doehla, 1777–1785; "I flatter myself," The Campaign That Won America, p. 163–164; "We are so deeply laden with cannon," Eyewitness to the American Revolution, p. 274; "This is in consequence of intelligence," Eyewitness to the American Revolution, p. 275; "over a country covered with woods and roads," Diary of A French Officer, 1781; "I would be very glad to send an opinion," The Campaign That Won America, p. 165; "to proceed with all dispatch for New York," The Campaign That Won America, p. 166; "they are absolute masters of navigation," The Campaign That Won America, p. 242; "is in no immediate danger," The Campaign That Won America, p. 242; "Before this letter, I always took it for granted," Observations on Some Parts of the Answer of Earl Cornwallis to Sir Henry Clinton's narrative.

Chapter 20

"Not one grain of flour in camp," The Campaign That Won America, p. 173; "Every day we lose now is comparatively an age," Letter, Washington to Gen. Lincoln, 9-15-81, Writings of George Washington, v. 23, p. 119; Tarleton's report, Tarleton's A History of the Campaigns of 1780 and 1781, p. 365–366; "Mr. Washington is moving an army to the southward," Letter, Clinton to Cornwallis, 9-2-81, Tarleton's A History of the Campaigns of 1780 and 1781, p. 416–417; "I think the best way to relieve you is to join you," Letter, Clinton to Cornwallis, 9-6-81, Tarleton's A History of the Campaigns of 1780 to 1781, p. 418; "If I had no hopes of relief," Letter, Cornwallis to Clinton, 9-16-81, Tarleton's A History of the Campaigns of 1780 and 1781, p. 419–420; "a feeble action," The Campaign That Won America, p. 166; "a proper reception," The Campaign That Won America, p. 138; "stand or fall together," The Campaign That Won America, p. 243.

Chapter 21

"*Mon petit general,*" George Washington in the American Revolution, p. 449; "departure at the 15th of October," George Washington in the American Revolution, p. 449; "coup de main," George Washington in the American Revolution, p. 449; description of *feu de joie*, George Washington in the American Revolution, p. 450; "*fie so violent,*" The Campaign That Won America, p. 142; "be prepared for the worst," Letter, Cornwallis to Clinton, 9-16-81, Tarleton's A History of the Campaigns of 1780 and 1781, p. 419–420; "that de Grasse is not so sound asleep," The Campaign That Won America, p. 246; "At a meeting of the general and flag officers," The Campaign That Won America, p. 197; "detain us here to the 5th of October," Tarleton's A History of the Campaigns of 1780 and 1781, p. 422–423.

Chapter 22

"Nothing but hard labor goes on here," Letter, 9-1-81, Historic Resource Study. The British Defenses of Yorktown, 1781, p. 20; "everything has hitherto succeeded to our wishes," Letter, Washington to Forman, 9-24-81, Writings of George Washington, v. 23, p. 132–133; "may drive us leeward," George Washington in the American Revolution, p. 451; "unable to describe the painful anxiety," Letter, Washington to de Grasse, 9-25-81, Writings of George Washington, v. 23, p. 136–139; "The plans I had suggested," The Campaign That Won America, p. 185; "bitch of an open launch," The Campaign That Won America, p. 185; "Every officer will have his men," The Campaign That Won America, p. 185–186; "an unbounded confidence in our commanders," Eyewitness to the American Revolution, p. 279; "not the least objection to any of the inhabitants," Letter, Cornwallis to Nelson, 9-26-81, Historic Resource Study. The British Defenses of Yorktown, 1781, p. 20; "inch by inch," Tarleton's A History of the Campaigns of 1780 and 1781, p. 375; "shall soon retire within the works," Letter, Cornwallis to Clinton, 9-29-81, Historic Resource Study. The British Defenses of Yorktown, 1781, p. 93; "Come on, Mr. Washington, I'm glad to see you," The Campaign That Won America, p. 194; "now confined to within pistol-shot," Historic Resource Study and Historic Structure Report. The Allies at Yorktown: A Bicentennial History of the Siege of 1781, p. 131; Washington cannonball episode, George Washington: Soldier and Man, p. 237–238.

PART FOUR—SIEGE PREPARATIONS
Chapter 23

"In a narrower circle," Memoirs of the Marshal Count de Rochambeau, Relative to the War of Independence of the United States; "an unmilitary move," Historic Resource Study and Historic Structure Report. The Allies at Yorktown: A Bicentennial History of the Siege of 1781, p. 153; "far from laughing," Letter, 9-30-81, Historic Resource Study and Historic Structure Report. The Allies at Yorktown: A Bicentennial History of the Siege of 1781, p. 154; "parapets are not thick," My Campaigns in America: A Journal Kept by Count William de Deux-Ponts, 1780–1781; "no one is allowed to drink water from wells," Orderly Book Kept During the Siege of Yorktown, Virginia, September 26–November 2, 1781, p. 18–27; "may very well decide our struggle," General Orders, 9-30-81, Writings of George Washington, v. 23, p. 154; "I'll bet a beaver hat," The Campaign That Won America, p. 200; "doing everything in my power," Tarleton's A History of the Campaigns of 1780 and 1781, p. 424–425; "so serious a light," The Campaign That Won America, p. 247.

Chapter 24

"Negroes lie about, ailing and dying," The Campaign That Won America, p. 274; Description of British fortifications, Historic Resource Study. The British Defenses of Yorktown, 1781. Colonial National Historical Park, Virginia, p. 67–87; "through a country whose population is too scattered," Letter, Washington to de Grasse, 10-1-81, Writings of George Washington, v. 23, p. 160–165; "reduced only to calculation," The Revolutionary Journal of Baron Ludwig Von Closen, 1780–1783; "oak plank," Letter, Knox to Captain Shilds, 9-30-81, Historic Resource Study and Historic Structure Report, The Allies at Yorktown: A Bicentennial History of the Siege of 1781, p. 159; "at least take a more menacing position," Letter, Washington to de Grasse, 10-1-81, Writings of George Washington, v. 23, p. 160–165; "after having wounded several of our men," Journal of Barnadus Swartwout Jr. During the American Revolution from November 1777 to June 1783; "dodge for these buggers," Diary of Captain James Duncan of Colonel Moses Hazen's Regiment in the Yorktown Campaign, 1781.

Chapter 25

"Fleet consists of twenty-three sails of the line," Letter, Clinton to Cornwallis, 9-24-81, Tarleton's A History of the Campaigns of 1780 and 1781, p. 424–425; "better state of defense," Letter, Cornwallis to Clinton, 10-3-81, Tarleton's A History of the Campaigns of 1780 and 1781, p. 423–424; "carry that home and show it to your wife and children," George Washington in the American Revolution, p. 454; "terribly afraid of gunshot," The Campaign That Won America, p. 206; "eager to shake hands with the French Duke," Historic Resource Study and Historic Structure Report. The Allies at Yorktown: A Bicentennial History of the Siege of 1781, p. 175; "handsomely in a pudding beg," Letter, Weedon to General Greene, 9-5-81, The Spirit of 'Seventy-Six, p. 1218–1219.

Chapter 26

"Congratulate the army upon the brilliant success," General Orders, 10-4-81, Writings of George Washington, v. 23, p. 171–173; "the sale of liquors and refreshments," General Orders, 10-4-81, Writings of George Washington, v. 23, p. 171–173; "return the enemy's compliments with interest," Letter, St. George Tucker to Frances Tucker, 10-5-81, Historic Resource Study and Historic Structure Report. The Allies at Yorktown: A Bicentennial History of the Siege of 1781, p. 179; Martin's encounter with Washington, Private Yankee Doodle, p. 231–232; "resolution of this reporting structure must be resolved," The Campaign That Won America, p. 248; "too late to give relief to Cornwallis," The Campaign That Won America, p. 249; Vauban's fifty-five numbered paragraphs, General Orders, 10-6-81, Writings of George Washington, v. 23, p. 177–185; "so it could be said," Private Yankee Doodle, p. 232; Asa Redington story, Narrative of Asa Redington.

Chapter 27

"Ready in the blink of an eye," The Journal of Johann Conrad Doehla, 1777–1785; "the enemy must capitulate," Alexander Hamilton: A Life, p. 241; "Whether it is practicable to relieve Lord Cornwallis," Letters Written from the West Indies by Sir S. Hood in 1781-2-3 by Extracts from Logs and Public Records; "desperate cases require bold remedies," Letters Written from the West Indies by Sir S. Hood in 1781-2-3 by Extracts from Logs and Public Records; "do not hold the meeting for me," The Campaign That Won America, p. 248; Description of allied artillery and first parallel, Historic Resource Study and Historic Structure Report. The Allies at Yorktown: A Bicentennial History of the Siege of 1781, p. 185–210; "embarrassed, confused, and indecisive," The Campaign That Won America, p. 217; wagered a pair of silk stockings, The Journal of Lieutenant

William Feltman of the First Pennsylvania Regiment, from May 26, 1781, to April 25, 1782, Embracing the Siege of Yorktown and the Southern Campaign.

PART FIVE—THE SIEGE
Chapter 28

Washington's first shot, Eyewitness to the American Revolution, p. 283; "the contrast was humiliating," George Washington in the American Revolution, p. 455; "horribly many cannonballs," The Journal of Johann of Conrad Doehla, 1777–1785; "Allies deprived us of the suspicion," The Journal of Johann Conrad Doehla, 1777–1785; "either be Monday's Point," The Campaign That Won American, p. 250.

Chapter 29

Allied gunner procedures, Historic Resource Study and Historic Structure Report. The Allies at Yorktown: A Bicentennial History of the Siege of 1781, p. 60–71; "subject to disappointment," Letter, Clinton to Cornwallis, Tarleton's A History of the Campaigns of 1780–1781, p. 424–425; "the ships were miserably ruined," The Journal of Johann Conrad Doehla, 1777–1785; "more horrible or more beautiful spectacle," Historic Resource Study and Historic Structure Report. The Allies at Yorktown: A Bicentennial History of the Siege of 1781, p. 253; "some of our shells," Eyewitness to the American Revolution, p. 283–284.

Chapter 30

"Must evacuate these miserable works," Tarleton's A History of the Campaigns of 1780 and 1781, p. 379; Tarleton's plan, Tarleton's A History of the Campaigns of 1780 and 1781, p. 379–383; "nothing but a direct move to York," Letter, Cornwallis to Clinton, Tarleton's A History of the Campaigns of 1780 and 1781, p. 425; "no other armed vessel of consequence," Letter, Washington to de Grasse, 10-11-81, Writings of George Washington, v. 23, p. 208–209; "five guineas," The Campaign That Won America, p. 221; "you may say to the Baron," The Campaign That Won America, p. 221–222; "make good the boast," The Campaign That Won America, p. 222; "you even cover your general's retreat," Historic Resource Study and Historic Structure Report. The Allies at Yorktown: A Bicentennial History of the Siege of 1781, p. 266; "upwards of a thousand shells," Historic Resource Study. The British Defenses of Yorktown, 1781, p. 107.

Chapter 31

"Stopping the disturbing practice of stealing," Orderly Book Kept During the Siege of Yorktown, Virginia, September 26–November 2, 1781; order for the men to stay away from dying Negroes, Orderly Book Kept During the Siege of Yorktown, Virginia, September 26–November 2, 1781; details of second parallel, Historic Resource Study and Historic Structure Report. The Allies at Yorktown: A Bicentennial History of the Siege of 1781, p. 300–307; "siege will not last more than twelve days," Historic Resource Study and Historic Structure Report. The Allies at Yorktown: A Bicentennial History of the Siege of 1781, p. 267; "to instill terror by unremitting fire," Journal of Ebenezer Wild; "a cask of wine to each corps," Historic Resource Study and Historic Structure Report. The Allies at Yorktown: A Bicentennial History of the Siege of 1781, p. 275; details of Major Cochrane's death, The Hessians and Other German Auxiliaries of Great Britain in the Revolutionary War, p. 279; "both are again in need of repairs," The Campaign That Won America, p. 249.

Chapter 32

De Viomenil's argument with Lafayette, Historic Resource Study and Historic Structure Report. The Allies at Yorktown: A Bicentennial History of the Siege of 1781, p. 277; "we have it," Alexander Hamilton: A Life, p. 242; "My children, I have great need of you tonight," The Campaign That Won America, p. 226; Washington's knees shook, Historic Resource Study and Historic Structure Report. The Allies at Yorktown: A Bicentennial History of the Siege of 1781, p. 278; "You must be brave and firm," George Washington in the American Revolution, p. 456; "Wer da?" The Campaign That Won America, p. 230; "Olney's company from here," The Campaign That Won America, p. 228; "I am a dead man," Narrative of Asa Redington; "Rush on, boys," The Campaign That Won America, p. 228; "Remember poor Scammel," Historic Resource Study and Historic Structure Report. The Allies at Yorktown: A Bicentennial History of he Siege of 1781, p. 282; "I am in my redoubt," Historic Resource Study and Historic Structure Report. The Allies at Yorktown: A Bicentennial History of the Siege of 1781, p. 283; "Vive le Roi," The Campaign That Won America, p. 233; "you have the liberty to step back," Eyewitness of the American Revolution, p. 285; "It is a spent ball," Historic Resource Study and Historic Structure Report. The Allies at Yorktown: A Bicentennial History of the Siege of 1781, p. 287; paraded up and down the lines as a "skulker," Narrative of Asa Redington.

Chapter 33

"Success of the enterprise last evening," General Orders, 10-15-81, Writings of George Washington, v. 23, p. 223; "taken by assault on the evening of the 14th," Letter, Washington to president of Congress, Writings of George Washington, v. 23, p. 227–229; "surest way to keep the besieged," The Revolutionary Journal of Baron Ludwig Von Closen, 1780–1783; "blood flowing out of his nose and mouth," Autobiography of Philip Van Cortlandt, brigadier general in the Continental Army; "the enemy carried my two advance redoubts on the left," Letter, Cornwallis to Clinton, 10-15-81, Tarleton's A History of the Campaigns of 1780 and 1781, p. 425; "enemy began to fire so fiercely," The Campaign That Won America, p. 435.

Chapter 34

"What troops," Historic Resource Study and Historic Structure Report. The Allies at Yorktown: A Bicentennial History of the Siege of 1781, p. 298; "battered our works so badly," Extracts from Volume IV, Diary of the American War, 1776–1784 by Captain Johann Ewald, Hessian Field-Jager Corps; "you fire better than the French," The Campaign That Won America, p. 220; Knox and Lafayette incident, Historic Resource Study and Historic Structure Report. The Allies at Yorktown: A Bicentennial History of the Siege of 1781, p. 312–313; "two nights ago, my Eliza," Alexander Hamilton: A Life, p. 243–244; "constantly crowded by spectators," General Orders, 10-16-81, Writings of George Washington, v. 23, p. 225–226; "sixteen large boats are to be in readiness," Historic Resource Study and Historic Structure Report. The Allies at Yorktown: A Bicentennial History of the Siege of 1781, p. 314; "Thus expired the last hope of the British Army," Tarleton's A History of the Campaigns of 1780 and 1781, p. 388.

Chapter 35

"The whole peninsula trembles," Eyewitness to the American Revolution, p. 286; "all our major guns are dismounted," the Journal of Johann Conrad Doehla, 1777–1785; "I went into one of the redoubts there," Extracts from Volume IV, Diary of the American War, 1776–1784 by Captain Johann Ewald, Hessian Field-Jager Corps; "think it inhuman to sacrifice the lives of this small body," Letter, Cornwallis to Clinton, 10-20-81, Tarleton's A History of the Campaigns of 1780 and 1781, p. 427–433; "I cannot recommend that the fleet," Letter, Cornwallis to Clinton, 10-15-81, Tarleton's A History of the Campaigns of 1780 and 1781, p. 426; "we stand prepared to improve the advantage," Letter, Robertson to Lord Amherst, 10-17-81, Letters Written from the West Indies by Viscount Sir. S. Hood in 1781-2-3 by Extracts from Logs and Public Records; "the most delightful music to us all," Military Journal of Major Ebenezer Denny, An Officer in the Revolutionary and Indian Wars; "I propose a cessation of hostilities," Letter, Cornwallis to Washington, Tarleton's A History of the Campaigns of 1780 and 1781, p. 433.

PART SIX—THE SURRENDER
Chapter 36

"Soldiers on the parapets killed," Historic Resource Study. The British Defenses of Yorktown, 1781, p. 119; "a farce or if His Lordship is in earnest," Historic Resource Study and Historic Structure Report. The Allies at Yorktown: A Bicentennial History of the Siege of 1781, p. 322; "an ardent desire to spare the further effusion of blood," Letter, Washington to Cornwallis, 10-17-81, Tarleton's A History of the Campaigns of 1780 and 1781, p. 434; "detail," Letter, Cornwallis to Washington, Tarleton's A History of the Campaigns of 1780 and 1781, p. 434; "to avoid unnecessary discussions and delays," Letter, Washington to Cornwallis, 10-18-81, Tarleton's A History of the Campaigns of 1780 and 1781, p. 435; "If you choose to proceed to negotiation," Letter, Cornwallis to Washington, 10-18-81, Tarleton's A History of the Campaigns of 1780 and 1781, p. 437; "a very harsh one," The Campaign That Won America, p. 261; "Cornwallis and his army are ours," Alexander Hamilton: A Life, p. 244.

Chapter 37

"Settled between His Excellency General Washington," Tarleton's A History of the Campaigns of 1780 and 1781, p. 438–442; "done in the trenches before Yorktown," The Campaign That Won America, p. 262; "the play, sir, is over," Letter, Lafayette to de Vergennes, 10-20-81, Historic Resource Study and Historic Structure Report. The Allies at Yorktown: A Bicentennial History of the Siege of 1781, p. 329; Von Steuben–Denny incident, Military Journal of Major Ebenezer Denny, An Officer in the Revolutionary and Indian Wars; "gratitude due the officers and soldiers of this army," General Orders from Cornwallis, 10-19-81, Historic Resource Study. The British Defenses of Yorktown, 1781, p. 123; "appeared in splendid triumph," Eyewitness to the American Revolution, p. 290.

Chapter 38

"Sir, you are mistaken," Historic Resource Study and Historic Structure Report. The Allies at Yorktown: A Bicentennial History of the Siege of 1781, p. 331; "just a guard-mounting," A Hessian Soldier in the American Revolution: The Diary of Stephan Popp; "their step is irregular," Eyewitness to the American Revolution, p. 289; "put off swords and cartridge boxes," The Revolutionary Journal of Baron Ludwig Von Closen, 1780–1783; "I had just cause to thank my God," The Journal of Johann Conrad Doehla, 1777–1785.

Chapter 39

"Congratulate the army," General Orders, 10-20-81, Writings of George Washington, v. 23, p. 244–247; "a divine service will be performed tomorrow," General Orders, 10-20-81, Writings of

George Washington, v. 23, p. 244–247; "a reduction of the British Army," Letter, Washington to president of Congress, 10-19-81, Writings of George Washington, v. 23, p. 241–244.

Chapter 40

"I have the mortification to inform you," Letter, Cornwallis to Clinton, 10-20-81, Tarleton's A History of the Campaigns of 1780 and 1781, p. 427-433; "his manner seemed to say," Memoirs of the Marshal Count de Rochambeau, Relative to the War of Independence of the United States; "really doesn't matter what happens to my head now," Eyewitness to the American Revolution, p. 302; "saw houses riddled by cannon fire," The Revolutionary Journal of Baron Ludwig Von Closen, 1780–1783; "one could not take three steps," The Revolutionary Journal of Baron Ludwig Von Closen, 1780–1783; "furniture and books were scattered," Eyewitness to the American Revolution, p. 292; detail of captured items, Historic Resource Study and Historic Structure Report. The Allies at Yorktown: A Bicentennial History of the Siege of 1781, p. 343–344; Tarleton–Day episode, Eyewitness to the American Revolution, p. 292; "past three o'clock and Cornwallis is taken," The Campaign That Won America, p. 278; "Cornwallis had given up," The Campaign That Won America, p. 283.

PART SEVEN—EPILOGUE

"Security and relaxation," Letter to Robert Harrison, 11-18-81, Writings of George Washington, v. 23, p. 351–352; "the deep and solemn distress," George Washington in the American Revolution, p. 471; "as though he had taken a musket ball to the chest," World Almanac of the American Revolution, p. 292; "Oh, God, it is all over," World Almanac of the American Revolution, p. 292; "I retire from the great theater of action," George Washington in the American Revolution, p. 526.

978-1-58348-198-1
1-58348-198-2

Printed in the United States
85332LV00003B/27/A